RIVER SONG

Also by Di Morrissey
In order of publication

Heart of the Dreaming
The Last Rose of Summer
Follow the Morning Star
The Last Mile Home
Tears of the Moon
When the Singing Stops
The Songmaster
Scatter the Stars
Blaze
The Bay
Kimberley Sun
Barra Creek
The Reef
The Valley
Monsoon
The Islands
The Silent Country
The Plantation
The Opal Desert
The Golden Land
The Winter Sea
The Road Back
Rain Music
A Distant Journey
The Red Coast
Arcadia
The Last Paradise
Before the Storm
The Night Tide

Di MORRISSEY
RIVER SONG

Pan Macmillan Australia

Pan Macmillan acknowledges the Traditional Custodians of Country throughout Australia and their connections to lands, waters and communities. We pay our respect to Elders past and present and extend that respect to all Aboriginal and Torres Strait Islander peoples today. We honour more than sixty thousand years of storytelling, art and culture.

This is a work of fiction. Characters, institutions and organisations mentioned in this novel are either the product of the author's imagination or, if real, used fictitiously without any intent to describe actual conduct.

First published 2024 in Macmillan by Pan Macmillan Australia Pty Ltd
1 Market Street, Sydney, New South Wales, Australia, 2000

Copyright © Di Morrissey 2024
Lyrics to 'River Song'/'On the River' © Goldheist Music 2024

The moral right of the author to be identified as the author of this work has been asserted.

All rights reserved. No part of this book may be reproduced or transmitted by any person or entity (including Google, Amazon or similar organisations), in any form or by any means, electronic or mechanical, including photocopying, recording, scanning or by any information storage and retrieval system, without prior permission in writing from the publisher.

 A catalogue record for this book is available from the National Library of Australia

Typeset in 12.5/16 pt Sabon LT Pro by Post Pre-press Group
Printed by IVE

Endpaper composition by Belinda Huang, design by
Deborah Parry Graphics

Chapter image credits: Prologue, Kwest/Adobe Stock; Chapter 2, Gavin/Adobe Stock; Chapter 3, Tommy Lee Walker/Adobe Stock; Chapter 4, Kathryn Lincoln; Chapter 5, EkaterinaKiseleva/Adobe Stock; Chapter 6, CReadius/Adobe Stock; Chapter 7, Stephen D/Adobe Stock; Chapter 8, Kwest/Adobe Stock; Chapter 9, cauayanislandresort/Unpslash; Chapter 10, Michael Moloney/Adobe Stock; Chapter 11, themorningglory/Adobe Stock; Chapter 12, Pixabay; Chapter 13, oneinchpunch/Adobe Stock; Chapter 14, lovleah/iStock; Epilogue, junce11/Adobe Stock; Author's Note, Grainger Museum collection, University of Melbourne.

The author and the publisher have made every effort to contact copyright holders for material used in this book. Any person or organisation that may have been overlooked should contact the publisher.

 The paper in this book is FSC® certified. FSC® promotes environmentally responsible, socially beneficial and economically viable management of the world's forests.

*Dedicated to my darling Boris . . .
25 happy years together. I miss you.*

Acknowledgements

The love and support of my children, Gabrielle and Nick, and grandkids, Sonoma, Everton, Bodhi and Ulani, has so helped me through a hard year.

Thank you also to editor and great dear friend Liz Adams, who has shared the journey.

Ross Gibb, Praveen Naidoo, Ingrid Ohlsson, Bernadette Foley, Alex Lloyd, Tracey Cheetham, Clare Keighery, Katie Crawford, Lily Cameron, Belinda Huang, Brianne Collins, the super sales team and all at Pan Macmillan, now and then . . . it's been a happy 30-book marriage!

So many have thrown in their advice, ideas, wishes and information for this book – including the lady in a newsagency who was buying a lottery ticket. When I asked what she'd do if she won, she said, 'I've actually never thought about it . . . but yes, I know . . . I wouldn't tell my kids!'

Thanks for input from Gayle Cameron, Greta Gertler, Usha and Reg Harris, Missy Higgins, Jenny Huxley, Nawal Maharaj, Gabrielle Morrissey PhD and Di Rayson PhD.

And thank you, Goldheist (the lovely Hester Fraser) for 'River Song/On the River' (see the QR code at the end of the book to hear the song).

Prologue

LEONIE SAT ON THE western verandah, an empty chair across from her and a solitary glass on the small side table.

She wished she could paint. The spread of sky, all gold and rose, had melted over the clouds now the sun had set. Each evening was different. She had always enjoyed sitting with Tony to watch the sunset. They would have so much to talk about or laugh over, or they'd just sit together quietly as the sky changed from pink and orange to black. She closed her eyes, the familiar pain clutching at her.

'Are you all right, Mum?'

Her twelve-year-old son Corby, his hair tousled from soccer training and his cheeks pink, came out onto the verandah.

'Oh, hi, darling. Yes, I'm fine, thanks. Just missing Dad. You okay? Done your homework?'

'Just about to start.'

She smiled and reached for her son's hand.

'I miss him too.' Corby leaned into her and Leonie wrapped her arms around him. 'I'm scared I'll forget him. That I won't turn out good enough,' he said.

'Not possible, my love. He'll always be a part of you. And you know, you look so like him. He would want you to just be you: Corby Foster!'

He pulled away with a wry smile.

Leonie reached up and held his face in her hands. 'Darling, no matter what you do, he'd be proud of you. I know I am. To me you're the world champion of cheering people up, just like your dad. That's a big deal.'

Corby straightened up, giving her a small grin. 'Yeah, I know.'

'Go do your homework, I'll be in shortly.'

'What's for dinner?'

'Moussaka,' she called to his back. 'You'll like it.'

*

Night was tiptoeing towards the window where the figure of the young woman was silhouetted at the piano.

Her hands were attacking the yellowing keys, shoulders hunched, her sweet voice trilling, as if calling to be set free and rush into the shadowed clouds. She sang and played as emotions, feelings, laughter and tears exploded from her body, soul and heart.

Above the glorious music came a hammering at her door.

'For goodness' sake, Maddie! Keep it down. Dinner is ready!'

She closed her eyes and lifted her hands. The last notes reverberated around the room, sliding through the open window to sail into the last light of the fading sun.

'All right. I'm coming.'

The young woman leaned forward, her forehead hitting the keys in a discordant clash of sound.

'Aaargh. Almost there, it's almost there.' She sat up and glared in frustration at the piano keys. Then she rose and slammed the piano lid shut as if trying to keep the last notes from escaping.

*

Chrissie lay still, her face pressed into her pillow.

He gave her a playful slap on her naked hip and got up, his feet padding across the floor.

She did not move at the sounds of the shower running, the footsteps, the opening of a drawer.

Soon a door slammed and a car drove from their driveway.

She raised her head, the chill of the early evening making her shiver, but then let it fall again. She lay still and silent, lost in time, until she heard another car arrive, doors slam and children's voices calling.

'Mummy, we're home.'

Chrissie sat up, pulling on her clothes. 'Be right there . . .' The TV went on, and she could hear the fridge door opening. Smoothing her hair, she went out to greet them.

'Hi, kids. Did you have fun at Nana's house?'

'Yes. Where's Daddy?'

'He's gone out with friends.'

'What's for dinner?'

Sighing, she glanced out the window, where the darkness of night had crept in unnoticed.

*

Sarita peered into the wardrobe in the back bedroom. It was her sewing cupboard, jammed with leftover fabrics, a basket of buttons, ribbons, pins, needles and zips, a tape measure and packets of beads. There were hatboxes and shoeboxes filled with trimmings and accessories she'd accumulated from her years of sewing costumes for the Riverside Players theatre group. Some unfinished, abandoned costumes drooped from hangers. Her gaze fell on a small box at the bottom of the closet. She stared at it, wondering what she'd put in there.

Sarita pulled it out and opened the lid. Inside was a favourite doll she'd carried with her when her father brought her to Australia after the death of her mother in Fiji. And beneath it, folded neatly, was the dress her mother had stitched so carefully for three-year-old Sarita.

Lifting it out, Sarita fingered the neat rows of stitches. Was this where her love of sewing had come from, she wondered.

She carefully refolded the dress and put it back in the box. Maybe one day she'd have a granddaughter to give it to.

The daylight had gone from the room, and she realised she'd forgotten what she'd been looking for in the first place. Quietly she left, shutting the door behind her.

*

The trees were still, the surface of the river glassy. Cows were statues. Birds fell silent, settling to roost. Here and there, in the town and dotted across the hills, along the river and gullies, lights came on one by one as dusk brushed over the families of Fig Tree River, ushering in the night.

For each of these women, evenings were ever thus. Did they ever pause to wonder what tomorrow might bring? No, they were busy, distracted, following the pattern of their lives.

But for these four women, life was about to change.

I

THE BUILDING DWARFED HER as she stared up at it from the sidewalk on Fifth Avenue, New York City. How grand and prestigious it must have been in the 1920s.

Fleur Livingston stepped close to read the plaque on the side of the building.

**THE FORMER AEOLIAN BUILDING
689 FIFTH AVENUE**

She walked into the foyer and headed up in the elevator to the eighteenth floor, where a woman was waiting for her.

'Thank you for agreeing to meet me,' said Fleur.

'Happy to help. How was your trip to White Plains?'

'The old Grainger home is very, very interesting. Now I'm keen to go to Melbourne and see the museum there.'

'Yes. Quite. Well, fortunately the office space you asked about is free at the moment, so we have permission to look around.' The young woman led her along a corridor and opened a door.

'Oh. It's very modern, isn't it!' Fleur said. 'I guess my head is still back in the twenties.'

'Well, since the remodelling it's all very different, of course. That's the window where it happened, over there. I couldn't do what she did.'

Fleur glanced around, trying to imagine a heavy desk and armchairs, maybe a lounge; perhaps a framed concert poster on the wall, a vase of flowers or a pot plant. She went to the window and caught her breath.

'It's terribly high.' She peered down, then said quietly, 'It must have taken a lot of guts to jump.'

'Or desperation. She landed on the roof of the building thirteen storeys down.'

'Horrible for them to deal with. Percy and his mother were very . . . close. I don't know any particular details, though,' Fleur added hastily.

'Apparently Mr Grainger's manager had left the room to get her some medication. When she came back, Mrs Grainger was gone. But it's hard to know what really happened – it was so long ago.'

'1922,' said Fleur.

'I doubt many people would even remember them now,' said the younger woman. 'Is there anything else I can help you with?'

'Well, I was wondering if all the pianos have gone. It was such an impressive showroom in its day, I believe. A shame really,' Fleur said, and sighed.

'Oh yes, long gone. Piano recitals aren't such a big deal now as they were in the roaring twenties! That dance, what was it called?'

'The Charleston? I don't think it was Percy's thing. He loved folk music, classical, and of course his own compositions.'

The young woman shrugged. 'Is there anything else?'

'No. And thank you for your time.'

'You're welcome, Ms Livingston. Safe travels to Australia.'

*

A few weeks later, Fleur drove down a narrow road, and at the turning she spotted a jacaranda tree splayed over the entrance to a short dirt lane with white double gates at the end. Both sides of the lane were bordered by fences across the back gardens of houses. One side was screened by trees, the other by clumping bamboo, so she had no clue what the homes might be like.

Fleur was suddenly concerned that the cottage she'd rented from a couple she'd met in Melbourne might not be as the online photos represented, but there was nothing for it now but to press on. She stopped at the big white gates and saw the garage to one side. She eased the car into its dusty dimness.

When she opened the side door of the garage, she stepped into a charming garden and discovered that the house was built on a rise. She walked around to the front.

A white wooden fence framed the garden like a painting, and beyond it a sprawl of trees leaned over to see their reflection in the smooth wide river. From one advantageous branch, a fat rope swung above the water. Older trees, gnarled and throwing deep shade, rose up the hill from the opposite bank. Beyond the river fringe were distant paddocks dotted with fat brown cows, the whole scene roofed in warm blue and fluffs of white clouds.

Fleur turned and studied the small white cottage, happy that a verandah faced this tranquil picture.

She turned the house key, charmed by the front door's old glass panel featuring a delicate painting of a kookaburra and native flowers.

Stepping inside, straight away she drew a deep slow breath. Everything would be just fine. She walked through the wooden house, admiring the surprisingly large, airy rooms, the stained-glass windows, the old polished wooden floors. She felt sure this was a place of comfortable, warm and happy memories.

It was simply furnished, with white walls, so it was clean and bright. A thoughtful bunch of white daisies sprang from a jug on the kitchen counter beside a spare set of keys and a note from the real estate agent with details of services and contact numbers.

Fleur thanked her lucky stars that she had fortuitously met the owners and they'd offered to rent their house to her for the rest of her stay in Australia, however brief it might be.

She looked through the sliding glass doors that opened onto the verandah, with the river view beyond, and drew a deep breath.

Manhattan was a long way from this New South Wales country town.

*

Leonie drove towards home as dusk was spreading like golden honey across the sky, burnishing the underbelly of the clouds. It was calming.

Flocks of birds speared through the air alongside her, swooping to the river and then on, to roost in The Scrub – the main attraction for tourists stopping here on their way from the coast.

She smiled as she drove past the side road that led to The Scrub. It was not the Big Scrub – a rainforest being saved and restored further north – but this small remnant rainforest was close to the wide meandering river, old trees screening the native vegetation from the mown lawns of the riverside picnic area. Ancient littoral rainforest remained in this pocket of roughly ten hectares – an isolated island where her husband's parents and grandparents had played.

It had been overgrown then, the giant fig trees that gave her town its name slowly being swallowed by voracious creeping tangles of blackberry and cat's claw vines. But thanks to a dedicated local horticulture group, The Scrub had been rescued and revived before it was smothered.

She turned at the town roundabout, known as the sewer lid, a boring cement circle at the bottom of the main street. She had always visualised an antique lamppost with twin arms holding electrified old-fashioned lanterns in the centre of a flowerbed, but the local council had no such ideas. A sewer lid was maintenance free.

On a whim, Leonie drove to the top of the street and pulled up in the car park next to the Riverside Playhouse. Turning off the engine, she peered out at the silhouette of the grand old theatre, which stood against the skyline in the now fading sunlight. It could have passed as a weatherboard church save for the wide façade and entrance.

It had started life as the town hall, then became a theatre and music hall, and in the 1950s was converted into a cinema. In the seventies a large cinema chain with more comfortable seats moved into the main town, across the river, and eclipsed the Playhouse. The old building had come perilously close to being demolished until a small group stepped in, helped by the energetic Country Women's Association, who lobbied to save it and have it somewhat 'tarted up' as a multipurpose theatre, though the council considered it 'restored'.

And so it had become home to the Riverside Players, and much to the community's surprise and delight they turned out a production each year of quite professional quality. Leonie, as the theatre's director, was the driving force, and had made it her goal to find hidden talent in the community and produce top-notch productions. She was proud that the shows always sold out.

A ping from her phone announced a notification, and she saw a message from Corby saying his soccer coach was driving him home so she didn't have to collect him after all. With that reprieve, she allowed herself another moment to gaze at the theatre that meant so much to her. Having recently turned forty, widowed for five years, the theatre productions had filled a vast gap. They were her one passion and interest outside managing Wilde Wood, her husband's family property, and, if she were honest, the one thing – along with her son – that had made her life feel fulfilled after her husband's death. She recalled with concern the rumours she'd been hearing since their last production that the council might have other plans for the glorious old theatre. Nothing had come of them, though, so she hoped that was all it was – just talk.

Giving herself a little shake, she tucked her thick, shoulder-length chestnut hair behind her ears and brought her focus back to the here and now. She had to make dinner and then go through her notes in her ideas book to decide on the next production of the Riverside Players. She felt a frisson of excitement run through her. Finding a project, auditioning talent, preparing costumes and sets, rehearsing for months for the next production was always an interesting and fulfilling experience.

*

Madison idly wiped down an outside table. The main street was nearly empty and trade was slow. It was that quiet time in between afternoon and evening. She only had an hour to go of her shift. And then what? She was so bored. Her best friend was overseas, another was graduating university, but most of her schoolfriends, like her, were doing mundane jobs in the town where they'd grown up.

Hearing footsteps behind her, Maddie turned to see a woman approaching. She indicated the table.

'Okay if I sit out here?'

Maddie nodded, struck by the woman's American accent. Fig Tree River didn't usually attract many tourists.

'Of course. I'll bring you a menu and some water.'

'Thank you, honey.'

As Maddie poured iced water into a jug in the café kitchen, her boss, Jordan, yawned. 'Nothing much happening, you may as well call it a day.'

'Okay. I'll just take an order for the lady outside, then I'll go.'

Maddie moved away, but could feel Jordan's eyes on her. *What a creep*, she thought. She'd seen him leering at Sandra, the new waitress. While they appreciated the cash payments including tips, she knew the other staff felt like she did, that Jordan was a lecherous pain, but in this small town you took what work you could get.

She handed the woman the menu and poured her a glass of water.

'I'll come back for your order.'

'Oh, it's fine. I really only want coffee, and maybe some biscotti?'

'I don't think we have that. Is it a cake?'

'An Italian type of cookie. That's fine. Just a large iced coffee, no cream, please.'

Maddie went back inside, prepared the drink, and then delivered the tall glass to the American. The woman was casually but smartly dressed, her blonde hair done up. As old as her nan, Maddie guessed. Perhaps in her seventies.

'Wonderful. Thank you. My, this is a pretty town. You from here?'

'Yes, I am. Are you just passing through?' asked Maddie.

'Well . . . that depends. I'm undecided. I've rented a cute little cottage, so I will be staying for a little while, but for how long, I don't know.'

'Oh, well, yes.' Madison was thinking of how house rentals had gone crazy a few months back, with holiday-makers and tree-changers from the city seeming happy to pay a bundle for a place in Fig Tree River. But it had quietened down since then. 'Have you been driving around the country?'

'Not yet. I spent the past little while in Melbourne and Sydney, so I thought it might be time to get out of the cities and explore. I rented a car in Sydney, drove north, and here I am. This is my first day here.'

'And you have a house already!'

'Yes, I sure lucked out there! And it's even cuter than I imagined.'

Jordan stuck his head out the door. 'Any food wanted here?'

'I'm trying to talk this nice lady into having a pumpkin scone,' said Maddie.

'None left,' he said, and grumped back inside.

'Your boss?' The woman raised an eyebrow. 'What's a pumpkin scone like?' She pronounced it 'sc-OH-ne'.

Maddie smiled. 'I was just having a dig at him. He ate the last two for lunch.'

The older woman chuckled. 'Well, I'll come back another day and try a pumpkin sc-oh-ne, or rather, *scone*, shall I?'

And she did. Fleur Livingston came almost every day after that, when she had finished her morning walk.

Maddie thought the American woman was such a warm person, and looked forward to seeing her. She did wonder, however, why Fleur had chosen Fig Tree River as a place to spend some down time when she said she lived in New York. Why would anyone choose Fig Tree River over New York City?

*

Fleur Livingston was equally curious about Madison. There was something about Maddie that set her apart from other young women Fleur had met – a softness, a dreamy quality. Yet there was no doubt she was efficient and down-to-earth, too.

As Fleur pulled off her sunglasses and sat down at her now regular table a few days later, Maddie came over.

'Have you been out jogging?' she asked, looking down at Fleur's running shoes.

'How polite of you to think that I jog.' Fleur laughed. 'I've been out walking, so I need sustenance. Sparkling water, please, and surprise me with a treat, Maddie.'

Maddie came back with a pistachio and date slice, and Fleur smiled in delight. 'Oh, this looks delicious. I'd better have a coffee to follow. But not just yet.' She glanced around. 'I've noticed you're not busy at this time of day; do you have a moment to chat? I'm curious, Miss Maddie, what do you do with yourself when you're not working? Anything interesting?'

Maddie hesitated, then said, 'I mess around with my guitar and an old piano. I sing a bit.'

'Are you taking lessons?'

'Ah, no.' Maddie looked down. 'I just play for myself. I write songs. The music comes, then I find the lyrics. Or sometimes the words come first.' She stopped. 'It's nothing really, just something I do for myself. Shall I get your coffee?'

'Sure. Thank you.' Fleur looked thoughtful as she watched the young woman walk away.

*

Maddie's body was beginning to protest as she pushed down on the pedals as hard as she could, her mind focused on moving forward.

As the long shadows of the trees began to reach across the road, Madison went harder. She'd never meant to ride into the looming dark like this, but she'd agreed to stay late and do the afternoon shift and then help clean up at the café. Anyway, there wasn't far to go to reach home and she knew every inch of the road.

The car came out of nowhere, passing so close to her that it clipped her handlebar and her bike spun out of control, skidding and plunging her into the grassy verge alongside the road.

As the vehicle roared off, she rolled carefully onto her back, trying to breathe as panic overwhelmed her.

Suddenly there was a shout from behind. 'Are you all right?'

Madison struggled to sit up, gasping for air as a comforting arm and familiar voice steadied her.

'You okay? Here, let me help you.'

There was no mistaking the accent. In a daze, Maddie stared at Fleur Livingston.

'Take deep breaths. You're okay, honey.' Fleur stroked Maddie's hair. 'Don't move for a minute. Where does it hurt?'

'I'm . . . not sure. Just shocked, I think. My hip hurts where I landed on it. What happened?'

'That car clipped you. Try to relax; can you straighten your arms? Legs?'

'Yes. I think so.'

'All right, let's get you home. Can you stand up? Here, let me help you. I'll put your bike in the trunk of my car, then I'll drive you home.'

'No, no really, I can manage . . .' Maddie climbed gingerly to her feet and felt a throbbing in her hip. It was very tender but she didn't think anything was broken. She didn't fancy getting back on the bike, though. 'Well, okay, thanks, if it's no trouble.'

Fleur pushed the light frame of the bicycle into the back of the four-wheel drive, then she helped Maddie into the front seat.

'So how far away are we from your place?' she asked as they set off.

'Just a couple of kilometres down this road. It's a long-ish ride from town but it's pretty. I come this way a lot, but not usually so late in the day . . .' Maddie stopped and took a breath.

They were silent a few moments, then Fleur said

quietly, 'You're wondering why the driver didn't stop?'

Maddie nodded. 'Anyone local would have. Did they know they hit me? It was scary.'

'It overtook you like a mad thing. Do you want to report it to the police? I'm happy to go with you, as I saw what happened.'

'Really? Maybe I should. Thanks, Fleur.'

'We can go now, if you feel up to it?'

'I have the day off tomorrow. Let's do it then. I just want to get home now and have a hot shower.'

'Sure, honey. Why don't you phone me in the morning and I'll meet you at the police station.'

'Well, that would be great.' Maddie glanced at the woman beside her, grateful she'd come along when she had. 'Thanks so much, Fleur.'

'No problem.'

They drove in companionable silence for a little while, and Maddie began to wonder about her new friend. She asked, 'Do you have family? Kids?'

'No. I have a brother in Canada with a lovely family. I never married.' Fleur glanced at Madison. 'That's not to say I haven't had love in my life. I've been a career gal, I suppose.'

'Oh. I see. What sort of career?'

'I'm involved in the music business, actually. It's my passion.'

Maddie's ears pricked up. 'Really? What do you mean? You teach music? Like classical or modern?'

'Does there have to be a difference?' Fleur gave her a quick smile. 'Music is emotive in that it appeals to one's emotions, possibly popular music more than classical in some people's opinion. But we shouldn't be judgemental, should we?'

'I've never thought of music like that,' said Maddie. 'So do you play professionally?'

'I play piano and I've lectured on all sorts of music from bluegrass to ancient Japanese court music.'

Maddie glanced out at the quiet country road. 'So why are you staying here?'

'Resting up, thinking. Doing some writing. I've been working on a project –'

'Oh, turn here, this is the lane to my place,' Madison broke in.

Fleur pulled in at the gateway and leaned over the steering wheel to look at the garden.

'What a lovely old house. Is it a farm?'

'No, just a few acres. My dad keeps a couple of old goats and chooks. Just pets.'

'Here's my phone number.' Fleur pulled a notepad and pen from her handbag. 'I'll meet you at the police station when you're ready.' She tore the sheet of paper off the small pad and handed it to Maddie. 'Okay. Let me help you with your bike.'

Fleur opened the back of the car and lifted the bike out. Maddie pushed it along the driveway towards the front door as a light came on.

'That you, Maddie?' her mum called out.

Maddie turned and gave Fleur a quick thumbs-up then headed towards the house.

*

Leonie glanced at her phone – 8.15 pm. Was it too late to call Sarita? She decided to chance it.

'Hey, Sarita, it's Leonie. Not too late to chat?'

'Not at all. We're watching a boring movie. I was about to head off to bed with a book. Do you have any ideas yet?'

'Not yet. The productions I'd love to do would cost far too much for an amateur group like us.'

'Oh, pity. Too bad we don't get any funding from the council,' Sarita said. 'We should, you know – our shows are always sold out.'

'True. But we all agreed we didn't want the restrictions from above that taking money from council would involve. This way we can be bold and adventurous.' Leonie laughed.

'And do something like *Hair* with the nude scene, or raunchy and fun like *Priscilla*?'

'Absolutely. There's nothing wrong with those. Great music,' said Leonie.

Sarita laughed, but then she said, 'Maybe it's time we *did* do something different. Not a light musical. Something a bit meatier.'

'Perhaps, but it can't be a heavy drama. It needs to be interesting, entertaining, different. I think I'll call the drama committee together to ask if you can all come up with some ideas.'

'I'll try. My forte is really only costumes, though, Leonie, as you know! But it would be fun to do something a bit crazy and out there. Stir things up.'

'You don't "only" do costumes, Sarita! You are a master creative costumier!'

Sarita chuckled. 'Thanks, Leonie. I do love working on our shows. So when's the committee meeting?'

'I'll let you know. Sometime next week? But I'll catch you at the Saturday markets. How's your veggie garden?'

'Overflowing! Ray went mad with the fertiliser and we're growing monsters. See you Saturday.'

Leonie enjoyed her friend's energy and always felt good after talking with her. They did need to find something adventurous and unusual for their production this year. Sarita was right, and she'd given Leonie lots to think about.

*

Maddie watched Fleur as she parked in front of the police station.

'Are you sure about this?' Maddie asked her. 'I just feel they'll think I'm being silly. I mean, nothing happened . . .'

Fleur looked at her. 'Nothing happened *this* time. Sure, it may have been an accident, but if it was, why didn't he stop?'

'Do we know it was a he?' Maddie said.

'I don't know many women who drive a big heavy car with all those macho toys attached and a souped-up motor,' said Fleur dryly.

The policewoman at the desk was noncommittal as she took their names and details of why they were there.

'No number plate? No description of the driver? Type of car?'

'It came from behind me, then I was on the ground, so I didn't see it,' said Maddie.

Fleur opened her mouth to speak just as a tall, solid policeman in his fifties came to the desk.

'Got a problem, ladies?'

'Hit and run,' said the policewoman.

'So you're here to report it?' he asked. 'Who was the victim?'

'Me,' said Maddie.

'I was driving some distance behind,' said Fleur. 'I saw it happen. He just kept going as I stopped to help Madison, who'd been knocked off her bicycle.'

'Why don't you both come and sit down and give me what details you can. I'm Sergeant Franks.'

They followed the officer around the counter as the policewoman answered the phone. He gestured to two chairs in a small office and sat on the other side of the desk.

'Right, so when did this happen?'

'Yesterday evening,' said Maddie.

'So it was dark?' He raised his eyebrows.

'Not really,' said Maddie.

'Five twenty-five pm,' said Fleur. 'I glanced at the time as I stopped.'

'You were following her? You're related? Friends?' he asked.

'Well, we're sure friends now,' said Fleur with a smile. 'I was just driving along when I was overtaken dangerously by this driver and was so annoyed I tried to catch up to get his number plate. But then I saw the girl on the bicycle. It seemed to me the big vehicle made no effort to miss her. He might even have deliberately nudged her. I stopped to help and realised it was Madison, whom I met at the café here in town. Luckily she was okay.'

'Well, let's get down to the details,' said Sergeant Franks briskly. 'We appreciate you coming in. Little bits and pieces can add up – tell me all you know.'

*

'This is a cute place, such a gorgeous setting, thanks for suggesting it,' said Fleur as she sat down at the table, facing the view to the river, which hugged a curve of mangroves without a house in sight. A refreshing breeze wafted over them on the wide verandah of the old home, which had been tastefully converted into a restaurant.

'What's the history of this place?' Fleur asked, looking around.

Maddie passed her the menu. 'There's not much on the menu but everything is so good. Um, I think it was the old children's hospital or something. The current owner lives out the back, she does all the cooking. My mum loves it here. She always comes here as a special treat, so she thought you'd like it, which is why I brought you here!'

'She's right. I look forward to meeting her sometime.'

'I'm treating you, by the way,' said Maddie. 'To say thanks. I was nervous about that police interview. He – Sergeant Franks – was nice, but it was all so . . . you know. Official. But you made me feel confident we were doing the right thing.'

'For sure, but I doubt you'll hear anything. Put it behind you, honey. Now, what are you having?'

They ordered and Madison found herself relaxing and laughing, surprisingly enjoying the company of the older woman, who was entertaining as well as interesting. She looked at her new friend's outfit; Fleur had such a particular style. She was wearing a white embroidered blouse and floaty skirt in a dreamy, floral silk, and had a chiffon scarf twisted around her curly hair. It was hard to tell if the streaks in Fleur's blonde hair were natural or the work of an expensive hairdresser.

Maddie realised she'd been lost in thought when Fleur asked her, 'Tell me, Maddie, I so enjoy chatting with you, but I mean, how does one meet other people in a town like this? If you're someone new, like myself?'

'Oh. I don't know. I know people because I grew up here. School, where I work, my parents, friends . . .'

'In the US, if you move into a new neighbourhood,

there's generally a neighbour who's part of their welcome wagon group. They turn up with home-baked goodies and introduce themselves, invite you to a local get-together to meet neighbours, that sort of thing.'

'Really? We don't have anything so organised. I'll ask my mum to invite some friends over to meet you, if you like. She belongs to several clubs.' Maddie smiled. 'The CWA – the Country Women's Association – does a lot of fantastic work. And there's the Red Cross –'

'Right, though I'm not sure that's my kind of thing. Tell me, what do you do with yourself outside your job?'

'Oh, you mean my music?'

Fleur nodded. 'Tell me more about it. How come you never did classes?'

Maddie shook her head. 'I never wanted to do lessons. For as long as I can remember I just knew how to play . . .' She paused, not sure what else to say.

'Go on. You mentioned you have a piano.'

'Yes, an old one, it was my grandmother's. My mum did classes when she was young but she didn't like playing. She didn't want to get rid of the piano, though.'

'So you taught yourself?'

'Yeah, I guess. My music just happens. I started plinking and plonking away. My fingers find the tune, the words just come, and so I sing them. Then I write the words down in case I forget them. I don't know how to write down the music. I keep that in my head.'

'How long have you been doing that?' asked Fleur quietly.

'Hmm. Since I was about four or five. When I was around twelve I bought a second-hand guitar with my pocket money.' She gave a small smile. 'I stayed in my room and played. I think my parents listened at the door and if they heard music, they knew I was okay. It's just something I do for me, really.'

The waitress brought their meals, and after a few moments of tasting and exclaiming how delicious it was, Fleur asked, 'What are you doing now, here in Fig Tree River? Is the café your calling, your dream job, Maddie?'

Maddie looked away. 'I've never thought of a job as being like that. But sure, I like it.' She paused. 'Maybe I'll record my songs myself one day. Actually, now that I think of it, that's my dream.'

'How fabulous!' Fleur said. 'Start small, start local, sing in a bar, do party gigs, try a lot of different styles . . .'

Madison leaned back in her chair. 'Oh, no, I couldn't do that. I'm too shy to sing in front of an audience.'

'Then what do you want to do with your music? Recording is a tricky exercise,' said Fleur, taking a bite of her meal. 'You mentioned the clubs your mum is part of; is there a music club, or a choir?'

'Choir isn't for me, but the Riverside Players are fantastic and put on shows here. They often do musicals and seem very professional. But I don't have any experience, so I wouldn't fit in,' said Maddie.

'I think you might find that in a small place like this, many in the cast wouldn't have had a lot of professional experience either. They probably started out with none at all, just like you. Some might even be middle-aged before they decide to have a go. You have to start somewhere. The earlier the better,' Fleur said robustly.

'Do you think I could?'

'Yes, absolutely. Would you like to be my age, sitting here saying, "I wanted to be a singer and write music, but gee, I didn't have the courage to have a go," as you Aussies say?'

Rather stung by her words, Maddie nevertheless realised Fleur might be right. 'I'll think about it,' she said quietly.

Fleur straightened up and continued, 'The Riverside Players sound interesting. I wouldn't mind meeting whoever it is that runs the group. Do you know who it is? How would I find out?'

'Yes, the director, Leonie, comes to the café. I'll ask her for her number,' said Maddie.

'Thank you, Maddie.' Fleur smiled. 'It could be interesting.'

*

Leonie looked around at the committee members sitting at the table that ran along the verandah at Wilde Wood.

Except for Sarita, she didn't socialise much with the others as they all led very different lives, although she was happy to have a chat if she ran into them in town. She liked that they were a mixed bunch with various jobs and interests, who came together because of the Playhouse.

Sarita Golding was warm and caring, with a generous smile that would light up her face. Although they were friends, Leonie didn't know much about Sarita's past except that she'd been born in Fiji, was married to a charming man, Ray, and they had three sons. For all her modest demeanour, Sarita was something of a legend among the Riverside Players for the amazing and inventive range of costumes she and a group of volunteers had made over the years for the chorus and lead stars.

Christina Webster was a pretty young mum, and always reminded Leonie of a delicate flower – soft, sweet, shy. But despite her delicate appearance she was surprisingly strong and could wield a hammer and saw with the best of them. She designed and built the sets, sometimes with assistance from a couple of young lads and an electrician.

Roger Lowe was chubby and balding, with cherubic features and a riotous, ribald sense of humour. He was also a pianist of powerful talent, who trained and accompanied the singers.

His partner, Freddy Jones, was tall, gangling, with glasses that slid down his patrician nose. He had a brilliant musical mind and a gentle nature, until the conductor's baton was in his hands, and then he really took command. He could assemble and conduct a scattergun group of amateur musos and turn them into a cohesive and competent small orchestra by opening night.

After a bit of catching up over a pot of tea, Leonie called for quiet. 'It's good to get together,' she said. 'Like a family reunion. Thanks for coming, everyone. Now, I want us all to put on our thinking caps. While I don't expect any grand ideas right now, by our next meeting, I *do* want to hear some inspired suggestions for our next production!'

'When you say "grand", do you mean grandiose, or grand opera formality, or just bloody big budget?' asked Roger.

Leonie laughed. 'You know I don't mean that sort of grand – you've seen our usual budgets! So no grand opera. I mean, thinking outside the box, something we haven't done before, something different.'

'Like a dark moody drama?' asked Christina.

'How depressing,' interjected Sarita. 'I don't think the locals would go for a kitchen sink drama. When they come to our shows they want to have a good time.'

'Hell, yes. Escapism,' agreed Roger. 'Don't you agree, Freddy?' He turned to his eternal shadow.

'Sure. But you don't want to talk down to them. I've found a lot of our audiences are pretty smart.'

Leonie nodded. 'We can't underestimate our audience,' she agreed.

'So are you thinking a drama or a musical?' asked Chrissie. 'Or a mixture of both?'

'I like the sound of that,' said Sarita.

'Me too,' said Leonie. 'But this year needs to be our best yet. We've all been hearing the whispers that council might be considering other plans for our Playhouse. While it might all be just hot air, we need something with a big pull to show how important the theatre is to the town.'

'Oh dear, I hadn't heard about that. It sounds bad,' said Chrissie.

'Surely the council wouldn't mess around with the Playhouse, would they?' said Sarita.

'Our council has no respect for heritage,' sniffed Roger. 'They just want bucks. They could turn it into anything.'

'They could leave the façade and gut the interior,' added Freddy.

'Please, let's not jump to conclusions. But I think we need to do a bang-up show to prove how valuable, needed and loved the Riverside Playhouse is to the town,' said Leonie, and the others all nodded their agreement.

'Do we have a budget, Leonie?' asked Sarita.

'Well, we still have a nest egg from last year's show.'

'Yes, our shows always fill the theatre. Not like those dreary has-been pop stars and wannabes touring around the country,' said Roger. 'They never sell out.'

Chrissie laughed. 'Yes. Audiences love seeing the local

butcher dancing the Jitterbug or the local hairdresser appearing as Maria in *West Side Story*.'

'So where do we start?' asked Freddy.

'Well, as I say, you're all welcome to throw in ideas,' said Leonie.

'You've done brilliantly every time,' said Sarita.

Leonie smiled. 'Thank you, but it's a team effort. Think about this and let's see what we come up with. Perhaps chat to friends to find out what they'd like to see.' She picked up the teapot. 'In the meantime, I'll make some more tea and we can brainstorm.'

They all nodded, knowing that Leonie would turn up at the next meeting with copious notes and suggestions. But privately, each was hoping they'd find some idea that proved how popular and necessary the Playhouse was.

2

MADDIE PARKED IN THE laneway outside the white gates, which stood partially open. Getting out of the car, she edged through the gap into the garden, where a Hills hoist was tucked into a corner beside a small toolshed. The lawn was trimmed, banks of hydrangeas grew along a wooden fence and a lush vine clambered over the small porch.

She was about to take her shoes off to add to the ones by the door when Fleur came out to greet her.

'Don't worry about your shoes, Maddie. Come in.'

Maddie wiped her feet on the doormat anyway, noticing the painting on the glass insert on the door.

'Love the kookaburra.'

'It's cute, isn't it? Come and take a look at the view, it'll knock your socks off.'

'Oh, wow,' said Maddie as Fleur led her onto the verandah, where she had mugs and a plate of biscuits set out.

'Pretty damn cool, eh?'

Maddie nodded. 'The river looks stunning. I sometimes forget that we have such a beautiful river on our doorstep. I take it for granted, but this is really special. And you're right in town, too.'

'I have neighbours on either side but I never see them. Not just because of the trees and the bamboo – they seem to keep to themselves. I hope my music doesn't bother them.'

'Gosh, did this house come with a piano? If it did, the neighbours are probably used to it. What do you play for them?'

Fleur chuckled. 'My unseen audience? Well, like you, I prefer to play my own music, but the project I'm working on is still a work in progress. And the piano was one of the reasons I rented this house, it's perfect for me. Sit down, Maddie. Tea or coffee?'

As they sat chatting over their mugs of coffee, Maddie reached for another biscuit. 'I love these, what are they?'

'These, my dear, are biscotti. I kept a stash in the car when I drove up from Sydney.'

'I'm hooked,' said Maddie with a grin. 'I'll have to get the café to start stocking them.'

Fleur sat forward a little. 'So. I always enjoy chatting with you, but I asked you over for another reason, too. As you know, I'm in the music business. I'd love you to sing for me. Something you've written.'

Maddie gulped and put down her mug.

Without giving her a chance to say no, Fleur rose. 'Let's go in to the piano.'

Maddie followed her inside, feeling nervous. 'You play something for me first,' she said.

'Okay.' Fleur sat at the piano. 'How's this?' She started to play.

Maddie tilted her head, eyes closed. Then Fleur sang softly,

If all the world was wilderness
How shall we find our way,
If all the world was emptiness
who shall we call to play,
If all our world is done and changed
Who will we blame today . . .

And the sweet notes suddenly clashed, making Maddie shudder.

'Sorry, Maddie. Just a little rant about the mess we – they – have made of our earth.'

'The music was so gentle, then sad. I blame the politicians,' said Maddie.

'That's too easy. We all have to do more. Seems we never learn. Have you heard this one?'

Fleur played again on the piano and sang along. Maddie shook her head.

'That was a song called "The Universal Soldier" by my favourite artist, Buffy Sainte-Marie,' Fleur said quietly. 'She wrote it during the Vietnam War.'

'It's beautiful,' said Maddie.

'I think so too, and so impactful. But enough of me. It's your turn.' Fleur stood up and ushered Maddie to the stool.

Nervously Maddie sat at the piano and began to play, singing softly, but soon she gained confidence as she noticed Fleur had closed her eyes and seemed to be listening intently.

> *It's only a mile way,*
> *A day and life away*
> *When we planned to meet*
> *And start a life together.*
> *But fate stepped in*
> *to cheat us of our dreams*
> *and now each day I see your grave*
> *keeping us far apart. So now it seems*
> *My world is neither here nor there,*
> *When you're only a mile away.*

Maddie lifted her fingers from the keys as the last notes lingered.

Fleur smiled. 'That was beautiful. You wrote that?'

'Uh-huh. Well. It came into my head. Mum thinks I'm going a bit nuts with music and lyrics bubbling away in my brain half the time. It doesn't bother me. Sometimes I just tune out . . .' She smiled at her own pun.

'And you don't read or write music,' said Fleur thoughtfully. 'Hmm, well, at least you write down the lyrics. And you could learn to read music, you know. You have a lovely voice. Now, let's go finish our biscotti.'

Maddie wasn't sure how she could learn to read music, but it was nice to hear Fleur's flattering words.

*

'Is this Leonie? Hi, my name is Fleur Livingston. Madison Murray gave me your name. I was wondering if I could come and see you to chat about the Riverside Players?'

'Oh, yes. Madison is a lovely girl. She told me to expect a call from you. Said you were in the music business?'

'Indeed I am. I'm in town for a break to finish a project in peace and quiet. But Madison said there was a theatre group here and that you create some wonderful productions. Then, when I heard Maddie sing, I was surprised she's never been to audition. She's super shy, but has some voice.'

'Really? She's never let on at all. Goodness, we can't have local talent hiding their light under a bushel.'

'I agree. But actually, it's not Madison I wanted to discuss with you. I really want to find out more about the Riverside Players and I've been told you're the person to speak to.'

'Yes, I'm the director. I'd love to talk to you about our group. Why don't you come over to my place, and we can chat about it, if that's convenient?'

'You're not too busy?'

'Well, we're not doing a show at the moment, but work on a farm never stops.' Leonie laughed. 'How about Thursday afternoon?' She gave Fleur her address and the two women arranged a time to meet.

*

Leonie and Fleur leaned on a fence, gazing at the distant cattle.

'This is a magical place,' said Fleur.

Leonie nodded. 'My late father-in-law, Arthur Foster, once told me, "We're lucky to be here, kiddo, but this land really belongs to all the animals, the trees and good grasses and creeks. So you have to look after it." I couldn't imagine living anywhere else, now.'

'I can understand that. I'm so much more aware of

the natural surroundings since coming to Fig Tree River. New York feels a world away.'

'Yes, I was a city girl once, too. I couldn't believe how beautiful it was when I moved here from Sydney.' Leonie gave a small smile. 'This was my husband Tony's special time of day. He was out of the house at dawn to see to the cattle and the endless maintenance and routine of a property. So we'd catch up at dusk and pause and chat over a drink before the evening busyness. He passed away a few years ago now.'

'Oh, I'm so sorry, Leonie.' Fleur put her hand on the other woman's arm. After a moment she went on, 'Did you work at all when you moved here? I mean, other than being wife, mother, and running things too, I imagine,' Fleur said.

Leonie nodded. 'When I first came here I was a teacher at the public school. But I had Corby, my son, and then Tony's father died, and there was so much to do here I gave up teaching. I still miss it, though.' She paused, staring across the paddocks to the hills that marked the boundary of Wilde Wood. Then she went on thoughtfully, 'Tony's great-grandfather came here as a soldier settler, adding more land to the property over the years. So Tony was the fourth generation to grow up here and continue as the caretaker of this wonderful land.'

'Sorry, but what's a soldier settler?' asked Fleur.

'Oh, it was a plan by the government after World War I for returned soldiers to be given land to farm. It was intended to help develop the country while at the same time rewarding the soldiers for their service. Of course, it was a lottery. Some got great land like this, others scratched around in poor country and couldn't make a success of it. Tony said his father was told to always be grateful for this place. Sometimes life really is all about luck.'

'I see,' said Fleur.

'Anyhow, times changed and Tony started to explore new ideas and talk of other ways to farm, raise beef cattle, not use chemicals, learn about regenerative farming. Of course, he was pooh-poohed by lots of his mates. Some locals considered him a bit of a ratbag, for changing how things had always been done. Told him to go and hang out with those other hippies.'

Fleur smiled. 'I was at Woodstock . . . all that mud and music. I suppose I went for the music, but what happened there became a lifestyle and a movement.'

Leonie nodded. 'Tony was ahead of his time. His dad always did things like his father. But now things are changing.'

'They certainly are. The fires, floods, logging, loss of habitat and wildlife. I've read about it, and it's not just here. It's a threat on everyone's doorstep!' Fleur looked around and then said gently, 'It must be hard, running all this alone.'

Leonie nodded again and stood up straight.

'Tony's cancer diagnosis was sudden. In weeks we went from having a happy normal family life to basically living in a hospital room.' She paused, then said, 'In the end I brought him home, so he could see his land in his dying days. It gave him some peace, I think.' She turned to Fleur, her face twisted. 'But it's all so hard.'

'I can imagine it is,' said Fleur quietly.

Leonie drew a breath. 'I've learned a lot since I've been on my own. I have a fantastic farmhand, Harry, who worked with Tony and has stayed on. He's a godsend. But I've had to cut back on the big plans Tony and I had.

Now I just want to make sure that I can protect the legacy that is this land for my son, Corby. I'm trying to keep that dream alive.'

Fleur nodded. Her heart went out to Leonie, who now seemed lost in thought.

'Sorry.' Leonie shook her head. 'I was off with the pixies. Let's head back to the house. I'm hanging out for a cold drink. Or a hot tea.'

Fleur smiled. 'Sure thing.' As they walked back to where Leonie had parked the four-wheel drive, she said, 'It's so peaceful here. Lovely place to raise a family.'

'I'm grateful I have Corby. Sometimes I worry I'm swamping him, using him as a link to his dad. He looks so like Tony.' Leonie sighed.

'Thanks for the tour,' said Fleur as they climbed into the car and bounced over the rough paddock to the dirt track that led back to the house.

*

Just as they'd decided on a glass of wine, Corby came out to the verandah. His mother made the introductions and he shook hands with Fleur.

'Homework done?' Leonie asked.

'Nearly. What's for dinner?'

'Steak and salad. Fleur, would you like to stay and eat with us? It's no trouble.' Leonie smiled.

'Why, thank you, if you're sure. I'd love to.'

And they enjoyed a wonderful meal, chatting easily about Fleur's life in New York, Corby's school and soccer, and Leonie's involvement with the Riverside Players over the years. Later, Fleur and Leonie lingered over coffee as Corby went off to finish his homework.

'It sounds like you do a brilliant job with the shows at

the Playhouse,' said Fleur, eager to pick up where they'd left their conversation at dinner.

'Oh, I've always loved the whole scene,' Leonie said. 'When I was a child, I sang in the choir and played in the school orchestra. Did some amateur productions, saw every show I could. Then when I moved here I joined the Riverside Players, which was run by a marvellous woman, Beryl Thompson. She'd been in theatre, performed in a few big productions over the years before she, too, married a farmer. But she never lost that showbiz itch. She taught me so much. I was her right hand, so when she sadly died, everyone expected me to take over. And I did. Learned the hard way.' Leonie smiled. 'It takes a lot of time, patience, strength and passion to mount a show. But there's nothing like a standing ovation.'

Fleur nodded. 'Opening nights are hell for me. I stay in the background if I'm involved in a production.'

'Do you work alone?' asked Leonie.

'Only until a show goes into production. I do like collaborating, though. I wish I could see some of your efforts. Have the shows you've done been filmed at all?'

'Some have, although I don't tend to revisit them.' Leonie chuckled. 'I try to keep moving forward. If you get too intense and analyse stuff you go nuts wanting to change things or wondering if you could have done better and so on. A bit like life, actually.'

'Do you work with a piano?' asked Fleur.

'Not me, but I spend ages with my brilliant guys, the musical director and the conductor. They're a couple, and so talented! Never a dull moment. They pretend to be temperamental prima donnas but they're caring, good blokes. Couldn't do it without them. You'd be surprised at some of the talent that's around in a small town like this.

And, according to you, that might include some I haven't found yet.'

'Mmm, yes, I bet,' said Fleur. 'You should ask Maddie to sing for you sometime.'

'I'll do that. So how long are you going to be here?' asked Leonie.

'As long as I need to be,' said Fleur. 'I really have no ties but my work.' She rose. 'Well, it's getting late and I expect you have to be up early, so I won't hold you up. This has been a lovely visit. I'll return the favour. Perhaps we can talk more over lunch or dinner at my cottage?' she said.

'Sounds wonderful. I'm keen to see your place!'

'Sure makes a change from New York,' Fleur chuckled.

'I'd love to get there one day,' said Leonie with a sigh.

'Maybe you might take a show there sometime,' Fleur said. 'Now, before I go, let me help with the dishes.'

'No, thanks, it's fine. Corby and I can stack the dishwasher for the morning. We run it once the sun is high. We're nearly all solar-powered now.'

'Oh, that's so great. And water? You're a long way from town.'

'The original small dams that Tony's grandfather made are still here. And we have a decent tributary off the main river. But we mostly rely on tanks, and the biocycle for sewerage. Tony invested in batteries so we're pretty much off the grid,' said Leonie.

'Good for you. We have to rethink things. You'd be surprised at the green spaces, community and rooftop gardens in New York,' said Fleur as they walked towards the front door. She turned and smiled at Leonie. 'Good night, thank you again, and say goodbye to Corby for me, he's a sweet kid.'

*

When Fleur arrived home and pushed open the front door of her cottage, she glanced at the painting of the kookaburra whose bright eyes always seemed to be looking at her.

She nodded at the bird. 'Well, that sure was a lucky meeting. Things happen for a reason. Right, buddy?'

The shadow of a leaf on the trailing vine flickered against the dim painting. Or was that a quick wink from a sharp eye?

Humming to herself, Fleur closed the door behind her.

*

Leonie was thoughtful as she carried the dishes into the kitchen and quickly rinsed them. She was thinking about Fleur's words that her only ties were to her work. Leonie couldn't imagine life without commitments, obligations, family. For a moment she envied Fleur, but the thought of Tony and Corby and their special place quickly brought her back to reality.

'Hey, Mum, that's my job!' said Corby, coming into the kitchen.

'Oh. Of course. Well, here, take over. Did you have a nice evening?'

'Yep. That American lady was pretty cool. What was her name again?'

'Fleur Livingston. I hope she stays in town for a while. She writes and composes music and has worked with some big orchestras and, I think, famous names.'

'Is she helping you with the Riverside Players?'

'Wouldn't it be great if she did? Maybe I'll ask her. I just have to find the right show first.'

*

Chrissie parked near the grand old museum and shepherded her two children from the car. As she turned, she saw Sarita walking up the street arm in arm with a man she didn't recognise. Sarita flung back her head and laughed. It was an intimate moment, but the man was not Sarita's husband or anyone Christina knew from among Sarita's many friends. Feeling uncomfortable, she grasped her children's hands and hastily turned away, but Sarita called to her.

'Chrissie! Hey. Come say hello.'

Chrissie and the children walked over to the pair.

'Hi, Chrissie, hi, Thomas, Mia.' Sarita smiled at the two kids, who shyly mumbled hello. Before Chrissie could think what to say next, Sarita turned with a huge smile to the man beside her, saying, 'I don't think you know my brother, Brett Harper.'

Chrissie looked at Sarita in surprise. 'You have a brother?' She didn't want to state the obvious, that while Sarita was deeply olive-skinned with dark eyes and hair, Brett was fair with sun-streaked blond hair.

'He doesn't come to visit as often as I'd like. I'm the big sister who gets to boss him around.' Then, seeing the confusion Chrissie was trying to hide, Sarita said, 'We have the same father, different mother. Otherwise we could be twins, right?' She laughed.

'Ah, weren't you born in Fiji . . .?' Chrissie was trying to recall what she knew of Sarita's background.

'Yep. I came here as a toddler.'

'Rita was telling me about the theatre group she's in. Are you one of them too?' asked Brett.

'Is she what! She not only designs our sets, she builds them,' said Sarita.

'Well, I do get some help,' said Chrissie. 'And there's

no way I'm climbing up into the gantry. We have some guys who do that for me.'

'But you're the boss,' said Sarita.

'So you're good on the tools?' Brett asked.

'You bet she is,' Sarita said, smiling at her friend. 'We joke, nicely, that it's best not to get in the way when she's got the hammer in her hands!' Sarita turned and waved at the rambling old building behind them that was a popular tourist stop. 'I'm taking Brett round the museum,' she explained. 'It's all been renovated – quite stunning what they've dragged out of storage.'

'Oh, I must find the time to take my two to look around,' said Chrissie, tugging their hands as she moved away. 'Nice to meet you, Brett. See you, Sarita.'

*

Fleur sat in the darkness on the verandah. The soft night breeze cocooned her as she gazed out at the rising moon, the glimmer of the river. No traffic, no voices, no sounds other than the murmur of the water and nearby night creatures. She guessed that if she could see through the hedge and bamboo she'd see the glow of lights, perhaps a TV screen in a dim room. Once, she'd heard a soft voice urging an old dog back indoors.

She was secure and relaxed in her own bubble. When she came inside, she closed the doors to the verandah and sat at her piano. She hoped she was blending into the ambient background sounds of life and nature, her music simply sending the message – you are not alone.

She smiled to herself as she shuffled together papers, sheets of music, and a folder of photographs.

It was now or never. This was not at all how she had planned on breathing life into such a deeply held, passionate project. But obviously she'd landed here out of the blue for a reason.

*

'Leonie? It's Fleur. I'd love to meet up . . . there's something I'd like to run past you. I'll explain when I see you . . . Have you got an hour or so? No, not a café. In fact, why don't you come over here? . . . Fabulous, see you then.'

*

'How stunning is this!' declared Leonie as she looked at the view from Fleur's verandah. 'Why would you bother with a café?'

'I like to stop in and see Maddie after my morning stroll and before I start my work,' said Fleur. 'Please, come in.' She led Leonie into the lounge room and invited her to sit down by the coffee table.

'Now, let me show you what I really want to discuss with you.' She indicated the tabletop. 'Here, I've spread it all out for you.'

Leonie rifled through typed pages stapled together and some sheets of music, then picked up the bundle of photographs.

'What a beautiful woman! This is the flapper era? The twenties?' she said as Fleur made coffee in the adjoining kitchen.

'1928. Her wedding day.'

'How beautiful is this dress!'

Leonie was shuffling through the photographs in absorbed silence when Fleur came back over with their coffees and sat beside her.

'What an interesting-looking man . . . her husband?'

Leonie pointed at one photograph. 'This is in Europe, isn't it? There's something about him . . .' Her brow furrowed in thought, and Fleur smiled, jumped up, and sat at the little piano and started to play.

'Recognise this?'

'Liszt? Or is it . . .? An unusual interpretation.' Leonie frowned.

'How about this one?'

At the tinkling chords Leonie smiled. 'Of course. Beloved of school bands – "In an English Country Garden" by Percy Grainger.'

'Yes, though the piece is actually called "Country Gardens". It's ironic that of all the magnificent music he wrote, his most recognisable and popular piece was a ditty he was very dismissive of,' said Fleur. 'Much later, in a concert he gave, he told the audience, "The typical English country garden is not often used to grow flowers in; it is more likely to be a vegetable plot. So you can think of turnips as I play it."'

Leonie laughed. 'He sounds like a real character.'

Fleur nodded. 'It's quite a story. A musical one. Drama, fame, infamy, glory, passion . . . You can't tell it without the music.'

The penny dropped. 'You've written a musical . . . about Percy Grainger?' said Leonie.

'Look at the front of the folder.'

Leonie turned the folder back over and read aloud the words Fleur had printed on the front: *'Percy and Ella.'*

'I've spent ages in the Grainger Museum in Melbourne as well as other places around the world where he lived and worked. It's certainly a saga, and has been a challenge, but now I need to workshop what I've written,' Fleur explained.

'It sounds like a brilliant idea. I don't know much – well nothing, actually – about Percy Grainger.'

'Well, you will,' laughed Fleur. 'As they say, you couldn't make this up! Look, don't judge till you've read the whole extraordinary story – well, my take on just part of his life, anyway. Actually, it's not Percy, per se, it's told through his wife Ella's eyes. To do Percy's life justice would mean doing a miniseries! Hours and hours!' Fleur turned back to the piano. 'Here's Ella's theme. He called it "To a Nordic Princess".'

Leonie closed her eyes as Fleur played, and the haunting, sweet notes floated into the room. Each time she played it, Fleur saw the gleam of an icy lake, shadows from snowy peaks, a figure striding through winter woods, the shimmering image of Ella Strom's beautiful face as she slowly smiled . . .

Two hours sped past as Fleur outlined how she saw each act, occasionally playing a song, singing a chorus. Finally, she took a breath and looked at Leonie.

'Eventually, this would be a major production. But I see no reason why we can't do a trial run here in Fig Tree River. Not a full production; just a chance to see and hear it on stage, without all the bells and whistles. Would this be something you'd be interested in?' asked Fleur. 'It would help iron out potential issues for me.' She smiled. 'Give the Riverside Players a chance to do something unique.'

Leonie took a moment to let it all sink in. 'Fleur, I don't know what to say . . . It's fabulous! So exciting. I already feel as if I'm watching the show unfold in my mind and working out how it could be staged.' Leonie clapped her hands. 'I'd kill to do this!'

Fleur grinned delightedly. 'Let's run it past your

musical committee. See what they think,' she said. 'But perhaps call your music men first,' she added. 'I need feedback!'

'But don't tell them what you want before they give an honest opinion,' laughed Leonie. 'Oh. My. God, as they say. This is unreal!'

*

Leonie arranged for the four of them to get together at Freddy and Roger's home, a quaint 1930s cottage with an elaborate garden.

'It's my passion, darling,' said Roger proudly as they stood on the front path surveying the lush flowerbeds. 'Wait till you see Freddy's ruddy "collection".' Roger did melodramatic air quotes and nodded meaningfully towards the house, then he stepped up onto the verandah and opened the front door for Leonie and Fleur.

Freddy smiled as he came to greet the two women in the hallway. 'Hi, Leonie dear, so lovely to see you. And very nice to meet you, Fleur.' He kissed their cheeks and ushered them into a formal lounge room.

Fleur looked at Leonie. 'Lordy, you didn't tell me they live in showbiz heaven,' she said, looking around in wonder.

'Movie world, actually,' said Leonie with a smile. 'Freddy is a collector of film memorabilia.'

'Roger collects too, but he just collects rubbish,' sniffed Freddy. 'We have enough Willow plate to cover the Eiffel Tower.'

Fleur tried to take in the assortment of china, glass, vases, ornaments, pictures, posters, paintings and pieces of period furniture that mingled with old movie cameras, red velvet cinema seats, lights, the paraphernalia from studio sets and props. The lounge room curtains looked to be replicas of stage curtains in red velvet with gold tassels.

They followed Roger and Freddy through to the kitchen, where Fleur saw modern cookware that would delight the best chef, and a row of copper pans hanging by a woodfire stove which, seeing the jug of flowers and crystal goblets on the hotplates, she realised was past being used. Open shelves were lined with a fringe of painted paper triangles. Along with the collection of early English cups and serving dishes were distinctive bold modern jugs and plates, and vintage mugs, which caught her eye.

'Ooh, I love those mugs. Art deco?'

'Well spotted. Aren't they gorgeous? They're very collectible, by Clarice Cliff, that great English ceramicist.'

'Do you both cook?' asked Fleur.

'Freddy does, he is a divine cook,' said Roger. 'I grow superb vegetables out there and he works the magic in here.'

'I'll make tea, you do the farm tour,' said Freddy.

'You weren't joking,' said Fleur as they headed out the back and wandered among large waist-high tubs of vegetables, including lettuce and tomato plants.

'How are the old girls?' asked Leonie, pointing at the plump chickens pecking in a well-kept, wire-framed chook pen.

'Oh, Rudolph the rooster went to heaven and the chorus line is a bit out of sorts. Poor darlings are getting a bit past it too, but they still strut their stuff,' said Roger.

'It's all wonderful,' said Fleur.

'Well, it took us a while to get to this point. Life can be a bitch. But here we are – and now we're considered a respectable boring old couple in a small town,' said Roger. 'Come, let's go back in, Freddy's made ginger cake. I'm dying to know what this meeting is all about.'

They made their way back to the sitting room, which had a piano in a corner. It was one of the few objects without decoration, although piles of sheet music and notebooks were stacked on top. When they'd finished tea and cake, Freddy wiped crumbs from his hands and said, 'So. Are we ready?'

Roger sat at the piano as Fleur placed several sheets of music in front of him and stood to the side, ready to turn the pages. 'I'll sing the lyrics so you get the idea.'

As Roger skimmed the sheet music, gently tapping a note or two, humming quietly, Fleur turned to Leonie and Freddy.

'As Roger plays, let me set the scene.' She opened a file of pages and began to read while Roger swept into the opening bars and through to the trailing finale of the first scene.

'Scene Two. This is the first meeting of Ella and Percy,' said Fleur. 'We can skip this chunk of dialogue –'

'No! I want to know what they say!' Leonie said.

'I want to hear more music,' said Freddy firmly.

Fleur turned the page. Roger leaned forward, intently studying Fleur's rows of dancing musical alphabet, which suddenly took flight as he found the rhythm.

'Oh, how divine,' whispered Leonie.

Freddy closed his eyes, murmuring, 'Hints of the classics . . . but the interpretation! And you wrote this, Fleur? You are a genius.'

Occasionally Roger swore when his fingers stumbled as they raced across the keys.

Freddy, now reading the music over Roger's shoulder, occasionally murmured a correction, 'No. D flat . . .' and started to hum as he read the music. Fleur's voice brought life to the lyrics as she turned the pages for Roger, and each of them followed the storyline carried by the music, which ranged from formal to fun, serious to faintly tribal.

Finally Fleur slid the last page onto the cradle and Roger banged the keys, reaching the crescendo finish. He was sweating and flushed.

'My God, Fleur, it's divine,' said Freddy when the last note had faded away. 'It has everything.'

'It is all singing, all dancing, all drama! What a trip. So this is like an overture with bits of the whole show?' asked Roger.

'Full orchestra?' asked Freddy.

'We don't quite run to that,' laughed Leonie. 'But it's utterly mesmerising, Fleur. It sweeps along like a saga one minute, then so sweetly sad the next, and so . . . passionate.'

'Has this been performed before?' asked Freddy.

'We will be the first,' said Leonie proudly. 'Fleur has asked the Riverside Players to premiere it! Of course, it's too big for us to do, too intricate, so Fleur just wants us to do a basic run-through so she can see where she can make any changes and improvements.'

'Broadway, here we come,' said Roger, jumping up and flinging out his arms.

'Just one thing, darling,' said Freddy, looking at the other three. 'Do we have the talent here? Roger is a great pianist, but he's hardly suitable to play the lead. So can we find a handsome, wild, eccentric but brilliant pianist who becomes a hero but hides a dark past and can actually sing?'

'I believe so . . .' said Leonie thoughtfully.

'And a beautiful young woman, his dreamed-of Nordic Princess, who can sing like a nightingale?' added Roger.

'It will be an adventure finding out,' Leonie said. 'What do you think – shall we do it?'

Roger turned to Freddy. 'I think this town is about to hit the headlines!'

Leonie grinned but said, 'Let's not get ahead of ourselves. We all know the dramas that can happen along the way.'

'That's why we do it, darling,' shouted Roger.

They all fell silent for a moment, each thinking about what they were embarking on . . .

'I'll get the bubbles,' said Roger. 'I knew it, I just knew we'd fall over something spectacular!'

'Get the good glasses,' added Freddy. 'This calls for a toast.'

Leonie took hold of Fleur's hands and pulled her into a hug.

At that moment, seven antique clocks of all sizes and shapes suddenly began chiming the hour. It was a strange symphonic cacophony that sent shivers down the spines of the two women.

As the clocks subsided, they heard the popping of a champagne cork, and they all let out a sigh and exchanged warm smiles.

3

DAWN WAS BREAKING AS Leonie pulled on her boots, the leather softened with wear to the comfort of a sock. She remembered the day Tony had taken her into the store in town that stocked the famous Aussie riding boots.

'I don't have a horse,' Leonie had said.

'You will. And you'll need boots to wear on the farm. These'll last you a lifetime. The more you wear them, the comfier they get,' he'd told her, and he'd been right.

She loved her boots and kept them polished and lined up alongside Corby's and Tony's and all the gumboots on the back verandah. Corby often polished his father's boots and waited for the day they'd fit him.

As Leonie headed to the shed to check on the feed for the hens and horses, her mind kept spinning back to

Fleur's music and lyrics. Mentally she went through local talent she would love to cast in such a show, including musicians. Even doing a pared-back version without a full production would be a great experience.

She'd ignore the rumours of the council's plans for the old theatre, or whatever was in the works. The fate of the theatre was a problem for another day. Now there was a show to produce.

Leonie turned when she heard the clump of Harry's boots as he came into the shed.

'Morning, Leonie. Just been in the eastern boundary paddock, bit of fence down.'

'Can you fix it right away, please? Don't want the wildlife in there,' said Leonie.

'Yep. Few wallabies about, nothing too hungry.'

'Not like the wild boars up in the territory, eh?' Leonie smiled, knowing how Harry loved to recount adventures he'd had when working as a young jackeroo up north.

'We'll be in bloody strife if we get wild pigs around here. We got enough trouble with them kids and motorbikes racing through the bush.'

They ran through a quick checklist for the day ahead.

'Right, see you round morning-tea time then,' said Leonie.

'Nope. Thanks. I'll grab a fancy coffee in town as I've gotta get to the produce store and do a couple of other bibs and bobs.'

'Righto. See you later.'

Back in the kitchen, Leonie sat down with a coffee and a pencil and paper. Corby had gone to school. The morning chores were done.

She had a full breakdown of the musical from Fleur and was ready to begin what she thought of as her surgery – dissecting the scenes and seeing which characters were in each one, reading the script and making an initial list of what they'd need for the sets and props.

By the time she'd finished, two hours had passed. She shook her head to clear it and bring her mind back to all the other things she had to fit into her day. But wow, what a show this would make! And she loved it. Her instincts told her this was a hit that could take on the world.

She picked up the phone.

*

The following week, Leonie and an assortment of the Riverside Players gathered at the old theatre, though without Sarita and Chrissie, neither of whom could make it to the meeting. Leonie felt a great sense of homecoming being back in the beautiful space. When they had a show in the works, the Playhouse became like a second home, so it was always a wrench when the show ended and they didn't spend so much time there. A shiver of excitement coursed through Leonie as she sat in the front row, with Freddy on one side of her and Fleur on the other. Roger was at the piano. A few other stalwarts and some new faces perched on nearby chairs, waiting to audition.

'Are we ready?' Fleur asked quietly.

'I guess so. Not a big roll-up,' said Leonie, looking around, 'and no one who looks quite right to play Percy or Ella.' She felt a little disappointed. 'I expect our regulars would prefer to do a full show rather than a run-through.'

'Well, it might be a pared-back version, but it will be done in front of an audience, so it will still be a public performance,' said Fleur.

'True. I just hope we can find the talent to do it justice,' Leonie said.

At that moment a tall man in a checked shirt and jeans came through the door.

'Sorry I'm late. I saw your ad up on the noticeboard. Is it okay to audition?'

'Of course, you're very welcome. I'm Leonie Foster. And you are?'

As Leonie held out her hand, Fleur broke into a big smile. 'You're Sergeant Franks!'

The man gave an embarrassed grin. 'Er, actually, I am.' Then he added, 'Oh, you're the American lady, who came in with the hit-and-run girl.'

Leonie and Freddy stared at Fleur. 'What?'

'It was an accident Madison had which I felt she should report. In fact, where is Madison? I asked her to come along tonight.' Fleur frowned, looking at the group.

Leonie introduced the others to him then said, 'Please, Sergeant Franks, take a seat with the rest of the group.'

'Call me Wade. I'm off-duty.'

'Fine. What's your vocal range, by the way?' she asked.

'I'm a hearty baritone,' he answered cheerfully as he went and sat with the others.

Freddy turned to Fleur. 'Who's Madison?'

'A lovely young woman with a wonderful voice. She's very shy about her singing, though. I was hoping she'd come along.'

Leonie walked onto the stage and looked around at the earnest faces. 'Hi everyone, thanks for coming. First, let me introduce Fleur Livingston, creator of this show – *Percy and Ella*. Fleur is a composer, conductor and producer of some productions staged in New York.'

This elicited some surprise and awe, and several people glanced at each other.

'She has written a musical drama based on several years in the dramatic and fascinating life of the Australian composer and pianist, Percy Grainger.' Leonie smiled. 'You may not be familiar with his name, but he was a musical genius, one of the greatest composers and musical arrangers Australia has ever produced. So we'll let the play unfold, and our audience will be enchanted, shocked, wowed, or just swept away by the music, romance, drama, and the sheer outrageous wonderfulness of Percy.'

'Who's playing Percy?' asked Wade. 'Sounds like he'll have to be able to play the piano and sing, right?'

'Well, yes. That's a challenge.' Leonie glanced at Fleur, who nodded. 'What we need to do initially is get a sense of the pace of the show and the passion of the voices, and how the lyrics, music and dialogue come together.'

'Is this the first time anyone has done this show?' asked a woman Leonie knew from a previous production.

'Sure is, Amy. When this show is a smash hit on Broadway we can all say we were the first to perform it.' Leonie glanced at Fleur again and smiled.

The door up the back opened, and the two women turned at the sound.

Madison waved a brief apology as she hurried in and sat down a small distance from the rest of the group.

Fleur gave her an encouraging smile and looked from Freddy to Roger.

'This is Madison Murray. I told you about her. I asked Maddie to come along and help with one of the roles,' she said.

The small group welcomed her and Maddie gave them a shy smile.

'Okay,' said Leonie. 'Let me set the opening scene. It's 1924. We're on board the steamship SS *Aorangi*, sailing towards Cape Town, South Africa, where Percy first meets Ella.'

An hour or so later the atmosphere in the room had changed from cautious to collaborative, tentative to enthusiastic. Captivated by the storyline and music, everyone was talking, making suggestions and asking Leonie if they could try singing one of the parts or reading aloud some of the dialogue.

Finally, Leonie banged on the table. 'Right, I think we're ready to do a first run-though. Just to see who suits which character.'

Roger played some of the musical interludes and songs as the group followed along, humming or singing the lyrics quietly.

Fleur and Leonie circulated among the dozen people, listening as each sang a stanza or two before deciding who would sing which part. Several were singing the leads to see whose voice suited those roles. There was an atmosphere of friendly competition.

Eventually, Freddy handed Madison some sheet music.

'I can't read music,' said Maddie nervously, looking across at Fleur. 'But if Roger plays it first, then I should be able to follow.'

Maddie stood by the piano, nodding and reading the words as Roger played.

Leonie joined them. 'Are you ready now to try singing the songs?' she asked Maddie.

'I guess so.'

'Good, just have a go.'

Madison began softly, Leonie leaning forward to hear her over the background chatter and vocals.

As the song built and Roger played more emphatically, Maddie's voice rose with more confidence and enjoyment.

The room quietened and conversation stilled as everyone turned to look at Maddie, who, oblivious to those behind her, sang the lyrics from the sheet she held, her eyes closing as she came to the final stanza.

The music stopped, and her last notes quivered in the now silent room. As she drew breath and opened her eyes, everyone broke into applause.

'Wow!'

'What a voice!'

'Well done, Madison!'

Maddie flushed and looked embarrassed.

Leonie nodded and looked at Fleur, who folded her arms and grinned.

'Right, settle down, let's move on,' said Leonie. 'Who hasn't sung Ella's role yet? Anyone else want to try it?'

'Why?' said Wade. 'There's Ella right there.' He pointed at Maddie.

'Oh, no,' started Madison.

'Perhaps,' said Leonie diplomatically. Privately she agreed, but she didn't want to put Maddie on the spot or make anyone feel they couldn't try out for the part. 'Okay, let's move on to the chorus number in Act Two.'

After a couple of hours and several more songs, Leonie thanked the group for their efforts and called it a night. Everybody trailed out of the theatre, talking animatedly.

Leonie walked over to Maddie, who was putting copies of the lyrics into her bag.

'You have a lovely voice, Madison.'

'I was right about her, wasn't I?' said Fleur, joining the two women.

'Thank you so much. I really don't consider myself a . . . performer,' said Madison. 'I mean, I don't think I could do that on stage.'

Leonie went to speak but Fleur stepped in. 'As I told you, Maddie, this performance is really for my benefit, to hear how it all works with music, lyrics, voices. I'm so glad you came.'

'I'm sorry I was late. I had just about talked myself out of it,' Maddie admitted. 'But I didn't want to let you down. I suppose I could sing a part, if it would help you with your project.'

Roger and Freddy came over after packing away the sheet music.

'You have a voice, girl,' said Roger.

'She writes her own songs too,' Fleur added.

'Amazing,' said Freddy.

'Yes, thank you, Maddie,' said Leonie. 'We'll see you next Wednesday evening for a first run-through. You'll be singing the part of Ella.'

Maddie's face lit up with surprise and delight.

*

'Hey, Sarita, can I help?'

Sarita straightened up to see her brother walking down the path. 'Sure, can you help me finish weeding this row?' She pointed at the neat vegetable plot. 'Ray's been busy working late this week, checking the auditor's report for council, so he hasn't had time to do it.'

'Are you still taking veggies to the monthly markets?' asked Brett as he set to work pulling out weeds.

'Yes indeed. The extra income's handy and we enjoy talking to the customers.'

When the gardening was done they headed inside

and Brett made coffee as Sarita washed her hands at the sink.

'Hmm, that coffee smells good. Do you want a biscuit?'

'Why not.' Brett smiled.

'I'll miss you when you go back to Sydney. This has been a lovely visit.'

'It's a nice break for me too, while I'm kind of mulling over my options,' Brett said. 'I do love it up here.'

'What options? With your job? I thought you liked what you were doing? Or is it your love life?' Sarita grinned. 'You're a great catch. What's taking so long?'

'Ah, it's not from a want of trying,' he chuckled. 'I'm not sure, I never met the right person, I guess.'

'Maybe you're too fussy,' joked Sarita.

Brett smiled and shook his head. 'I keep thinking the rest of my life is a long time. I don't want to make a mistake. I would like to have kids, though. You and Ray are doing a great job with the twins and Billy.' He sipped his coffee as Sarita looked thoughtful. 'They're good kids. You'll miss them when they've all flown the nest. When do the twins start uni?'

Sarita sighed. 'Not long now. They're applying for a different university from Billy. They want to be independent and don't want their big brother having to look out for them.'

'They're twins, they'll look out for each other. They're doing different courses, though?' asked Brett.

'Right. We hope we end up with a vet, a civil engineer and – well, who knows with Billy. His Arts degree could lead to anything. But, you know, even though he has a part-time job, he's costing us a packet.'

'Yeah, I can imagine. Living in Sydney doesn't come

cheap. City kids can stay at home and go to uni, country kids have to leave. That's one drawback to living in the country. But it'll be a great opportunity for them,' said Brett.

'Coming up with the money isn't easy,' said Sarita. Then she shook her head. 'I just don't know how we'll manage when we have to pay rent for all three boys. Not that we resent it or anything, we want the best for them.'

'Of course you do.'

'So, what are the plans you're mulling over?' asked Sarita.

'Well, I love my job, but it's twenty-four-seven on some cases. It can be very full-on. It does offer the chance to travel, so I'm thinking of maybe taking a position overseas, change of scene.'

Sarita looked up at him. 'Really? What does Mum say?'

Brett shrugged. 'She doesn't want to stop me from doing something new, but she's worried I might settle there and not come back for years.' He paused and said thoughtfully, 'Do you think Dad would've come back to Australia from Fiji if your mother hadn't died?'

'Who knows. So many unexpected upheavals, I suppose. I think life was difficult in Fiji at that time. And, of course, losing my mother when I was just a toddler . . .' Sarita sighed. 'Anyway, I am so glad he made a happy life for us all with Mum.' Sarita thanked her lucky stars for it – Brett's mother, the woman she knew as Mum, had loved her as if she were her own.

'Do you remember anything at all about Fiji?' he asked gently. 'You and Dad never mention it.'

'No, I don't think so. I was so young! I didn't know what was going on. I think those early years when Dad and I came here must have been hard for him. All my mother's family were in Fiji and Dad has hinted to me that they didn't exactly approve of the marriage, so they lost touch. But Dad always said his folks here were wonderful and helped him with me. Then he remarried and, like I say, I got a whole new family.'

'So you never think about Fiji? Never wanted to go back there?' he asked.

'No. Why would I? My life is in Australia with Ray and we're happy. I enjoy working in the dress shop and Ray will stay on at council till retirement . . . unless we have to move to a unit in Sydney to be near the boys.'

'But you wouldn't want to leave here, would you? You seem so settled in Fig Tree River, doing the shows at the theatre and stuff.'

Sarita reached out and patted his hand. 'Listen, it's not your problem. We'll figure something out if we need to. But it's true, I love doing the costumes for the theatre group. It's a chance to be creative. Oh, by the way, Leonie's just started working on a new show. It's going to be amazing.'

'Oh, what is it?'

'Well, it's just the vocals and music, not a full-on production. So there probably won't be any costumes, but Leonie asked me along to a read-through anyway. This American woman is staying in town for a while, and she wrote it. Apparently she's a composer and musician.'

'What's an American composer doing in Fig Tree River?'

'Good question. She's rented a place by the river and she's using her time here to finish working on the play. No idea where she'll take it from here.'

Sarita stood up and carried their mugs over to the sink.

'It's really interesting to see it come to life with the singers they've chosen. It's like going into another world when you step inside the theatre,' she said.

Brett looked at her and smiled. 'I'm glad you're doing that, Rita. Don't worry about the boys, they're good and they're smart, they'll be fine.'

'Thanks, Brett. I know that. But don't forget I'm your big sister and I'm always here for you, too.'

*

It was Saturday and Corby had gone to soccer with his mates. Harry had the weekend off, like he usually did unless they had a big job on with the animals or a farm issue. Leonie decided to jump in the ute and check the water troughs linked to the creek. Driving across the paddocks where she and Tony had worn a path through the tall grass, following the cattle tracks, she pulled up at the stand of casuarina trees that fringed the creek. The water fed into the river, which wound its way down to the sea. Here it was crystal clear and fresh, flowing from the high hills and the distant mountain range where occasionally, in a cold winter, snow fell. She and Tony used to bring a picnic here and watch Corby clamber along the bank looking for a turtle or a platypus when he was a toddler.

Leonie frowned as she saw the detritus in the creek and the brown, muddy water. She couldn't remember any heavy rain in the area recently. She wandered a little further along the bank, then heard voices. *Where were they coming from?* she wondered. Her property stretched some distance to the base of the hills. Across the creek there was a narrow dirt road and a fire trail very rarely used except in emergencies like bushfires, or floods from run-off from the hills.

Then she heard the whine of a motorbike.

'Bloody hell. Don't tell me bikies have gate-crashed us,' she said aloud. She didn't want to confront a group of bikers, or racist Nazi flag wavers that she'd heard had been seen in nearby areas. Of course, they could just be kids on bikes exploring. Just as she turned to go back to the ute, she saw them.

Two men were standing at the narrowest breach of the creek, looking across at the trees that shielded Leonie from sight. They were well dressed and seemed business-like. She stepped out and headed along the creek bank.

'Hi there! Can I help you?' she called.

The men looked up in surprise; they'd been studying a large map that they held between them.

'Are you lost?' she called in a friendly tone.

'I don't believe so,' said one.

'You are on my property,' said Leonie pointedly.

'Just checking out this land parcel. It's not being used?'

'It's very much being used, and you're trespassing. The land is not for sale, you know. Who gave you the idea it might be? What are your names and why are you here?'

'It doesn't look like you're using it, so why don't you sell it?' one asked affably.

'But I *am* using it. And what I do on my land is none of your business. I'm asking you to leave my property. Now, please.'

She folded her arms. The men took no notice and consulted the map again.

Leonie took her phone from her jeans pocket and began to take photos, zooming in on the two men.

One looked up. 'Hey, stop that!'

'I asked you to leave my property.'

They turned their backs and spoke together, then folded the map and walked away towards the trees.

Leonie found she was shaking. What the hell was that about?

She leaned against her ute, checking the photos. Neither man looked familiar. As Leonie got in the vehicle she heard the motorbikes again, whining their way back up the hill.

She couldn't ease the sense of violation and the niggling concern that the men hadn't just stumbled onto her land by mistake. She jammed her foot on the accelerator more heavily than she meant to and lurched forward towards home.

4

Corby looked rattled when he came home from school and saw his mother in the side garden with a policeman. He dropped his bag and hurried along the verandah.

'Hi, I'm home.' He gave Leonie a questioning look.

Leonie saw his expression and smiled. 'It's okay, sweetie, this is Sergeant Franks. He's in the show we're doing with Fleur Livingston.'

'Hi, son. Corby, isn't it? Wade Franks. I was just passing by and thought I'd drop in for a quick chat about the rehearsals.' He held out his hand. 'My schedule is a bit all over the place at the moment.'

'Oh, I see.' Corby shook his hand. 'Nice to meet you.'

'Afternoon tea is in the kitchen,' said Leonie. 'I'll be there in a minute.'

Corby turned and went indoors.

'Looks like a good kid.'

'Yes. Hard for us without his dad,' said Leonie.

'You want to bring him down to the PCYC? We have a lot of activities after school and on weekends. Sports, clubs, games, camps. He'd be welcome. They're a great group. Lot of good male leadership.'

'That's a terrific idea. He's so wrapped up in soccer, but I'd love him to widen his interests as the soccer season will end in a couple of months. Also, I'll be tied up with the musical,' said Leonie. 'By the way, I'll just mention this as you're here, there were a couple of well-dressed men walking around on my property, down by the creek. Had a map of the district, I think, and they were not friendly. What do you think that might be about?'

'Not from the council? Hmm. Does it look like a paddock? Is it fenced? Animals? Machinery there?'

'Well, no. Tony and I called it our nature reserve. It's a sort of untouched habitat between us and the start of the hills.'

'But you own it?'

'Of course, from when Tony's family settled here. His grandfather cleared a lot of it because of bad bushfires, but it's grown back. We keep the creek banks cleared as a firebreak.'

'Isn't the council planning a dam around here somewhere?'

'God! I hope not! I'm not selling or breaking up this property. It's going to stay in the family. Corby's family,' said Leonie firmly.

Wade nodded. 'Do you have koalas? That'll make it difficult to clear the land for a dam.'

'Yes, we do.' She smiled. 'We've got a small colony

there. I've promised Fleur I'll take her bushwalking and show her.'

'Ah, yes, Fleur. Well, actually, that's why I dropped in.'

'Oh, sorry, Wade, I got distracted. Would you like to come inside?'

'That's okay, Leonie. I don't want to be pushy or anything, but I wondered how you were going with singers, you know, for the main part.'

'Percy? Well, Brian Pearce, our star singer who can also play piano, is away on a long trip to Europe. Whoever plays the role has to be able to play the piano like a demon as well as carry off the singing and acting too.'

Wade nodded enthusiastically. 'Grainger must've been amazing to see.'

'Do you play?' asked Leonie.

'Me? Heck, no. Well, I can pick out a few chords. And I can get a decent tune from a guitar when I sing. But no.' He gave a loud laugh. 'But it came to me that I might know someone who could play the role of Percy.'

'Oh?' Leonie didn't want to get her hopes up, but she'd been getting nowhere with this problem so was keen to hear Wade's suggestion.

'A couple of months back we were called to an incident at the town hall, and there was this youngish chap who'd got into a bit of a fracas there. He'd been caught once before, got into the museum.'

'That doesn't sound good!' said Leonie.

'Oh no, it was fine. It turned out he just wanted to play the piano in there. He seemed like a decent bloke, if a bit, well, out there. Crazy about playing the piano. It's like it's some sort of therapy for him. He doesn't own one so he seems to be making a habit of getting to a piano when and where he can. He sings, too.' Wade grinned. 'Not very smart if you've snuck into a joint to then start pounding a piano while singing at the top of your voice!'

'And you're suggesting this fellow could be our Percy?' Leonie raised her eyebrows incredulously.

'I know, I know. Some of the others at the station think he's a bit of a nutter, but, well, I do appreciate music, maybe more than most. So I kinda stuck up for him. I know when a pianist and a singer are damned good, and he is. He was a bit evasive about his background when we spoke to him. Won't talk about himself, apart from telling me his name because he had to – Julian Halstead. I helped him to get some work out on a property but he hated being out of town. Said he'd rather sleep down by the river.'

'Mmm, he sounds odd. Or trouble,' said Leonie doubtfully.

Wade held up his hand. 'Yeah, I know. But there's just something about him. He's very affable and friendly, and he's got a remarkable talent. Like Percy.'

Leonie laughed. 'Wade! For a cop you're sounding very much like a talent scout!'

'Not really. I just get the feeling he's a good bloke. I'd really like to help him.'

'Sounds like he just needs a second-hand piano, or somewhere to play. I mean, is he a vagrant? He could be dangerous.' Leonie was surprised that this seasoned police officer was so concerned about this strange-sounding man.

'I tried not to pry. He's not a beggar, or a whinger, for that matter. I bought him a cup of coffee once, but he refused to accept any food from me. I think he's very proud. It's just that he was the first person who came to mind when you said you were looking for a character who could sing and play the piano like a madman.

He has a sort of . . . *aura* about him.' Wade shrugged. 'Not to worry. It was just an idea. I'd better get back, see you Wednesday night.'

'Thanks, Wade. I'll think about it. See you,' Leonie said, then waved as he got into his car and drove away.

'So that policeman's in your show?' asked Corby as Leonie pulled off her boots at the door.

'Yes. But not a big part. By the way, he suggested that you might enjoy going along to the PCYC to check it out one night.'

'But I have soccer. Do they play soccer there too?' Corby asked, but with little enthusiasm. 'What's PC whatever stand for?'

'Police Citizens Youth Club. Wade said they do all sorts of things. I thought you might like to go along when I have rehearsals instead of having Harry stay with you.'

'Maybe. If I get bored of soccer, I could try that instead. But Mum, I'm not ever going to be bored with soccer,' said Corby with a big grin.

*

Fleur and Leonie were sitting on Fleur's verandah overlooking the river. Leonie had her large notebook open.

'Now, a few other things,' Leonie said. 'It would be good to film the performance, but there's no one currently in the group who could do it.'

Fleur leaned forward. 'Well, I was thinking that too, and I've found a local guy who seems to have a decent little video business. He does weddings, commercials for businesses in the area, that sort of thing. I phoned him and he got the idea straight away. We'll shoot the piano interludes separately and cut them in. He gave me a reasonable quote.' Fleur grinned at Leonie. 'I'm hoping he'll get so swept up in it all, he'll do a bit more than that for me as a means of promoting himself.'

Leonie shook her head as she laughed. 'Brilliant. I can see how your mind works, Ms Livingston!' She looked down at her notes. 'Next on the list – what should the cast wear? Our budget rules out full-blown costumes. But . . .?' She gave Fleur a questioning look.

'I thought they could all be in black, very simple, so as not to detract from the music and dialogue.'

'Like a choir?' said Leonie.

'Not quite. I want some interaction between the cast members.'

'All right. In that case, maybe you, Sarita and I should discuss some ideas.' She reached over and refilled their water glasses. 'We also need to catch up with Chrissie to see if she can make some sort of backdrop.'

'Good idea. Let me know when we can meet with them.'

'Will do. That brings us to the big hole we have to fill.' Leonie sipped her water.

'Percy.'

'Yes.'

'I just know he's out there somewhere,' sighed Fleur.

Leonie hesitated. 'It's a shame Brian is away. Wade Franks mentioned he knows a guy who's a demon pianist and singer. He's been hauled up by the cops once or twice, though –'

'Where is he? Who is he?' Fleur asked excitedly.

'It doesn't sound like he'd be reliable. As I say, he's been cautioned by the police for breaking into places. Sounds a bit wild and out there . . . too risky, I reckon.'

'I'd still like to meet him.'

'Do you really think that's a good idea?'

'I think it's worth a try. Give me Wade's phone number and I'll ask him about this guy. He sounds promising.'

'If by promising you mean unpredictable,' said Leonie.

'Like Percy himself!' Fleur said. 'I knew we'd find him.'

'I'm not sure about this, Fleur,' said Leonie.

'Honey, this is how the world works! Trust in fate, put it out there to the great orchestral conductor in the sky!' she exclaimed, spreading her arms enthusiastically.

'Then promise we'll talk about it again before you commit to this man. And if you track him down, do not arrange anything without me there,' said Leonie.

'Of course not.'

'I don't want any trouble,' said Leonie. 'We have to be sure we have the right person.'

'Right,' agreed Fleur cheerily. 'So let's call Wade Franks.'

*

On Wednesday night, they were all gathered in the old theatre for rehearsals. Fleur stood by the piano talking to Freddy and Roger, and Leonie was sitting at a table in front of the stage, with the script in front of her. Wade, Maddie and the other cast members sat in small groups, chatting quietly.

The door opened and a man came in, a small camera bag over his shoulder. He was tall and slim, in his late twenties, his hair tied back in a ponytail. He wore glasses and had a big smile.

'Hi, I'm Charlie Carr. The video guy. Oh, hi, Fleur.'

'It's good to see you again, Charlie,' she said. 'Let me introduce you to the boss.' Fleur smiled and nodded at Leonie, who stood up to shake his hand.

'Hi. I'm Leonie Foster, the director. Thanks for coming.'

'No worries. Just want to find out what's involved before I lock down any ideas.' He glanced around. 'Are we shooting it in here?'

'Yes, with a backdrop behind the stage,' Leonie said.

'So what kind of show is it? I think you mentioned a musical, Fleur?'

'Well, the storyline is told in dialogue and musical sections,' explained Leonie. 'We'll do some choreography, movement, but not dance, per se. If you'd like to sit down and watch part of the run-through, you'll get the idea, I hope.' Leonie smiled as she led Charlie to the piano and introduced Freddy and Roger.

Charlie nodded. 'Okay. Doesn't sound like I need a big crew, then.'

'No, probably not,' Leonie said, then nodded at Chrissie who was walking down from the stage. 'Christina is our set designer. Charlie, maybe you and Chrissie should talk about some ideas for visual effects with lights, silhouettes, that sort of thing.'

'Good to meet you, Charlie,' said Chrissie. 'That's right, Leonie, we can do a lot with lighting.'

'Absolutely. What about a screen backdrop with video clips or stills of some scenes?' Charlie suggested.

'Yep, that could work well too,' said Chrissie.

Leonie gave a light clap. 'Right, everyone, let's make a start.' She turned and pointed. 'Wade, can you please sing Percy's role . . . just for now?'

Wade grinned. 'I'll give it a shot. Till you find Percy.' He looked through the sheets of music and dialogue and took a deep breath.

There was a scraping of chairs, a shuffling of pages

and clearing of throats. Freddy stood in front of them, ready to cue the singers and conduct them through the musical numbers. Roger was at the piano and Leonie at her little table, pen poised, ready to make notes. Fleur stood to one side, her arms folded, watching them.

'If you stumble on a cue or miss a note or a word, just keep going,' said Freddy.

Maddie was frozen, her hands shaking.

In the background Charlie lifted his camera, not turning it on, but to frame the scene in his viewfinder.

The overture resounded through the auditorium and they were away. Eyes flicked from scripts to Freddy, voices rising and falling through the opening song and into the dialogue.

Some voices were overly loud, projecting too hard, while others were too soft, or trembled slightly as the singers stumbled over lines.

Then Freddy turned his gaze to Madison, lifting his arm as the opening chord of her first song began.

She paused a fraction, her eyes on Freddy who gestured and . . . Madison burst into tears. Roger stopped playing.

'I can't do this,' Maddie sobbed. She dropped her face into her hands.

Chrissie, sitting behind her, reached over and embraced her. Everyone stopped.

Leonie walked over to Maddie, gently removed the young woman's hands from her tear-stained face, and held them.

'Maddie, it's okay. It's very normal to be nervous.'

'I'm not nervous,' she managed. 'I'm terrified. I can't do this . . . with other people listening.' Maddie pulled her hands free and covered her face again.

The singer on one side of her put an arm around her shoulder. 'We all feel like that sometimes, Maddie. You have a great voice.'

'C'mon, Maddie, we need you as Ella,' said Toby, another regular in Leonie's shows.

Maddie let her hands drop, but she still looked stricken. She glanced across at Fleur, who gave her a nod and a thumbs-up.

Roger struck a key. 'Shall we go again?'

Freddy lifted his arms. 'Right, gang. From the top of Ella's entrance. On three, Maddie, one, two, three.'

Maddie's voice was a bit tremulous but within a minute it grew stronger. She stood up again, reading the lyrics as she sang and following Roger's lead on the piano. She'd practised the song over and over in her bedroom and now that same confidence began to strengthen her voice as she sang with clarity and heart.

They continued, Wade struggling with the tenor role, but while there were hiccups and stumbles, the group put everything they had into their efforts, even when they occasionally tripped over their lines.

As the music, lyrics and dialogue rolled through the room, Charlie slowly lowered his camera. He simply sat, watching, his camera cradled in his lap.

'And, voilà! Finale!' Leonie stood and clapped.

Charlie, Fleur, Chrissie, Freddy and Roger did the same. Then everyone started talking, laughing, gushing with relief.

'Well done, folks. Relax a few moments then I'll give you some notes,' Leonie said.

Over the chatter, Charlie turned to Fleur.

'That's all so interesting,' he said. 'Who was this Percy guy? And . . .' He looked over at Maddie. 'Ella – she was . . .' Words seemed to fail him for a moment. 'Why isn't this a full-on show? Or a movie?' he asked.

'Oh, I have plans,' said Fleur. 'This is a pared-back version of what I hope will one day be a full stage production. It's a sort of test run, if you like. Which is why I need some visuals to screen behind the actors. Do you have any ideas now?'

'You should include shots of those two,' Charlie said, pointing to Freddy and Roger. 'The pianist and the guy conducting the singers. You going to have a full orchestra?'

'One day, I hope, but not for this run-through. One step at a time,' said Fleur.

'Who's going to be Percy?' asked Charlie. 'The woman singing Ella is great.'

Fleur smiled. 'Yes, she's very talented, and now I think she's going to find her confidence as a singer.'

'Absolutely. What a voice. Count me in, Fleur, it's fascinating.'

'Thanks, Charlie. We need your skills.' Fleur turned to Leonie. 'I think he gets it.'

'You've done a brilliant job, Fleur, rough as that was for a first run-through,' said Leonie.

'Team effort,' said Fleur happily. 'Okay, let's do the surgery and dissect all this. Over to you, Leonie.'

Fleur and Charlie moved away as Leonie joined the chattering group again.

'Thank you, everybody. That was a mammoth effort. And well done, Wade and Maddie. I just have a few notes to go through with you and then we'll call it a night.' Leonie sat down and everyone gathered around her.

Freddy squeezed onto the piano stool beside Roger.

'So. What do you think?' he asked quietly.

'If Fleur can flog this in the right places, it'll take off everywhere,' said Freddy.

'Not without the right Percy, it won't.'

'Mmm, true. Maddie is tentative, but she's only just starting out. She has no idea of her own abilities yet,' said Freddy.

'I don't quite get what Fleur is planning. Who's going to watch a video of a run-through without appropriate costumes or anything?' said Roger. 'In the past, we've recorded some shows for our own archives, but that's all.'

'Just go along for the ride, sweetheart. Leonie and Fleur know what they're doing,' said Freddy calmly.

As Maddie said good night, Leonie gave her a hug. 'Well done, you really got into the swing of it by the end.'

'Thanks for your help,' said Maddie. 'I hope I can get there.'

'You will, you will. You're jumping in the deep end – you just have to start swimming. Try to enjoy it.'

'I get overwhelmed by the music . . . by all of it,' Maddie said shyly.

'Just keep paddling, sweetie.'

Charlie joined them and shook Leonie's hand. 'Thank you for letting me sit in. I'm blown away, and it was only a rehearsal.' He smiled at Madison. 'Have you done anything like this show before?'

'Oh no. Not at all!'

'Well, I thought you were great.' Charlie turned to Fleur as she approached them. 'Thanks for contacting me, Fleur,' he said. 'This has been quite a night.' Looking back at Maddie, he added, 'You got transport? Happy to drop you anywhere.'

'I have my mum's car. But thanks.' She gave them a wave and headed for the door.

'Okay, I better go too. I'll be in touch again soon, Leonie,' Charlie said.

Leonie thanked him, then looked around the room – a few people were still talking enthusiastically, not ready to go home. She felt an excitement and energy she hadn't had for a very long time. This was going to be unlike anything she'd done before, she thought.

*

The following morning, Fleur took her usual table at the café, keen to talk to Maddie.

'How are you feeling about the show?' she asked when Maddie brought out her coffee. 'Are you enjoying being part of it?'

'I still can't quite believe I'm doing it. I hope I don't let everyone down,' said Maddie.

'Think of the rest of the cast as family. You tend to bond quickly in these situations.'

Madison nodded. 'I feel like I'm stepping into some new world.' She glanced over her shoulder as Jordan called out to her. 'Oh, I'd better get back to it,' she said.

Fleur smiled and pulled her phone from her bag. She was scrolling through messages when someone said hello and she looked up to see Charlie standing by her table.

'Hi, Charlie,' said Fleur. 'Do you have time for a coffee?'

'Sure, thanks.' He sat down, and the pair were deep in conversation about the rehearsal when Maddie walked out to take his order.

'You work here?' Charlie asked, noticing her long apron.

She gave a brief mock curtsey. 'Not really. I just

thought I'd wear this apron with *The Jolly Café* on it for fun.' She smiled at him. 'What can I get you?'

'A strong black, thanks.'

Maddie headed back inside, and Charlie shot Fleur a surprised look. 'Maddie seemed much more reserved last night.'

'She's not when you get to know her. But she is very shy about her music.'

'I wouldn't be shy if I had a voice as good as hers.'

'She also writes her own songs. I think she's got loads of potential, but convincing her to do this one-off performance has been a delicate job,' said Fleur. 'So you're enthusiastic about filming our production?'

'Yes, it's very different from my usual work for businesses in town, which makes it all the more interesting for me. Who are you going to pitch the video to?' he asked.

'What makes you think I'm doing that?' asked Fleur.

'Well, why not? And why else would you want a professional job instead of a home video?'

'If I do something, I like to do it properly,' said Fleur. Looking up, she noticed Leonie on the other side of the road and waved to her to join them.

'Hello, you two,' said Leonie. 'I've just had a check-up at the dentist, so I'm ready for a cup of coffee.' She pulled up a chair beside Fleur. 'I thought things went very well last night.'

'Yes, Charlie and I were just talking about it.'

Charlie grinned. 'I'm interested to know who's going to be the male lead.'

Fleur leaned forward. 'Ah, funny you should ask. We're hunting down our Percy, too. Except we're not sure how to find him.'

As Charlie looked puzzled, Leonie briefly explained

what Wade had told her about the mysterious man called Julian Halstead.

'It turns out he was let off any charges because he didn't actually break in anywhere. The town hall was open and the side door at the museum was found to be faulty and easily accessible. And as nothing was taken or damaged – he just wanted to play the piano – he was cautioned with a warning for trespassing.'

'What else do they know about him?' asked Charlie.

'The police have no address so tracking him down would be difficult, and it's possible he's not even in the area any more. All Wade said is that he is in his thirties and fair haired. Until our Percy breaks in somewhere to find a piano, I've no idea how to trace him,' said Leonie. 'And there's no piano shop in town.'

'Of course not,' said Maddie as she placed Charlie's coffee on the table. 'I wish there was.'

'You want to buy a piano?' Charlie asked.

'Well, sort of. I have my grandmother's old one, but a new one would be nice. Or even just someone who knew how to tune it. Flat white, Leonie?'

'Yes, please, and a slice of fig tart,' she said.

'That sounds good. I'll have a piece too, please,' said Charlie.

Fleur looked thoughtful. 'I don't want to hold you up, Maddie, but if you were looking for a piano, where would you look?'

'Facebook. The local newspaper. Stick up a message on the community noticeboard.'

'Hmm. Okay. Thanks,' said Fleur.

She turned to Leonie as Maddie went back inside.

'Do you know where I could get a second-hand piano?'

'No idea. Why do you want one?'

'What better bait for our elusive pianist than a stray piano?'

Maddie returned with Leonie's coffee and two pieces of fig tart. 'Fig season. They're delicious.'

Charlie smiled. 'Thanks, Maddie. What else do you do besides sing, write music, and work here?'

'Actually, I picked the figs.' Maddie pointed to the two pieces of tart. 'A neighbour has a tree.'

'That sounds like fun. Could you take me fruit picking some time?'

Madison stared at him. 'Well, sure. I suppose so.'

'Only when you're not busy,' Charlie said, suddenly sounding shy.

Jordan called to Maddie again and she glanced inside. 'Oh, excuse me.' She hurried back in to attend to a customer at the counter.

Leonie grinned at Charlie and was about to say something when Fleur said, 'We need to find a piano.'

'There's the piano in the Playhouse,' replied Leonie. 'But Fleur, you can't just camp in there and hope Halstead turns up!'

'No, I know,' agreed Fleur with a laugh. 'But there has to be some way we can trap him into using that piano.'

'I could set up a security camera and link it to my phone. I'd call you if it goes off and we could go there. What you think?' said Charlie.

'Possibly. I don't want to frighten him off, though,' said Fleur.

'How will you let him know there's a piano waiting for him? And how would he get in?' said Leonie.

Fleur smiled. 'I know. What Maddie said just now gave me an idea. Leonie, what if you advertise for a piano tuner for the Playhouse piano and give your phone number?' She paused as Charlie stared at her then burst out laughing.

'Genius! After all, how many piano tuners would there be in Fig Tree River?' Leonie said, chuckling.

'Not many, if what Maddie said is anything to go by,' said Charlie, shaking his head.

'Most likely he won't have the tools to tune it, but I doubt he'd resist the chance to play it,' said Leonie.

'And you'll just happen to have the music for *Percy and Ella* under your arm.' Charlie smiled.

'It will be ready and waiting on the piano shelf, opened to the overture,' Fleur said.

'There's one thing you've missed in this plot,' Charlie said.

'Tell me.' Fleur leaned forward again.

'You don't know what sort of a bloke you're dealing with. I'm happy to hang around with a big stick, just in case.'

'Thank you, Charlie, but hopefully all we'll need to do is applaud.'

Maddie hurried to their table. 'Sorry, I got held up in the kitchen. Want anything else?'

As Fleur shook her head, Maddie turned to Charlie. 'I finish at three. We can go to the orchard then, if you like?'

Leonie and Fleur looked at the two young people and smiled broadly.

'Charlie, you can tell Maddie about the plans to find our Percy,' said Fleur. 'Now, I'd better make tracks. See you all soon.' Leaving the money for her coffee, she picked up her bag and phone and joined Leonie as they walked to their cars.

'Who's "our Percy"?' Maddie asked Charlie.

'I'll tell you when we meet at three,' said Charlie.

5

Leonie and Harry stood by the ute, looking at the creek.

'What do you think, Harry?' asked Leonie.

'I reckon it's a dumb idea. A dam's not needed, especially here. There's better ways to secure water. It's going to cause more spoilage and deforestation, and mess up the environment. Then there's the hassle of clearing the land and the disruption when they're building the jolly thing. I reckon it's just a vote-getting exercise.'

'I was hoping you'd tell me what you really thought,' said Leonie, and laughed. 'I love that you speak your mind, Harry.'

'No point in beating around the bush. Not that we can do anything about it, if they want to put one in.'

'Why not? Of course, this is all still a rumour at the

moment, but if it becomes a reality, we will have to stand up for our rights, what we believe in.' Leonie knew Harry was a straight shooter, and she respected him for that. But he was not prepared to challenge authority. It was a trait that sometimes irritated her. Harry was seventy-two, but seemed to live by the same rules and ideals as his father and grandfather had, whether or not it still made sense to do so. 'I know water is precious, but if you think it's just a political play, we have to call it out,' said Leonie. 'If they flood the upper valley we'll lose those great mature trees there. And what about the koalas? I know there's koala habitat in that valley. A dam would wipe them out.'

'Well, you find the people who want to build this dam and tell 'em that, or whoever has the bright idea to make a buck or three out of clearing the place for it.'

'I'll do that, Harry.' Leonie sighed. 'But I don't know how many wars I can fight,' she muttered. Things felt like they were getting on top of her. Costs for the farm were spiralling, its income was patchy, and there were a dozen things to do around the place. Tony's idea of rewilding with regenerative farming was becoming harder to manage. She straightened up. 'We'd better keep our eyes out for any signs that there have been trespassers, and I'll make some enquiries about the dam.'

'I haven't heard anything on the news,' said Harry as he opened the passenger door.

'If you do, then we'll have a fight on our hands,' said Leonie, banging her door shut with some force.

*

'Sorry to interrupt, just wondering what's happening about dinner tonight? Want me to cook?' asked Ray, poking his head into Sarita's sewing room.

'That would be great, I just want to finish this.'

'Whose funeral are you doing?' he asked, looking at the swathes of black fabric Sarita had draped around her sewing table.

'Ha! No such thing. I'm making the shirts for the cast. To go with white pants. We're going with a black-and-white piano theme.'

'Ah. Sounds a bit boring.'

'Well, it's not a full production. Not yet, anyway. Chrissie and I came up with the idea, and we'll have a stark white and black background.'

'Right. Could look good. I'm sure Leonie would love to stage the whole thing with all the frills but we'd never get the budget for it.'

'Hmm.' Ray paused. 'I heard some news in a meeting at work today.'

Sarita stopped and looked up at her husband, frowning at his expression. 'Like what? What's the council up to now?'

'I was doing a bit of number crunching, as they're looking at ways to raise money –'

'Flog things off, you mean?'

'Now, that's unfair. It's called harmonisation.'

'So?'

'The Riverside Playhouse was mentioned. It might be closed down.'

'No way!' cried Sarita.

'Hang on, Rita. They're not pulling the building down. At least, that's what they're talking about at the moment.'

'We'd lose all the magic of having the theatre in the heart of town! Leonie was right to be worried about the rumours we all heard a while back. What do they plan to use it for, then? Riverfront highrise luxury apartments? And isn't it heritage listed?'

Ray put up his hands placatingly. 'I'm not sure! If I hear anything more I'll pass it on.'

'Hearing about it is one thing, *stopping* it is another,' said Sarita.

'Don't tell anyone yet, nothing has been decided. I don't want to start a panic.'

'Of course. Just keep an eye on it, though. Forewarned and all that.' Sarita sighed in frustration and turned back to her sewing, but Ray paused at the door.

'There was one other thing that was floated in the meeting – they're thinking of building a new dam,' said Ray.

Sarita looked up again. 'What about it?'

'The site they're considering sounds pretty close to Leonie's property. Has she mentioned anything about it?' he asked.

'No, nothing. Why? Could it be a problem?'

'Maybe. Water's always an issue – not enough or too much and it floods. And dams can harm the environment, especially big ones. I can't imagine this would be a monster, but dams can cause issues for the natural waterways.'

'There's that beautiful creek that runs through Leonie's property. It has platypus and turtles in it!' exclaimed Sarita. 'I reckon she must not have heard about it. Surely she would have mentioned it if she had.'

'Maybe it's just another thought bubble from the mayor.' Ray rolled his eyes. 'Anyway, this show you're doing sounds different from anything you've done before,' he continued, changing the subject.

'Yes, it is different, not choreographed or a full-on production. A concert format, Fleur calls it,' replied Sarita.

'Gotcha. So why is Fleur doing it here? No offence to the magnificent Riverside Players, but it's a far cry from Broadway.'

'Chrissie and I were wondering the same thing. I think she just happened to stumble across Leonie and the Riverside Players,' mused Sarita.

'And decided to try it out in Fig Tree River?'

'I guess so,' said Sarita. 'Maybe it was fate.'

'Oh, you and your airy superstitions,' he said, laughing. 'Back to whipping up those tops. You're not sewing the pants too, are you? Though, given you've outfitted everyone from Cleopatra to Chewbacca, I wouldn't be surprised if you were.'

'Don't forget Cinderella and Captain Hook!' She laughed. The costumes were all stored at the theatre and it occurred to her that it might be time to sort through them and check they hadn't been attacked by moths or mould. She couldn't help thinking of the costumes she could do for *Percy and Ella* in a full production of the show.

'I'll let you know if I hear any more rumblings about the theatre or the dam,' said Ray.

'Okay, thanks,' answered Sarita above the whirring of the sewing machine.

'Spag bol for dinner?'

'Sounds wonderful,' said Sarita, not looking up.

*

Maddie and Charlie were hiking along a bush trail at the edge of town. Since they'd caught up after she'd finished work and gone fig picking, they'd formed a pleasant, easygoing friendship. Their mutual interest and involvement with Fleur's show gave them common ground.

They had slowed their pace as the track was now wide enough to stride side by side.

'So there's been no contact from the ad Leonie put in the paper looking for the piano man?' said Maddie.

'Nope. But it's only been three days.'

'Why did she ask for a piano tuner and not just a pianist?' said Maddie.

'Yeah, well, I guess she didn't want to be bothered with a bunch of wanna-be-famous pianists. Do you play?'

Maddie shrugged, looking where she was stepping on the rocky track. 'I guess so. I mean, I just taught myself.'

'Ah. Right. So have you thought of studying music?'

'Not really. I've hardly left Fig Tree River,' said Maddie.

He stopped and looked at her. 'Why not?' he asked.

Maddie turned and stared at him. 'Why would I? Most of my friends are here, my family is here, I know everyone, I have a job, I'm happy here. I have my music.'

'But that's just it – you have real talent! I don't know much about songwriting and shows, but I've heard you sing and I think you're really gifted.'

Maddie smiled. 'Thanks. I love music, it's just my own thing, you know?' she said simply. 'Why would I go and try to compete and struggle to get known? I like my life as it is.'

*

Leonie heard someone calling out to her and she turned to see Troy, Chrissie's husband, smiling broadly at her. 'Hi there. How are things doing, Leonie?'

Chrissie was lagging behind him, holding her children's hands. Thomas's Under 10s soccer match had come to an end and the older boys had just started.

'Hi, Leonie, is Corby playing?' Chrissie asked as she joined them. 'Thomas's game ran late today.'

'Yes, he's out there in the chaos.' Leonie smiled, waving a hand at the field.

'Might be chaos to the uninitiated. To us experts, it's like a finely honed game of chess.' Troy winked. 'There's a girls' game next Saturday but I wouldn't waste your time watching it. They can't match up to the boys.' He laughed.

Leonie bristled. She found Troy to be a bit of a loud-mouthed know-it-all. 'You might be surprised,' she said archly. 'Think of how the whole country came together to watch the Matildas. Your Mia might like to try it.' She nodded down at Troy and Chrissie's daughter, then turned back to the game.

Leonie loved the town's oval and the adjacent park, encircled by shady trees, though a few concrete eyesores like the sporting club and an office building had replaced some older gems over the years.

'I'll wait for you and the kids in the car,' Troy said to Chrissie. 'See you, Leonie.'

Leonie and Chrissie watched Corby's game for a few more minutes while Chrissie's children kicked a ball around on the grass behind them. 'I'd better get going too, I guess,' said Chrissie. She paused awkwardly, then said, 'And I'm sorry, Leonie, but I won't be able to do those backdrops for you. For the show.'

Leonie looked at the younger woman in surprise. She had always been so enthusiastic and keen to be involved in their productions before. 'Oh, Chrissie, that's a shame. You'll be missed. But of course, no problem if you have other commitments. Feel free to come back anytime if you change your mind,' she said.

'I'd love to, but I just have things on at home. It's hard to get away, especially in the evenings. The kids . . .' She glanced down at the youngsters. 'Anyway, I gave Sarita my notes and ideas.'

'Yes, stylish simplicity, and I love the black-and-white theme,' said Leonie. 'No one else will do them nearly as well as you, though, you know. We'll be very sorry to lose you. I do hope you can come back and re-join us someday.'

Chrissie looked at her, then said hesitantly, 'Well, maybe I could make the backdrops at home in Troy's shed? It's certainly big enough.'

'Oh, that would be great, if it's not going to inconvenience you?' said Leonie quickly. 'We'll fit in around you.'

Chrissie nodded, then glanced towards the car park, where a car horn beeped. 'I'd better go.'

'Right, enjoy the rest of your weekend. Maybe we can catch up soon?' said Leonie gently.

'Sure. See you later, Leonie.' Chrissie gave a quick wave and called out to her children, who grabbed the ball and ran to her. Then she hurried them over to the car, where her husband was waiting.

*

Fleur had her laptop open on the dining room table as she FaceTimed with New York for the fourth time that day.

'Agreed.' Fleur smiled. She had dealt with New York impresarios before and knew how to sell a show. 'I'll have the video of the run-through to you as soon as it's ready. Then let me know how you'll be pitching it.'

After more assurances and a friendly goodbye, Fleur signed off from the call and sat looking thoughtfully at the blank screen. Then her phone started to ring.

'Hi, Leonie, what can I do for you?'

'Fleur, I've found Percy! At least, I mean, he's answered the ad!'

'You're not serious!' Fleur said excitedly. 'When can we meet him?'

'I didn't push it. He asked a lot about the piano. He seemed intrigued when I said it was in the old theatre, but I told him that Mrs Lang, the building manager, is there this afternoon from three o'clock and she can let him in. I'll meet you there before that and we can wait for him to turn up.'

'We should tell Charlie, as he was in on the plan as well.'

'All right. Can you ring him, Fleur?'

Fleur did just that.

'You make it sound like it's a first date,' laughed Charlie, when Fleur told him of their plan. 'I'll leave the delicate tiptoeing around to you, but since you have no real idea of what he is like, I'm glad to come for backup. Do you want me to bring my camera?'

*

It was cold in the Riverside Playhouse as Fleur, Leonie and Charlie sat in the front row, waiting for the mysterious pianist to arrive.

To pass the time, Fleur asked Charlie about his dreams beyond Fig Tree River.

'I don't want to be doing weddings or real estate and car sales commercials forever. I'd throw it in tomorrow if a better offer came along. Especially to travel. I've been to a few interesting places, but . . .'

'Hollywood beckons?' Fleur smiled.

'There's no beckoning. That's the problem. I plan

to save enough to go and knock on doors with a decent showreel.'

'Good idea,' she said. 'If you find yourself in New York, you can stay with me until you find your feet.'

'I'll take you up on that. Thank you,' Charlie said.

They had left the door to the theatre open, and the trio couldn't help glancing over their shoulders occasionally as they sat waiting.

'This place is spooky,' whispered Charlie.

'Oh, I rather love it in here. The smell and the atmosphere, the empty stage . . . it's like waiting for the magic to happen,' said Leonie.

'Da-dummm . . . and the curtain rises and . . . *There's no business like show business, like no business I knowwww . . .*' sang Charlie with a flourish of his arms.

There was the sound of clapping behind them and they turned to see a figure coming down the aisle.

'Bravo!' said a cheerful voice.

The man was tall and slim, fair haired and neatly dressed in a leather jacket and jeans. Fleur rose to greet him, guessing him to be in his early thirties. Up close she noticed how good-looking he was, with even features and a pleasant smile.

'Hi there, you must be Julian. I'm Fleur, and these are my friends, Leonie and Charlie.'

'Hello. Why are you all here?' Julian asked, looking slightly perplexed.

'I admit, we've been hoping to run into you, Julian,' said Leonie. 'You have been recommended to us as an excellent pianist and singer, but we didn't know how to find you, hence our ad. We're putting on a run-through for a show and we're hoping you might be suitable for one of the parts.'

'Oh, well, sure.' Julian shrugged, as though this sort of proposal happened to him all the time. 'Best way to test that out is to play for you.'

'Hang on and I'll turn on some lights,' said Charlie, heading to the wings as the two women and Julian stepped up onto the dim stage where the piano stood.

Julian sat at the piano and immediately leaned forward to look at Fleur's sheets of music. He skimmed the pages, taking it all in. Then he tapped his finger on a key, his head cocked.

At that moment Charlie flipped the master switch and the stage was flooded in light.

To their immense shock, Julian lifted his arms high and slammed his hands down on the keys in a startling punch as he ripped through the opening bars of the overture to *Percy and Ella*, never taking his eyes from the sheet music.

Charlie rushed across the stage, camera to his eye, filming, while Julian flung each page to the floor as he played.

Fleur stood motionless near the piano, watching Julian's hands fly across the keys without pause as if he'd been playing this music all his life. Leonie realised that much as she appreciated Roger's skill, his piano playing was pedestrian compared to this. The themes of the musical numbers – the bravado, romance, sadness, wistfulness and joy – rolled through the theatre, giving the audience of three goosebumps as the show came to life in a way it never had before.

Julian stopped when he came to a second set of musical scores and peered at it.

Fleur leaned towards him, saying quietly, 'There's lyrics to this section.'

Unperturbed, Julian nodded and picked out the notes of the opening bars one by one. Then his hands fell on the keys like before, and he began to sing as he played.

Charlie was moving quietly around the stage, panning up to Fleur's face as she stood by the piano watching Julian gently sing the wistful, haunting song. Tears were running down her cheeks and she held fingers to her smiling lips as she watched her Percy come to life.

Seeing her expression through the lens, Charlie switched his focus to his ears rather than his eyes, still holding the shot steady as he listened.

Julian sang with a light warm voice until he came to the underlined chorus . . . *'And you left me, left me, oh so high, still I ask you why . . . why . . .'* and it seemed he hit the notes with his fist and repeated almost in a shout of pain . . . *'I still ask why . . .?'*

He lifted his hands as the notes and his anguished voice echoed around them and faded away. He looked at Fleur.

'Who *is* this?' he demanded.

She stared at him a moment, deciding what to say, then said simply, 'Percy Grainger.'

Julian rolled his head back and looked up into the gantry, his face breaking into a smile. Then he thumped the top of the piano with the palm of his hand.

'I thought so! This is reminiscent of . . . ah, what was it called . . . when his mother died?' He frowned as he thought.

'"The Nightingale and the Two Sisters",' said Fleur.

'Yes. Yes, that's it. Such wistful music,' said Julian. 'He never recovered, really, did he?'

'No. I don't believe so.' Fleur paused then said, 'I have a lot of questions to ask you. Who are you?'

'Just Julian.' He smiled. Then, as Charlie moved around to focus on his face, Julian lifted a hand and ran his fingers along the piano keys. 'This piano is perfectly in tune.' He glanced at Charlie, gave a flutter with one hand as if brushing him away, and smiled.

Charlie straightened up, lowering the camera, and glanced at Fleur and Leonie.

'Let's sit down,' Fleur said.

She and Leonie sat in the front row. Julian sat between them. Charlie sat on the edge of the stage, cradling his camera.

Fleur was trying to think how to ask Julian about his personal situation; though he looked clean and tidy, the jacket was well worn, but then leather was like that. His gold-blond hair was a bit long and curly but maybe he just preferred it that way. He was certainly attractive and also very much at ease.

'So, you're not a local, and neither am I. You play and sing exceedingly well. What has your career path been?' she asked bluntly.

'Crooked. Not in the legal sense! But my life has taken a few twists and turns.' He shrugged. 'Music has always been a part of it. I studied at the Conservatorium in Sydney and then I got a scholarship to a music academy in Germany. After that I travelled around the Scandinavian countries. When people I met in musical circles found out that I was Australian, they mentioned Grainger. I did some concert tours but after a few years I got over the touring and performing. I wanted to do my own thing. So I came back.'

'What's your connection to Fig Tree River?' asked Leonie.

'None at all. My family is from the 'Gong.'

'Gong? Where's that?' said Fleur.

Julian flashed a smile. 'A bit south of Sydney. Near Kiama.'

Leonie laughed. 'He means he came from Wollongong, Fleur.'

'So how come you're here?' asked Charlie.

'I'm working my way north. Doing odd jobs when and where I can. I took up painting and I've sold a few of my works, too. I try to keep in practice with my music. Have to admit, it's not too easy to find a free piano, though,' he added rather sheepishly.

'So we heard.' Leonie smiled. 'That's how I found out about you.' She explained about hearing about him from Wade.

'Oh yeah, I got hauled in by the cops a couple of times. That guy was pretty good, actually. He found me singing as I went for it in the town hall late one night, and in the museum another time.' He shrugged. 'It's been hard to get work. I have to be a bit careful about what I do.' He lifted up his hands. 'Heavy labour wrecks me. If I break a finger, I'm stuffed.'

'Where are you living?' asked Fleur.

'Boarding at the pub, but I hate it. Smells and it's noisy as hell – but cheap. I actually went and slept in the park a few nights. Too cold for that now, though. And anyway, I'll be moving on soon.'

'What if we could arrange for you to use this piano whenever you wanted?' said Fleur. 'Well, for a few weeks or so, anyway? We could pay you a small stipend if you'd be in our show,' she added, glancing at Leonie, who nodded in agreement.

Julian was, Leonie decided, quite eccentric, but absolutely right for the part of Percy.

His face lit up. 'Well, that's an offer I can't refuse.'

Fleur grinned delightedly then clapped her hands together. 'No one else seems to know about Percy, it's wonderful that you do.'

'May I ask what all this is about?' asked Julian, looking between the three of them.

'Fleur is a composer and conductor,' said Charlie. 'She's written a show about Percy Grainger.'

'Is that what I was just playing? *You* wrote that?' Julian looked impressed.

'I did. Are you surprised?'

'Oh, well, yes, but not that you wrote it,' said Julian. 'This is a small country town. I didn't expect to meet an American composer here, who has not only heard of, but appreciates, one of Australia's most famous and colourful composers.'

Fleur smiled. 'To tell you the truth, honey, I never expected to end up here either! I needed time to relax and polish my score, after almost drowning in Grainger memorabilia in his museum in Melbourne. And now I've found a singing pianist who is like Percy Grainger reincarnated . . . who would ever have guessed?'

'So, are you keen to join our show then, Julian?' asked Leonie.

'Hell, yes! Whatever it is, count me in.'

*

Later that evening Leonie rang Fleur to talk about Julian.

'Finding him was like a movie plot, but he's real. And he can sing! I can't wait to get him and Maddie together.'

'I know,' replied Fleur. 'It was such good luck. I'm going to move him out of the town hotel – pub – to a B&B that's a bit quieter and more comfortable. It will be great if you can arrange for him to use the theatre's piano to practise, plus he can come to my place sometimes to work through the score with me on my piano. We need to bring him up to speed on the project.'

'He's not so weird, is he?' asked Leonie.

'No way. He's quite charming. Charlie says the video he took when Julian first appeared is a bit rocky but riveting! Charlie was telling me he wants to follow the production of the show as well as filming the show itself, as he thinks it could be a good short documentary.'

'Gosh, this is all getting bigger than *Ben-Hur*! How about we meet up with Maddie to tell her the news before the next rehearsal? When is good for you?'

'Give me a few days; how about Saturday? It's Maddie's day off. Why don't we meet for a quick lunch?' suggested Fleur.

'I'll ask Chrissie and Sarita to come along as well. They'll get such a kick out of this, that is, if Chrissie can get away. She seems to have a lot on these days.'

*

Leonie had suggested they all meet for lunch at the Lucky Moon, a Chinese restaurant in the main street, as it was easy to park outside and the food was pretty good.

They chose a table upstairs on the old-style balcony looking down onto the street.

'It's very authentic food here, Fleur,' said Leonie. 'Even though Mr Ying, the owner and sometime chef, has never set foot in Asia. His great-grandfather came to Australia to make his fortune on the goldfields, and he passed down his love of cooking to his family, who later opened this restaurant. It's a bit of a gem in Fig Tree River.'

'It's true. I love coming up here. I always wonder

why the other shops along here don't use their upstairs balconies instead of closing them in,' said Maddie after she'd greeted the others.

'Let's look at the menu and we can each pick something different to share,' said Leonie.

They were giving the waitress their order when Chrissie arrived, looking flustered. 'Oh, hi, everyone. So sorry to hold you up. Had to leave the kids with my mother and I was already running late.'

'Here, sit down and relax,' Leonie said, pulling out the chair next to her.

'Do you have any favourites here?' said Sarita.

'No, no, order for me, that's fine. I'll just have a lemon squash, please,' said Chrissie.

They had a bit of a catch-up and then the food arrived as Fleur was in the middle of describing their meeting with Julian.

'He sounds too good to be true,' said Maddie as she spun the lazy Susan to try something from the various dishes. 'Where's he living?'

'Fleur's arranged for him to stay at a B&B. She's generously paying for him,' said Leonie.

'Good on you, Fleur, that's very good of you,' said Sarita. 'I wish someone could help us out that way. Money's tight in our family at the moment with the boys all going off to university in Sydney soon.'

'But you and Ray both have good jobs,' said Chrissie.

'We do, but just you wait till your two are teenagers. They are so expensive, especially since Ray and I want them to be well educated. What we wouldn't do with a bit more money.' She sighed.

'I know what you mean,' said Leonie. 'Wilde Wood sucks up cash. I feel as if I'm walking a tightrope trying to produce an income while rewilding parts of it. Just for once, it would be nice not to have to worry about how to pay the next bill.'

'You sound like my mum,' said Madison. 'My parents always seem to be struggling and Dad would give anything to be able to return to the land.'

'Heavens, we all sound so poor!' said Leonie. 'But let's put this into perspective, none of us is destitute.'

'No, we're not,' said Chrissie quietly.

Sarita sipped her drink and sat back in her chair. 'What a gloomy lot we are. Let's talk about the show instead – after all, that's what we're here for.'

'What got you interested in Percy Grainger in the first place?' Chrissie asked Fleur. 'I'd never heard of him before.'

Fleur steepled her hands together in front of her. 'That's a long story. I'd never heard of him either, until I was working with a symphony orchestra in New York and I was very taken with their concert pianist. Nice guy, and we were chatting in a break one day and I asked how he got into playing the piano. He told me his aunt had been a curator for the Grainger home in White Plains, which is now a museum. Said he'd visited the house in Westchester County, not far out of New York, several times, and he became interested in the Australian composer and arranger. In fact, he called him a musical genius.'

'Really?' said Leonie. 'That would have been enough to make me want to find out more.'

'Absolutely. I looked into him after that and got a bit excited about Percy's story. So I decided to visit White Plains too,' continued Fleur. 'Percy and his mother Rose came to the US from Europe at the beginning of World War I and moved to White Plains a year before Rose died.

After Percy married Ella, the two of them basically lived there the rest of their lives. They visited Australia several times to set up the Melbourne museum.' Fleur paused.

'Keep going, I want to hear more,' said Maddie, smiling.

'Well, I went to the White Plains house quite a few times, though it would take months to absorb all the things crammed in there. More than memorabilia, there was an aura about each room . . . So that started me on my quest to find out more about Percy and Ella and Percy's mother Rose. Tragically she died by suicide and her death really affected Percy . . .' Fleur stopped. 'All in all, Percy's story is amazing. Sadly his career faded a bit by the end of his life.'

'Oh, that's so sad!' exclaimed Sarita.

'He was Australia's leading pianist, arranger and composer through the 1920s and '30s, colourful, crazy and super clever,' Fleur said. 'He pioneered the collection and recording of folk music and invented his own "free music" machines. His personal life was even more colourful and controversial. He and his mother Rose were very close and had a fascinating relationship, but I decided to write this musical about a later period of his life, when he meets Ella, his Nordic Princess. I've read so much I could spend a week talking about him.'

'And in your musical, the story is told through Ella's eyes as she unravels the mystery of Percy,' said Maddie.

'Got it in one,' said Fleur.

'It's a great achievement, Fleur, bringing this story to life,' said Leonie.

'Thank you, Leonie, but don't forget, we're a team,' said Fleur. 'As a composer and arranger I can only go so far.

The interpretation of Ella and Percy will come from the performers and musicians, and from you.' Fleur smiled. 'As the director, Leonie, you have to know and understand the libretto – the storyline and lyrics – the characters, themes, context. You're the one who's in charge of the overall look and feel and who basically keeps everything in the context of the playwright's, and in this case, the composer's, vision.'

'And you are brilliant at that,' said Sarita.

'That's enough now. You'll make me blush,' laughed Leonie. 'When will you have the backdrop ready, Chrissie?' she asked, changing the subject.

'I've been working on it at night so it's been slow going, but I'm nearly done. I just need a couple more bits and pieces to finish it off,' said Chrissie. 'Would someone be able to pick it up and take it to the theatre when it's done?'

'No problem,' said Leonie. She checked her watch. 'Well, this has been so lovely, but I'd better get going.'

The others agreed and they all gathered their things and headed downstairs. As they waited at the front counter to pay, Leonie glanced outside.

'Hey, look at that sign outside the newsagency . . . megabucks to be won in a special lotto draw next month! Let's buy a ticket between us, shall we? We can share the winnings.' She laughed. 'That would solve all our money problems.'

'We'd be lucky to win twenty dollars, the way these things work, but I'm game,' said Sarita.

'Not me,' Fleur said firmly.

'What if we win and you miss out?' joked Maddie.

Fleur shook her head adamantly. 'That'd be great for you! It's a thing I have, Maddie. My parents raised me to believe that gambling was evil so I never will, but don't let that stop you.'

'Let's do it,' said Sarita. 'We will all put in equally.'

As Chrissie fumbled for money in her handbag, she muttered, 'Oh, I'm a bit short.'

'By how much? Here, I'll lend it to you,' said Leonie.

But Sarita shook her head. 'That's bad luck.'

'Oh, for goodness' sake, I'm sure I have some coins in the car. Let me go look,' said Chrissie, and she hurried across the street.

'Are you sure about not joining us in the ticket?' Sarita asked Fleur, but the older woman was staring at something over the road and didn't answer.

'Maddie,' Fleur said quietly.

'What's up?' asked Maddie, coming over to her.

'Look at Chrissie over there . . .'

'What about her?'

Chrissie was leaning into the driver's seat of a car, looking for coins.

'Not Chrissie herself, but look, Maddie, the car! It's the one that ran you off the road. I know it!' hissed Fleur.

'What! Are you sure? It all happened so fast I didn't really see it.'

'I can see that car hitting you like it's a movie clip rolling over and over in my head.' Fleur frowned.

'Look, I'm okay. It was an accident and we'll never know who it was – it definitely wouldn't have been Chrissie. C'mon, let's go to the newsagency,' said Maddie.

Fleur shook her head firmly. 'Not me. I'll wait outside for you.'

The newsagent looked a bit bemused when the four women handed over the equal portions of money for their ticket as a syndicate.

After registering Leonie's phone number, the newsagent gave her the ticket. 'Good luck, ladies.'

'I bet you say that to everyone,' said Sarita.

'Yep. I do.' He grinned. 'And they always come back to try again.'

'My grandmother used to put names on her lottery tickets,' said Leonie. 'Let's call this our Percy ticket.'

'As in p-u-r-s-e-y?' chuckled Sarita as they walked outside.

As they parted ways, Fleur looked back at the four women and suddenly felt warm and teary. In the most unlikely of places these women were helping her achieve a long-held, seemingly impossible, dream.

6

Fleur slowed her pace from a brisk walk to a stroll as she stepped up onto the old stone bridge, taking deep, slow breaths. Then she smiled as she saw Maddie jogging towards her on the other side.

She waved and called, 'Hey, Maddie! Not working this morning?'

Maddie looked momentarily startled, then smiled and crossed over to join her.

'Hi! No, I'm starting late today. I didn't know you walked this way,' she said.

'I thought I'd change my routine. It's getting colder these mornings, so I don't feel like going too far.'

They walked off the bridge onto the path. 'Are you happy with how the show is shaping up?' asked Maddie.

'Of course! Landing here in Fig Tree River has been my lucky touchstone. It's incredible that I found you all. There's so much talent. I keep having to pinch myself.'

Maddie smiled. 'You sound like Leonie. She says there's amazing talent in country towns, if you give people the right opportunities. Also, I suppose things like the local theatre group help to bring people together, too.'

'That's true,' Fleur said. 'Living in a big city can be isolating sometimes. Though if you have a passion, you seek out like-minded people, and doing just that is a big part of my life in Manhattan.'

'That's the big time. Must be exciting.'

'Sure can be.' Fleur glanced at Maddie in her running clothes and knitted beanie. 'Would you be up for the big time?'

Maddie shook her head. 'I wouldn't know where to start in a place like New York!'

'But you know me now.' Fleur smiled.

Maddie nodded, though she couldn't ever imagine herself actually visiting Fleur in New York. 'I know you have a brother in Canada, but do you have any family in New York?' she asked.

Fleur shook her head. 'No. Not anymore. I moved there when I was young and met the love of my life. He was a conductor and quite a bit older than me. He died a few years later. He encouraged me to stay in New York and pursue my career. So I did.' She gave a small smile.

'I'm so sorry, Fleur,' said Maddie.

'I'm okay, I have a tight group of friends, Maddie. The music world is quite small, if spread across many countries, so I know lots of people and I keep in touch, travel and work with them. This is the first time I've lived for any length of time in a place where I didn't know anyone.

But, well, I seem to have been swallowed up by the locals! Which I'm thrilled about,' she added.

'But you won't stay?' said Maddie.

'No. I might be in my seventies but I'm as busy as I've ever been. Indeed, if I get *Percy and Ella* up, who knows where it'll go!' She glanced at Maddie. 'You have to grasp opportunities when they come along, Maddie, or they might pass you by.'

'And Leonie? Is she talented enough to go further?'

'She's terrific, but she has a life here, a child to raise. I can't see her heading to the big time, really.'

'Yes, you're right. We all have ties here in one way or another,' agreed Maddie.

'It's a bit different for you, though, Maddie,' said Fleur gently. 'I know you have family and roots here. But you're young, gifted, and your whole life is still ahead of you! You should get out into the world. Your problem is you don't realise how good you are! I've seen talent that's been lost, or never pursued, or taken down the wrong road. Success requires making the right decisions. Which is sometimes difficult.'

'Hmm. I s'pose so,' said Maddie dubiously.

Fleur stopped and took her arm. 'Maddie, believe me, time evaporates, so don't waste it. You have a raw and natural gift. You could do something with it, or just have a nice hobby writing songs and singing them. To whom? For whom?' She looked at Maddie's startled expression. 'It might seem impossible to you to move out of Fig Tree River and aim for more. You're happy here, I know. But, believe me, one day you'll wonder, *Could I have...?*' Fleur dropped Maddie's arm. 'Sorry, sweetie. I don't mean to be pushy, but chances don't come along very often in life. If you don't take them, there's nothing worse than regrets, than dreams not only unfulfilled, but never dreamt.'

They walked on in silence. Finally, Maddie said quietly, 'I've always thought my music was something just for me.' She turned and looked at Fleur. 'What if I'm no good? If no one wants to know about the songs that I write and sing for me?'

'Well, find out! You enjoy what you do. If no one else does, then keep doing it just for you. That's your decision. You have to totally believe in yourself, to hang in there no matter what.' She looked at Maddie and smiled. 'No pressure.'

Maddie burst out laughing. 'Okay, I'll lock myself in my bedroom and think about it.'

'In the meantime, have fun and enjoy what you're doing with Leonie and the gang.'

'We're all doing it with you, too, Fleur,' said Maddie.

Fleur nodded and picked up the pace. 'Let's get moving, okay?' But her voice was husky as she stepped out ahead of Maddie.

*

Sundown. It was Tony time and Leonie sat on the western verandah watching the sky melt into burning gold clouds as Corby juggled a soccer ball in the twilight. She'd been thinking about how to tackle the issue of the dam. Then she had a thought. She picked up her phone.

'Hi, Sarita, how's it going?' she began.

'Oh, hi, Leonie. Good, thanks. Have you rung about the show? I'm really looking forward to meeting Julian.'

'Well, that's one reason I called. We'll have a run-through next Wednesday. Julian is getting his head around it all first. But actually, there's something else I wanted to ask you. You once mentioned that your brother is an environmental lawyer, as I remember?'

'Brett? Yes, what do you want him for?'

'Something's come up and I don't know what to do –' Leonie realised her voice was shaking.

'What's happened, Leonie?' Sarita sounded concerned.

She took a breath. 'I've heard that a dam might be put in above my land. Could be disastrous – it would certainly devalue the place and damage habitat and so on.'

'Good heavens. Ray did say recently that the council were tabling plans for a dam in the area, but he didn't have any details. He might know more now, but yes, perhaps it would be best to talk to Brett.'

'I'm not sure I can spare the time to go to Sydney to see him, and I can't really afford him just yet, but if he wouldn't mind a quick chat to guide me, that would be amazing.'

'Of course, and I can help – Brett's visiting us this weekend to clear his head between cases. He's here for a few days. Why don't you come over?'

'Really? Well, that'd be wonderful. Thanks, Sarita.'

*

They sat in Sarita's sunroom and made small talk for a short time, then Sarita stood up.

'I have a couple of things to do. Call me if you want more tea or something stronger,' she said, and left them to chat.

Leonie liked Brett immediately. He was warm and friendly, very like Sarita, she thought.

'Well, Leonie, I can't offer too much advice yet, as it appears to be early days,' he said after she'd explained the situation. 'Dams are expensive and highly contentious, so the red tape is endless. I'd say you should start by getting some confirmation of the plan, which could be difficult. Try to find out why it's being considered now, and why in that location. How big will it be? You might also try to find out what the Environmental Impact Study says – they'd have to get one done.'

'I understand,' she said, but wondered how she'd ever find out all those details.

'When you have some solid info, let me know, then we can move to the next step.' He smiled. 'And feel free to drop into any conversations about the dam that you have a lawyer to advise you.'

'That's so kind of you. I really appreciate your help,' said Leonie. 'Our area is such a special place. My late husband loved it and so do I.'

'Have you always raised beef cattle, or was it dairy? There's a lot of dairy farms around here.'

'Tony's family always had beef cattle. There was a bit of a family rift in the early days, I believe. One of the brothers wanted to clear all the trees, but the rest of the family considered it too hard and dangerous to log. When Tony took over, his plan was to diversify what we produced and rewild part of it, regenerate the land around the creek and back paddocks that had been farmed for so many years.'

'Tony was probably considered a bit radical?' Brett smiled.

'Yes, among some of the older farmers. Most people hadn't heard of rewilding or regenerative farming.'

'It sounds like a big project. Keep me in the loop about the dam and we can talk next time I come up. I love coming here, not just to see Rita, Ray and the boys, but I just love Fig Tree River.'

'But you and Sarita grew up in Sydney?'

'Yes, and it was great, but these days I enjoy having a break from the city sometimes.'

Sarita stuck her head in the door. 'Leonie, you're not driving your ute, are you?'

'No. Why?'

'I have some materials for Chrissie to use for the backdrop. Some plywood and tins of paint and stuff.'

'I can fit them in the back of my four-wheel drive,' said Brett.

'Well, if you wouldn't mind driving them over to her, that'd be great,' said Sarita. 'Everyone is dying to meet Julian. Is it okay if I come to the afternoon rehearsal?' she added.

'Of course. You still on holiday from the shop then?' said Leonie.

'Permanently, it seems.' Sarita grimaced. 'Margaret has decided to close the dress shop and retire. I'm out of a job.'

'Oh no!' exclaimed Leonie. 'I'm so sorry, Sarita.'

Brett looked shocked. 'Rita, I thought you said you'd taken some time off while I was here. Are you okay?'

'Sorry, Brett. I didn't say anything before because I didn't want to spoil your visit,' she said. 'I'm looking for another job, but this couldn't come at a worse time, really.'

'How can I help you, Rita?' asked Brett, sounding concerned.

'Oh, I'm sure we'll be all right. Ray is hoping to get a raise and I'll find another job. We'll manage.'

Leonie stood up and gave Sarita a quick hug. 'I'll keep an ear open in case I hear of anything.' She turned to Brett. 'Thank you again for all your help. I'll let you know what I find out.'

After Sarita walked Leonie to the door, she came back into the lounge room. 'C'mon, Brett, I'll give you the stuff for Chrissie.'

'An address would be helpful, too,' he said, and Sarita chuckled.

'She's at the edge of town, not far.'

*

Brett was pulling into the driveway when Chrissie came outside, shading her eyes as she looked to see who it was.

He wound down the window. 'Hi, Chrissie. It's me, Brett. Sarita's brother.'

'Oh. Right.' She looked confused, so Brett pointed over his shoulder towards the rear of the car.

'I've got some building stuff for you.' He got out of his four-wheel drive. 'For the show?'

'Oh, wonderful.' Her face cleared. 'Would you mind helping me bring it into the shed?'

'Of course not.' Brett handed Chrissie a tin of paint, then pulled out the sheets of plywood. 'I'll come back for the rest – where's your workshop?'

He followed her around the house past fruit trees and vegetable beds and stopped in surprise.

'Wow, now that's a shed!'

'The previous owner built it to store his machinery and tractor. My husband Troy keeps all his plumbing supplies and tools in there. I have a workshop tucked in a corner.'

'Troy's lucky to have so much space,' said Brett.

'I suppose so. This is my area over here. Thanks so much for bringing this, Brett. I'll get to work later. I'm looking forward to it.'

After he brought in the last of the materials from his

car, Brett glanced at the array of tools all neatly stacked and hung on a wall next to a workbench.

'Who taught you how to build?' he asked curiously.

'My grandad, actually. I did woodwork at school. I liked it better than cooking or any of those kinds of subjects. But it's just a hobby. You know, a bit of an escape. Some people knit or paint pictures – I build things.'

'I see.' Brett suddenly felt uncomfortable, though he wasn't sure why.

'Do you have a hobby?' she asked.

Brett looked down at her green eyes and pretty face.

'Ah. Not really. It feels like I always have too much work on. But if I have a chance I like bushwalking.'

They stared at each other, wondering where to take this small talk. At the sound of a car driving in, Chrissie startled and turned away. 'Gosh, I'd better go. I left something on the stove. Thanks again for bringing this over.' She gave him a small wave and hurried away.

Brett rounded the house to find a man staring at his four-wheel drive.

'Hi! Troy is it? I'm Brett, Sarita's brother.' He smiled and extended his hand.

Troy raised his eyebrows, taking his hand.

'You delivering something?'

'Yes. My sister asked me to drop some building materials over here. For the set of the musical.'

'I didn't think they were doing anything fancy this year, just recording it or something? You in the show?' asked Troy, looking puzzled. 'New around here?'

'Just up here for a short break, staying with Sarita and Ray. And no, I'm not in the show. Can't sing to save myself!'

'Right. I see.'

'Must be great having a wife who's so handy on the tools,' said Brett.

'Maybe. But she can't cook to save herself,' said Troy with a grin. 'You staying around long enough for this show thing?'

'No, but I might come back to see it,' said Brett as he opened his car door.

'Well, thanks. Saved me a trip. See you round.'

He turned and went inside as Brett started his car and drove back out onto the road.

*

There was an atmosphere of excitement and curiosity among the cast. Freddy and Roger, looking as nonchalant as they could, handed out the librettos while Charlie adjusted his lighting. He was going to shoot a practice run even though this was just a rehearsal. All were waiting for Leonie and Julian to arrive.

'C'mon, folks, let's have a warm-up,' suggested Freddy.

They gathered on the stage, then Roger ran them through the warm-up exercises.

'What scenes are we doing?' asked Wade.

'I think Leonie wants to run it from the top,' said Freddy. 'In fact, here they are!'

Everyone turned to stare at Leonie and Julian as they came down the shadowy aisle and stepped up onto the stage.

Roger rose and gestured to the piano stool. Julian gave him a small bow and sat at the piano, then started playing 'Country Gardens' at double speed, then laughingly ran his fingers along the keys and stood up. 'It's good to meet you all.'

The mood was suddenly relaxed and comfortable as they all welcomed Julian.

Wade pumped his hand. 'Well, I didn't expect to meet you again, but I'm glad I have. Very pleased to see you here.'

'I believe I have you to thank for suggesting me to Leonie,' said Julian.

'Oh, I had no trouble remembering you.' Wade laughed. 'Never heard anything like it when I found you in the town hall that time.'

Leonie smiled at Fleur, who'd just arrived, then clapped her hands. 'Okay, everyone. Let's begin.'

She ran through the preliminaries, checking in with all those playing the main roles. Everyone settled down, taking their seats in the ring of chairs on stage, shuffling through the pages of their scripts.

Julian sat down next to Maddie and said, 'Hi, Ella.'

Maddie grinned. 'G'day, Percy.'

Roger began to play and Freddy spread his sheets on top of the piano and lifted his arm ready to cue the opening chorus.

Julian sang well and his personality was infectious. Leonie noted with satisfaction how the rest of the cast stepped up, allowing their characters to shine. What's more, they all looked like they were enjoying themselves.

When it came time for a scene where Percy himself was to play the piano and sing, Roger and Julian exchanged places.

As Julian began playing, the group fell silent and turned to look at him, open-mouthed. When he turned to deliver his next line and saw everybody just staring in awe at him, he laughed.

'Cut it out, guys!'

'Let's take a break,' said Leonie, glancing at Fleur, who was grinning from ear to ear.

The ice had been broken, and everyone milled around, talking about the show. Julian had become one of the gang.

Roger turned to Freddy. 'It's easy to see that Fleur and Leonie have put a bit of time into getting Julian up to speed,' he said.

'The coaching certainly paid off,' agreed Freddy. 'Plus, he's a natural.'

'Natural genius?' said Roger. 'Some miracle that they found him. He won't be looking for work after this.'

'Or looking for pianos,' Freddy chortled.

Maddie walked over to Charlie, who was checking his camera.

'Did you get that? Julian's playing?'

'I sure did. And your faces as everyone was watching him. It's great footage.' He smiled at her.

'So are you going to film all our rehearsals?'

'Not all of them. Although I want to do some separate segments. Some backgrounders of you, Julian, Fleur and Leonie, so that we get to know who you are before you turn into Ella.'

'Ah, okay. Sounds interesting. You'll have more than enough material, I guess.'

'That's an understatement.'

'I hope everyone else falls in love with Julian as Percy, just as all of us have,' said Maddie.

'They'll all fall in love with you too,' said Charlie softly.

*

Sarita was seated in the front row of the theatre when Fleur joined her.

'Maddie sings so beautifully,' Sarita said. 'A glorious voice. She and Julian should keep performing together after this show, they're both extraordinary.'

'Yes, their voices really complement each other,' Fleur said. 'How are you going with the costumes?'

'Nearly finished.'

Fleur smiled. 'You know, Percy made a lot of his own clothes. He loved towelling, wore caftans and did African beadwork. Even made shoes for himself. Fabulous things! His mother sewed for him too.'

'Really? Wow, he was the gift that keeps on giving,' said Sarita.

'Indeed he was,' Fleur said.

Up on the stage, Leonie clapped for everyone's attention. 'Act Three, please.'

*

Charlie rang Maddie as she was pulling on her bike helmet.

'Hi, Mads, have you finished work?'

'I'm just getting on my bike to ride home. Why?'

'I'm going to check out a dairy farm for a TV commercial. The owners have opened up a creamery café and a shop selling their cheeses. It looks like a cute place. Thought you might like to come? I could pick you up at your place in forty-five minutes or so, if you're keen?'

'Sure. Sounds fun. You know where I live?'

Maddie raced home and changed in ten minutes flat, into her favourite jeans, a knotted T-shirt and pink sneakers. She let her hair down and threw on some lip gloss but didn't bother with anything more elaborate. She liked Charlie. He was fun and easy to be with, which suited her fine. She'd had one passionate relationship, which had ended badly, and she didn't feel quite ready to fling herself into another yet. She was too busy with Fleur's show, anyway. But she enjoyed having a friend to hang out with.

She saw Charlie pull up and ran down the driveway.

'Hi,' she said as she opened the passenger door and got in. 'So where is this farm?'

'Not too far south. In a pretty area. Picture-perfect dairy country. Fat cattle, green paddocks, and old trees along a shady creek, from what I saw on their website. I think their shop only opens on the weekend; they're too busy during the week, I suppose.'

'Is this the first time you've been there?'

'Yeah, I want to meet with them at their property and find out more about their ideas and what I can suggest. Talking to them on the phone, they sound really interesting. They want to do a TV ad to help market their products – cheeses, gelato, all things dairy – and meat.'

'Oh, they eat their cows?'

'Waste not, want not, I guess. I might not focus on that in the ad,' Charlie said dryly, and turned and smiled at her.

'Do you ever make things look better than they are?' asked Maddie.

'You bet. And people. With all kinds of effects and now with AI. But I prefer to keep it real as much as possible.'

'I suppose you can also use music to create a feeling in a film.'

'Definitely. Music is a big one,' agreed Charlie. 'It sets the mood.'

'Hmmm.' Maddie was silent as she looked at the rolling hills patched with dark green forests. 'Could you live out here?' she asked.

'I'm not sure I could live this far out. I couldn't manage a property, and besides, I like to be near the sea, or a river. Could you live in a city?'

'No, I don't think so. I mean, not permanently. I'm a country girl.'

'Your parents live in town, but are they from the land?'

Maddie hesitated a moment. 'Yes and no. My father was, but we had to sell up when there was that terrible drought around here, years ago. Mum is a town girl. Though I think she'd like to move to a city or a bigger town, really. Anyway here we are,' she said quietly. 'My dad's dream would be to have enough money to go back onto a property, though.'

'So they both compromise,' said Charlie. 'But I can think of a lot of places worse than Fig Tree River.'

Maddie nodded as Charlie turned off the road and pulled up in front of the gates to the dairy farm.

*

The owners, Margot and Laurie, were enthusiastic about their plans and dreams for their farm as they showed Charlie and Maddie around in their four-wheel drive. They drove up a hill and stopped beneath some shady trees.

'This gives you the best view,' said Margot as she led them to the very top of the hill.

'My God, it looks like a movie scene,' said Maddie.

'Stunning,' said Charlie.

A river glittered like new steel, surrounded by marshy wetlands, and in the distance a tide of rolling hills grew into the peaks of the surrounding ranges.

Margot and Laurie grinned. 'Pretty cool, eh?' Laurie said.

Directly below them on the farm was a wide creek fringed with grasses and pools, and standing in and around the marshy water were several dozen water buffalo, their wet dark hides gleaming, heads crowned with large semi-circular horns like dramatic headdresses.

'You milk buffalo? Not cows?' said Charlie.

'Both,' said Margot, laughing at Charlie's surprise. 'We churn out mozzarella, feta, pecorino, haloumi, havarti, burrata, parmesan and quark, as well as gelato, yoghurt and labna!'

'Sounds delicious. Do you round these guys up?' asked Charlie, thinking how good footage of the water buffalo ploughing through the creek and charging across paddocks would look.

'Not really, it's more of a stroll,' said Laurie. 'The dogs nudge them along. They're pretty mild mannered – unless they're upset.' Laurie chuckled. 'Which we try to avoid. Bad for their milk.'

'They plod into the sheds to be milked; they have the hang of their routines,' added Margot. 'One of them has been hand-raised so is a bit of a pet.'

'Do they have names?' asked Maddie.

'Yes, they do,' admitted Margot. 'The pet one is called Sooky.'

By the time they'd toured the property, had afternoon tea in the little café with its stunning views and bought some cheeses from the farm store, Charlie was brimming with ideas for a commercial.

'We just need a hook for the storyline,' he said. 'I'll keep thinking, and please let me know if you have any ideas.'

Laurie nodded. 'Will do. Great to meet you both.'

Maddie and Charlie thanked the couple and said goodbye before walking back to the car.

Charlie stopped, looked around and waved his arm. 'What about that view? You couldn't paint a better picture of bucolic peace and beauty! Anything grown here must be touched with magic.'

Maddie stood beside him. 'You're right. It is magic. It's the greenest green I've ever seen.'

She turned around and gave a strangled cry.

'What the . . . Shit! Stand still, don't move,' she gasped.

Standing between them and Charlie's car was a chubby buffalo, its head slightly lowered as it stared at them from large brown eyes. It didn't look fully grown but what surprised Maddie was its white face in contrast to its smudgy grey hide.

She took Charlie's hand, saying quietly, 'Walk backwards.' Without losing eye contact they edged away.

'I think it's young; look at its horns, they're not so big,' said Charlie quietly.

'Big enough,' muttered Maddie.

The buffalo watched them then took several tentative steps and stopped.

'What do we do? You're the country girl,' Charlie said, trying to sound relaxed.

'Stand still. I know if you run from a cow it chases you.'

A shrill whistle suddenly blasted towards them.

'She's okay! Won't hurt you!' shouted Margot. She put two fingers in her mouth and gave a couple more short whistles, and to their surprise, the young water buffalo turned around and trotted obediently towards her.

'Gee, look at that,' said Maddie. 'That buffalo's like a dog!'

'That's Sooky, the pet I was telling you about. Sorry

she scared you – she loves visitors. I wondered where she'd got to.'

Charlie was looking at Margot as she rested her hand on the back of Sooky's neck.

'Margot, could Maddie have a photo with Sooky?' he asked.

'Sure. She's a real ham, loves having her photo taken. Sooky, that is,' smiled Margot.

*

In the car, Maddie opened the bag of cheeses she'd bought. 'Wow, these look so yummy. I think I bought too much, though.'

Charlie glanced at her. 'We could buy some bread and olives to go with them and have a picnic, sometime in the next few days. What do you think? I have a kayak and know a few places downriver that are good for a swim with platypus.'

'I thought you were a city boy,' said Maddie in surprise. 'Water's too cold to swim in at the moment, but kayaking sounds great.'

'Okay. Let me know when it fits in with your schedule.'

'I have Wednesday off,' she said. 'I'll bring the picnic, you bring the kayak.'

'Done.' He glanced at her and grinned.

'No camera, though.' She nodded at the camera bag on the back seat.

'That will be hard,' Charlie said. 'Once you've been a camera operator for TV news you're always ready to film any action for that night's bulletin.'

'I didn't know you worked for a TV station,' said Maddie. 'Do you still do that sort of work?'

'Not any more. I only worked in TV for a while to earn a crust and get some experience. I like to be able to control what I'm filming.'

'It makes my life sound so ordinary,' Maddie said.

'How do you define ordinary, Mads?'

Maddie chewed her lip. 'Hmm. Routine? Never expect the unexpected? Does that sound boring to you?'

Charlie tempered his reply. 'It sounds safe. Happy. You're lucky.'

'I just started to realise that I've never thought about the future. My mother tells me to take one day at a time. My father thinks I'm a dreamer and not very practical.' Maddie looked down at her hands.

'Fleur and Leonie have pushed you out of your comfort zone,' said Charlie quietly.

'Yes, well. Not for long. Once we've done *Percy and Ella*, that'll be the end of my showbiz career.'

'What makes you say that?' asked Charlie.

Maddie shrugged. 'Well, once the Playhouse is gone, there won't be any local opportunities.'

'What do you mean?' exclaimed Charlie.

She glanced across at him. 'You haven't heard? Dad told me. Apparently the council has plans to redevelop the old theatre.'

'What? Do you know for sure?'

'Some mates of Dad's work for a demolition outfit. That's how he heard about it.' She looked at him. 'Developers don't care that it's old and beautiful.'

'Surely it's heritage listed. Have you said anything to Leonie?'

'No. I didn't want to upset her, especially when she's working on the show. Anyway, she's probably heard the same rumours. It's hard to keep things secret in a small town.' She turned to Charlie. 'I don't see how we can stop it, either.'

'Surely they couldn't destroy it. We'll have to try to find out more,' Charlie replied.

It was sunset as he pulled into Maddie's driveway.

'Thanks for inviting me along today. I had a great time,' she said as she opened her door and got out. Charlie got out too and came around to her side.

'So did I, Maddie. Don't tell anyone about Sooky, I don't want them to steal my idea!' he said, laughing. Then he leaned in and surprised her with a quick hug.

She lifted her face to his and kissed him. It seemed the most natural thing to do in that moment, and a wonderful feeling.

They both gently pulled away.

'I'll see you Wednesday, okay?' Charlie said softly.

Maddie nodded and smiled. 'You bet.' She watched him get back in the car and drive away. It had been a special afternoon.

*

Leonie clapped her hands. 'Attention everyone, we're starting the Battle of Hastings Scene.'

'This is where we need an orchestra,' Julian whispered to Maddie.

'It would be nice,' she agreed. She turned and glanced at him. He'd had his hair trimmed – or was it styled? – into the tousled blond curls flopping onto his forehead. He wore faded jeans, old boots that he'd polished and a loose white shirt with full sleeves, giving him a flamboyant, piratical air. He still had his leather jacket. She wondered if Fleur was giving him money to buy clothes. But then these could just as easily have come from the op shop. It was a very different look from his first appearance. He still had his charm and self-confidence, and he seemed very relaxed.

Leonie walked over to them with a page of notes in her hand. 'There is a subtle change in the mood between Percy and Ella from this scene on, although Percy remains at arm's-length, to a degree,' she said.

'Is that change Ella's idea, or his?' asked Maddie.

Julian dropped his arm around Maddie's shoulder. 'Percy's idea. Silly man.'

Leonie put a finger to her lips. 'Now, this would be a big full chorus scene with the mock battle on the beach. The town's recreation of its history and so on. But it is the first romantic connection between Percy and Ella. Please, take your places.'

In the stalls, Sarita and Fleur watched as the two leads stood together, sharing pages of the libretto. Roger readied himself at the piano, and Freddy stood poised to conduct. Behind Maddie and Julian, the rest of the cast prepared to do battle in song.

'Imagine the fabulous choreography we could stage in a full production,' whispered Fleur.

'In full fake chain mail and helmets,' said Sarita.

'Charlie's also disappointed we're not doing that, but it's not practical,' said Fleur.

They sat quietly, absorbed in the scene on the stage as Julian and Madison went through their lines and then into their duet, 'A World Awaits', where Percy first kissed Ella after asking her to come to America to his house at White Plains.

Maddie loved this duet, but she was taken aback when Julian swept her into his arms and kissed her passionately at the finale.

At the applause from the rest of the cast, she pulled away, frowning at him. Julian might have thought the kiss was just part of the play, but she had found it too intense.

'Let's take a break. Then notes,' called Leonie.

As everyone broke away to chat and rest, Julian turned to Maddie. 'You're special,' he said softly. 'And beautiful. We're beautiful. We're meant to be together.' He held her gently by the shoulders, looking into her eyes and speaking quietly but intensely.

'It's only a show, remember, Julian,' Maddie said firmly, but she felt a bit rattled.

'Ah. But the magic is there. You'll see. This is only the beginning.' He stroked her hair. 'I'll write a song for you.'

She quickly brushed his hand away. 'You can stop being Percy now, Julian. And anyway, I have enough to memorise for the moment, thanks.'

As she walked away, Maddie was glad Charlie wasn't at the rehearsal. Julian's behaviour had made her uncomfortable.

7

IT WAS ONE OF those near-perfect days. Charlie wished he had his camera as he pulled up in a shady clearing, but he'd promised Maddie he would leave it behind this time.

Through the trees, the creek sparkled like a diamond band as it wound between the old silky casuarinas.

Maddie stood beside him. 'Oh wow, how cool is this? I had no idea this place was here. Did you bring your camera?'

Charlie slapped his forehead. 'Damn. *Of course not!* You told me no camera. This is a fun day.'

Maddie laughed. 'Yes. And I was right. Besides, it might get wet.'

'I would never let my camera get wet,' he replied archly. 'Anyway, we have our phones if a photo op presents itself. C'mon, can you help me get the kayak down?'

'So what's the plan?' asked Maddie as they slid the orange craft into the water and Charlie secured it to a tree.

He passed Maddie her backpack and slipped his own over his shoulders. 'Well, you've brought lunch and water, I have survival gear and a bottle of wine for later.'

She gave him a look. 'You're joking, right? I mean, about the survival gear.'

'Not really. I was a scout, they trained me well. I have fishing stuff, a first-aid kit, knife, compass, flare, matches, space blanket –'

'A space blanket? Are we spending the night?' She raised an eyebrow.

'Not unless we get lost.'

'We have a flare and a compass. Just how far are we heading?'

'Relax. I have this stuff with me all the time. If we catch a fish, we can cook it.'

'Okay,' said Maddie doubtfully.

But once they had life jackets on and were paddling down the river, she leaned forward and said to Charlie, 'This is gorgeous.'

They travelled a little further, then Charlie lifted his paddle and said, 'Just let's drift a bit, listen . . .'

At first Maddie was tempted to ask, 'Listen to what?' But then she heard it, the quietness – a soft swish of leaves, the swift movement of a bird, a gurgle of creek water against a log, all so soft, so much a part of the scenery. Maddie realised she was holding her breath as they drifted along.

Charlie glanced over his shoulder and gave her a wink.

She nodded. Neither wanted to break the spell by speaking. He pointed up ahead and gently dipped his paddle into the creek, and as Maddie followed his movements, he guided them towards a flat area of the bank.

Softly he said, 'It's easier to get out here where there's a level bit.' He pointed at the small area of muddy sand.

They slid the kayak up onto the bank and Maddie followed Charlie through the grass towards a shady patch of trees.

'Ah, there it is.' He pointed to a ring of large river stones with a metal plate propped in its centre. 'Looks like no one's been here since the last time I came and rearranged the stones.'

'I hope that doesn't mean you're planning to hunt something to add to our lunch,' said Maddie.

'Want to have a go at catching a fish?'

'Maybe in a minute. Can I rest?' She slung off her backpack as Charlie unfurled a groundsheet and spread it out.

'I'm going to throw a line in. Just for fun,' said Charlie.

Maddie pulled out her sweater and balled it over her backpack as a pillow. Leaning back against it, she stretched out, gazing up at the leafy patterns patchworked onto squares of blue sky far above the whispering trees.

The next thing she knew she was opening her eyes and smelling something cooking. She sat up.

Charlie was squatting by the fire.

'Don't tell me you caught a fish?'

'Of course.'

'It smells delicious.' She peered at the foil-wrapped fish sitting on a hot stone in the glowing embers.

While Charlie served the fish onto plates, Maddie unpacked the cheese, bread and olives she'd bought, as well as a couple of salads. They sat in companionable silence for a while, enjoying the food and the beautiful, tranquil setting.

'It's just so gorgeous here. How'd you find this place?' Maddie asked eventually.

'You'd be surprised what I stumble over when I go out on location surveys looking for places to film. Anyway, I was chatting to the barmaid in the pub –'

'As you do,' nodded Maddie.

'Turns out her uncle is a local Elder and she put us in touch. Uncle Clarrie took me around, showing me all kinds of hidden places. He told me a bit of their history. That's how I found out about this area, and I've taken lots of photos here at different times of day.'

'I understand now why you and your camera are a team. Where're you going next? I can't imagine you will want to stay in Fig Tree River forever.'

'Depends how Fleur and Leonie's show turns out. And what about you, Mads, where're you going next?' He gave her a smile. 'You're going to be a hit.'

'I don't think so! Anyway, why would I leave Fig Tree River? I mean, you appreciate how beautiful it is here,' said Maddie.

'But you have talent, Maddie,' he said seriously. 'It would be a shame not to see where it could take you.'

Maddie scraped the last of the fish from her tin plate. 'Maybe. And what about Julian? He's really gifted.'

'Uh-huh, he is. But you also have to have the drive, the hunger. That's why I admire Fleur. She's very focused and driven, and she's devoted to her career.'

'Yes, she sure is. I don't think I could be like that. Which reminds me, I told her I'd practise my big solo.'

'Well, go on then, let's hear it,' said Charlie.

Maddie hesitated, then put her plate to one side and stood up, taking several steps away from the fire and turning towards the trees so Charlie was out of her line of sight.

First light, soft and bright
Beckons from the long dark night . . .
To see and feel the warmth of light.
Open my heart to thee,
Oh caring, protector, shady tree . . .
Spread your branches and welcome me . . .

She sang with growing confidence and passion, her eyes closing before the final notes floated into the surrounding bush.

Maddie jumped in surprise as Charlie came up behind her, giving her a gentle hug.

'That's beautiful, Mads. What's the significance of that song?' he asked softly.

She turned around, circling her arms around him. 'Percy's love of Australia never left him, even though he lived most of his life abroad, so Fleur told me.'

'Beautiful. Like you.' He kissed the side of her neck and then gently kissed her smiling mouth.

Maddie pulled back and looked at him. 'You had to lure me out here to kiss me?' she teased.

'Nope. It just suddenly seemed like a good idea.'

'Yes. I think so too.' She kissed him again as the trees rustled in a soft breeze that rippled across the surface of the shining creek.

It was a kiss like none she had ever experienced. What began as something light-hearted suddenly grew to a mind-blowing, body-shaking surge of feelings. It came to Maddie in an illuminating flash that this was the moment she'd dreamed and wondered about. How did you know, really know, if someone was that special one? Now she knew. She grasped Charlie tightly, as if he might disappear if she didn't.

Charlie gently eased his mouth from hers. 'Whoa, let me catch my breath. What've you done to me?'

Maddie simply stared at him. 'Now, I get it. You . . . and me, this is it. I mean –' She felt flushed. 'I mean . . .' All the clichés, the dreams of a little girl about falling in love, swept over her. 'I've never felt like this before.' She was suddenly embarrassed, shy, flustered.

Charlie drew her to him and hugged her. They stood holding each other for a moment, then kissed again.

*

Rehearsals were getting more intense as the one-night show and video recording loomed.

'We've sent out invitations, and please tell your family and friends that tickets are now on sale,' Leonie told the group gathered on the stage. 'We'll have drinks and cheese afterwards in the lobby, kindly provided by The Big Cheese – thanks to Maddie for persuading them! Also, do let people know that Charlie might take some video of the audience milling about afterwards, in case anyone doesn't want to be filmed,' she added.

'We have our costumes,' said one of the girls in the chorus, 'but when does the backdrop arrive? The bare stage is a bit boring.'

'Chrissie has it under control. She emailed me some photos and it looks terrific – very Art Deco, a black-and-white piano and music theme along with some cut-out figures in wonderful poses. It's really very effective,' said Leonie enthusiastically.

'Sounds great,' said Roger.

'Does she want someone to collect it from her place?' asked Sarita.

'Yes, I think she mentioned that. I'll check with her and let you know. One more full rehearsal and then . . . the big night!'

Julian squeezed Maddie's arm. 'Nervous?'

'I am a bit,' said Maddie quietly. 'It's not like we can fix anything the following night. It's one hit and that's it. What about you, are you nervous?'

'Nope. Should I be?'

She shook her head. 'You're incorrigible.'

'I'm doing something I enjoy. What's not to like?'

'You're not nervous about forgetting a line, or hitting the wrong note or something?'

Julian shrugged. 'I'll deal with it if it happens. But my advice is, just enjoy yourself. Be yourself.'

Maddie wondered if Julian was really as confident as he sounded. Anyway, in a couple of days it would all be behind her, and she'd go back to her real life.

*

Sarita had to make some minor adjustments to a couple of shirts for two of the men in the production.

'Why are you still sewing? A bit last-minute, isn't it, with the show on Saturday night?' asked Brett, when he walked into her sewing room.

'Almost finished. You are staying over to see the show?' she asked, looking up.

'Yes, if that's okay. I thought I might go over to Leonie's place and check out where she says they're going to put that dam.'

'Good idea. Thanks, Brett. Want to put the kettle on? I'm nearly done.'

As he filled the kettle in the kitchen, Sarita's phone rang on the counter. He knew she couldn't hear it, so he picked it up and noticed it was Chrissie calling. He accepted the call.

'Hey there, Chrissie, Sarita is sewing, I'll just take her phone in –' He paused as Chrissie burst into a distraught outpouring on the other end. 'Wait, wait, calm down. Did you just say your house is on fire?'

'What's going on?' Sarita came into the kitchen.

'Here, it's Chrissie, her place is on fire.' Brett looked bewildered.

Sarita grabbed the phone. 'Chrissie! What's happening, are you okay?'

Sarita listened, rubbing her head in dismay. 'Okay, okay. Are you sure you're all right? Where are the kids? Is the fire brigade there? Is everything under control?'

'Should we go over there?' asked Brett.

'Chrissie, Brett is here, we can come over to your place –' She stopped as Chrissie broke in. Sarita listened then said, 'Look, if you're sure. Please don't worry, we'll think of something. No, no, I'm sure it's not your fault, don't feel like that. It'll be okay, Chrissie . . .'

'What's happened?' asked Brett as Sarita hung up.

'A fire in her shed, while she was cooking dinner in the house. They don't know the extent of the damage yet, but we've lost the backdrops for the show.'

'Oh, bloody hell! Is she okay? That was a big shed.'

'I think she and the kids are fine but very shocked. I'll call Leonie after Chrissie's rung her. What a blow. Poor Chrissie, she feels dreadful. She says Troy told her she must have left a power tool on and it shorted, or something. He's pretty mad.'

'So long as she's all right,' said Brett. 'You sure we shouldn't go over and see if anything is salvageable?'

'Let me talk to Leonie first. She will let us know if we can do anything.'

Brett made a pot of tea while his sister called Leonie.

'Poor Chrissie, she's devastated,' said Sarita.

'It could have been worse if the house had caught fire,' said Leonie grimly.

'So what do we do? Just go with lighting effects, or something? Have you spoken to the others?' asked Sarita.

'Not yet. I'm about to call Charlie and see if he has any suggestions. You've got the costumes under control?'

'Yep, for all the cast. Just going to add some final touches for Maddie and Julian.'

'Okay. Thanks, Sarita. I'll be in touch.'

*

For once, stepping into the dim interior of the old Playhouse didn't hold its usual mystique and magic for Leonie. It felt cold, dark, dingy and miserable.

Then the theatre lights flooded the empty stage, and she shivered, feeling apprehensive for the first time. 'Hi! Who's there?'

'Just me,' called Charlie.

'Ah.' She walked down the aisle. 'So. Where to now, Charlie?'

He stepped from the wings into the light, shading his eyes to see her. 'Is Chrissie okay?'

'She's desperately upset at letting us down. And I'm at a bit of a loss. The timeframe is so short. We have a bunch of people on stage all dressed in black and white, singing and speaking – with just a piano. I was thinking we could add some more music . . . instruments, but there's not the time for it.'

Charlie hopped down from the stage and sat beside Leonie in a seat in the front row.

'Yeah. Forget that, it's in the too-hard basket, I think. Now, I'll have three cameras set up. I can do a lot with the lighting, and I've called in favours from a couple of friends, audiovisual guys, to help me.'

'Oh wonderful. Are they expensive?'

'Not if they can use some of Fleur's piece as a demo later. They're smart guys. They do album videos, that sort of thing. And they owe me,' said Charlie.

'Sounds like a plan,' said Leonie, feeling somewhat relieved.

'Give us a few hours and then bring Fleur in, see what she thinks. I'll set up the cameras so they won't intrude on the stage,' said Charlie calmly.

'Thanks so much, Charlie. I'll let Chrissie know, too. She'll be relieved, I'm sure.'

'Chrissie's coming along to the show, though, right?'

'I'm sure she'll be here. Of course.'

*

Sitting in the dressing-rooms backstage, being fussed over while their hair and make-up were being done, everyone was hyped up and nervous.

'There's quite a few people in the audience already,' said Sarita as she checked how everyone was looking, then walked to the door. 'See you all in the lobby for drinks afterwards. Break a leg, folks!'

She passed Leonie coming into the dressing-rooms. 'Hi. They all look great and seem ready to go for it,' said Sarita.

'Oh, good. Have you seen Chrissie? I'm surprised she isn't here yet. Everyone else seems to be, it's a full house now.' Leonie grinned excitedly.

'I'll check if she's out the front. She can be quite shy.'

'I just hope she doesn't feel badly and won't come,' said Leonie.

'If I can't find her, I'll ring. Brett is here and he knows where she lives so he can drive over and collect her if need be. We need all our gang here,' said Sarita. 'I saw that Fleur is in the front row.'

As everyone gathered quietly on stage behind the closed curtains, Leonie spoke softly. 'So here we are, we made it! Enjoy yourselves tonight. Don't fret if you make a mistake, just move on. And remember what Charlie wants – even if you don't have anything to do for a section or two, keep in character, pay attention. You won't know when a camera is on you. There's one in the centre taking in everyone, plus one on the solos, and one taking random footage.' She turned to Roger and Freddy. 'That includes you two.'

Roger, seated at the piano, threw up his hands, whispering, 'I'm ready for my close-up, Ms DeMille!'

Smiling, Leonie put her finger to her lips. 'Remember, we're doing this for Fleur and the Riverside Playhouse.' She blew them a kiss and tiptoed into the wings.

The lights dimmed over the audience as a recording of Grainger's orchestral version of 'Country Gardens' was played. When the opening strains faded, the curtain lifted.

Maddie stood and sang beside Julian at the piano. She looked very nervous, but determined. At one point, Leonie glanced from the stage to Fleur in the front row and saw tears on the American woman's cheeks.

There was no mistaking the magic between Julian and Maddie. Their voices married as if they'd sung together all their lives, the electricity between 'Percy' and 'Ella' soaring into the audience. And as Julian slid from the piano seat to take Ella in his arms, the orchestral strains of Grainger's 'To a Nordic Princess' flooded the theatre's sound system. As they kissed, Roger sat back on the piano stool.

At the finale, the audience roared and cheered, leaping to their feet as they clapped.

Fleur had her hands over her mouth as Julian and Maddie stepped forward, beckoning her onto the stage. She grabbed Leonie's arm and together they stepped up to receive the applause and cheers of the cast, Roger and Freddy, and the enthusiastic audience.

'Speech, speech,' called Brett from the front row.

Fleur hesitated, then, as the applause quietened, she stepped forward.

'Thank you, thank you. Tonight you've seen a dream become a reality. I never expected to find the talent, the friendship, the fruition of years of work brought to life in a small Aussie town. I owe it to this incredible cast ensemble. This is a birth you have witnessed tonight. Thank you, Madison, Julian, and all the cast, thank you, Freddy and Roger, Charlie and his crew who have filmed this magical event tonight, and thanks to Sarita, Chrissie and the team backstage. And thank *you*, our audience! I hope you will follow the fortunes of this event and be able to say, "I was there for the first performance of *Percy and Ella*." Finally, please thank our brilliant director, Leonie Foster!'

There was no formal bringing down of the curtain as friends and family swarmed onto the stage to hug and congratulate each other.

The gaiety carried on out into the foyer, where tables were set with drinks and food.

None of the cast changed out of their costumes. Freddy and Roger were telling friends they were packing for Broadway, while members of the audience were shaking their heads, saying, 'I had no *idea* there was such talent in our little town!' 'We want to buy the video, the album.' 'It was *stunning*!'

Leonie caught sight of Charlie walking among them, filming and receiving effusive comments. Then, behind her, she heard Brett saying to Sarita, 'Oh look, Chrissie *is* here!'

Turning, Leonie saw Sarita rushing over to their friend. 'Chrissie, you made it! I called earlier but you didn't answer. Did you see it?' cried Sarita.

'Yes. I crept in. Mum picked up the kids and dropped me off. I missed a lot of the rehearsals so it was totally magic to see it tonight! And Charlie did a fabulous job with the lighting effects, but I feel so terrible about my backdrops –'

'Don't,' said Brett quickly. 'Accidents happen. And this has been a fantastic night.'

'I'm so glad I didn't miss it,' said Chrissie quietly, after Sarita excused herself to help in the dressing-room.

'I'm glad you came too,' smiled Brett.

A few people began to leave the foyer and Freddy and Roger invited the cast, crew and friends over to their house for drinks.

Leonie was talking to Ray and Sarita when the manager of the theatre came over to congratulate her. 'That was truly wonderful,' she exclaimed. 'I do hope it will be done as a big show here next year.'

Ray jumped in and said, 'Well, it won't if the GM at council has his way. They're talking about closing this place and redeveloping the site.'

'What rubbish! The Playhouse is part of the town's heritage,' said the manager. 'Let's hope it's just gossip.'

'We'll help you clean up here,' said Leonie.

'Thanks, but that's fine. I have a cleaner coming in the morning. You go off and enjoy yourselves. Go and toast your success.'

*

It was nearly midnight and the group was ensconced around the fire pit in Freddy and Roger's back garden, all but Chrissie who'd had to get home to her kids.

'What do you reckon you got on the video, Charlie? Enough to make the entrepreneurs race for their wallets?' asked Wade.

'The big job of editing all that footage is still ahead for Fleur and me. But if I've caught half of the magic I saw on the screen, it'll grab attention.'

'Whaddya reckon, Fleur?' asked the police sergeant.

'Frankly, I'm just enjoying relaxing with a glass of wine. I've been a bit overwhelmed by people's lovely comments. It was so wonderful to see the audience's response and hear the feedback.'

'You deserve a break, Fleur,' said Leonie. 'Just enjoy the town and the beautiful house you're in.'

'You have all made me feel so at home. I hope I can repay you in some way.'

'Seems strange to be going back to work and normal life, with nothing to look forward to . . . like going to rehearsals.' Maddie sighed.

'Maddie, I reckon the world's your oyster if you wanted to have a crack,' said Roger.

She wrinkled her nose. 'But I don't want to sing in public . . .'

'But you just *did*!' said Wade, laughing.

As everyone laughed along with him, Maddie

glanced at Charlie, who raised an eyebrow and gave her a crooked smile.

'So what are your plans, Julian?' asked Roger.

'I don't do plans,' Julian answered smoothly.

'What's that mean?' asked Charlie.

Julian shrugged. 'I take life as it comes.'

Fleur spoke up. 'You created magic tonight, you two. It was very, very special.'

'I s'pose you're going to ask if the magic will still be there after two hundred performances?' teased Julian. 'And I say . . . it will.' He leaned towards Maddie, who stood up quickly and went to top up her drink.

Sarita interjected, 'You're very talented, Julian. And I think the show was – is – stunning. It's an omen. Everything happens for a reason.'

'Yes, my sister is very intuitive,' laughed Brett. 'I was knocked out by the show. I'd love to see it with all the trimmings.'

'Well, couldn't we do the show with the full works? When you're ready, of course,' said Freddy to Fleur.

'You mean after its Broadway premiere?' said Roger.

'Maybe have the Australian premiere for the full-scale musical at the Riverside Playhouse!' said Wade.

'The Playhouse might be gone by then,' said Roger soberly. 'From what I've heard, they want to put up some big development on the site.'

'The space isn't big enough for that. It's just perfect for the Playhouse, though,' said Leonie.

'I reckon half the town was built around that theatre,' said Freddy.

'And what would the town do for entertainment with no Playhouse?' asked Sarita.

'Sport, movies, stay home and stream. Maybe if you're desperate, read a book,' said Brett, half in jest, but no one laughed.

'Let's not spoil the party,' said Leonie. 'Just enjoy the moment.'

She glanced around at the group. A few months ago, some of them had been strangers. What a journey they'd been on. She hated the thought that they'd soon be back in their own lives and would rarely cross paths – until, hopefully, the next show. It was always like this after a show finished its run; the letdown after all the adrenalin was inevitable. But Fleur, Maddie, Charlie, Julian . . . they had their own paths to follow. She glanced at Sarita and wished Chrissie was here, too. Their tight-knit little group now included Maddie. But would Maddie really stay when her talent was recognised?

Enough already, she told herself.

Sarita and Ray stood up. 'We'd better go. You coming, Brett?'

'Yes, I have to drive back to Sydney tomorrow for work on Monday. I'm so glad I came, though. Once-in-a-lifetime experience, I reckon. Thanks to you all.'

Others rose, carrying plates and glasses inside.

'You right to get back, Julian?' asked Brett.

The young man gave a thumbs-up. 'Wade is dropping me off at the B&B and taking Fleur home.'

Charlie stood up too. 'See you tomorrow arvo, Fleur.'

'Wow, you guys aren't wasting any time,' said Leonie.

Maddie gave Fleur a hug.

'Thank you for getting me into this . . . and through it!' she said, smiling.

'This is just the beginning for you, Maddie.'

Julian kissed Maddie's cheek. 'That's what I keep telling her.'

Maddie shrugged. 'Tomorrow I'm back to making chai tea and lattes.'

She turned to say good night to Charlie, but he had gone.

*

Charlie and Fleur sat side by side, looking at the large computer screen as applause and the finale music played while the cast took their bows.

'Bloody fantastic! Even if I say so myself,' said Charlie.

'You've done a brilliant job!' said Fleur. 'I can't thank you enough. You didn't charge me anywhere near what this is worth.'

'Look what I had to work with!' He smiled. 'I hope this works out for you. Let us know how you go back over there in the Big Apple.'

'Of course I will. You have my details. Anything I can help you with, just shout out. I have contacts in LA when you're ready. Now, please make sure the others understand, it's a tough gig to get a show up. But, well, fingers crossed.'

'Can I drive you to the train station tomorrow? I can't believe you're going down to Sydney on the train,' said Charlie.

'Thanks, but no. I've booked a taxi to collect me after I drop off my hire car in town. Listen, there's one thing ... keep working on Maddie's confidence, would you? I'm very fond of her and I think she just needs to start believing in herself more.'

'Sure, will do. Do you think she'll make the move out of Fig Tree River?' he asked.

'That's up to Maddie. She has a gift, but you need more than that. You need the hunger. Let's wait and see.' She leaned over and gave him a hug. 'Now I better head home. I have an early departure.'

'I feel bad, just leaving you. Letting you go to the train on your own,' said Charlie.

'It's fine. I'm used to it. I'm a solo traveller, Charlie. But I'm sure our paths will cross again.'

He leaned over and kissed her cheek. 'I feel like you've changed our lives, Fleur. Safe travels.'

*

Sarita pulled up at Chrissie's, and as she got out of the car, Chrissie came around the side of the house. 'Oh, hi, Sarita, how was the afterparty? The show was a big hit.' She wiped her forehead. 'I feel so badly about everything.'

'Please don't, it all worked out in the end. How bad is the damage to the shed?'

'Not as bad as I thought. I feel so stupid.'

'Can I see?' Sarita strode around the back to the shed, which, she thought with surprise, looked to be just fine. Chrissie hesitated, then quickly followed her.

Inside, however, Sarita could smell that something had been burnt. But she had to look closely to see the damage.

A pile of ash, burnt wood, a twisted metal frame, a scorched bench and a blackened tin wall was all she saw.

'Lucky you got it out so fast, before it could spread,' said Sarita. 'All Troy's gear seems to be okay. Is everything insured?'

'Troy says it's not worth claiming for my disaster area here. I only lost some tools.'

'Well, you have to replace them,' said Sarita.

Chrissie shrugged. 'We'll see. I have enough to do, what with the kids and house. Would you like a cup of tea?'

Her invitation was polite but didn't sound enthusiastic.

'Yes, I'd love one,' said Sarita firmly, and they went into the house.

'The kitchen is a bit of a mess, sorry. I haven't tidied up since the kids left for school,' said Chrissie as she took out mugs for their tea.

'No worries. So, what are your plans, then?' asked Sarita.

Chrissie looked puzzled. 'Plans?'

'Well, getting your little workshop going again. Remember you made those wooden toys for the charity drive at Christmas? A friend of mine has a darling boy turning four, and I was going to ask if you could make him something. I'd pay you, of course.'

'Oh, not till I can afford to get my tools and stuff replaced. I'll let you know.'

Sarita sipped her tea. 'Well, even though the show is over now, we thought we'd all get together for a morning tea or lunch or something. There's a bit of drama brewing about the Playhouse being knocked down or moved –'

Chrissie gasped. 'So the rumours are true?'

'Looks like it. We're still trying to find out what's actually happening and what's just gossip,' Sarita said. 'What day and time suits you to have our get-together?'

'Thursday mid-morning,' Chrissie answered promptly.

'Done.' Sarita smiled, feeling pleased. It was often difficult for Chrissie to join the others. 'I'll see you then.'

*

Maddie carefully poured the milk into a large flat white and then walked outside and put it down in front of Julian.

'So, what have you been up to?' she asked him.

'Nothing much. You?'

'I'm here, aren't I?' Maddie gave a hint of a smile.

'Written any good songs lately?' he asked.

'Maybe. Why?'

'Just curious. I thought you might be getting a portfolio ready to storm New York.' Julian raised an eyebrow.

'I could ask you the same. Are you working?'

'Depends what you call work.' He smiled.

'Do you have enough to pay for your coffee?' She gave him a quizzical look.

'Of course. I've been doing odd jobs, but mainly I've been messing about with pianos. I thought you might want to sing with me.'

'Oh? Like where? You mean as a paid gig? That's not really my thing.' Maddie glanced at a couple who'd put down the menu and were looking at her expectantly. 'Got to go, I have to take an order.'

'We can make beautiful music together, Maddie.' Julian gave her a wink.

She rolled her eyes. 'Give me a time, a date and a place and I'll think about it. Don't forget to pay my boss for your coffee.'

'See you, Maddie.' He blew her a kiss.

'Yeah, sure.' She shook her head. Julian was talented, handsome and annoyingly mysterious, she thought. But he was a bit too sure of himself, and he was pushing her in a direction she wasn't sure she wanted to go. At the same time, she felt a bit lost without the fun and excitement of the show.

Where to now? she wondered.

*

'What's up, my beauty?' asked Ray. 'Are you bored?'

'Maybe. Nothing personal.' Sarita laughed. 'I suppose it's just the letdown after all the intensity of the show. And with Fleur leaving, and no job to go to, I feel sort of empty, at a loose end.'

'You always feel like this after a production. Maybe you need a break. A holiday? Then you can look for another job.'

She shrugged. 'That would be nice. But we can't afford any extras at the moment.'

'C'mon, we could go away somewhere close by for a weekend. Been a while since we had a romantic escape.'

Sarita smiled at him. 'Sounds nice. Maybe that's what we need. Until the next thing comes along.'

'The next show, you mean?'

'Maybe. I think we all feel a bit adrift. I worry about Chrissie; she's so upset about the fire, and she really thinks she let us down. I think we need something we can all get our teeth into again, as a distraction from our day-to-day lives.'

'I doubt you'll have another experience like Fleur and *Percy and Ella*! It will be interesting to see if we ever hear from Fleur again.'

Sarita looked at him in some alarm. 'Really! You think we'll never see her again?'

'C'mon, Rita. It was strange that she even turned up in Fig Tree River, let alone produced a show like she did! Like you *all* did. If I didn't know better, I would have thought she'd made Percy up!'

'You couldn't make Percy up.' Sarita chuckled. 'I feel sad that he was so famous, such a character, yet hardly anyone remembers him now.'

'That's life, babe,' said Ray with a shrug.

Sarita looked thoughtful. 'How depressing. Makes you wonder about all the people over time who've made a difference and are now forgotten, while people envy, imitate and go bananas over some TikTok star who hasn't done anything special.'

'No one will remember that fleeting "fame" those so-called influencers have on social media in a year's time, I bet. Now. Let's plan a naughty weekend somewhere nice.' He leaned over and kissed her. 'I feel so lucky I have you.'

*

Leonie tethered her horse and walked across the paddock, stopping here and there to crouch down and dig into the soil. She'd kept the cattle out of this paddock for six months and she and Harry had regularly turned the soil. The tillage was paying off; it was less compacted, crumblier, holding the moisture but letting heavy rain soak in and not wash away the surface soil. Enriching the soil had been hard yakka, as Harry described it, but if she could regenerate on a bigger scale over her property, it would make a great difference. Livestock, while giving her an income, was not conducive to restoring the depleted soil that had been compacted by the presence of generations of heavy cattle.

She'd have to decide which way to go with the farm soon, Leonie told herself. Caring for the environment while juggling a home, her son and the farm income was hard for a one-woman band. She sighed. Not only that, Harry was getting on and had begun dropping hints about newer and more efficient methods than 'an old bloke with a crook shoulder' could handle. He was right, but new machinery and her regenerative plans were expensive. Keeping Tony's dream alive and a future for Corby were what drove her. Though this, plus the worry of a possible dam near her property, nagged at her constantly.

She rode back to the home paddock, unsaddled her horse and gave him fresh hay. Checking her watch, she saw it was time to get ready for morning tea with the girls. That would cheer her up.

But Leonie was feeling restless. She missed the excitement and challenge of staging the musical. Looking at Charlie's final cut of the filmed version of *Percy and Ella* had been eye-opening. To see it objectively and appreciate the music, the voices and the acting only frustrated her, as she could see how wonderful it could be as a fully professional production with an orchestra. She hoped Fleur could get the backing to produce it. And what of Maddie and Julian, what could be in store for them? What would she do if she was in her twenties with talent like that instead of carrying all her responsibilities single-handedly? While she had never considered marrying again, she thought that it would be nice to share her burdens with someone close. Harry was a good man and understood what she was going through, but he was an employee and looking forward to retirement. She knew that in other circumstances he would have retired by now, but he was loyal to her and Corby.

Leonie showered and got dressed. Then, as she combed her hair, she stood back and looked in the mirror, really seeing herself for the first time in a while. And she was shocked.

She needed her hair cut and styled instead of wrenching it into a ball on her head like she usually did. Was that a wrinkle? She knew her nails were trashed, and she hadn't paid much attention to her skin, make-up or, well, anything, for ages. There was never time.

She hadn't made much of an effort for the show night either, figuring it was best to spend the time helping the cast and crew.

My God, I need to take myself in hand, she thought. And then a small voice seemed to say, *Why?*

For a minute Leonie hesitated, then pulled open the bathroom drawer and looked at the jumble of half-used cosmetics and make-up. She slammed it shut.

'It's only the girls,' she sighed. Leaving the room, she launched loudly into the chorus from 'Tomorrow' from the musical *Annie*. Tomorrow would get here soon enough – she would start then.

Leonie picked up her car keys and shoved her mobile phone in her pocket. As she pulled the front door closed, her phone rang. Fishing it out again, she glanced at the screen and saw she had several missed calls from a number she didn't recognise. She hesitated, ready to reject the call, but something about all those missed calls made her answer as she hurried over to the car.

'Hello? Yes, I am Leonie Foster. Sorry, what's this about?' She stood still. 'Wait, sorry. Can you please slow down and start again?'

Leonie leaned forward, bracing herself against the roof of the car with one arm as she pressed the phone against her ear. Her hand started to shake.

'My God, are you saying we won some money? In that lottery? . . . Yes, I understand. Yes, we had a syndicate. Four of us . . . *How* much have we won?'

Leonie flung herself into the driver's seat. 'I . . . I'm sorry. Can you repeat that? Yes, I'm all right, I'm sitting down now . . . I just can't believe it. Is this for real? No, it can't be . . .' Leonie's hand was shaking so much she could hardly hold the phone. She listened, gripping the steering wheel with her other hand. Finally tears began running down her face. 'I really can't believe this. This had better not be a trick.'

She listened. 'Okay, thank you. Yes, I'm just going to meet them. Should I tell them? Are you sure?'

Leonie nodded as the calm voice assured her the call was genuine and explained what the next steps would be. Leonie could hardly take any of it in. They'd won the jackpot. All of it!

Eventually the lottery agent ended the call and Leonie sat in the car resting her forehead against the steering wheel, taking deep, slow breaths. Her mind was spinning. The weird euphoria was overwhelming. It was a lot of money – an almost unimaginable amount. It would change their lives... which was wonderful. So why did she have a nagging fear? She started the car and drove slowly and carefully, thinking hard.

She pulled up a little way from the tearoom on the river where they'd chosen to meet, got out of the car and rang Sarita.

'Hi. Where are you, Leonie? We're all here waiting for you.'

'Listen. I'm at the park across the road. I feel like a walk, can you all come over? I need to talk to you in private, not in a café. Bring everyone with you.'

'Oh, good grief. What now?' asked Sarita. 'What's happened, are you okay?'

'I'm fine, but I have some news. Just come over.'

Leonie stopped pacing and sat on a park bench. Her legs felt wobbly. She looked at her friends as they walked quickly towards her.

'What's up?' said Maddie.

'Is Corby okay?' Sarita asked as she sat down beside

her. Chrissie sat on her other side and Maddie stood in front of them.

Leonie flung up her hands and laughed. 'Sorry. Don't panic . . .' She paused, trying to find the words, then just blurted out quietly, 'We won the lottery!'

There was a moment of stunned silence. Then all three spoke at once.

'What?'

'You're kidding. Don't do that to us!'

'No way. Really? How much? If it's peanuts after all this drama, I'll shoot you,' said Sarita, laughing.

Chrissie held her hands to her mouth and started shaking. 'Did we really win something?'

'If we split it between four, can I buy a new car?' asked Sarita.

Then seeing Leonie nodding and nodding and nodding, Maddie gently took her by the shoulders.

'C'mon, don't tease us, Leonie. How much is it?'

'Ninety.' Leonie swallowed. 'Million.'

There was a strange, loaded silence as they all took this in.

Maddie sat on the ground and stared up at them. Sarita and Chrissie looked at each other.

Then they all started to babble and hug each other and cry and laugh.

'No way. That can't be right. Did they ring you up or something?' Chrissie asked.

'How could anyone spend that sort of money?' wondered Maddie.

'I got the call just now, as I was leaving the house. The syndicate was in my name, remember? So they had my number. Listen, we have to talk about this. First, we can't tell anyone –'

'What! Are you nuts? People will find out,' exclaimed Sarita.

'Well, let's work out a plan first. Of course we can tell our families. I googled lottery winners once. There are warnings of beggars, con artists, sob stories and bad luck cases. Most people say they wish they'd never won the money. We need advice, and I think it would be best if we keep the news quiet until we've spoken to a lawyer or a financial advisor, or both. Thankfully we ticked the box for no publicity if we won.'

'Oh, that's all true,' said Maddie. 'I don't mind giving some money away, but not being hassled for it.'

'So, what's the plan, Leonie?' asked Chrissie. She looked worried.

Leonie stood up. 'Let's go into the tearoom and have a slap-up morning tea.'

'Can we order champagne?' said Maddie.

'It's 11 am!' said Sarita.

'So?' said Maddie.

And they laughed.

Linking arms, laughing and talking, the four women strolled back across the road to the tearoom.

Briefly, Leonie glanced over her shoulder, looking back at the empty park bench. Had they left all their troubles behind them? For a moment she felt she saw a darkness on the bench, then she decided it was just the shadow from the tree branch above. But she knew one thing for sure: their lives would never be the same again.

8

SIX MONTHS LATER

LEONIE WAS PERCHED ON the fence, her boot heels hooked on a railing, while she watched Harry and Steven, the new kid, as Harry called him, plant a row of swamp gums along the paddock fence line. After a couple of minutes, Harry strolled over and leaned on the rail next to her.

'He's got the hang of it. We'll have a whole koala corridor to link the forest going up the hill,' said Leonie.

'Yep. He seems a good kid, where'd you find him?' asked Harry.

'Scotty the butcher recommended him. Said Steven wasn't cut out to butcher carcasses,' she said. 'He wants to work on the land.'

'Doesn't know much about it, though,' said Harry. 'Says you're paying him real good.' Harry gave Leonie a look.

'What's that mean?'

'Lashing out lately, aren't you?' he asked as a smile crinkled around his eyes. 'That pay rise you gave me; young Steven there. You haven't been so concerned about spending a bit of cash these days.'

'Why do you say that? I have to invest in this place to set it up for Corby.'

'Just wondering,' said Harry casually. 'I saw that sign in the newsagency a few months back.'

'What sign was that?'

'Some group bought a big winning ticket in the lottery from Fig Tree River Newsagency.'

'And you think it was me?'

'Four people. I figure you might be one of them.'

'And if I had won the lottery, what do you reckon I'd do with it?' asked Leonie with a smile.

'Keep doin' what you're doin',' said Harry. 'Mind you, I wouldn't let on either, if I was you. Too many weirdos and con men out there.'

'So. We'll keep it between us, eh, Harry?' said Leonie calmly. 'You know you can ask me for help or anything you need any time.'

'Thanks. I'm doing fine. You just keep doing this for Corby.'

Leonie nodded, suddenly on the verge of tears. 'I just wish it'd happened before . . . before I lost Tony.'

'Ah, they say things happen for a reason,' said Harry sagely.

They stopped talking as the young man walked over to them.

'Morning, Mrs Foster. Harry, I've run out of seedlings. Where to next? That soil is pretty thin, y'know, not much goodness.'

'You reckon?' said Harry.

'It's been dry,' said Leonie. 'Also we stopped using chemical fertilisers. I didn't want any runoff heading to the creek.'

'Yeah, that's good. So you just let this paddock go wild for a while to heal itself?'

'You know a bit about the land, then?' asked Leonie in some surprise.

The young man shifted, looking a bit embarrassed. 'I wouldn't say that, I've just been reading up, like . . . you know, about regeneration and stuff. I'm really interested in it.'

'Leonie calls it rewilding,' Harry said.

'Oh really, wow, that's great.'

Leonie smothered a smile. 'Yep. My late husband was into it. That's why we're giving it a go, and I believe it's important too, of course.'

'Lend Steve some of those books you showed me,' said Harry. 'He'll probably read them.'

Steven looked enthusiastic. 'I'll take good care of them, Mrs Foster.' He shuffled a bit. 'I really want to thank you for giving me a go here.'

'Well, it'll be up to you, Steven . . .'

'Er, just one thing.' He looked embarrassed. 'Everyone calls me Stevie. Is that okay?'

Leonie and Harry exchanged a glance.

'Then Stevie it is,' Leonie smiled.

*

When Corby came home from school, Leonie put out a cold drink and asked, 'How about we go fishing? Just to the creek. We haven't done that for ages.'

Corby threw the gear in the back of the four-wheel

drive and they headed across the paddocks to their special spot along the creek.

Each time Leonie went there, memories came to her of swimming naked with Tony after decent rain, teaching Corby to fish, lying on the wet rocks to cool off, the picnics the three of them had had in the leafy green coolness, and the quiet stillness where you might glimpse a platypus.

'What are we using for bait?' Leonie asked.

'I took some worms from your worm farm,' said Corby.

Leonie cast her line and sat down in a fold-out chair with a book as Corby fished further along the creek. The sun was still warm as it dipped towards the horizon in the late afternoon and she relaxed drowsily back into her seat, just enjoying the peacefulness. That was, until she noticed Corby jerk his line upwards and start winding furiously.

'Hey, you caught one!' she called. 'Excellent. Well done. Maybe we should head back; it's cooling down now.'

As she watched Corby unhook the fish and pack up his rod and gear, she suddenly asked, 'Corby, what would you say to going to Disneyland for a holiday?'

He did a double take. 'I'd say fantastic . . . unreal!' He paused and looked at her closely. 'But what about the farm?'

Leonie gave him a smile. She had decided not to tell Corby about the lotto win until he was older, but she figured a pared-back version might help explain things. 'I reckon we can do it. I've got a bit of money saved. I could buy some new gear for the farm, or –'

'Or we go to Disneyland!' shouted Corby. 'Are you

joking, Mum?' He began leaping around. 'Yay!' Then he stopped. 'You're not kidding me?'

'No. We can go.'

As he danced around her, Leonie knew she'd have to tell him how much she'd won at some stage. But it could wait.

Corby couldn't stop talking as they gathered their gear and turned back towards the car. He looked behind to make sure he hadn't left anything – he'd learned that lesson the hard way on previous outings – then he paused.

'Hey, Mum, what's that up there on the other hill?'

Leonie turned and shaded her eyes to look in the direction Corby was pointing. 'What do you mean? What is it?'

'Dunno. Some red thing. A cloth, or flag or something.'

Leonie spotted the red shape on the hillside.

'I've no idea, but I don't like it being there. I wonder if it was put there by those men who were here a few months back.'

'What men? Will I go and get it?'

'Yes, why don't you.'

She watched her son wade through the creek and clamber up the hill through the undergrowth, then she turned back to pack up their things. A few minutes later, a panting Corby returned.

'I pulled it out. It's some sort of flag.'

'Show me.' Leonie laid the flag out flat and examined it grimly.

'It's got a number on it. What is it, Mum?'

'Something to do with putting a dam in up there, I reckon.' She looked to the ranges. 'A great big dam on the main river. It'll kill all the tributaries and our creek!'

'Oh no! Can we stop it?' exclaimed Corby.

'Not sure yet, sweetie. But we'll give it a go.'

*

Ray and Sarita stood at the bay windows staring out at the garden.

'It looks like one of those intimate gardens they use for weddings,' sighed Sarita contentedly.

'And I don't have to look after it,' said Ray. 'Now that we have a gardener to help!'

'I just love this house,' said Sarita. 'It's perfect for us. So well designed, very gracious. It must have taken years to get the garden like this.'

'Well, you said you didn't want to buy a brand new house,' said Ray.

'Yes, this place feels lived in, with warm and happy memories.'

'You sure you don't want to go out for dinner?' asked Ray. 'The move has been pretty hectic.'

'Not really. I want to cook in my dream kitchen.'

'How about a glass of red?'

'Yes, please. I just had an email from the twins. They're having a ball in that van we bought them,' Sarita smiled. 'They're heading to Broome next. Maybe we should fly over and meet them. Do you think they'll get bored being beach bums and just cruising around for a year?'

'They can't be beach bums forever,' said Ray. 'They'll have to get jobs eventually.'

'Right. I'm glad they have no idea how much we won; it might make them feel they can just do nothing. I want them to learn to stand on their own two feet and earn a living, like everyone else,' said Sarita.

'I reckon they could cope with the news about your

win. I don't like keeping it from them. We raised them to be responsible young men.'

'But, Ray, the twins are still teenagers. They could easily give up on a serious career! They won't want to work if they know they don't have to. The same goes for Billy.'

'I think you're underestimating them,' said Ray.

'Well, maybe, but you haven't worked for six months!' said Sarita with a raised eyebrow.

'I'll always have a job! I'm our financial advisor, remember. Besides, I'm busy setting us up in our new house. Don't you love it?' He waved his arms around the large sitting room with its French windows facing a view of the river and distant ranges.

'Of course!' said Sarita. 'It has everything, but I still have plans for it. For us.'

'Don't tell me you want to set up a hydroponic greenhouse! We don't need to sell food at the markets anymore, love.'

'I just think it's a great way to grow healthy food and share it,' said Sarita.

'So, are you serious about Broome?' asked Ray, handing her a glass of shiraz.

Sarita smiled. 'I don't care. Why don't you surprise me with a fabulous holiday somewhere.'

Sarita's phone rang. 'Hi, Leonie.'

'Hi, Sarita. How did the move go?'

'Great, thanks. We're just sitting here having a glass of wine admiring our new home and garden. I can't wait to show it to you. I love being out of town and not having neighbours on top of us. So, how're you?'

'Crazy busy. I'm taking Corby to Disneyland. Can you believe it? We'll go in the school holidays. I have a good friend in Los Angeles who I haven't seen in years and years, and she said we can stay with her for a couple of nights. She was a bridesmaid at my wedding.'

'That sounds terrific. Corby will love it! We've been discussing holidays, too. How long is it since you've been away from the property?' asked Sarita.

'Years now, the last time was just after Tony died. It was meant to be a distraction for Corby, but it rained and we were both so unhappy we came back early.' She sighed. 'I was only saying to Harry recently how I can't help wishing this windfall had happened when Tony was alive. So, where are you thinking of going?'

'Ray is going to surprise me!'

'Really? I'd be dropping hints,' said Leonie. 'Up the star rating!' She paused. 'It still seems a dream to just decide to do something because I can afford to do it, not just *wish* that I could, you know? I still worry that I'm going to wake up and find it never happened! Have you told all your family?'

'Only my brother. I still think it's best to fly under the radar. After you told us what you saw online, I've read such horror stories about lottery winners,' said Sarita. 'Fortunately, most people in town haven't put two and two together. Have you heard from Maddie lately?'

'No, but it's always been this way with most of the people I know through the shows. We see a lot of each other when we're doing the show, then we go our separate ways until the next one. She's obviously not working in the café any more. And what about Chrissie and Troy?' asked Leonie.

'Last I heard, they'd moved up the coast to Port Haven. I just wonder how Chrissie is doing, though. She didn't really seem herself when we were doing *Percy and Ella*. Oh, hey – any news from Fleur?'

'Yes, actually!' said Leonie. 'She's moving forward

with the show, but slowly. Said she's trying to get it produced at a popular off-Broadway theatre.'

'Oh, keep us posted,' said Sarita.

'I will. But listen, Sarita, that proposed dam being built on the main river above my place looks like it's moving ahead. Corby spotted a marker flag.'

'What! Oh no. Well, that would be a massive project. They can't keep it under wraps for too long, surely!'

'That's right. I need to get in early and stop it. It's an insane idea.'

'I agree, but good luck convincing the politicians,' said Sarita.

'I know. I was just wondering if you think I could ask Brett for some advice, now that it looks like it's going ahead. Happy to pay him, of course!'

'It's the sort of thing he does, that's for sure. He's just been working with the Environmental Defenders Office on a project they're taking to court. He asked how things were going with you the other day.'

'That's good of him. Will he be in town any time soon, do you know? It'd be easier to talk face to face.'

'Yes, it would,' said Sarita. 'He also asked how Chrissie was doing, and I said I had no idea. I'll call him now and see if he'd like to come up and visit again soon. He can see my new digs while he's at it!'

*

'Hey, Charlie, it's me. What's happening?' Maddie asked cheerfully when Charlie answered the phone.

'With what?' asked Charlie.

'The buffalo. The Big Cheese buffalo dairy cheese commercial!'

'Oh, right. Yes, all good, we're finally back on

schedule, after Margot had to put the project on hold for a while. We start shooting in two days. I had to find a few handlers as well as crew!'

'Oh, can I come? I won't get in the way,' promised Maddie.

There was the briefest hesitation before Charlie said, 'Sure, if you want to. It'll be a bit crazy; we've been run off our feet. Can you get yourself out to the farm, though? I'm with the crew.'

'Of course. I'll keep out of the way.'

'Sure. See you bright and early on Tuesday, then.'

'Yes, see you then. Is there anything you'd like me to bring?' she asked, but he'd already hung up.

*

By the time Maddie arrived at the farm at 7 am, things were well under way. She greeted Margot and Laurie, who seemed a bit frazzled by all the activity with the film crew, staff and handlers, and the cast of a dozen or so buffalo who were the least fussed by all the activity. Margot was giving Sooky, the star of the show, a final brush. A little girl, dressed in shorts, T-shirt and matching pink hair ribbons, was holding a rope around Sooky's neck.

The director stood beside Charlie and his camera. A woman with a clipboard gave the little girl directions and then stepped to one side.

As Maddie watched from the back, Charlie nodded and the woman called out, 'Off you go, Sally!' then turned to the onlookers, her fingers to her lips.

Unperturbed by the crowd of people around her, the little girl led Sooky behind a small rise and disappeared. The director shouted, 'ACTION! C'MON, SALLY.'

Instantly Maddie saw what Charlie was doing. It was

a bucolic setting with lush fields and river flats, the spread of sky and fluffy clouds. Suddenly the girl leading Sooky walked towards the camera, then passed out of the shot, leaving the scene empty save for the stunning vista. There was silence until the director called loudly, 'Cut!'

Charlie gave a thumbs-up. 'Brilliant. Gorgeous.'

Someone broke into the chorus from 'The Sound of Music', much to everyone's amusement.

'Right, let's set up in the milkshed,' called Charlie.

'Oh, that's just too delicious,' said Maddie, coming over to him as everyone started moving the equipment. 'Really. Do you have music to go with it? A theme song?'

Charlie, who was lifting the camera off the tripod, glanced at her. 'You want to write something?'

'I will, if you want!' said Maddie brightly as she walked beside him. 'So, what's next?'

'Sally sitting on a tree stump drinking a big glass of milk with Sooky hopefully munching grass at her feet.'

'It's charming.' Maddie looked thoughtful. 'It needs some Fleur music.'

'We have to pay for the music, we can't just use anybody's.'

'Okay, leave it with me,' Maddie said with a smile.

Charlie looked at her. 'You're serious? Okay. Give it a go.'

As he hurried away, Maddie said aloud, 'I'll do better than that, Charlie boy.'

She didn't hear from Charlie for a week or so after that, but she knew he was working day and night on editing the footage. And she lost track of time herself as she was swept away writing the music for the Sooky commercial, as she thought of it.

She composed a sweet yet haunting melody to

accompany the vista of the valley and the buffalo, then as the camera zoomed out and the figure of Sally, swinging a bucket and leading placid Sooky, came over the crest of the hill, Maddie sang:

As fresh as morning dew, as sweet as a smile,
Sooky and Sally bring the finest milk supply . . .

The theme music, soft, catchy and unobtrusive, continued under the sequences Charlie had listed.

It all added to the feel Charlie was aiming for – wholesome, fresh, natural and appetising. He called her back a few hours after she sent it to him.

'Hi, Maddie. Thanks for the link to the music. It's fabulous, Margot and Laurie are over the moon,' Charlie said. 'I can't thank you enough. I realise we didn't talk about a quote, though, sorry. Just send me your invoice when you're ready.'

'Of course not! No, this one's on me. It was fun to do. I did it for you, because I wanted to,' said Maddie.

Charlie paused. 'Well, thanks again. But I don't want you doing stuff for free. This is a business, so we have to make sure it's copyrighted for you.' He hesitated, unsure what to say. 'I'm not prying, but have you sorted out what you're going to do with your winnings? I hope you're being smart. And careful.'

'Don't worry, I took advice. It feels good to be able to look after my parents financially after they've struggled for years.'

'You should look after yourself, too, Mads,' Charlie said softly. 'It's not my business, of course.'

'Thanks, Charlie. And don't worry. I know what I want to do.'

Maddie was glad she'd told Charlie about her win, but hadn't told him exactly how much she'd won. She didn't want anything to get in the way of the happy relationship they had established but, she admitted to herself, something seemed different anyway. She wasn't sure if it was the win, or the fact that Charlie had been swamped with work ever since the show, but things hadn't been the same between them for a while now. She sometimes wondered if that picnic on the riverbank had only ever been a lovely dream.

There was silence on the line for a moment. 'Mads, you have masses of talent, you should use it,' said Charlie eventually.

She shrugged and gave a laugh. 'We'll see.'

*

'Oh . . . my . . . God!'

The small private jet descended, and Sarita gazed out the window as the emerald dot grew larger in the ocean of sapphire blue, a gold trim of sand ringing it. 'It looks like a picture postcard!'

Ray leaned across her to peer out the window. 'Doesn't look like there's anything on it at all! Certainly not a splashy luxury resort. They must have bures hidden among the palm trees. What have I got us into?' He grinned.

'Well, Fiji was your idea. I just suggested upping the ante. You said this was very, very private,' said Sarita.

'I hope that doesn't mean we have to catch our own fish and cook it,' said Ray wryly.

Sarita glanced over at the other passengers: one couple and a man who looked like he was on a business trip. While he wasn't wearing a suit and tie, his linen jacket and trousers didn't shout 'holiday wear'. The woman hadn't lifted her eyes from her book, and the man beside her was tapping on a laptop. They were casually dressed but Sarita recognised that they were wearing exclusive labels. 'Do you think we're going to fit in?' she whispered to Ray.

'When we boarded and they rolled out the champagne, I was struggling to look nonchalant!' Ray winked. 'We're certainly going all out.'

'I thought we did very well. My guess is that the other couple have done this before. The flight attendant obviously knew them – she gave them the Krug without asking – but she asked us what we wanted,' said Sarita.

'I had the feeling that if I'd asked for a cocktail with chilled Icelandic water and moon dust on top she would have smiled nicely and said "Certainly, sir,"' Ray chuckled quietly.

On the tarmac the other couple nodded to them.

'Enjoy your stay,' they said politely. They stepped into a waiting golf buggy and were whisked away.

'Apologies, your buggy is on its way. Have a cold drink if you wish while we get your luggage,' the flight attendant said to Ray and Sarita.

But at that moment a buggy drove towards them and stopped. They settled themselves in the back seat as their luggage was put next to the driver.

He was apologetic for being late. 'I will be your driver while you're here, or you are welcome to take the buggy yourself. There are many things to do here. Or just do nothing!'

'That sounds great,' said Ray. 'We're looking forward to exploring a bit.'

'And relaxing,' added Sarita.

As they set off, Sarita felt as though she was wearing 3D glasses, looking at another world around her.

'It's almost too beautiful. It doesn't look real,' she said quietly. 'It's like every gorgeous plant, flower and palm tree has been made just for this spot. It's crazy,' she whispered.

After a short drive, the driver dropped them off in front of their private bungalow. They were greeted by their hostess, a woman who introduced herself as Angelica, who seemed to appear from nowhere just in time to invite them to take a seat on the cool, shaded verandah. She offered them their choice of drinks from fresh juice to champagne, and described the activities that were available. They could scuba-dive, swim at sunrise, and picnic on a deserted atoll with a hamper of their favourite foods and wines.

'Are there many guests here?' asked Ray.

'Several. Most like to keep to themselves, although we have casual cocktails every sunset at the Beach Bar on the terrace. You have butler service, so you can choose to have meals prepared for you at your bure or eat in the dining areas. There's a choice of breakfast and lunch venues, or you can enjoy those in your own bure as well,' explained Angelica.

'So many choices!' said Sarita.

'It's just a few minutes' walk to the dining areas, or you can use your buggy,' she said. After giving them some more details about the resort, Angelica wished them a happy stay and left so they could make themselves at home.

Sarita and Ray walked inside and admired the casual but elegant décor. Perfume from delicate and expensive-looking candles wafted past them as they padded through to the bedroom, where they discovered their bags had been unpacked, clothes hung and toiletries set out in the bathroom, where there was also an array of expensive soaps and lotions. Their bed was draped with mosquito netting, more for effect than necessity, they thought, and faced the sea. It all looked like a romantic painting.

'S'pose we'll sleep okay in here, do you think?' said Ray, as Sarita rolled her eyes, quite speechless at the luxury of it all. It was even more upmarket than she'd imagined.

'Man, they've thought of everything. Dine inside or outside, here's the button for the butler/housekeeper/driver/manager.' He shook his head then looked at Sarita. 'I did more than okay finding this place!'

'I feel like I'm dreaming.' She reached up and wound her arms around him, giving him a kiss.

After another drink they decided to stroll around their garden. The mellow wooden bure was cleverly designed to blend into the tropical setting, taking advantage of the breezes and views. It was discreetly private, with its own swimming pool and spa.

Walking out onto the path, they discovered that it led to a cluster of palms where a small waterfall splashed into a decorative pond.

Later in the day, as Sarita lounged on the daybed by their pool overlooking the ocean, Ray came back from the beach.

'Hi, you look relaxed. And very sexy, too.'

Sarita glanced down at her new swimsuit and matching sarong. 'I can't believe I'm wearing hundreds of dollars' worth of gear that doesn't even cover all of my body.' She waved her hands at him. 'Notice that the nail varnish matches. I had a very extravagant mani-pedi poolside!'

'If we were so inclined, this is the sort of postcard photo people take for Instagram and their Christmas card picture,' said Ray.

'No way are we doing any of that! How was the beach?'

'Beautiful. Unspoiled. I don't think there's anything else here.'

'It's a private island. Maybe the staff come in each day by boat,' said Sarita. 'Although, didn't Angelica say she's always here? And there's probably someone else who stays with her. I bet we could ring for the butler at 2 am.'

Ray yawned and stretched indulgently. 'So, do you want to have our chef prepare us something in our amazing bure or go for the sunset cocktails?'

'I'm on holidays, I don't feel like getting dressed up for cocktails,' said Sarita.

'I'm pretty sure it's just guests who want to mingle.'

'Do you think there could be someone famous staying here?' asked Sarita.

Ray burst out laughing. 'Look around you! Look where we are! I'm sure there would be, but I suspect famous people like to keep to themselves.'

'True. Well, let's make the most of our first night here and go to the cocktails. I'll have a shower and get changed.'

As they walked through the lawns and gardens to the bar, they couldn't see any other accommodation.

'Where is everyone?' wondered Sarita.

'Tucked away in villas overlooking the sea or on the beach. We chose beachfront. Each one is totally private,' Ray said. 'You can sunbake nude if you'd like.'

'Why would I do that?' She waved an arm at herself. 'I came tanned.'

Ray looked at his wife, and caught his breath. It was like seeing her for the first time, when he'd instantly fallen in love with her. Those bright brown eyes, glossy thick dark hair, dazzling smile and skin like velvet. She was beautiful, funny, bright and caring. Dressed in her elegant sarong with matching chiffon shawl dotted with yellow hibiscus flowers and a fresh hibiscus tucked in her upswept hair, Sarita looked vibrant and carefree. Apart from her wedding band she wore no jewellery, though her gold sandals added an elegant touch.

She caught Ray looking appreciatively at her and took his hand.

*

The sliding doors that led down to the beach were open. Several people sat at the lavish bar along one wall or in private alcoves facing the sea. Out on the deck, lounges and deep chairs were spaced between tables laden with exotic appetisers, flower arrangements and crystal glasses. It looked very casual, but each lounging area was semi-private, screened by the flowers and far enough apart that conversations wouldn't be overheard.

The staff wore uniforms of casual red and white – the men in traditional white sulus and red shirts, the women in long red and white floral dresses. All the staff seemed cast from the same mould of shapely, fit, attractive, smiling and polite people.

They were swiftly welcomed by name. 'Mr and Mrs Golding, *bula*, welcome. Do you prefer inside or out on the terrace?'

'I think outside, please,' said Sarita. 'It's so balmy.'

Settled with their champagne flutes, it became obvious that social interaction occurred around the hors d'oeuvres table. So while two couples were hovering, holding plates and picking at the food, Sarita nudged Ray.

'Let's get a morsel or two of that delicious-looking food.'

As they chose from the array of delicacies, they exchanged smiles with one couple.

'These look wonderful,' said Sarita.

The other woman, dressed in a flowery silk caftan and accessorised with elaborate gold chains, gold earrings and a matching ring, all set with large colourful stones – rubies, sapphires and emeralds – seemed to assess Sarita, and gave a small smile.

'Yes, beware, or dinner can be an anticlimax. We tend to eat late after this,' she said in a soft American accent.

'Sounds sensible,' said Ray.

'Work it off in the sauna,' said the man standing beside the woman. He looked to be younger and fitter than all of them. 'I also swim a mile or so each morning.'

'And no sharks, I presume, as we're inside the reef?' said Sarita.

'Ah, you must be Australian. Thought I could tell from your accent,' he grinned.

The woman nodded at Sarita's outfit. 'Is that an Australian designer?'

'Ah, no, it's one of mine,' smiled Sarita.

The woman looked interested. 'You're a designer! What label?'

'No label. I make my own clothes,' said Sarita.

'She does all the costumes for the shows at our local theatre, too,' chipped in Ray proudly.

'Oh. How fascinating,' said the woman coolly. She sounded bored.

'So. Where in the US are you from?' asked Sarita, changing the subject.

'Houston, Texas, ma'am,' answered the young man.

The woman turned back to their seats. 'I'm ready for champagne,' she announced, stepping away. The fellow gave a smiling shrug and followed her to their lounges.

Ray turned back to the table. 'Texas oil, would you say?' he murmured. 'Son or boyfriend?'

'Shush, Ray.'

'Okay, I'll just be cool,' he said.

'I can't believe this food,' sighed Sarita.

'Well, shall we sit down and eat it? Or do we have to socialise?' he asked in a low voice.

'I'm going to sit and eat,' said Sarita.

Smiling staff hovered and topped up drinks as two other couples joined a group who were sitting in an alcove. All radiated cheerful self-confidence and had seemingly made no effort to dress up for cocktails.

There was a burst of laughter from the bar. Ray glanced inside.

'I might go in and get a cold beer, see what they've got. No more bubbles for me. Do you mind being alone a moment?'

'Of course not.'

But as soon as he walked away, a Fijian hostess joined Sarita.

'Is everything to your liking, Mrs Golding? Are you dining in your bure tonight, or a venue? There's also a casual beach barbecue where we do anything you might like: Asian, seafood, any kind of meat, perhaps? Or we can barbecue on your patio for you.'

Sarita shook her head. 'We might save that up for another night. I'll talk with my husband about where we'll eat tonight and let you know. Thank you.'

'Well, I hope you enjoy your stay with us. Please,

anything you would like at all, let me know. My name is Lavinia.'

'Thank you, Lavinia.' Sarita smiled at her.

Ray made his way back to her and sat down, putting his glass of beer on the table. He rolled his eyes.

'How're the rich and famous?' asked Sarita quietly, with a grin.

Ray frowned. 'Bloody pain, actually. Some young jerk in there fancies himself the next Tom Cruise and wanted to juggle all the bottles in the bar. Dropped several of them, made a big mess.'

'So who's in there with him, Bryan Brown?' asked Sarita.

'Some hot movie star kid I've never seen or heard of. Apparently he's just filmed a surfing movie out on the reef here. Seems surfer films are in fashion again.'

'So what shall we do tomorrow?' asked Sarita.

'I'm not thinking that far ahead. I might have another beer. Nah, on second thoughts, I don't want to tangle with the junior movie star.' He drained his glass. 'Too much, too soon,' said Ray, stretching his legs. 'Fame. Gone to his head. I say we ask for some of that seafood to be brought to our bure. Fancy a moonlight picnic and a naked swim?'

'That sounds like a plan,' said Sarita. 'Maybe we'll meet some nice friendly people tomorrow.'

*

The following day, as Sarita lay in a hammock reading a book, Ray wandered up to her.

'I think I'll go for a walk along the beach to the little rocky point that we saw from the plane.'

'Good for you. I'm engrossed in this book. And I'm feeling too relaxed to move,' she said, stretching indulgently.

By the time Ray returned, Sarita was asleep in the shady hammock. She stirred as she heard him.

'Hi. How was the walk?'

'Great. I met a fellow, English, we're going fishing.'

'But you don't have any fishing gear.'

'I do now,' he said, grinning and pointing to tackle and a rod. 'Ask and you shall receive . . . the sports director had it here for me in a flash.'

'There's a sports director?' Sarita shook her head in wonder. 'Is it lunchtime yet?' she asked.

'Any time is mealtime here. What do you feel like?'

She swung her legs out of the hammock. 'I wish there were local markets to wander around.'

'We don't need any food!' said Ray in alarm.

Sarita laughed. 'I know! Just to soak up the local colour. See how they compare to our markets. Maybe find some gifts. Anyway, you be careful fishing. So who is this guy?'

'I don't know. He looks to be retired, speaks well, one of those people you chat to and they seem like old pals in no time.'

'Nice. Enjoy the fishing. If you bring fish home we'll have the chef cook them on the barbecue. I'll see you later.' Sarita blew him a kiss.

She wandered inside and, on a whim, pushed the butler button.

A large, smiling Fijian man walked quietly into the room, greeting her effusively.

'Could someone take me for a drive, please?' Sarita asked. 'I'd like to take some photos. Also, is there a local market I could visit?'

He gave a broad smile. 'We bring a special market here tomorrow, on the front lawns. There are many good things to buy.'

'Oh! That sounds lovely. I'll certainly be there. But today, maybe I can just go for a drive.'

He nodded. 'Certainly. Like a small tour. And Mr Golding?'

'He's gone fishing. I'm ready any time.'

'I'll get your driver.'

*

The western side of the island was lush, green, and dwarfed by jagged mountains sliced by rocky, fast-moving streams. A cluster of thatched huts was surrounded by fields stretching towards the jungle. There was not a shop or business of any kind in sight. It all looked like a toy land.

'Who lives there?' asked Sarita.

'Just workers for the resort,' the driver answered.

As he drove through the verdant landscape back to the exquisite architectural novelty of the luxurious resort nestled into the hillside, Sarita couldn't help but compare it with the simple cluster of huts in the tiny village she'd glimpsed.

Back at her bure, Sarita changed and headed to their pool. She stretched out in the shade and, without asking, her favourite cold drink served in a coconut shell quietly appeared beside her.

Sarita closed her eyes and dozed. Shadowy images, voices, a song, drifted through her mind. Vague memories, the sense of being held, being loved, sent a surge of warmth through her. But as she surfaced to wakefulness, the images and sounds faded like wisps of cloud.

'Hey there. How's your afternoon been?'

She looked up at Ray. 'A lovely drive. And there's a market here tomorrow. How was the fishing?'

'*Very* impressive. That was no plain old fishing boat – it had everything. A person to bait the hook, hand you a drink, take off the fish,' he laughed.

'That's not fishing!'

'No,' said Ray. 'But it was fun. Andrew – Andy – was just a bloke on the beach with a fishing rod when I met him. But it turns out he seems to have something of an entourage in tow. Couple of young women hanging around. They were bored silly.' He sat down next to her. 'So are we going for cocktails again?'

'I guess so.' Sarita wasn't too enthusiastic but didn't want to disappoint Ray.

Ray gave her a look. 'What's up?'

'I had a funny sort of episode . . . nothing serious. It was like a dream. Suddenly. Memories of some kind. It made me feel . . . strange.'

Ray took her hand. 'Like what?'

'I don't know. Something just felt familiar. Weird.' She shook her head.

'And now? Is it better? Do you feel okay?' asked Ray.

'Yes. I don't know why, but something just kind of hit me.'

'You should feel relaxed! Look where we are! We have more money than we could ever need in the bank, well invested. What can go wrong? Stop worrying, my love.'

'Is that how you feel?' Sarita asked, sitting up. 'It's still hard to take in that we can buy whatever we want – within reason.'

'Within reason?' Ray raised his eyebrows.

Sarita couldn't help laughing. 'I could blow the lot on a mansion or a huge cruiser.'

'Listen to your financial advisor! Let's relax and enjoy

our time here.' He sat up and looked at her. 'You know, it's not that surprising you felt you might have remembered something. You were born here, you lived here a while when you were very young. Perhaps we could try and find your family while we're here in Fiji?'

Sarita frowned. 'Actually, that hadn't occurred to me. Why would I? Anyway, after all this time, I'd have no idea where to start.'

'Fair enough. Come and have a swim in our private pool.' He pulled her to her feet.

*

There were a few more people in the bar and on the terrace than the previous evening. The low hum of voices was punctuated by small bursts of laughter.

'Is that your fishing mate?' said Sarita, looking over at the group.

'Yep, and the others must be the mates he told me were joining him,' said Ray.

Sarita stopped, staring, and grabbed Ray's arm.

'*That's* the Andy you went fishing with?' she whispered. 'Oh, good lord . . .'

'What's up? He's a nice enough guy.'

'Ray! That's Andrew Cucello! The movie star!' she hissed.

'Is it? Well, I'll be damned. So it is, I thought there was something familiar about him, couldn't put my finger on it.'

'Don't say anything. Just be casual.'

Andy saw Ray and lifted a hand. 'Hey, matey! Come on over!'

Sarita gave Ray a wide-eyed look but he just smiled and led her over to the group. Andy slapped Ray on the shoulder. 'Everyone, this is my Aussie fishing pal,' he said. 'And this is?' He smiled and held out his hand to Sarita.

'Andy, meet my wife, Sarita.'

'Hello, lovely to meet you.' Andy grabbed her hand in both of his, squeezing it, then lifting it to his lips. 'What a beauty you are. You must come out on the boat with us.'

'Why, thank you,' Sarita managed. 'I'd love to.'

Ray gave her a look.

Waiters hovered and drinks were passed around. Sarita excused herself and went to a table out on the terrace. She wanted to text Leonie that she was in the same room as a mega movie star, but realised she didn't have her phone. Instead she glanced around just in case there was another famous face, but she only spotted the couple from Texas. The young man gave her a smile and a nod, but the woman didn't glance in her direction.

*

Ray stared at his plate in the warm glow of the candlelight and mellow lamps in the resort's main dining room. 'I think I understand now why people take photos of their food.'

'Don't you dare,' said Sarita. 'It is amazing, though. This tuna is to die for.'

Ray picked up the handwritten menu. 'I have hollowed urchin shell – with all the spikes on it – filled with fresh urchin roe, delicate shrimps marinated in walnut oil, herbs, mirin, olive oil, egg yolk jelly, topped with a necklace of seaweed and caviar. I don't even know what half those things are.'

'Anything would taste good here. I mean, we're in paradise,' said Sarita.

They both turned to look at the glimmering ocean

reflecting the moonlight. Sarita heard the brush of palm leaves and breathed in the perfume of night blooms.

'Even when I went on the drive through the jungle, I always sensed that we are on an island,' said Sarita. 'I like that. Makes me feel safe.'

'Mmm, really? Actually it makes me feel somewhat isolated, but it's fine being here with you. I think I prefer the big island. Australia.'

Sarita smiled. 'Yes, of course, that's home. But now we have the freedom to . . .' She paused.

'Please tell me you don't want to do cruises on big ships!'

Sarita shook her head. 'Gosh no. I'd feel trapped on one of those big liners!'

'Why? Some of them are bigger than this island!'

'Dessert, Mrs Golding?' Lavinia hovered, smiling. 'Our chef is an award-winning chocolatier.'

'Oh, yes please, you got me there. Please bring me his best dessert!'

Ray waved his hand. 'Not for me, thanks. But I'd like a cheese platter . . . a selection, please.'

*

The following day Ray returned from an early-morning walk along the beach. He poked his head into the bedroom where Sarita was reading under the cloud of mosquito netting.

'The market is here. Doesn't look too exciting. I wouldn't rush out there,' he said.

'Come back to bed then.'

'That's an invitation I won't refuse,' smiled Ray.

*

It was late morning when Sarita ambled over to the market, which comprised a few sellers sitting before bamboo mats spread on the lawns. Handicrafts, knick-knacks, souvenirs like kava bowls, baskets, woven grass hats and some local fruit were laid in front of them. Several guests, including the Texan woman, Andy, and a couple Sarita didn't recognise, were chatting as they looked at some of the wares.

Sarita was behind them and they were unaware of her presence, but she could hear them talking, especially the American woman, who was gushing at Andrew Cucello.

'I adore your movies. What are you doing at present?'

'Having a break! Hanging out with some pals. Say, you want to join us for drinks tonight?'

'Ooh, love to. Who will be there?'

'Just my friends.'

'Oh, sounds great, Andy. Ah . . . you're not including others? I mean, that Australian man with his Indian wife. He must have picked her up in Suva.' She gave a derisive laugh. 'Didn't expect someone like that to be here. *And* in her homemade clothes.'

'She looked okay to me. Took her husband out on my boat. Not doing that again. Not the wittiest guy. Said he was a public servant. Who knows what they're doing here! Say, I might get our hostess with the mostest to whip us up some drinks. What's her name again?' He turned to a man beside him. 'Kavilani?' He started clicking his fingers at some nearby staff.

Sarita turned away, tears stinging her eyes, and hurried to the reception lounge, the first refuge she saw.

The young Texan man was coming towards her.

'Hi there. Checked out the markets?' he asked.

'There's nothing of any quality or taste out there,' blurted Sarita, and kept walking.

'Right. I'll give it a miss.' He turned towards the bar.

Ray was in a lounge chair by their bure pool with a sulu wrapped around his wet swimsuit.

'Where'd you get to? Did you find anything nice?'

'No. Except I overheard that rude American bitch,' said Sarita. And burst into tears, repeating what the woman had said.

'Not our kind of people,' said Ray calmly.

'No. They're not. And frankly, Ray, this place is all a bit over-the-top too.'

'What do you mean?' He sat up. 'I thought you were enjoying yourself?'

Sarita sat beside him. 'I thought it would be a lovely idea. But this isn't us. I want to leave. Let's just go.'

He looked at her. 'Right now?'

Sarita nodded. 'Is that okay?'

Ray leaned over and kissed her. 'Whatever floats your boat, my lovely.'

She kissed him back and started to laugh. 'Ray, that is such a silly saying! Let's find another adventure. With real people!'

9

Leonie collected Tony's maps and spread them across the dining table. Some had belonged to his grandfather and were old and out of date, but they all showed the land that had been in Tony's family for several generations. She studied the back paddocks near the creek, following the ridgeline above, where there was a dotted line and a handwritten note: *Falls and main river*.

'Corby!' she called.

Her son came in from the kitchen munching a sandwich and she asked, 'Do you ever remember Dad or anyone saying something about a waterfall up the hill above our creek?'

He shook his head. 'Don't think so. Maybe ask Harry?'

'From this map it looks to be high in the hills. If they

put a dam up there it could definitely affect the main river and our creek and everything in between,' said Leonie.

'And take the water from our creek? No way!'

'Or if the dam overflows, or is breached, or something else goes wrong, not only do we lose the water, but the habitat and wildlife could be seriously affected by flood or lack of water flow. Either way a dam just doesn't sound like a sensible idea. I need to find out more and quickly. I wonder who else knows about this? Whoever is building this dam is keeping quiet about it until a deal is done and dusted, I suppose.' Leonie frowned.

'So what are you going to do?' asked Corby.

'I'm thinking,' said Leonie. 'I was going to wait for Brett to visit, but Sarita is away at the moment. I think Chrissie has his mobile number, though.'

'Who's Brett?' asked Corby.

'Sarita's brother, he's an environmental lawyer. He came up for the show, he visits her and Ray a lot.'

'Oh yeah. I remember.'

*

'I guess you've settled into Port Haven?' Leonie asked Chrissie when she finally answered her phone. 'Are you enjoying it?'

'Hmm. It's different. I miss the familiarity and friends. I'll get used to it, I guess.'

'What about the kids? How're they adjusting?' asked Leonie.

'They're trying hard. The teachers seem fine, but the other kids . . . well, it's tricky. The kids at the new school all have their own friends, and don't seem to socialise outside their own circle. It's nothing like the school at Fig Tree River.'

'Changing schools is always a huge adjustment, I suppose,' said Leonie. 'And what about you?'

'I'm doing okay. Same as the kids, trying to fit in.' Chrissie seemed to be making an effort to sound light-hearted. 'Of course, now we're in an apartment I don't have my tools or anything – I left them at my parents' place. I'm trying to focus on the kids and getting the apartment sorted.'

'Well, I hope it all comes together soon,' said Leonie. 'Listen, Chrissie, the reason I rang is that I'm trying to contact Brett, Sarita's brother. Do you happen to have his phone number? I remember he delivered some building materials to you once.'

'Oh – yes, I guess it's in my phone. Why, what's up?'

'He's an environmental lawyer and I'm worried that there's a plan to put a big dam above us on the main river.'

'Whoa, that doesn't sound good. What if it overflows or something?' said Chrissie.

'Exactly. Now that I can afford to pay Brett to help with this, I want to contact him.'

'I'll text you his number if I still have it,' said Chrissie.

'Thanks. Talk soon.'

Within minutes Chrissie had texted through Brett's mobile number, and Leonie called him and explained briefly what she knew.

'That does sound concerning,' he said.

'I don't think this is a mega dam, but from what I've read, even middle-sized dams can cause problems,' said Leonie.

'That's right. There are issues with the flow of the river which can stop fish migration, prevent nutrients being carried into estuaries, damage habitat and limit leisure activities, and they can cost at least double the original estimate in time and dollars. And that's just for starters,' Brett added, sounding professional, which is exactly what she needed.

'So you think we could get it knocked back, then?' said Leonie.

'Don't underestimate those who lobby for dams to be built. But I'm happy to help, so what do you want to do?' said Brett. 'Should I come up and have a look at the projected site?'

'Well, we'd love to see you, of course. But I'm not exactly sure where the proposed site is. Seems to be under wraps at the moment. I'm having great trouble getting any info, but as soon as I do, I'll call you.'

'When you know the proposed site, you could hire a drone and get a survey of it,' said Brett. 'Then I'll head up when I can.'

'Thanks so much, Brett. Have you heard from Sarita and Ray, by the way?'

'No!' He laughed. 'I assume they're swanning around with the jet set. They deserve it, though. You too, Leonie. Have a bit of fun with Corby.'

'I intend to. Disneyland is on the agenda.'

'You're a brave person to tackle that! Talk soon.'

*

Chrissie sat on the beach watching Thomas and Mia play in the gentle waves. Being able to walk to the beach was a novelty and luxury they still couldn't believe. Thomas insisted they go early each morning just to check it was still there – clean swept, only a few walkers and dogs, and the silhouette of surfers.

Some apartments faced the beach and, behind them, Chrissie and her children had discovered the man-made canals where each home had moorings complete with a jetski and speedboat. All the houses looked alike – glass boxes with patios, pools and jetties – and the owners shared their prosperity and pretension.

Troy was revelling in spending. A sports car, flashy clothes, their new highrise apartment – the gauche gloss of the nouveau riche. Chrissie hated it.

She didn't like Troy's new friends, either. She didn't trust them for a minute and they seemed to know it, so they avoided her. She didn't say anything to Troy, though. Chrissie knew Troy was presenting himself as a successful man, newly arrived in town. Port Haven was burgeoning with development, piloted by a network of wheeler-dealer businessmen linked to other coastal developments; the epitome of the group once known as the white shoe brigade. Troy was out nearly every night with them, splashing money around.

Fortunately, Chrissie had found an unpretentious café near the children's new school, which she would go to each afternoon to wait to collect them in her new, but modest, car. She enjoyed sipping a coffee and reading the local newspaper.

When the café owner saw her there one day, he paused to chat.

'You're becoming a regular. Interested in the local news?' he asked, indicating the paper.

'Well, I guess so. We've just moved here. My children are at St Patrick's.'

'I figured that. So where are you from?'

'Fig Tree River,' said Chrissie.

'Ah. Just down the road. Moved to be near the school, then?'

'Well, that's one reason. It was my husband's idea.'

The man nodded. 'I see. And you? What do you do with yourself?' he asked.

Chrissie felt slightly flustered. 'I make stuff. You know, woodwork, carpentry, that sort of thing. Well – I used to.'

'Really?' he said with a friendly smile. 'You can't fix cupboards, can you? The pantry at the back is a mess.'

'Actually, I could help you out. I've built all sorts of things. I used to make the sets for the shows at the Riverside Playhouse in Fig Tree River, that's –'

'I know it! My wife and my mum, we go to see their shows! Good as anything in Sydney or Brissie, I reckon.'

'Really? We think so too!' Chrissie's face lit up. 'Seriously, do you want me to take a look at your pantry?'

'Oh, I don't want to put you out. I was going to go to the Men's Shed to ask if someone could do the job. They're just down the road.'

'Oh – well, fine, that's a good idea,' said Chrissie, rather disappointed he hadn't taken her seriously.

'If they can't help me, I'll let you know.'

'That'd be good.' Chrissie smiled and glanced at her watch. 'Oops, I'd better be going. See you later.'

'Have a good one!'

As she paid for her coffee, Chrissie realised she couldn't remember the last time she'd laughed.

*

Madison wished she still had a job to escape to as she pulled her pillow over her head to block out the raised voice of her father as he argued with her mother on the phone.

This was not how it was supposed to be. She could be doing anything she wanted, and right now all she wished was that she was serving coffee and cake in the café without a care in the world. She felt confused that her great lucky windfall was turning into a nightmare for her family. Her parents were doing nothing but argue over what she was trying do for them.

Beside her parents, Charlie was the only other person she'd told about her lottery win – and he didn't know the true amount. He had suggested she get financial advice, invest some of her money and then forget about it, so she had a nest egg safely stashed away for the future. So that's what Maddie had done. Now Charlie was away on a job somewhere and must be out of range, as he hadn't answered any of her messages.

Sighing, she left her bedroom and wandered into the kitchen.

Her father was making himself a mug of instant coffee.

'How can you drink that stuff, Dad? Let's get a proper coffee maker. Those capsule ones are so easy.'

'This is fine by me. You go buy yourself a fancy coffee machine if you want one.'

'Maybe I will.'

'Have you spoken to your mother?'

'Nope. But I heard you on the phone with her just now.'

'She's having a good time with her cousin looking at bloody Gold Coast units,' muttered her father.

'What for? A holiday for you both?' exclaimed Maddie.

'Nope. She wants to move there.'

'What! Why? You'd hate that, Dad.'

'Yeah.' Her father sat at the table staring into his coffee mug. 'No way would I move up there. And I'm not staying here on my own. I miss my farm.' He looked at her. 'Why don't you buy us a farm, Maddie?'

'What? Dad, for goodness' sake.'

'You've got enough money. Nothing wrong with looking after your parents. After what we've done for you.'

Maddie was about to retort but held her breath, then said slowly, 'Dad, I appreciate everything you and Mum have done for me. But I thought you'd be glad that now we can all be secure. I can do my music, travel, do things I always dreamed about but knew we could never afford. You and Mum have security now, and some extra cash. So why don't you two do things like take a trip, have a proper holiday –'

'Buy a racehorse?' He gave a bit of a smile.

'You're not serious,' said Maddie. 'Dad, I can't give you money for a horse, or whatever! But I can give you enough for you and Mum to have a holiday, and the security to know you'll always have plenty to get by. I'm investing the rest for the future. Isn't that the main thing?'

'Yeah, of course, Maddie. I understand and you're being sensible.' He drained his coffee and put the cup in the sink. 'But you'd better tell your mother that too, in case she is serious about this Gold Coast caper.'

'Why don't you go up there? Join her just for a break?' suggested Maddie. 'No harm in that. You might even have fun.'

'I might do that.' He looked at her. 'Mads, you're smart and you've got your music. You do what you want to do. Just be careful of fellas who sniff out that you might have money.'

'Dad, don't worry.' She watched her father leave the room, and sighed. Why did money complicate things rather than make them easier?

*

A driver was waiting for Sarita and Ray when they flew into Nadi.

'We're going to Vuda Point,' Ray told him.

'Ah, yes. You can go to many places from there, it's very beautiful. Very special,' the driver said.

'Are there any markets along the way?' asked Sarita.

'Not on the way, but the Lautoka markets are not much further. Very good. Very . . . local,' he added.

'Lautoka. That's where my mother came from,' Sarita said quietly to Ray. She turned back to the driver and asked, 'Could we go there first then, please?'

'Okay. Lautoka markets, here we come,' said the driver with a smile. 'The markets are very big, but they are under cover. Let me know if you want to stop anywhere to take photos, too.'

'That's okay, thank you,' said Sarita.

'Lautoka is a very old place. Centre of the sugar industry,' said the driver.

'Yes. My father worked there many years ago,' said Sarita.

'Ah, so you have family here?' he asked.

'Oh, here and there, probably,' Sarita said vaguely.

Ray looked at her. 'Do you think any of your relatives might still be there, love?'

'I have no idea.'

'What's their name?' asked the driver curiously.

Sarita glanced at Ray, who gave a slight shrug as she said, 'My mother's family name was Chand.'

The driver slapped the wheel. 'From the Chandirastaram family! Everyone just calls them Chand. Much easier.' He laughed.

'I guess so,' said Sarita. 'It doesn't matter.'

'Who are the Chand family?' asked Ray.

'Oh, big business people. They run Chand Printing Company,' said the driver. 'The family have businesses in Suva and Nadi too. Important people in Lautoka. You will see them?'

'No. We're just here on a holiday,' said Sarita.

Ray looked at her and reached across, taking her hand. 'Why? You're not interested?' he asked gently.

'Why should I complicate my life? Especially now,' said Sarita firmly.

'The markets are along here,' said the driver as they edged down a crowded narrow street in the township.

'Good grief, it's enormous!' said Ray. 'A huge complex, not just a few sellers outdoors.'

'Anything particular you want? I can drop you close,' said the driver.

'No, we just want to have a look. We won't be long. Sorry, what is your name?' asked Sarita. She hadn't expected the driver to be quite so chatty.

'Sanjay, madam.' He stepped from the car to open her door with a swiftness that defied his age. 'You have my mobile. I won't be far.'

'What time did we say we'd be at Vuda Point?' Ray asked Sarita.

'No worries, sir. They will wait for you to come,' Sanjay reassured him.

'Okay. Right.' Ray took Sarita's arm. 'Of course they'll wait for us.'

An hour later, they headed back to the car.

'Now that's what I call a market,' said Ray. 'Seems a shame we only bought a pawpaw.' He smiled.

'Yes. But look at the size of it,' Sarita said. 'They don't grow them like this at home!'

*

From Vuda Point, they headed to a small exclusive island retreat, where they were to stay for a couple of nights. After their last experience, they had chosen it because they would be the only guests – well outnumbered by staff, according to the website.

'This has been much more relaxing, if less salubrious than the other place,' Sarita said over a late breakfast on their last morning.

'You didn't miss having people to talk to?' asked Ray.

'I don't miss the movie stars. I talked to the staff while you were having a swim earlier. Very interesting, but what they had to say was shocking,' said Sarita. 'These islands are going to get swamped by rising tides.'

'How depressing,' said Ray. 'What will happen to everyone who lives here?'

'They'll be forced to leave, I guess,' said Sarita. After that they ate in silence for a while, both thinking about what the near future held for the local people.

'Well, I really enjoyed swimming and scuba-diving in safety inside our little reef,' Ray said eventually, to lift the mood.

'And playing Robinson Crusoe, but with all the trimmings,' she laughed. 'I love how no one intrudes here, food just appears, everything disappears again afterwards and if we want something it arrives almost before we've asked for it. We should do this again with the boys.'

'Yes, they'd love it. This holiday has been unbelievably special,' agreed Ray. 'But back to reality soon, I suppose. Well – our new reality. When do we get the boat back to Vuda Point?'

Sarita checked her watch. 'In a couple of hours,' she said.

'What would you like to do after we've checked into the hotel there?' asked Ray.

'We could look around Vuda Point,' Sarita said. 'Maybe Sanjay could suggest something. I'll give him a call to check what time he's coming to collect us.'

*

The next morning, Sarita went out to the parking area of their hotel at the marina, where she saw Ray and Sanjay in animated conversation by the car.

'Sarita, Sanjay has found your family!' Ray said as she walked over.

'What?' She frowned, trying to take this in. 'I mean, why? How?' She looked at Ray.

Sanjay gave a brief bow. 'Madam, you mentioned your family name, and as I said, they are a very well-known family. I know someone who works for them. I mentioned that they had a relative visiting here; please forgive me for . . . for interfering. They are surprised.'

'Not as much as I am,' said Sarita. 'I don't imagine they want to meet me after all this time.'

'Oh madam, they are nice, very good people. They would like to meet you now, after I explain . . .' Sanjay clasped his hands in some dismay, as if he'd done the wrong thing.

'What did you explain?' asked Ray gently.

Sanjay waved his hands with a small, knowing smile. 'Ah, that you stay in very good places, you very good people.'

Ray and Sarita exchanged a look. Ray rubbed his fingers together discreetly.

Sarita nodded. 'If we'd been ordinary tourists they wouldn't be interested,' she said to Ray quietly.

'The Chand family is very important in Lautoka, Nadi, Suva.' Sanjay pulled a slip of paper from his pocket and handed it to Ray. 'Here is the phone number for Mr Chand.'

Sarita reached over and took the slip of paper from Ray. 'Thank you for going to the trouble, Sanjay. Now, we thought we might drive out to the old sugar plantations and look around,' she said briskly.

Ray raised his eyebrows. This was the first he'd heard of this plan. He turned to Sanjay. 'Well, thank you. We'd like to see where CSR had its operations back in the old days.'

Nodding quickly, Sanjay opened the car door for Sarita. 'Yes, sir, madam. I know it very well. My family, my great-grandparents, worked in the sugar fields.'

Sarita looked at Ray and said quietly, 'Dad was a manager at the sugar refinery. I'd like to see where he lived and worked.'

'Sounds like your mother's side has done well too,' Ray said. 'It wouldn't hurt to call them. You know, maybe our boys would be interested in knowing about their maternal grandmother one day.'

'Ray, why?'

He shrugged. 'Just a thought. I think it could be interesting and we never need mention it to anyone if it doesn't work out.'

Sarita leaned forward towards the driver's seat. 'Sanjay, what is the Chand family expecting, exactly? What did your friend say?'

'They would like you to come to dinner to meet them at the big house. Please, you can phone and speak to Mr Chand.'

'I'll do it, if you like,' said Ray, reaching for the slip of paper.

'Whatever,' said Sarita tightly, feeling ill at ease.

As Ray pressed the numbers she said, 'You might as well put it on speaker. We all seem to be interested.'

Mr Chand's voice was youthful, educated, faintly British sounding.

Ray introduced himself, but before he could explain further, the man knew at once who he was.

'What a pleasant surprise this is,' he said. 'And, I gather, quite accidental?'

Sarita raised her eyebrows. Was there a faint accusatory tone?

'Well, sometimes this is how things happen. My wife did not want to disturb your privacy after all this time, but our splendid driver here seems to be a magician as well,' said Ray.

'Fate, perhaps. Well, of course, I gather you are relaxing, but we would like to invite you both to a dinner, a small gathering of family.'

'We don't want to inconvenience you at such short notice,' began Ray.

'Not at all, my wife likes to entertain. It would be our pleasure to meet you both. Your driver knows our home. Would 6 pm tomorrow suit?'

Ray raised his eyebrows at Sarita who hesitated, then shrugged. 'That sounds lovely, thank you,' he replied.

'We look forward to meeting you both. Ray and Sarita Golding, yes?'

'Yes. Thank you.' Ray ended the call. 'You know their residence?' he asked Sanjay, who nodded furiously.

'Oh yes, yes sir. It's a very big house, they are important people!'

Sarita couldn't help but roll her eyes.

*

When it came to dressing for the evening, she said to Ray, 'What should I wear?'

'You always look wonderful. But maybe we should be on the conservative side. Did you bring anything other than shorts, swimsuits, sarongs?'

'Of course I did.'

'Perfect. I'm wearing my linen trousers and a casual shirt. I assume no one here wears a tie.'

'You didn't bring one, did you?' exclaimed Sarita.

'Of course not!' He paused. 'So how do you feel about meeting the rellies?'

'I don't know. They're strangers.'

'They're still your family,' Ray reminded her.

'They probably have as much interest in me as I do in them,' said Sarita. 'I can't help feeling they've only asked us because Sanjay told them we were staying at the most expensive places in the islands.'

'Yes. That crossed my mind too.'

'Ray, I don't know about going tonight. I haven't come on a search for my long-lost family. It's a mere fluke we've connected! And . . . I suppose I'm a bit nervous about what they'll think of me, after all this time.'

'It will be okay,' soothed Ray. 'Let's play it by ear.'

*

The house was imposing among the more modest homes around it.

A light came on as they pulled into the portico and a tall man was silhouetted in the entrance. He came down the steps as Sanjay hurried to open the car doors for Ray and Sarita. A woman appeared in the doorway behind him, watching as the three shook hands.

Aishik Chand led Ray and Sarita up the stairs and

introduced his wife, Indira. Several people were clustered behind her in a drawing room. All looked to be Fijian Indian.

Indira wore a white silk dress and elaborate jewellery, her hair wound in a chignon. She was attractive and expensively groomed. Sarita and Ray were introduced to the Chands' adult children. Then they were ushered out onto a terrace that faced a swimming pool and a tropical garden.

'How lovely,' said Ray. 'Your home is very beautiful, Aishik.'

'Thank you. It's a traditional house that has been modernised over the years. The old family home is in Suva. Please, make yourselves comfortable.' He gestured to the cane lounge setting as a young woman appeared with a tray of drinks.

Initially the conversation was slightly strained, as the women settled on the lounges and the men stood in a group. They avoided discussing any family history and talked instead about tourism, business and their children.

As the sun set, they went into a large dining room where many platters and serving dishes were laid out. It all smelled delicious.

'There are vegetarian dishes and also seafood, I do hope that is all right,' explained Indira as she invited them to take a seat.

'I recommend the coconut crab curry,' said their daughter, Dobra, who looked to be in her twenties.

The passing of dishes and chatter around the table made them all feel more relaxed. As the main course dishes were cleared away, Aishik lifted his glass to propose a toast.

'Sarita and Ray, we welcome you to our home, to

our island, and hope that we will forge a friendship going forward,' he said.

Sarita glanced at Ray, who responded, 'This has been an unexpected gift and surprise for Sarita and me. We thank you for your generosity and hope that we will share good times such as this evening together again.'

Everyone drank and the atmosphere became friendly and almost casual, Ray thought. Dessert followed, then Indira announced that coffee was being served in the sitting room.

Dobra and her brother, Ishann, excused themselves, Dobra saying, 'I'll bring Nani down, she'd love to meet Sarita. She wasn't quite up to a formal dinner.'

A few minutes later, Dobra returned, escorting a bright-eyed elderly woman into the room. Her hair was silver. She wore a colourful sari, and gold bangles jingled on her thin arms. Seeing Sarita, she beamed and clasped her hands together, and in a warm voice, said, 'Namaste, dear girl.'

Sarita responded, stepping forward to take the older woman's hands in hers.

'This is Purnima, Nani, our granny. Your mother's big sister,' said Dobra.

Sarita froze. She had seen photos of her mother and wondered if this was how she would have looked if she had grown old.

Ray hurried to his wife's side.

'How do you do,' he said. 'I'm Ray Golding, Sarita's husband.'

Sarita was still staring at the older woman.

Purnima gestured a greeting to Ray, saying, 'It is lovely to meet you both. I knew Sarita would find us one day. Welcome to our home.'

Sarita glanced at Ray, then said in a trembling voice, 'I wasn't expecting this.'

'Nani, sit down. I'll get you a cup of tea,' said Dobra. 'Please, sit down, Sarita. Ray, some coffee?'

Ray looked at Dobra and took the hint. 'Ah, yes please, I'll help myself.'

Sarita and her aunt sat alone on the sofa, and Purnima took her niece's hand in hers.

'You are so beautiful. Just like your mother. Her eyes . . . I would have known you anywhere. Do you remember her?'

'Only a little. I was so young.'

'Of course. It was all very sad. Times have changed. I'm sure my late mother wondered about you. But things were different then,' said Purnima. Her hands fluttered helplessly. 'Your mother was very strong. Knew her heart and her mind. But . . .' Her shoulders rose and fell. 'Our father ruled our lives.'

'My grandmother – your mother – never reached out to me,' said Sarita, trying to keep the bitterness from her voice. 'Did she think that my father was not good enough for your family?'

'Our family holds traditions very close. My father wanted your mother to marry the son of a business associate. Both families felt such a merger would be beneficial.' Purnima shook her head. 'Your mother must have loved your father very much to be so defiant.'

'And your father didn't care?' exclaimed Sarita, her eyes filling with tears.

'Did you know your mother worked with your father in his office, and that was how they met?' said Purnima gently. 'My father blamed himself for allowing that. He thought he was letting her be too independent.' The older woman twisted her hands. 'No one in the family went against our father.'

'Oh, I see,' said Sarita. 'You're telling me your father wouldn't let my parents marry because of a business deal?'

The old woman nodded, lowering her voice. 'But my sister had made up her mind and when she announced she was expecting a child with your father, that forced the situation. Our father said she had disgraced the family and none of us were to have anything to do with her again.' The old lady blinked back tears. 'It was so, so sad. We loved your mother, she was a wonderful and very special person, but we couldn't disobey our father.' She looked down at her hands. 'I sometimes wish I had been as strong and true as she was.'

Sarita kept her voice low, but the shock and sadness of this news slowly turned to anger as she realised that this was probably why her maternal grandparents had never once sought her out.

'So my mother and father married and moved to Suva and your parents never thought about me?' Sarita asked.

The old woman looked anguished. 'I like to think my sister would have tried to reconnect with us as you grew up, but she died so terribly suddenly.'

'Yes. I was three. I was a little girl. I can't help but feel that your family turned its back on me.'

The old lady's face fell and once again she took Sarita's hand in her long thin fingers. 'There is no changing the past, much as we might wish to. I hope you have had a happy life. I am glad you found us. I always hoped you would.'

Sarita nodded. She felt completely overcome. This had been a very unexpected revelation. She glanced at Ray, who quickly joined her.

'You all right?' he asked softly, seeing the tears in both women's eyes.

Sarita squeezed his hand, unable to speak.

Ray reached out his other hand and laid it gently on Purnima's. 'Thank you for seeing us.'

With Ray's help, Purnima rose, folding a length of her sari over her arm.

'Perhaps we may see you again?' she said.

Sarita took a deep breath. 'Perhaps. Thank you for telling me about my mother,' she said.

*

They were silent in the car on the way back to their hotel at the marina, aware that Sanjay was all ears.

In their suite, Sarita kicked off her shoes and sat on the balcony, looking at the boats bobbing in the moonlight.

'So. How do you feel?' Ray handed her a nightcap and sat down next to her. 'Nani Purnima was pretty cool, I thought. What did you think of the rest of the family?'

Sarita sighed. 'It's so hard to know. I wasn't expecting to feel as emotional as I did when I was talking about my mother with Purnima. But the others don't feel that same connection with me, I don't think. They just seem interested in us because we are "their" kind of people,' she said.

'Yes, they've twigged we've got money. Aishik suggested I take a share in a merger he's planning. A good investment and so on. Sounded like the minimum was a pretty big chunk of money, though. I got the feeling he was sounding me out about setting up his business in Australia.'

'What did you say?'

Ray smiled. 'I said I'd pass his proposition on to my financial advisor.'

Sarita was silent a moment. 'I've been thinking over the past few days. I didn't set out to look for my family, but now that we've found them, I'm more interested in my roots here in Fiji. They're our boys' roots, too. And when we have grandchildren, I'd love to bring them here, so they feel a bit invested and not just like tourists.'

'Is that really how you feel?' asked Ray gently.

'Yes. You were right when you said that our boys might want to find out about this part of their background,' she said, leaning over and taking his hand. 'And I really did enjoy staying on those little islands, even though I didn't like some of the other guests at the first resort. Maybe this place really is in my blood, and I just couldn't see it before.'

'Well, that's all good then,' said Ray.

'I've googled it, you know.' Sarita looked at him intently.

'What, the resort?'

'No. Buying an island.'

'You're joking!'

'When I searched the internet, I couldn't believe there is such a big market for islands,' exclaimed Sarita.

'Really? Won't they all be under water soon?' Ray said wryly, but seeing Sarita's expression he went on, 'Are you serious? What sort of price range? And what bang do you get for your buck?'

'Some are deserted. Some have rundown infrastructure or places partly demolished in cyclones that have never been rebuilt. We need a sheltered side and mooring access. They cost a few million, I believe,' added Sarita.

Ray laughed dismissively. 'Oh, for goodness' sake, get real, Sarita.'

Sarita went on as if he hadn't spoken. 'I don't like the thought of cyclones, so we'd need to invest in high-tech communication and warning devices, generators, that sort of thing.'

'You have got to be kidding.'

'I'm not,' she retorted.

Ray sat up straighter in his chair. 'Wait a minute. This is the first I've heard of this idea! Is it because you've got swept away with this family heritage thing?'

Sarita looked thoughtful. 'Of course, my island will be private, just for the family. But I would like to do something a bit philanthropic. I'm just not sure what.'

Ray slapped his head. 'Hell's bells, Rita. The sun has given you heatstroke. Let's not argue over a nutty dream idea.'

'Why is it nutty?' she asked calmly. 'I can afford it.'

'Let's discuss it later. C'mon, tomorrow's our second-last day. You said you wanted to see the Garden of the Sleeping Giant.'

Sarita did want to see the botanical wonder created by the Canadian actor Raymond Burr, who had established magnificent gardens to protect Fijian plants and flowers, but she didn't appreciate Ray's dismissal of her new idea.

'I do. It sounds beautiful,' she said finally. 'I'm impressed that that actor left behind a legacy that is both philanthropic and yet so beautiful...' She looked at Ray, suddenly feeling on the verge of tears. 'I don't know. I don't want to be selfish just because I got lucky.'

'Let's just take life day by day, okay?' He put his arm around her shoulders.

'Carpe diem,' replied Sarita.

*

The following evening, Sanjay dropped them at a quiet restaurant and bar in a local area near the waterfront for one last dinner before their flight home the next day.

'Very good food, very famous old place. Locals and foreigners like it,' Sanjay assured them.

The bar wasn't yet crowded. They sat at a table, their backs to the room, looking into the small, lush garden. They touched glasses in a toast.

'Thank you, darling. This trip has been enlightening!' said Sarita.

'So we'll come back?' asked Ray.

'Of course! We're island hunting, remember.'

'You're still serious about buying an island? Just for holidays, family and friends?' said Ray. 'I mean . . . really?' he added tentatively.

'Why not?' said Sarita lightly.

Ray rolled his eyes. 'But it would be such a huge undertaking. We'd need someone to help us. Manage it and so on,' he said, mainly to humour her. He hoped Sarita would let this dream go when they were back home in their new house and had settled into normal life again.

They were chatting together over a second round of drinks when a man appeared beside them.

'Hi, mate. Couldn't help overhearing you two talking. I know a fair bit about the islands around here . . .'

'Oh, well, we're just about to leave, actually. We've had a great time –' began Ray, but the man interrupted him.

'Mind if I join you?' He sat down without waiting for a response. He was grizzled and tanned, his Hawaiian shirt faded. He had an Australian accent and was carrying half a glass of beer. 'Aussies, eh? Me too.' He stuck out his hand. 'Stuart Shaw.'

'So you're a local here?' asked Ray, shaking his hand.

'As local as anyone gets here. Just don't call me an expat! Listen, I don't mean to be nosey, but I couldn't help hearing you guys talk about buying an island here. I mean, it's the dream, hey? The universal ultimate dream . . . escape . . . wish fulfilment . . . happy ever after.'

'Well, that's our business, but what if we were dreaming of owning an island?' said Sarita evenly.

'Don't,' said Stuart firmly.

'Why do you say that?' asked Ray. 'Have you lived on one?'

'Yeah. Worked on one. Several years. I've seen it all: the good, the bad, the ugly.'

Sarita was not about to ask him to explain, but he began to elaborate anyway.

'First, the weather. If it's not sunny, it's shit. No swimming, snorkelling, sunbaking, boating. Islands get bad winds, or cyclones. It's either unbearably hot or you're drowning in rain. There're bugs, bities, flies, and God knows what else that can make you sicker than a dog – and then you can't get off the island, because the weather's bad, or the sea is too rough, or the boat has broken down. The power karks it or the water supply has gone off or is non-existent. Tourists are a pain in the bum. And, ultimately, the whole joint is destined to go underwater 'cause of climate change. The seas are rising – so if you're not flooded, you might not have any island left at all. Apart from that, it's okay. So good luck if you're taking it on, mate.'

Ray looked bemused. 'Well, thanks for the tip, Stuart. We know what to look out for now.'

Sarita looked annoyed. 'C'mon, don't be such a pessimist. What about the tourists? The honeymooners, the holidaymakers, who save up to go to a tropical island paradise?'

Stuart slapped his head. 'They have the right idea! Come to Fiji for a good time, no stress or ties, party, live the good life. They don't have to worry about maintaining the bures they stay in, or what happens to all the rubbish they leave behind. What do we do with that? Can't bury it or throw it in the sea. But *they* can go home at the end and leave it all behind. The owner of the island can't. Why would you want to buy into all that crap?'

'Because we can,' said Sarita simply.

Stuart hesitated for a split second. Then he gave her a condescending nod. 'Well, ya got me there, love.'

'Can we buy you a drink, Stuart?' said Ray with a smile.

'Yeah. Bourbon and Coke'd be good. Thanks.'

They learned that Stuart had had his share of family dramas, businesses gone bust and failed romances.

'I'm doing okay with my fishing charter. Anyway, here's my card in case you or your mates are coming back and feel like throwing in a line or two. And listen, I don't want to put you off, but thought I could put you straight about island life, y'know? If you do decide to go down that path, I have some contacts who can help you.' He downed the last of his drink.

'Sure, thanks. Next trip,' said Ray, reaching out to shake his hand again.

Stuart stood up and gave them a sort of salute. 'See ya round.'

'Been a pretty different sort of trip than we're used to,' said Sarita as they watched Stuart leave.

Ray reached over and took her hand. 'You okay about . . . everything? Your mother, the family . . .?'

'Yep,' said Sarita. 'Now I know what happened, I

understand my mother and father's situation better. And of course, it can't have been easy for Dad going home and starting over without his beloved wife and with a toddler to care for.' Her voice wobbled. 'Now I know how much my mother loved Dad, too. Walking away from her family was probably the hardest thing she ever did to do.' She wiped her eyes. 'I'm ready to go home, Ray. This has been pretty eye-opening. But I need to digest everything.'

Ray leaned over, pulling her head to his shoulder, stroking her hair as they watched the tropical day melt away.

*

Maddie jumped up from the lounge, grabbed her phone and texted Charlie.

Wow, just saw the ad on TV! Looks fabulous – Sooky will be a star! Where ARE you? Love to catch up. Xx

He texted back a minute or two later.

Yeah, everyone is pleased. Buy shares in buffalo milk! Just been busy. I'll call you x

She felt ridiculously happy to hear from him. But he'd said much the same thing a few weeks ago, and hadn't called. So she punched his name into her phone and rang him.

'Hi. Thought I'd grab you while you're in range. Where are you at the moment?' she said.

'Ah, at my place. Just packing to head down to Sydney to do a job for a studio down there.'

'Another ad? I thought you wanted to make your own stuff?'

'Ads pay the rent. But while I'm there I might talk to film people about some ideas I have. I'm putting something together for a grant.'

'A feature film, or what?'

'No, it's a documentary. Early days. Has anyone heard how Fleur is doing in New York?'

'Not me. But I think Leonie keeps in touch.'

'What about the star man . . . Julian?' Charlie's question was casual, but Maddie thought she heard a strange note in his voice.

'I have no idea,' said Maddie quickly. 'Playing the piano somewhere, no doubt.'

'So, what are you doing with yourself?' asked Charlie.

'Just working on my own stuff.' Not wanting to get into another conversation about her future, she quickly added, 'I'm having a bit of an issue with Mum and Dad. Mum wants to move to the Gold Coast where her cousin lives. But Dad doesn't.'

'Bloody hell. That sounds tricky. I imagine your dad won't like that.'

'No, he's not keen. Charlie, can I see you, just for a coffee, to chat . . .?'

Charlie paused and Maddie held her breath. 'Sure, sure,' he said finally. 'It'll have to be tomorrow or the next day as I –'

'Tomorrow. Tomorrow is fine. What time suits you?' she cut in quickly.

'Afternoon. Four-ish? At the Riverbend Café?'

'Great. See you there.' Maddie ended the call, a sense of relief and warmth flooding through her.

She was there first the next afternoon, just sitting down at a table at the far end of the verandah when she saw Charlie walking towards her. He spotted her and gave a smile.

'Hey, you,' he said. He hooked his small backpack onto the back of his chair and sat down.

'Howdy, stranger.'

'Aw, c'mon, Mads, I've been busy. Not a lady of leisure like you.' He picked up the menu.

'Actually, I've been keeping busy too,' she retorted, trying not to show how his remark had stung her.

'That's good. Writing?'

She nodded as he put down the menu. 'Yep. Playing a bit more seriously, and I've found a teacher to teach me to read music properly.'

'Excellent idea. Now you can put down your songs so others can play them.'

'Sort of. It means I can put stuff out there for musicians and singers to share – well, if they want to,' she said rather shyly. 'I drive down to Newcastle to a music school once a week. So, what're you up to?'

'I'm a bit over doing commercials, but I've had a lot of offers after the buffalo milk one went to air. Sooky was a hit!'

'I knew she would be! That's great, and as you said, ads are good money, aren't they?'

He shrugged. 'Yeah. They're not what I want to make my name doing, but I can't knock back the bread and butter jobs. Not like you.' He gave a bit of a smile.

'I have plans,' said Maddie tartly, glad when the waitress arrived to take their orders.

Charlie waited till the waitress walked away before changing the subject. 'What's happening with Fleur's musical?'

'Still no news, I think.'

'And you haven't seen Julian? You two were pretty close, I thought.' There it was again – something in Charlie's tone that made Maddie sit up a bit straighter.

'Why would you think that? We were *acting*!' Maddie

was rattled. Was this why Charlie had seemed more distant lately? Had he forgotten their picnic, that kiss . . .? 'People are under the impression that we – you and I – are, or were, pretty close. I thought so, too . . .' She bit her lip.

Charlie reached over and took her hand. 'Mads, I'm sorry. It's just – I just feel uncomfortable. Your life is changing, you have the opportunity now to do whatever you want, it seems. I don't know how I fit in with that.'

'That doesn't mean you and I can't see each other.'

'No, I know. But I don't want to get in the way, I don't want you to feel obligated . . .' His voice trailed off awkwardly.

Maddie felt angry, hurt and confused. 'I can't believe you're saying these things. I thought we were friends, maybe more than friends.' She could feel tears stinging her eyes and she picked up her sunglasses and pushed them onto her face.

'Maddie, maybe I do want to be more than friends, but after the show – all your talent, and Julian all over you – and the money you won, well, it's all a massive opportunity for you. I don't want to stand in the way and then down the track you wonder what you might have done, what you might have become, if you hadn't . . . well, because of me and what I'm doing. I don't want to hurt you, I just don't want to hold you back. You need to spread your wings, and now that you have some money, you can.' Charlie spoke quietly and intensely, but Maddie pushed back her chair.

'I can't listen to this.' She jumped up and strode down the verandah, past several occupied tables where people glanced at her in surprise.

Charlie sat motionless, staring at the river. Then he

walked slowly to the counter and paid the bill, telling them not to bother with their order.

Maddie's car was gone. He got into his truck and slammed the door, then dropped his head onto the steering wheel.

'Oh, Maddie . . .'

10

CHRISSIE STOOD ON THE balcony, staring out at the line of highrises, the panorama of ocean spread before her. The tower blocks were set back from the dress circle and had uninterrupted views of the ocean. These cost more, but Troy only wanted the very best these days.

There was an irritating hum from the traffic below, which had multiplied since she'd first visited Port Haven years ago. Just over an hour away, Fig Tree River now felt like another country.

Port Haven had once been an attractive if sleepy beachside town favoured by country people and some city retirees. People bought small units as a home base, where they could just shut the door and roam the country in their caravan or motorhome for weeks on end. It was living the dream. Chrissie couldn't think of anything worse than caravanning or camping, but she wasn't loving the high-rise lifestyle as much as she'd thought she might, either. She and the kids missed having a backyard, and she definitely missed her small corner of the shed.

She'd mentioned to Troy that perhaps getting a job would give her an interest, but he had laughed at the idea. As another option, she was thinking of doing some volunteer work, perhaps with a charity or at the children's school, and she was trying to think of how to run that idea past Troy so that he would agree to it.

Sarita and Leonie had encouraged her to do something with her building skills, but she had no tools or workshop here.

Although her parents were only an hour away, Chrissie missed them popping in, and they missed the grandkids. Maybe she could ask them to take time off work for a holiday and stay in an apartment nearby, which Chrissie and Troy would pay for? Although she doubted that would work out. That wasn't the sort of thing Troy liked to spend their money on.

Sighing, she went inside to make herself a cup of tea. The kitchen looked like it was ready to be photographed for a trendy magazine: slick, shiny metal, low-hanging lights above the breakfast bar, everything out of sight so it looked clean, streamlined, and, thought Chrissie, as if no one ever cooked in it. This was partly true. Chrissie hated the kitchen; she missed her favourite pots and pans and the gadgets she'd inherited from her grandmother. Troy had insisted they get everything new – not that anyone else ever saw it, because they never entertained. The children were so afraid of breaking the new plates that Chrissie had bought them some cheap plastic dishes.

They had eaten out a lot at first, but the novelty had soon worn off and the kids and Chrissie preferred to stay home and eat in the kitchen. Troy still ate out regularly with his new business associates, trying every bar and restaurant on the coast. Chrissie didn't mind, even though she was lonely and bored.

She decided to invite Sarita and Leonie to come up for lunch one day during the week while Troy was at work and the children at school.

*

It took two weeks to settle on a date that suited Leonie and Sarita, but when the day arrived, Chrissie realised she was ridiculously excited to see them.

She wore a new dress and paid attention to her hair and make-up. She had booked a table on the terrace at a waterfront place that Troy thought was boring but which she had liked. It was quiet, private and had an excellent view over the ocean.

Leonie and Sarita had driven up together, and after hugging Chrissie, they were soon admiring the restaurant and talking nonstop. Sarita had them laughing as she recounted incidents from her Fijian holiday.

'But it does sound fabulous,' sighed Chrissie.

'It certainly was, much of the time. So I've decided to buy an island there,' Sarita announced.

Chrissie and Leonie stared at her in astonishment.

'Really?' said Chrissie.

'Why?' asked Leonie.

'Why not?' said Sarita, spreading her arms. 'It'll be an adventure. You can both come and stay. I have roots in Fiji, remember, so I thought I'd like to set up a philanthropic scheme of some kind.'

'What does Ray think?' asked Chrissie.

'He is sure I'm mad. He thought I was joking and that I'd forget all about it by now. But I'm researching, and it's very doable. A lot of work, of course.'

'Did you come up with this idea because you found your mother's family?' asked Leonie.

'Partly. And because I can afford it.'

'Are you keeping in contact with your Fijian family?' asked Chrissie.

Sarita shrugged. 'I'm taking it slowly. Finding the right island is my priority.'

Chrissie shook her head. 'I don't know what to say, that's so amazing.'

After Leonie had told her friends about her investigation into the mysterious dam on her property and the plans to take Corby to Disneyland, she smiled and said, 'So what are *you* doing, Chrissie?'

Chrissie hesitated. 'Well, we have the new unit, which is stunning, and the kids are in a private school, though to be truthful they miss their friends in Fig Tree River. As for me, I'm looking around for something to do, sort of.'

'Sort of? But are you enjoying this new life?' pushed Sarita.

Chrissie glanced down, and the mood shifted. 'Not much, to be honest. It's hard to meet people.'

'What about the school?' asked Leonie.

Chrissie wrinkled her nose. 'They all seem so established already. I went to a school function, but I was uncomfortable. People aren't as friendly as they are in Fig Tree River.'

'Snobs,' sniffed Sarita.

'Come to Disneyland with us, the kids would love it,' said Leonie kindly.

'Oh, but Troy would hate it . . .'

'Forget Troy. Just you and the kids. The school holidays are coming up. Seriously, I mean it,' said Leonie. 'I know your kids are younger than Corby but they're the perfect age for Disneyland. We can all stay in the hotel that's right there. Then you could come to LA with me, or take a trip down the coast . . . you can do anything you want, Chrissie!'

'Thanks, Leonie. I'll think about it,' she said.

'How about some dessert?' said Leonie. She was disappointed she couldn't get Chrissie to agree to come, so she changed the subject instead.

As they called for the bill, Sarita asked Chrissie, 'Can we stop by and see your place, before heading home?'

'Oh yes, I'd love to,' said Leonie.

Chrissie looked at her watch. 'Sure, I have time before I get the kids. I'll make us a coffee.'

Waiting for the lift in the underground car park of Chrissie's building, Sarita said, 'I guess the lift makes it easy to carry up your shopping?' She was trying to make conversation, as Chrissie had seemed quiet and a little anxious ever since they'd left the restaurant.

'Of course,' she said. 'I don't do a big grocery shop, though. It gives me something to do each day, picking up things for dinner. There's a supermarket across the road.'

Leonie glanced at Sarita behind Chrissie's back as they stepped from the lift. Considering buying groceries an outing was a worry.

Chrissie unlocked the door and they walked into a darkened room.

'Oh gosh, Troy has pulled the curtains. Hang on.'

She went to the windows and pushed a button and

the curtains slid back, flooding the room with light and a view of sky, gleaming towers and the vivid blue sea.

'Wow, it's stunning,' said Sarita.

'How high up are we?' asked Leonie.

'This is the fourteenth –'

'Chrissie, where've you been?' came a voice from another room.

'Oh, my goodness! Troy, you're home?' Chrissie's voice sounded tremulous.

Leonie and Sarita exchanged a swift glance as Troy strode into the room.

'Of course I'm home, who'd you think it was! You girls been partying, eh?'

'I just brought Sarita and Leonie in to see the apartment.'

'This is a fantastic place, Troy,' said Leonie quickly.

'It certainly is,' agreed Sarita. 'How are you enjoying being up here?'

'Suits me fine.' He looked at Chrissie. 'You going out again? You're all done up.'

'No, I'm not going anywhere now – except to get the kids,' she said hastily.

'Well, we must be heading home,' said Sarita into the awkward pause that followed. 'It's a bit of a drive. It was so lovely to catch up, Chrissie.' The two women hugged Chrissie and turned to go.

Over Chrissie's shoulder, Leonie saw Troy pick up his wife's handbag, open it and take out her wallet, which he put in his pocket.

It wasn't until they stepped outside the building that Leonie exploded.

'That Troy is such a creep. He took Chrissie's wallet from her bag!'

'Do you think he's spending her money?'

'Well, they're married – I'd say he definitely is. I hope she's put some away for herself,' said Leonie.

'Should we interfere?' asked Sarita. 'Some of the things Chrissie said at lunch worried me as well. She's always been a quiet type, but she doesn't seem happy. Something doesn't feel right.'

'I know what you mean, but what can we do? It might just be that she's still settling in. Troy has always been a loudmouth – getting him riled up won't help her. Chrissie will ask us if she needs us. I hope she makes some new friends here soon, though,' Leonie sighed.

'I wouldn't count on her going to Disneyland with you,' said Sarita.

'Me neither.'

*

Maddie banged her hands down on the piano keys in a jangle of clashing notes, then pushed back her stool and stood up. Nothing was coming together.

It had been over a week since she'd walked out on Charlie in the café. She knew he'd been busy but it was making her anxious that she hadn't heard from him. Telling her that he wanted to stay friends but didn't want to hold her back was all very well, but it was not what she wanted. What had changed? Why couldn't he share in her good luck? She was fuming as she stomped out to the kitchen to make herself a coffee.

The gleaming new espresso machine took up a chunk of space on the kitchen bench. Her father had refused to use it. He'd thrown his hands in the air, saying it was too fiddly and it sounded as though it was going to blow up.

'Your mother won't like it either,' he'd predicted.

Maddie hadn't asked when her mother was returning from the Gold Coast or what her plans were, but her father's moaning annoyed her. Suddenly she wanted to get on with her life, with or without Charlie.

She called Leonie to arrange to catch up.

*

Leonie gave her hug. 'Hello, lovely, how are you? Sarita and I were just talking about you, wondering what you're doing.'

'I'm keeping busy, actually. I'm doing a class with a music school to learn how to read music and I'm going to the gym every day. I was just wondering how everyone is . . . and have you heard from Fleur? How are things with her?'

'Oh yes, we keep in touch. Funny, I was thinking of calling you. Looks like she is going to get *Percy and Ella* up in an off-Broadway theatre!'

'Wow, that's so great!'

'What about you? Have you thought any more about performing? Or don't you want to go down that route?' asked Leonie.

'Well, not really. I mean, I loved doing the show, but mostly I enjoy singing when there's no pressure,' said Maddie.

'You sure that's not just nerves? Many wannabe singers would kill for your voice,' said Leonie kindly.

'You know, if you and Fleur hadn't pushed me, I wouldn't have done Ella. I didn't want to let you down.'

'It's good to stretch yourself, Mads. Push the boundaries. A fail here and there is a growing experience – no matter what your age. Look at Fleur – still having a go, doing something challenging at her age. And look at

Sarita, going on a super luxury holiday and now buying an island!'

Maddie's mouth dropped open. 'What? Sarita is buying an island? Where?'

'In Fiji! She got all swept up in the idea when she found her family there.'

'Wow! I can't believe that.' Maddie shook her head. 'How amazing.'

'Life's a matter of just moving forward. You should grab the world by the throat and shake it! Get out there and take risks, try things, travel!' said Leonie enthusiastically.

'And how are you grabbing the world?' asked Maddie with a crooked grin.

Leonie smiled. 'I'm working on it. I have a dam to stop. So far I just have my finger on the leak and am not sure what to do next, but I will certainly give it my best shot! Plus I have plans for my farm that I can now hopefully achieve, and I can support opportunities that come our way. By the way, how are your parents?' asked Leonie.

Maddie paused. 'They're okay. Why do you ask?'

'How have they reacted to your winning so much money?'

'It's turning out to be very disruptive, actually.' Maddie sighed. 'Mum wants to move to the Gold Coast and Dad wants me to buy him a farm so he can stay here.'

'Oh dear. That sounds difficult for you. And how's Charlie?'

'No idea. He's been totally flat out with work ever since the show.'

Leonie heard the tension in Maddie's voice.

'Don't lose touch with good friends, sweetie.'

'Yeah, I s'pose so. Why is it so hard for people to just be happy for me? Money shouldn't change anything.'

'Money changes *everything*,' said Leonie quietly.

*

'Sarita, this is madness!' shouted Ray as he clutched the side of the small cabin as the launch flounced and dipped across the roiling sea.

She glanced back at him from where she was standing next to the skipper, who was gripping the wheel tightly. 'It's exciting,' she called out.

Ray was feeling ill. Not just from the bouncing boat, but about the whole island idea. So far they'd seen three islands and he was already over it. He was tired of rushing from car to helicopter to another boat, then struggling ashore to look at either nothing, or abandoned buildings from an old motel-resort, derelict cabins or a half-finished mansion. He'd tuned out of the agent's romanticised sales pitch and also Sarita's enthusiasm, probing questions and copious notes. He wanted to go home to their nice new house and garden.

Sarita came and stood beside him, holding on as the boat dipped and banged over the waves.

'The skipper says it's hardly ever as rough as this,' she said cheerfully. 'Tail end of cyclone season somewhere or other.'

'I'd rather be somewhere else. I want a cold beer,' said Ray in a tired voice.

'There's plenty of cold beer in the galley fridge. I'll get you one.'

'No, no, Sarita. I can't drink it in this sea. I mean, I want to sit in a chair on our deck at home with a chilled glass.'

'You're no fun.' She pretended to pout, then looked sympathetic. 'Really? You want to go home?'

'Absolutely I do. This is just a crazy scheme, Rita. We should never have come back here.'

'Okay then. You fly home. I'll stay until I find something I want,' she said calmly.

Ray looked at her in disbelief. There was nothing he wanted more than to leave, but he couldn't let her stay here and deal with all this alone. Lord knew what she might actually decide to buy. She'd always been so careful and cautious; surely she could see the ridiculousness of this idea, or had some sort of money madness struck her?

Ray was vastly relieved when they were finally back at their hotel at the end of the day, and settled out on their terrace with cold drinks.

'Feel better now?' said Sarita chirpily, looking up from her notes.

'A bit, although my legs still feel wobbly. I'm not a good sailor, it seems. So no more boating for me,' he said.

'Oh, you won't notice it on a big boat like a cruiser. And once you're settled on the island . . . bliss, eh?'

'You mean, in between all the construction?' Ray said it lightly but from what they'd seen so far, all the islands needed a lot of work and money.

'Yep. That'll be half the fun, don't you think? To set things up the way we like? Just think how the boys will love it. Don't say anything, remember – we'll make it a super surprise.' She added thoughtfully, 'Of course, we still need to have a cause, do some good somehow . . .'

Suddenly it was all too much. Ray lost his cool, banging his glass down on the arm of his deckchair. 'For God's sake, Sarita! What's all this for? Why can't we just sit back and enjoy this time, our good fortune, in comfort?

Sure, we can help the boys, you can find some cause to support . . . but let's do it at *home*!'

Sarita was unruffled. 'You don't understand, Ray. I've been thinking, maybe this all happened because I was meant to find my original home, help my mother by doing something in her memory . . .' Her voice trailed off as she looked out to sea.

'Rita, for goodness' sake, you don't remember your mother; you never really knew her,' said Ray in an exasperated tone. 'It's a lovely dream that you feel you can afford to indulge, but that's all it really is – a dream, and totally impractical!'

'I can afford it. I want to do it,' she said stubbornly. 'If you don't like it, then you don't have to come here!' Sarita immediately looked contrite. 'Ray, just wait and see. You don't have to be involved until it's all done if you don't want to, but then you'll see how lovely our own island will be!'

'You'd go ahead with this crazy scheme without me?' asked Ray incredulously.

Sarita went to speak but bit her lip. Nevertheless, the unspoken retort hung between them: *It's my money.*

'Let's wait and see,' she said quietly.

*

'Dad, please come with me. It's been ages since we went to the Gold Coast. Mum will show you around – she and Julie have been exploring. We could have a nice time for a few days.'

Her father was shaking his head before she'd finished the sentence.

'Nope. I have no reason to go there. You go. Tell her to come back to Fig Tree River.'

'Dad, that's not fair.' Maddie was torn. She knew how much her father missed the old family farm, but she also knew her mother had no interest in living on the land. Maddie was at a loss as to what to do.

'Well, I'll go and visit Mum and Julie anyway,' she sighed.

*

Her mother's cousin Julie had been widowed ten years or more and she had made a comfortable life for herself in the new Sea Town Village, which was only a short walk to the beach. Her unit was spacious with plenty of room for her two guests.

'There's so much to do around here,' Julie enthused. 'Honestly, facilities and activities galore! I've made so many friends.'

'She's always going somewhere with them,' exclaimed Maddie's mother, Helen.

Julie gripped her cousin's arm. 'I'm so excited to think your mother might move up here, Mads.'

'Well, I'm not sure it's Dad's sort of thing,' said Maddie carefully. 'And it's rather a long way from Fig Tree River.'

'Michael can drive up here any time he feels like it,' said her mother lightly.

'Mum! You can't leave Dad alone in Fig Tree River.'

'Why not? He knows that I've been keen on a change of scene for years, and he won't even consider it. I want a life too, you know,' muttered her mother.

Maddie stared at her in shock. She hadn't realised things were quite this bad.

Just then the doorbell rang and Julie hurried away to answer it.

'Look,' said her mother quietly. 'I haven't said

anything to Julie, but you have all that money now! I'd love a place like this, I want to live on the Gold Coast. Is that too much to ask?' She looked at her daughter pointedly.

'Mum, let's discuss this when we get home,' said Maddie tightly.

Julie returned, saying, 'Sorry about that. Now, Maddie, your mother and I want to take you out for a bit of lunch. There's a great restaurant on the top floor of the shopping centre. You can see the beach from up there, and then we'll buzz around the shops, eh? What do you think?'

This was the last thing Maddie wanted to do.

'Uh, okay. Just a coffee and a sandwich will do me.'

Sitting in the plane on the way home the next morning, Maddie felt sad at the thought of her parents' relationship disintegrating after all these years.

*

Brett drove along Leonie's driveway, admiring the restored old farmhouse and gardens with their shady trees, and the paddocks spreading down to the creek where the thickly wooded hillside rose behind them.

Leonie came onto the verandah to greet him.

'Hi, Brett! So good of you to come over. I hope you didn't make a special trip up here.'

'Not at all. I'm coming up to Sarita's as often as I can at the moment. It's a good break from a big case I'm working on.'

'Well, it's very nice to see you again. We can go down to the creek now, or would you rather a coffee first?'

'No, let's go see what's down there.'

'Nothing. And that's the way we like it,' said Leonie.

She led the way across a bridge of fallen logs and rocks and up the rugged hillside on the other side of the creek.

'So what do you think about Sarita buying an island?' asked Leonie as they walked.

'Seems like a wild idea to me. I know Ray's not very happy about it, but she seems quite determined.'

As they reached a small plateau with a spectacular view, Leonie pointed. 'Down there, see? That's the spot for the dam, I'd say.'

'It'll ruin a beautiful valley. Is that koala habitat along there?'

'Sure is.'

Brett took out his phone and snapped some photos looking in various directions.

'I'll pass these on to a specialist who was recommended to me. He can assess the pros and cons and legalities of this dam proposal. Maybe we can launch a community fight to stop it.'

'That's helpful, thank you,' said Leonie. 'However, I guess not everyone is going to be against a dam. Water is a precious commodity.'

'Depends where it is and how it's used.'

Leonie nodded. 'True. Well, if we can get ammunition against the whole idea, I'm prepared to fight it.'

Brett smiled at her. 'Good for you!'

They clambered up to a rocky clearing.

'Wow, what a place to watch the sun rise and set,' Brett exclaimed. 'I'll just take some more photos.'

Back at the house, Leonie filled him in on all she knew, which still wasn't much. 'The response I got from the council when I asked whether a dam was planned for this area was total waffle and spin,' she said, 'but surely, legally, they will have to tell me more, if and when the planning progresses.'

'I sometimes think these media managers go to a special spin school,' said Brett dryly. 'A lot of talk that says nothing is quite an art. Well, I'll take these photos and whatever else I can find to the specialist I mentioned. Until I hear back from him, there's not much else I can do.'

*

Maddie was picking flowers to welcome her mother back home when a van pulled up at the front gate.

To her surprise, Julian stepped out.

'Behold, the beautiful maiden *avec fleurs*,' he said, smiling broadly and opening his arms.

Maddie smiled back, holding the flowers high so he wouldn't crush them as he gave her an awkward hug.

'What are you doing here?' she asked.

'What are *you* doing here? You're not at the coffee shop any more. I've been doing the rounds of rural hotels. Interesting clientele.'

'Pubs don't have pianos any more, do they?'

'Some of them do. And anyway, it was a stimulating experience. Are you going to invite me in?'

'Oh, yes, all right!' she said, turning towards the house.

He linked his arm through hers. 'You and I have a lot in common, Maddie.'

'You mean other than music?'

'Music is everything. Music is our *life*!' Julian exclaimed as he held the door open for her.

Maddie stopped and stared at him.

'I never thought of it like that . . .'

Julian leaned close to her and said earnestly, 'It's our passion, our joy, our challenge. You'd wither away if you couldn't play, sing, grasp those notes and wrangle them into beauteous melodies . . . right?' He stared fiercely into her eyes.

For an instant Maddie's heart lurched at the idea of not being able to sing or play music. She turned away. 'Well, that's not going to happen!'

Julian followed her into the kitchen. 'Maddie, be honest with yourself. Plunking away in the bedroom, trilling in the mirror – it's not getting you anywhere.'

Maddie turned to him, the heat rising in her cheeks. 'I do not plunk or trill in the mirror! In fact, I'm studying music notation right now.'

Julian's face lit up with a big smile. 'Great. I'm pleased. Then others could play what you write. Why don't we make music together?'

Feeling uncomfortable at his overfamiliarity, Maddie turned her back to him as she put the flowers in a vase.

Julian grasped her shoulders and spun her around.

Maddie leaned away, taken aback.

'Julian . . . we're friends and, as you say, we have a lot in common, but I want to do my own thing, maybe travel. My ambitions might be vague, but I don't want to get locked into anything,' she said firmly.

Julian stepped back, spreading his arms wide. 'Hey . . . I understand. You're talking to *doe . . . ray . . . meeeee . . .*' he sang.

Maddie tried not to laugh. 'I know. Now, sorry, but I have to tidy up. My mum will be home soon and the house is a mess. Let's catch up soon.' She gently pushed him out the door.

*

Leonie paced along the verandah, her emotions swinging between anger and sadness, and her thoughts churning wildly about what to do. She had just heard on the local radio that the Riverside Playhouse was going up for sale, and that the council had plans to allow the site to be completely redeveloped. She wasn't sure how she'd find the energy to protect it and stop the dam, but she knew she had to do something.

She gave a sigh of relief as Roger and Freddy's car appeared in her driveway and she hurried down the front steps to meet them.

'Thank you guys so much for coming over. I am beside myself! This is one of the dumbest ideas this council has ever had! Come inside and I'll make tea.'

Nursing their mugs at the kitchen table, Freddy said, 'The council's broke but they are hiding it as best they can. That's why they're flogging the Playhouse.'

'Surely there's something else they can sell rather than a charming, historic building,' added Roger.

'I don't think they care about history and charm and public enjoyment,' said Leonie. 'That site by the river is what's valuable.'

'Yeah, that land will fetch a motza,' said Roger. 'And save them the costs of the upkeep on the theatre.'

'The Playhouse is in very good shape, and it's functioning really well,' said Leonie, slicing the custard tart she'd made. 'I feel I should have seen this coming. The rumours have been swirling for a while now, but I didn't think they'd come to anything. When I rang and spoke to one of the council directors about our next production some time back, he was very evasive. Now I know why.'

'Is the theatre heritage listed?' asked Freddy.

'It's never been officially listed, and they've done a

lot of modernising inside over the years. The thing is,' said Leonie with some passion, 'it's loved by the community. And look at the enjoyment it gives locals who've rarely been to a theatre. Not to mention the talent we've nurtured within our own group – Maddie and Julian, for example. Without the Playhouse, they might never have got that chance!'

Freddy glanced at Roger. 'I feel like crying. It's bloody ridiculous. That Playhouse means a lot to all of us.'

'How can we help?' asked Roger.

Leonie put her mug down with some force.

'You know what? I've been thinking. I'll buy the Playhouse myself. That way we can keep it!'

The two men glanced at each other then stared at her. Freddy said quietly, 'That'd be a hefty sum of money, Leonie.'

She smiled at them. 'I came into some money recently. Perhaps that's why. It's the universe's way of allowing me to save the Playhouse.'

'A noble plan,' said Freddy slowly. 'But perhaps you should invest in your son's future, your own security.' He gave her a quizzical look.

'I think I can manage it,' said Leonie. 'Of course, this remains just between us.'

'Of course, of course,' the two men assured her, and glanced at each other.

Leonie wrinkled her nose. 'I am not one to draw attention to myself or make a scene,' she said, feeling tears spring to her eyes and a rush of affection for the two men. 'But if you ever need anything . . .' she managed.

Freddy took her hand. 'We get it. We're happy for you and Corby. You deserve it.'

Roger leaned forward, 'So who else . . . ?' Freddy

kicked him under the table and he clamped his mouth shut.

As Leonie rose to get more milk, behind her back the two men quietly punched fists together.

'So how do we do this? I mean, there'll be red tape and someone has to take responsibility and put their name on the contract,' said Leonie, suddenly all business.

'You'll need legal advice,' said Freddy.

'Couldn't we have a small committee, me, you two, someone else who's been involved with the Playhouse . . .' said Leonie. 'Maybe Ray? He's a very practical person and a good friend.'

'It will be your name on the contract, Leonie. Everyone knows you've devoted yourself to the Playhouse for years. Buying it might come as a bit of a surprise to people, though.'

'I'll just have to think about how to manage that.'

'Darlings, I have a suggestion,' said Roger. 'I say we go to the local community newspaper and tell them the story of Leonie wanting to save the theatre! That way she'll get community support and it will be very hard for the council to say no.'

*

The front page story caused a huge stir. Most people were outraged that the town could lose the beautiful old building, and many people commented that it was a showcase for local talent as well as a source of great entertainment. Many immediately intuited that the council was just out for a money grab. Mostly the locals were touched that Leonie was planning to purchase the old theatre for her late husband Tony, who had been a staunch supporter of community activities.

In the days following the newspaper story, Leonie fielded a lot of phone calls from locals asking what was going on and how they could help. Some people offered donations.

Leonie finally stopped answering her phone. When she told Harry he might have to take some calls for her, he quickly disappeared to a far paddock to fix something.

Late one afternoon the phone rang and she stared at the unknown number, debating whether or not to answer it. Then, sighing, she accepted the call and said, 'Hello. Who is calling, please?'

'Mrs Foster? My name is Alistair Broad. I was told about the situation regarding the Riverside Playhouse in Fig Tree River. I'm a heritage architect, so it goes without saying that I'm particularly fond of heritage buildings. It would be a tragedy to lose your theatre up there. I was wondering if I could help in any way?'

'Oh, thanks for calling – and for your interest,' Leonie said, feeling heartened. She liked Alistair's warm, friendly tone. 'Yes. I agree, losing the theatre is simply not on. Whereabouts are you located? I'm not sure the theatre needs an architect so much as a white knight,' she said, laughing. Then she felt silly. 'Sorry. I've been overwhelmed with interest about this, one way or another.'

'I can imagine. I just thought I'd reach out. It so happens I'm looking at a restoration job up the coast in a few days and will be going past Fig Tree River. I'd love to drop in and see the Playhouse. Perhaps I could give you a professional assessment of its value from a heritage perspective, if that would be useful?'

'Actually, that would be wonderful, very helpful.'

'It's heritage listed, I assume?'

'Locally it's considered heritage, but it hasn't been formally listed with the state government or such. We did receive some grants several years back, but the council doesn't consider the Playhouse as being essential to the town.'

'How sad. It doesn't sound a very balanced sort of council. I might check them out. And as I said, I'll be in the area so I can stop by – probably next Thursday?'

'Sounds great, thank you . . . Alistair, was it?'

'Alistair Broad. And it's my pleasure. I'll be in touch next week.'

*

On the appointed day, as Leonie parked in the theatre's car park, she saw a tall, good-looking man taking photos of the building's façade.

She walked towards him. 'Alistair?'

He held out his hand with a smile. 'Alistair Broad. Wow, this is quite a building.'

'Yes, it is, isn't it?'

He shook his head. 'Can't say I think much of your council.'

'Join the club,' said Leonie dryly. 'Would you like to look around inside?'

'Very much.' He followed her up the steps.

They toured the front of house, the projection and sound booths up in the gods, the props store and the dressing-rooms, and then they went out onto the stage.

The house lights were on and Alistair gazed at the rows of plush red seats.

'Pretty awesome, and much larger than I expected. It's certainly very professional. What's been your favourite show?' he asked.

Leonie shook her head. 'Oh, I don't have favourites. My shows are like children – I love them all. We've unearthed some great talent for a local town. In fact, our last production could be heading to Broadway.'

Alistair looked impressed. 'How fantastic. It'd be a tragedy if someone became a big name and said, I owe it all to the Riverside Playhouse . . . only to find the Playhouse no longer in existence.'

'That's what I've been thinking! And it's looming as a reality.' She turned to Alistair.

'Well, I'm happy to help as much as I can. This building is quite special.'

'Thank you. I'd be grateful for any ideas or suggestions you can give me about saving this place.'

'First up, try to get the government heritage people involved. This should be listed as a Local Heritage Site with the council, so you'd need evidence to support an application for heritage significance. A Local Heritage Site is usually listed on the LEP – Local Environmental Plan.'

Leonie frowned. 'Sounds complicated.'

'I'd be happy to help you through that process, for a start.'

Leonie nodded. 'I really appreciate that. Thanks, Alistair. Now, do you have time for a quick lunch? Perhaps I can show you some of the other buildings in town.'

*

They sat on the verandah at the Riverbend Café and ordered salads. Alistair was a good listener, and Leonie found herself talking about rewilding, regenerative farming and the possibility of a dam looming over her land.

'Sorry, I'm talking your ear off,' she said with a smile.

'Your farm project sounds fascinating. And the town is lucky to have you spearheading the campaign to save the theatre.'

'I'm just a figurehead, really, but then someone has to be,' she sighed. 'Thanks again for all your suggestions.'

'It's my pleasure. And I've been thinking – the Playhouse could be eligible to be listed on the State Heritage Register as an item of State Heritage Significance, as well. Which, of course, would add to its value, culturally as well as financially, and possibly makes it eligible for government grants in the future.'

'Noted. Again, I can't thank you enough, Alistair.'

'Please, keep me in the loop. I also have some good connections I can pass on. This kind of thing is right up my alley so I'm glad to help – and it doesn't hurt to have had such a delightful morning.'

Leonie smiled warmly as they shook hands. 'I've enjoyed it too!'

*

A world away, Fleur walked briskly along the shady tree-lined street in Manhattan's historic arts district of Chelsea with its dozens of galleries and theatres.

How would Madison and Julian fit in here? she wondered. What would her two discoveries from a small Australian country town make of it all, if she brought them over? It would be a massive leap for them.

She had no doubt that Julian would jump at the chance to come here. But what about Maddie? No matter what, Fleur reasoned, a dose of the big wide world would challenge them both to sink or swim. Especially Maddie.

11

'SARITA! YOU'RE NOT SERIOUS!' Ray jumped to his feet, dropping the newspaper.

Sarita put her bag down. 'I'm packed. Ready to go.'

'C'mon, you're kidding me.' He spread his arms.

'I told you I was going. I've arranged it all. Don't worry about me. My mind is made up. Just don't let the boys know. It's a surprise.'

'I'm the one who's surprised.' Ray sat down. 'Honestly, Rita, you've never done anything big like this on your own.'

'Are you saying I can't do it? I'm doing it for us. For our family.' Her voice softened.

'No, no, of course you're up to doing whatever you set your mind to! It's just . . . it's so far away, such a big deal.

Besides, we've always done things together,' he said, and they could both hear the note of hurt in his voice.

'You said you wanted no part of buying an island,' said Sarita quietly. 'You had nothing to do with the Playhouse productions. I had nothing to do with your job when you were working. I thought this would be a good project for us. Together. But perhaps not.' Sarita's face was tight.

Ray rubbed his forehead. 'I just have doubts that this is something we should do. It's like nothing we'd ever thought about doing before. And just because we *can* do it – afford it – doesn't mean we *should*. I just don't think it's for us.'

'How do you know?' Sarita said. 'Even when we couldn't afford something, it didn't stop us from dreaming about it.'

Ray felt rattled. 'You've been dreaming about buying an island in the South Pacific? Since when?'

Sarita looked past him, seeming to speak to herself rather than Ray. 'I'm not sure. I just get these feelings. Not memories, but ever since meeting the family, Nani Purnima, I have a sense of . . .' She paused, searching for the word.

'Loss? Your mother? Your Fijian family?' offered Ray.

Sarita shook her head vehemently. 'No. My family is *here*! You, the boys and my brother . . . No. This is . . . different.' She looked at him. 'I just know I have to do this. Maybe it's why I won the money.'

Ray looked at her and rolled his eyes. 'I've heard about this. People win a swag of money then go nuts. Buy houses, boats, first-class trips, everything! And they lose the lot or their lives become hell! Do you know how many say they wish they'd never won any damn money?'

'I am married to a financial expert. Or so I thought. I am not going nuts and being irrational,' she said flatly.

'Buying a tropical island, just for yourself, not as a business – isn't that a bit OTT?' he asked sarcastically.

Sarita glared at him. Then she turned away and said in a slightly choked voice, 'I have never been able to do anything important, interesting or challenging.'

'You don't have to win a pile of money to do that,' he answered.

'I'm not trying to big-note myself, if that's what you think.' Sarita seemed to crumple and looked teary. 'I just feel like I got the money for a reason.'

There was silence for a few moments as these words sank in. Then Ray took a deep breath and sighed.

'Okay, sweetheart. If you feel so strongly about it, I'll come with you. We'll do this together.'

Sarita wiped her eyes and shook her head. 'No. No, it's okay, Ray. You stay and look after things here. Maybe this *is* something I have to do by myself.'

'Sarita, darling, it could be difficult. Certainly risky. I don't think you should go alone.'

'I'm not. I've hired Stuart. Remember the Aussie guy we met in the restaurant before we left Fiji? I know he seemed a bit of a loose cannon, but I've been emailing and phoning him. He's being very practical and businesslike and he has lots of contacts.'

'But he tried to convince us *not* to buy an island!'

'I've decided he was being too negative. I'm doing this with my eyes wide open. It'll be fine,' said Sarita firmly.

'So why didn't you tell me about all this? How much are you paying him?'

'Just expenses, accommodation and meals while he takes me around places for sale, like an agent.'

'Tell him to buy his own booze,' Ray said caustically. 'Have you made contact with your family?'

'No. Not yet. My buying an island isn't their business,' said Sarita.

'I just thought they could be helpful. Have contacts. And keep an eye on . . . things,' said Ray.

'I'm perfectly capable of looking after myself,' said Sarita calmly.

Ray shook his head. 'You – we – have never done anything so big, so risky, so . . . out there. You've hardly left Fig Tree River!'

'Exactly.' Sarita straightened up. 'It's about time. And who's to say I can't step up and tangle with the world away from here?'

Ray studied his wife, suddenly seeing her for the strong-willed and determined woman she was. But he couldn't help adding, 'Just let me know instantly if you have any problems. Things can go wrong very easily –'

'And if they do, I'll deal with it,' she said shortly. 'Just promise me you won't panic or send in the cavalry if you don't hear from me for a little while. You know how poor telecommunications are out in the islands.'

Ray nodded. As Sarita glanced at her phone, he asked, 'You're really leaving? Right this minute?'

Sarita smiled. 'Yes, I'm really going. Don't worry, the fridge and freezer are stocked. Call a mate and go and play golf or tennis or something. I'll keep you posted. Remember, this island is for all of us.'

'I'll miss you and worry about you.'

Sarita was suddenly herself again. 'Oh Ray, you never took me seriously, and I didn't want to force you to go on this journey with me. I'll be fine. I have a car picking me up to go to the airport. I'll call you tonight from Suva. C'mon, give me a hug.'

The doorbell rang. Sarita held out her arms as Ray jumped to his feet and hugged her, then grabbed her bag as she headed to the door.

'The itinerary is pretty loose. With the unpredictable weather, boats, the locals on Fiji time, I'll expect the unexpected. But I've written out where I'll be when, roughly – it's on the fridge door,' said Sarita cheerfully.

'Okay then.' He handed her bag to the driver, who was hovering at the front door. 'I love you.'

She blew him a kiss as she went to the car.

Ray watched the car drive away, trying to match this adventurous Sarita with the Sarita who had once been happy spending hours surrounded by fabric, hunched over a sewing machine.

The house was suddenly very quiet.

*

Maddie reread the email from Fleur for the fourth time.

> *Dearest Maddie,*
> *I do think about you and my Fig Tree River friends so often. My news is that* Percy and Ella *looks like living again! A really wonderful off-Broadway theatre has agreed to do a limited season of it, between their regular program schedule. They like it for the obvious reasons but also the link with White Plains, New York. (You must visit Percy and Ella's home there one day – very evocative. Though, of course, nowhere near as intriguing as the Grainger Museum in Melbourne!)*
> *The reason I am writing now is that I'd like to*

invite you and Julian to come over. I have emailed him too. No promises, but I think you could have a shot at being our Ella and Percy in this production – ONLY if you want to, that is. I will help you cover your travel expenses, as well as Julian's. You can stay with me as long as you like. Julian can share with one of the musos who has a spare room in his lovely apartment. You also once mentioned giving songwriting a serious shot, so we can explore that too, if you like. Leonie tells me you're learning music notation – I'm so pleased to hear it! Reading and writing music will be a huge help, of course!

But what are you doing with yourself in Fig Tree River? You're at an age now where you can explore not only the world, but your own path, and see where it takes you. You've been given opportunities and the talent, you know. You want to be able to look back in years to come and know you used such gifts wisely with no regrets or 'should haves'.

I'm writing rather than calling so you can digest all this. But call me anytime. No pressure!

So looking forward to hopefully seeing you! Many hugs.

Fleur

Maddie drew a deep breath. Decision time. Her first instinct was to phone Charlie, but she stopped herself. She knew Julian would jump at the opportunity, and so he should. She knew this was a golden opportunity for herself, too – and not just as a possible career move, but as a broadening of her horizons. But she was hesitant, and it was because of Charlie. Damn him.

And that realisation made her annoyed with herself.

She'd promised herself she would move on, but stay friends, just as he'd suggested. Yet here she was, wanting Charlie to be the first person to hear the news of Fleur's offer, when she knew that what she really wanted was for him to come along on the journey with her.

Maddie sighed. Before any of that, she had to sort out her parents. It was time for action.

A few days later Maddie announced at breakfast, 'C'mon, Dad, we're going into town. I need your advice.'

'Since when?'

Maddie bit her tongue. 'Well, there are some things you know better than me. C'mon. We have to be there at nine.'

Grumbling, her father tucked in his shirt and followed her to the front door, where he reached for his hat, a cap with *Bullie Cow Sales* in peeling white letters on the front. But then he paused and hung it back up, reaching instead for his ancient Akubra. He brushed it off and jammed it on his head. Maddie didn't say anything but she was touched. It was a hat he had always worn when she went with him to cattle and clearing sales when she was little, and she hadn't seen him wear it in many years.

As they pulled into the car park behind the main street a young woman was waiting for them. 'Hello, I'm Victoria,' she said as Maddie got out of the driver's seat. 'Let's go in my car, shall we?'

'Hi, that sounds good, thanks. I'm Maddie and this is my father, Michael.'

'Where're we going?' whispered her father as Maddie opened the car door for him.

'Shopping,' she said lightly.

Maddie wasn't sure if her dad was paying attention

to the sales pitch from Victoria as she drove them out of town.

About twenty minutes later they arrived at a farm gate and Maddie got out to open it. As she got back in the car, her father tapped her on the shoulder.

'Why're we visiting old Mr Corbett?' he hissed.

'Oh. Mr Corbett passed away some time ago,' said Victoria over her shoulder. 'And Mrs Corbett has gone into a retirement village. So she's selling up. Pretty place, isn't it?'

'What's happened to his dairy mob?'

'They were sold long ago. Mrs Corbett leased the dairy shed and the yards to a man who's breeding kelpies. You know – the very expensive dogs that are so smart and muster up the cattle.'

'Remember Ginger, Maddie? Bloody good dog, he was,' said her father.

Maddie reached back and patted his hand. 'Yep, of course I do. He used to muster the chooks.'

Her father was smiling as they got out of the car.

'The house isn't fancy, but it's solid and nicely done up –' began Victoria, but Maddie interjected, 'Victoria, is it okay if we just let my father wander around, have a look?'

Maddie trailed beside her dad, who walked with his hands clasped behind his back.

'Still in pretty good nick. How much land they got?'

'Apparently Mrs Corbett sold some of it off, so there's only a couple of hundred acres left now,' said Victoria. 'Oh my . . .' She trailed off as four puppies galloped towards them, carefully watched by their mother and a man leaning against the fence.

'Sorry, I just let them out for a bit of a run,' the man called.

'You're the one who leases the land, then?' asked Michael as he stooped down to greet the enthusiastic pups.

'Yes, that's right. Then I take them over to the Milsons' place down the hill to train them with his cattle,' he explained.

Michael looked at Maddie and grinned. 'They need some cattle in here. These pups need to grow up with them.'

Maddie exchanged a smile with the man, who gave a whistle and the pups scurried back to him and sat, looking expectant.

'Hey, that's pretty good,' said Michael.

After they'd walked around the property, Maddie turned to her father and asked, 'So, have you seen enough?' They both looked towards the cottage, where Victoria was on her phone.

'Are you really serious about buying this place then?' asked her father. 'I gather that's why we're here.'

'Let's look inside the house, then we'll talk.'

The cottage had the traditional gun-barrel hallway with neat rooms off it and a large kitchen opening onto a shady back verandah, with views across the paddocks.

'Could you live here?' Maddie asked, although it was obvious that her father was delighted at the prospect of living on a farm once more.

'Sure could!' But then his enthusiasm faded. 'But your mother won't.'

'Dad, I've decided I'd like to buy this place for you. You and Mum will have to sort things out.'

He hesitated then said, 'She can come and go, maybe?'

'That's up to you both. I've got my own plans.'

He looked around again, his eyes soft, and said, 'Good on you, love. It's very generous of you. Your mum and I will work something out.'

She squeezed his hand. 'Thanks, Dad. Now, let me go and haggle with Victoria.' Maddie drew a breath. She'd never had to make such life-changing decisions before. Had she unwittingly forced a separation between her parents? *The money didn't just open doors*, she thought, *it closed them, too.*

She turned and watched her dad walk back to the pups and lean on the fence yarning with the dog trainer. He was pointing around the property, no doubt telling the other man what a wonderful dairy farm Mr Corbett had back in the day, and how he was going to run beef cattle here now.

*

Sarita wiped the perspiration from her face. Nobody was in a hurry at the boat terminal, which was actually more of an old jetty with a small wooden warehouse that also served as a waiting area. Several kids were fishing, and an old woman dozed in the shade. Sarita couldn't decide whether it was hotter inside the waiting shed or out in the air and sun. Her Fijian heritage didn't seem to help when it came to coping with the humidity and heat, she thought.

Stuart sat scrolling through his phone, unperturbed by the discomfort.

The flight from Sydney to Nadi, then a connecting flight to Savusavu, followed by a bumpy bus ride across to the coast, and now the wait for the boat Stuart had arranged to take them to the island they were seeing, had been exhausting. There had to be an easier way to get to Totoka Island, Sarita thought.

'Couldn't we just fly straight to the island?' she asked.

Stuart looked up. 'No landing strip. Could clear a chopper pad, I s'pose. Wind's often bad, though. You'll need to get a decent power boat if you buy it,' he added.

'I'll put it on the list,' said Sarita, unamused, and even more so when she realised he wasn't joking.

But as they set out in the launch Stuart had arranged and she finally saw a small green dot on the horizon, Sarita felt a tingle of excitement. Eventually she could make out the silhouettes of palm trees and then the gleaming strip of sand ringing the island.

Around a rocky point in the shelter of a cove jutted the stone seawall and the arm of a wooden jetty. As they motored closer she saw an old barge pulled onto the sand and a small powerboat tied to the jetty.

'Would that boat make it back to the big island?' she asked.

Stuart shrugged. 'Yeah; it'd be rough, though. It's more for fishing.'

'I'll have to take up fishing,' said Sarita dryly.

'I can find you a skipper if you want to go deep-sea fishing,' said Stuart.

'Let's wait and see if I decide to buy the place, and have a roof over my head first,' said Sarita.

She'd been told there was a structure on the island built by a previous owner who had run out of money before completing his dream hideaway.

'The island looks like a pretty bauble bobbing on the ocean,' said Sarita.

'It ain't going anywhere,' said Stuart. 'There's Varo on the jetty. He's the caretaker.'

The man in a flowered shirt and faded shorts greeted them with a big smile, and helped Sarita onto the wooden steps.

'*Bula*! I am Varo. Welcome to Totoka. It means "beautiful love",' he said.

'That's nice. Although I'm not looking for Love Island,

just a peaceful, happy place,' said Sarita, her legs feeling a bit wobbly from the bouncing boat ride.

'Here you are then!' He made a sweeping gesture and asked, 'So you want to be here alone? With your family? Or for business?'

'I don't expect to be alone. Holidays with family and friends,' said Sarita. 'So, what can you tell me about Totoka? What's its best feature?'

Varo pointed to the peak above them. 'At the very top, there is a small plateau. If you climb up there, you are indeed close to heaven! Fantastic views all round. Magic.'

'I'll wait here,' said Stuart. 'With the boat, and the esky.'

Varo looked blank for a moment. 'Ah, yes! For the cold beer, yes?'

Sarita looked at Stuart. 'You have an esky of cold beer?'

'Just in case. Don't want to be caught short. There's plenty of juices and fizzy stuff, too.'

'And food, I hope.' Sarita turned to Varo. 'Shall we?'

He hesitated. 'You want to go to the plateau?'

'Not right now. I'd like to see whatever has been built here and then sit in the shade with a cold water,' Sarita replied.

'Of course, of course. Follow me.'

The sandy path wound through tangled undergrowth and thick trees where insects clustered, zapping around her face.

Then suddenly they entered a large clearing surrounded by tree stumps in which there was a half-finished dwelling. The structure was almost swallowed by tropical plants and trees, and the remains of a woven coconut palm–leaf roof were barely supported by thick wooden posts.

Empty windows like hollow eyes and the gaping mouth of a carved double-door entry allowed Sarita to glimpse the framework of unfinished rooms inside, all covered by a tangle of vines and plants. It looked eerie, sad and forgotten.

Picking up a fallen branch, Sarita plunged in, brushing aside the forest debris as she ventured to the entrance and tried to visualise what the original plan for the building might have been. Varo hung back, watching her, his face expressionless.

Sarita took photos and returned to where Varo was sitting on a stump.

'Where do you stay while you're here?' she asked him.

He rose and pointed. 'On the other side of the island. Beach side. You want to go there? Maybe ten minutes' walk?'

'Okay, thanks. Let's go.'

They set off through the humid, silent bush. But as they headed over a small rise, a fresh sea breeze washed over them. Out in the sun and fresh air, Sarita drew a deep breath, and then saw that they were facing a stretch of untouched silver sand and the deep blue sea with nothing else in sight. She stopped still, speechless. It was staggeringly beautiful.

'Wow, this is just stunning,' she murmured.

'There's a lagoon around the little breakwater there.' Varo pointed. 'This is the side for bures, eh?' He smiled.

'Yes, but there doesn't look like anywhere to bring in a boat. Would that be possible?' asked Sarita.

Varo shook his head. 'No way. The island is long and narrow; the north side is the most protected, so that's where the jetty is, where we came in. Where the lagoon goes out gets good surf waves some of the year. You surf?'

'Not really. I like swimming in calm water. What about snorkelling?'

He spread his arms, 'Everywhere! The reef is best. When the tide is in you can see fish, stingrays, all kinds of creatures. When the tide is out, you can jump in and swim along the edge of the coral wall.'

They walked along the beach to the lagoon outlet, and in the shade of some palm trees was a small open-sided shack and a tent.

'Your place?'

Varo nodded. 'You want a cold drink?'

'Yes, please!'

He pulled out a plastic folding chair for Sarita and propped it in the shade. A small ring of stones fringed the remains of a fire. In the shelter was a large table piled with dishes, cooking pans, a chiller and a portable gas cooker, along with supplies in plastic crates. A fishing rod and net leaned in a corner.

'So you sleep in the tent?' asked Sarita.

'Yep. Too many bugs and bities outside. It's okay if the fire is going.'

'You don't have any power?'

'Plenty. I have a solar charger and my phone's on satellite link. I only stay here every few weeks. To keep an eye on things.'

'Like what?' Sarita couldn't imagine what would require watching. There didn't seem to be any animals except for birds, maybe lizards, and whatever lived in the reef and ocean.

'Boats sometimes come ashore. Tourists, fishermen.'

'You don't get lonely when you stay here?'

He shrugged. 'I have music. I'm not away from home too long. Sometimes my friends come over and stay and we party a bit.'

'Well, I guess you wouldn't disturb the neighbours,' said Sarita.

'What do you want to do with this place then?' Varo asked. 'No tourist resort?'

'No. Just for family and friends. My kids will love it,' said Sarita. 'But how would I get building materials and workers here?' she added.

He shrugged. 'Could be a bit tricky. Maybe ask Stuart. So, are you going to buy this place?'

'Depends,' said Sarita casually. 'There are a lot of problems to iron out first. I was led to believe the building was habitable, but it didn't look –'

'Oh, it's liveable,' said Varo. 'I didn't show you everything.'

Sarita drained her water and stood up. 'So could you show me, Varo?'

Retracing their steps to the half-built building, Varo led Sarita a little further through the trees to a small structure, constructed, Varo said, for the staff who would have worked on the island. Sarita walked around its small kitchen, screened sleeping areas, outdoor shower enclosed by a bamboo screen and a covered patio living area. While it was dusty, leaf-strewn and neglected, its roof was intact and it was certainly habitable.

'Why don't you stay here?' she asked Varo.

'I like the beach. More of a breeze,' he replied.

Sarita nodded, not wanting to look or sound too enthusiastic. But her mind was made up. She'd buy Totoka.

*

Sarita stared out the office window at the local marina, which was dotted with yachts. She was worried that she hadn't yet told Ray that she was going ahead with her crazy dream. She knew that he'd say it was up to her, it was her money and he'd said his piece, but she also knew he wouldn't be happy about it.

'Here we are, Mrs Golding, the final contract, if you'd like to go through it once more.'

Sarita raised an eyebrow at Stuart who was sitting beside her, and he shrugged.

'It'll be all right,' he said.

She'd come this far with Stuart so she felt she had to trust his judgement that the woman managing the sale was a reputable solicitor. When Sarita had mentioned to her that she'd been born in Fiji and had family here – the Chands – the solicitor had looked impressed and commented, 'A very good and important family in the islands.'

Sarita reached for the documents and started to skim through them. She couldn't see any significant changes, so she signed her name where required, momentarily catching her breath at the amount she was spending. *Who would ever have believed this?* she thought. For a moment she felt a pang of guilt about Ray, but she hoped he'd eventually come around when everything was sorted on the island and they were enjoying their own little piece of paradise.

*

Chrissie settled herself at her table in the coffee shop near the school. Lloyd, the owner, gave her a wave.

'The usual?'

'Yes please, Lloyd.'

The woman at the table next to her was reading the free newspaper and closed it with a sigh. She caught Chrissie's eye.

'Hi. Would you like to read the local rag?' she asked.

'Thanks, but I've read that issue.'

'It's really good. No help for me, though,' said the woman. 'Not enough classified ads. I s'pose I'll have to go online.'

'What are you looking for?' asked Chrissie. Then she thought perhaps this was too inquisitive. 'Sorry, I don't mean to pry.'

The young woman shrugged. 'It's okay. I'm so fed up with trying to get things fixed and paying a fortune to tradies. I don't know if they're ripping me off or not.'

'Are you building a house or something?' asked Chrissie.

'My husband took off with another woman so I'm living in my aunt's home. She's gone into an aged care facility. I'm grateful to live there but it's an old place that needs endless things fixed,' she said. 'My aunt let it go a bit the last few years.'

'Oh dear. How bad is it?' asked Chrissie.

'Just small things, but not small to me. Then when I get the invoices for the repairs it always makes me feel like I'm being taking for a ride.' She managed a smile and then, leaning over to Chrissie's table, held out her hand. 'Hi, I'm Penelope. Penny.'

Chrissie chuckled. 'I'm Christina. Chrissie.'

Lloyd put Chrissie's chai green tea in front of her. 'You two should share a table. You're both regulars.'

'Thanks. I was just having another whinge about tradies,' said Penny.

'Why don't you find a hunky Mr Fix-It and ask him to move in,' suggested Lloyd with a wink at Chrissie.

'In your dreams.' Penny smiled as she got up and moved over to Chrissie's table.

'Ask Chrissie here. She offered to fix my pantry shelves,' said Lloyd as he headed to the kitchen.

'Really? How do you know how to do stuff like that?' asked Penny.

Chrissie shrugged. 'I was lucky, I guess. I used to hang around a lot with my grandad and he taught me how to do things.'

'So can you change a tap washer, fix a squeaky door, unclog a drain . . . that sort of thing?' asked Penny.

Chrissie nodded. 'Yep. But I like to make things, build stuff, mainly.'

'Wow! How come most women are never taught to do that stuff? Mind you, some men aren't, either. My grandfather wouldn't have known a tap washer from a piece of fruit.'

'I also learned some things at school. I preferred woodwork to sewing,' said Chrissie. 'I make all the scenery and props for our local theatre productions. Well, I used to, when we lived in Fig Tree River. We only moved here recently.'

'Really? That sounds cool. I suppose you can change a car tyre too?'

Chrissie nodded and they both laughed.

'I'd be happy to help you. But our new place is an apartment so I don't have my tools or my old workshop,' Chrissie sighed.

Penny flung up her arms. 'I do! My God. I still have my late uncle's garage full of tools! I have no idea what to do with them. He loved playing in there. Had all the spanners and stuff lined up on hooks in graduating sizes, all neat as a pin. My aunt used to complain about how untidy he was in the house, but move anything from its place in the garage? Heaven help you.' She laughed. 'Not that I ever touched his tools.'

'What do you need fixing?' asked Chrissie.

'Oh – oh no, I'm not asking you to do anything . . .' began Penny. 'Sorry, I was just having a rant.'

'I'm not a plumber but I'm pretty handy on the tools. I'd be happy to pop over, truly. Where do you live?'

After that first day, the two women quickly became friends.

The first time Chrissie went to Penny's house she walked around the garage, admiring Penny's late uncle's tools and treasures.

'You're right, he was a tidy person. And everything is as sharp as a tack. What sort of things did he make?'

'Not a lot really. He'd fix things when they broke. We kids asked for a treehouse one time but that was a bit too much of a stretch. He seemed to just like tinkering with things, you know, pottering around in here.'

Chrissie smiled. 'Man Cave syndrome. Men like to mess about in their own space with their "toys".'

'So do women, I s'pose,' said Penny. 'I don't have a space. But then I don't have any hobbies.'

'Making repairs isn't just a hobby. It's pretty essential,' said Chrissie. 'I'm sure I saved my family a heap by doing odd jobs around our old place.'

'Your husband doesn't fix stuff for you?'

'Not really. He's a plumber but he never showed me how to fix a leaky tap or clogged drain or anything. I'm the one who did most of the work around our old home. There's not so much call for it in our new place.'

'Could you teach me?' asked Penny. 'I'm so over feeling like an idiot and worried I'm being ripped off for what seem to me to be pretty basic things. I'm happy to pay you.'

'Not at all. It's my pleasure,' said Chrissie.

In the house, Penny showed Chrissie the cupboard door hanging by one hinge.

'Easy-peasy, let me show you,' said Chrissie.

After Chrissie had finished several other odd jobs, they sat down over coffee and Penny looked thoughtful.

'You know what I'm thinking? You should teach other women how to fix stuff. I know heaps of people who'd be interested.'

Chrissie shrugged. 'Sure, I'd be happy to do that, ask your friends. Daytime, during school hours, is best for me.'

'Okay. Uncle Tim would be so happy to know that his tools are being used,' said Penny.

'Oh, I'll be very careful with them,' said Chrissie quickly, knowing what Troy was like with his equipment and all his new toys, like the jetski and his new sports car which she was not allowed to drive.

'I'll set it up,' said Penny.

*

Four women were ready and waiting when Chrissie arrived at Penny's home the following Thursday.

And to her surprise, they'd brought a few items with them that needed minor repairs. After she'd done those, they all trailed after Chrissie as she fixed a jammed window blind, replaced a washer and repaired a broken chair leg in Penny's house. As before, Chrissie refused to be paid, even though they all offered.

Over coffee and cake later, they exchanged stories about unreliable tradies, and appliances that barely lasted the warranty period.

'We have my mother's fridge for drinks out on the back verandah – it's still going like a train and it's over thirty years old,' said one. 'But newer things seem so much flimsier and less reliable.'

Others asked Chrissie for tips and advice, and they all seemed to laugh a lot. Chrissie realised she hadn't had so much fun in ages.

A few days later, Penny called her.

'Listen, that was great the other day. We all had a ball and it was so useful. The girls were all saying they know other people who'd want to come and see you about learning how to fix things for themselves. You've really started something.'

'It was your idea,' said Chrissie. 'I really enjoyed meeting them, and I'm happy to show them anything I can.'

'Well, we were thinking we should start a Women's Shed. Maybe you could give classes somewhere.'

'Oh, that sounds a bit difficult,' started Chrissie, already worrying about what it might involve. But Penny broke in.

'I had a feeling you might say that. But we know a place where you could give classes. We can have that space either on an afternoon or for a night class. It doesn't get used much, so they like the idea of holding a Women's Shed there. There're sanders and saws and all sorts of things I don't have a clue about. I can take you over to show you.'

Chrissie hesitated. 'It could be fun. Are there really enough women interested?'

'Absolutely! Also, it's a social get-together. Some of

them want to build things like, say, a storage box, or something for their husbands, just to show them they can! We can start a whole movement. Look at how the Men's Sheds took off. We could do a daytime class and perhaps one evening a week for those who're working.'

Chrissie felt a tingle of excitement. 'I'll have to run it past Troy.'

'Why?' Penny asked.

'Ah, um, because he'd have to look after the kids,' said Chrissie quickly.

*

That night after the children were in bed, Chrissie looked at Troy scrolling through his phone on the couch.

'Hey, I met a nice woman at the café before school pick-up,' she began.

'Mmm,' said Troy, not looking up.

'I fixed a couple of things at her house for her. Small jobs, tap washer and such –'

'Did she pay you?'

'Of course not!'

Troy shrugged and looked back at his phone.

'Um, she did ask me to help another friend or two and show them what to do.'

'Bully for you.'

'Troy, she wants me to – well, show them how to fix things, like classes. A Women's Shed sort of thing.'

This time Troy looked up. 'Bloody hell! What for? Why do women always want to do whatever blokes do? They just mess it up! For God's sake. If women were meant to fix things they'd start playing with a hammer instead of damned dolls when they're little. What a friggin' stupid idea. You women can't leave it alone, can you? Got to muscle in on everything. Women's Shed! What a waste of time. Is this because you big-noted yourself and told them you made stupid bits of wood backgrounds for those bloody plays of Leonie's?' He leaned forward, glaring at Chrissie. 'Women's brains don't work like men's, and you don't have the muscles and the smarts men have. Jesus, Chrissie, you can't even do maths, how would you measure anything, for starters? What a joke.' He turned back to his phone.

Chrissie was stung. 'I managed okay at the Playhouse! The newspaper always said how clever the sets were!' she said.

'You mean when they didn't fall over,' he sniggered.

'Or burn down,' she snapped.

Troy smirked. 'That was your dumb fault, Chrissie.'

Chrissie bit her tongue. She still couldn't understand how that fire had started.

'Well, I'm going to do the Women's Shed.' She wasn't sure where she found the confidence to say this – perhaps it was just that she really wanted to do it – but she walked from the room, steeling herself for a remark to be flung at her back. Instead she heard Troy punching numbers into his phone.

For the first time she could recall, a creeping sense of jubilation, of having stood up to him, flooded through her. She knew by his silence that she'd scored a hit.

However, just as swiftly came the fear of payback. Troy didn't like anyone answering back. She knew she'd better keep her head down and not ruffle any feathers for a while. She'd learned the hard way that it was better to keep out of his way when he was irked.

*

Maddie rolled over as the tapping at her bedroom door woke her.

'Yes. What is it?'

'Maddie, your boyfriend is here,' called her father.

'What? What time is it?' She jumped out of bed, wondering why Charlie had come by out of the blue.

She smoothed her hair, tugged at her pyjamas and opened the door.

'He's in the kitchen,' said her father with a smile.

'*Buongiorno, signorina! Que bella!* You slept in!' Julian threw his arms open.

'Oh. It's you.' Maddie paused, noting the disappointment that swept through her. 'Yes, I was up late. Why are you here?'

'Can't you guess?' Julian struck a pose and began to sing the first verse of 'New York, New York', as if he were Frank Sinatra.

'All right, okay. So you got a message from Fleur,' said Maddie grumpily as she headed to the coffee machine, still mad at herself for thinking it was Charlie.

'Yep. Fleur rang me. Kept telling me it's a long shot, no promises, see how we go, stay with a friend . . . but who cares! "I'm gonna be in New Yoik City."'

'Off-Broadway,' Maddie reminded him tartly. 'And you have to audition with everyone else, the role isn't yours yet. Please don't get your hopes up too much,' she warned.

'C'mon, Mads, have your coffee and brighten up. "It's a new day . . ."'

'Oh Julian, please stop! For God's sake.' But Maddie had to smile even though she was irritated. 'Sit down and I'll make you a coffee too.'

He sat waiting while she made the coffee, fidgeting, bopping and humming.

Julian was like a revved-up butterfly, she thought. Flitting from this to that, bringing laughter and colour and a smile as he went, but rarely anything substantial. Then, presumably, he would burn out and fall to earth to lie low for a while. Mercurial, magically talented, he was a strange combination of an open heart, ego and mystery. No one knew much about his history, family, or his life beyond the snippets he'd told them. He'd just seemed to arrive, out of the blue, ready to go, full of gifts and laughter, like some musical comet that had landed among them.

'So of course you're going then? How are you paying for the trip?' asked Maddie.

'Fleur is helping me, but I sold some stuff. Shall we go together?'

'Did Fleur say I was going? I'm not auditioning,' said Maddie swiftly.

'You won't have to,' he said.

'Rubbish. We would both have to audition. Are you up for that? This is your break-into-the-big-time chance, Julian. Take it seriously.' Maddie put the coffee mugs on the table.

'Oh, I am, I am! I spoke to Roger and Freddy and they've been drilling me on what to do, what not to do, and so on and so on.'

'Were they surprised by Fleur's offer?' asked Maddie.

Julian eyed her. 'Nope. Not surprised.' He paused. Then he burst out laughing, and reached over to squeeze her arm. 'Of course they asked if you were going too!'

Maddie pursed her lips. 'And what did you say?'

Julian suddenly looked serious, reminding Maddie again of his quicksilver nature.

'Well, I said it wasn't my business, but . . .' He leaned towards her and said softly, 'I said I'd try to convince you.'

Then he closed his eyes, pursed his lips and waited.

Maddie's first reaction was to laugh and pull back, but Julian remained still, a small smile curving his mouth.

'I'm not kissing you. We're not on stage now,' she said firmly. 'Stop throwing fairy dust over me!'

He opened his eyes again and lifted his arms in playful surrender. 'C'mon, Ella . . . you and I make wonderful music!'

'And that's all we're going to make, Percy,' she said dryly.

Julian drained his mug and took it to the sink to rinse it out as Maddie's dad walked into the kitchen.

'Oh, sorry to interrupt. Got a minute, Mads?' He was smiling.

Julian looked at Michael. 'I'll head off. Talk soon, Maddie.' With a wave he let himself out.

'I didn't mean to scare away your friend.'

'It's okay, Dad. This is your home.'

'Not for long.' He paused and then the words rushed out. 'Your mother thinks Corbetts' farm is a good idea.'

Maddie was stunned. 'Really?! Wow, that's a surprise. She's always made such a fuss about living out of town.'

'Oh no, love! She thinks it's a good idea for me. She wants to stay up there on the Gold Coast.'

Maddie's heart sank. She had privately decided that if she bought Corbetts' farm for her father, she would also buy something for her mother. But she hadn't really believed it would come to that. It wasn't the money that bothered her so much as the idea that this schism in her family would never have come about if she hadn't won the lottery. Charlie's advice to lock it away and forget it came back to her. How she wished she could talk to him.

*

Leonie had dug out the box of her show memorabilia and sat on her bed surrounded by programs, Playhouse posters, photos, scripts, sheets of music and notebooks.

So many memories! She knew that everyone who'd been involved in each production probably felt the same way she did. It was like living in a special bubble for the months of rehearsals, the adrenalin rush of each performance and the sense of loss and adjustment when life returned to the mundane.

And the core, the catalyst of it all, was the Playhouse Theatre. It would be such a loss to the town in every way if it were demolished. Looking at her assorted show things around her, she was more determined than ever to fight for the magical old building.

However, between stopping the proposed demolition of the Playhouse and the possibility of a dam being constructed on her local river, she was feeling overwhelmed. She couldn't help wondering why she was doing all this when she could be out doing fun things with Corby. But soon her usual steely mindset reasserted itself. Those things were just wrong, and someone had to stand up and say so.

And, of course, she had Disneyland to look forward to with Corby, although secretly she couldn't help wondering what the Italian coast might be like at this time of year. *Not to worry*, she thought. There was always next year.

Just then, Leonie's phone rang, and she was pleasantly surprised to see Alistair's name come up on the screen. He was driving and couldn't chat long, but he said he would be passing through Fig Tree River again the following week and could stop by, as he had a few more suggestions about ways to have the Playhouse heritage listed.

Leonie hung up feeling much more positive about saving the Playhouse.

*

'Why are you all dressed up?' asked Corby.

'I'm not. I just want to be presentable, an architect is coming over to help us save the Playhouse.'

'How's he going to do that?' asked Corby.

'Well . . . by fighting red tape with red tape, I s'pose,' said Leonie. 'It's all to do with laws and paperwork, which is not my forte.'

Corby shrugged. 'It's a nice old building. I'm going to write about it for our history class.'

'Really? A school project? What a great idea. Do you want to talk to Alistair when he comes?'

Corby wrinkled his nose. 'Not really. I'm being picked up to go to the PCYC. See ya.' He headed outside.

*

Alistair gazed over the paddocks from the verandah as Leonie flipped through the documents he'd given her, trying to make sense of all the jargon.

'What a wonderful serene place you have here. Not what I expected,' said Alistair.

'Oh, really? What did you expect?' said Leonie with a smile, pushing the folders to one side.

'Well, I thought I'd see cattle – where are you hiding them? It all looks very pristine.'

'My late husband felt the land itself was more valuable than mobs of cattle and feed for them. We have kept a few head to pay the bills, though. He was into regenerative farming, recognising that there is value in the soil, the clean water, the protection of the natural environment.

He thought carbon credit schemes were ineffective and a rip-off. Why claim carbon credits, say, for a forest that a farmer was never going to log in the first place? It's a financial juggle on paper that achieves little in the reduction of actual emissions,' said Leonie.

Alistair nodded. 'Makes sense. As you say, when you see a place like this, you can appreciate where the real value lies.'

'Would you like to go for a walk? I can show you our creek which goes into the river.'

'I'd love to,' said Alistair.

'Maybe you could explain a bit more to me about the legal issues and paperwork I'm facing with the Playhouse. I thought buying it myself would be the solution, but I know that alone might not be enough. The heritage stuff seems quite complicated. I suppose I'll have to talk to my solicitor,' Leonie sighed.

'Oh, don't go to that expense. You'll already have all the costs involved with filing papers, requesting information and so on, not to mention the sale itself! Let me help you go through all that, and then if there's anything we can't cover, you could ask your solicitor.'

'That's very kind of you, Alistair. I appreciate it,' Leonie said gratefully.

'Of course,' he said. 'I feel like I've become quite invested in your lovely Playhouse!'

Leonie smiled, thankful that Alistair seemed to know what he was talking about. Also, it was so nice to share things with someone supportive again.

'Have you got time for a drink before you leave?' asked Leonie.

He smiled. 'Of course.'

12

IT WAS BREAKING MORNING. A gentle breeze, glinting leaves and soft shadows lined the old bush road in that time between the dark of night and sunrise.

'So pretty,' said Leonie. 'I love first light. So did your dad. He was always up at this time of day.'

'It's so hard to get up early, though,' said Corby with a yawn. He was nursing his backpack in his lap, dressed in hiking gear and sturdy boots.

'You might need to get used to it, I'm sure you'll be getting up early at camp!' she said with a chuckle.

'And then, yahoo! Disneyland, here we come!' exclaimed Corby.

Leonie smiled. He was so thrilled that she had finally

booked the tickets, and, Leonie had to admit, she was feeling excited about the trip too.

She swung around the corner before the big dip down to the river crossing, and suddenly there was a blurred shape in her peripheral vision, a grey streak lunging, then an almighty bang, and the car swerving as Corby screamed . . . '*Muuuuum!!*'

It would remain a nightmare scenario for both of them for years to come, the crashing slide off the road, then hurtling towards a massive tree . . . and then nothing, until Leonie became aware of a noise, a motor of some kind. Then she could smell hot metal as she was cut from the wreckage, a roaring sound, a screaming siren.

'Corby . . . where are you? Where's my son . . .?'

'It's okay, it's all right, love, hold on, we'll get you out of here.'

'Where's my son?' she sobbed.

'He's on his way to the hospital in another ambulance. Let's get you out, hold still . . .'

Everything went black.

*

Leonie awoke in the blandness of a hospital room, gradually hearing voices near her, distant jangles and buzzing. Then it all rushed back to her and she cried out, 'Corby . . . where are you?'

As Leonie tried to sit up, alarms went off and she realised she was attached by a variety of wires and tubes to a monitor.

A nurse hurried to her side.

'Leonie, it's okay. Please. Stay still.'

'Where's my son, Corby? Is he – is he – all right?'

'He's in the operating theatre, Leonie. Please, he's getting the best care. Let me help you.'

'No, no, please, I must see him.' Leonie's face was wet with tears as the nurse gently eased her back down onto the bed.

'I'll let you know as soon as he comes out of theatre. Please, rest for now,' said the nurse quietly. 'Here, take this.'

Leonie swallowed the pill she was given and lay back down, closing her eyes, her body still racked with sobs.

She had no idea how long it was before she woke up again. She grabbed the buzzer and held her finger on it.

A different nurse arrived, followed by a surgeon, still in his scrubs, who leaned over her and touched her hand. He smiled and said, 'Your son is a very lucky boy, Mrs Foster. The air bag saved him from the worst of the impact and from possible broken ribs. However, he has some substantial injuries which will take a little time to repair.'

'What injuries?' she demanded.

'A broken collarbone, severe bruising, and we've checked him for internal injuries. He's concussed, so he'll need to stay a few days so we can observe him.'

Leonie shut her eyes and the blurred images of the accident unravelled like an old movie in her mind. 'It was such a beautiful morning, then we went around a bend, and suddenly a kangaroo – I think – leaped out and I hit it . . . the poor thing.'

'Sadly it's not an uncommon accident,' said the surgeon.

Leonie balled her fists. 'Dear god, make Corby okay,' she prayed.

The doctor continued. 'You've come out of the accident with no major problems, Leonie, but your leg is very badly bruised. You might need to use a walking stick for a few days, but other than that you have been remarkably lucky.'

Leonie nodded. 'Thank you, Doctor.' She closed her eyes.

When Leonie next woke she had no idea of the time and felt very disoriented. Painfully she rolled onto her side and then stopped and blinked.

A figure was seated next to her bed.

'How are you feeling?' he asked softly.

'Alistair . . .?'

He reached out and gently touched her shoulder. 'Yes. I came as soon as I heard. Corby will be okay. You were both very lucky.'

'I don't feel very lucky,' said Leonie. 'Thank you for coming.'

She leaned back on her pillow. 'I'm being well taken care of. Maybe you could see if you can check on Corby for me, let him know I'm close by and I'm fine . . .?'

'Of course,' he said. 'Shall I do that now, to put you at ease?'

'Oh, please do. I really appreciate this, Alistair.'

'No problem.' He stroked her hand and stood up. 'Want me to bring you anything to drink, eat?'

Leonie closed her eyes. 'Sweet of you to ask. No, just let me know how Corby really is, then I'll feel better.' She opened her eyes again. 'How did you hear about the accident?'

'When you didn't answer your phone or reply to my messages yesterday, I rang your farm. Your man there told me what happened. And look, I wanted to say, put the issue with the Playhouse to one side for the moment, Lee. I'll keep tabs on it for you and make some enquiries.

You concentrate on getting better.' He patted her hand and headed for the door.

'But I don't want it sold to anyone else . . .' Leonie found she was feeling drowsy from the medication and the words felt heavy in her mouth. As she drifted back to sleep, she felt relieved Alistair had checked on her and Corby.

A day later, Leonie was wheeled along corridors to Corby's room, and both broke into smiles at the sight of each other.

Leonie smoothed his hair. 'I'm so sorry this happened, honey. We're very lucky. Poor old roo. Wasn't his fault. How are you feeling?'

'Sad. I missed the camp.'

'There'll be other camps,' Leonie said softly.

The next morning Leonie was given the news that she could go home, albeit with a walking stick. She was torn; she hated leaving Corby behind in the hospital.

Just as she was packing up to go, there was a tap at her door, and Leonie looked up to see Brett. 'Well, what a nice surprise, hi, Brett!'

'Sarita and Ray sent me. Well, what I mean is, I'm up keeping Ray company while Rita's doing whatever crazy thing she's doing with that island! Ray was going to come too but he had an appointment, so I said I'd come and help you escape.'

'That's so kind of you. I want to go home but I hate to leave Corby here alone,' she sighed.

'As you told Ray yourself, Leonie, Corby's doing well. He'll be home in no time. Now, let's get you out of here,' he said as he helped her into the wheelchair.

'This makes me feel like an old lady! I can get along okay with the walking stick,' protested Leonie.

'Hospital protocol, apparently. Once we get you into my car you'll feel better. Ray told me to look after you, so no arguments.'

'How's Sarita doing over there? Does Ray know when she's coming home?' asked Leonie as Brett picked up the plastic bag filled with her things. 'Seems like she's been gone for months.'

'Yeah, tell me about it. I was thinking of flying over to surprise her. But she says she's coming back, and it's so hard to communicate from the island. Anyway, will I take you around to see Corby before we go?'

'Oh yes, please. Absolutely.' Leonie sounded teary. 'Alistair – a new friend of mine who's helping me with the fight to protect the Playhouse – has been very kind visiting Corby and me. It's been a real help.'

'Oh, that's nice of him. Where did you find this Alistair?' asked Brett.

'He's a heritage architect who contacted me when he read about the council's plans.'

'Good to have his advice, I'd say. Okay, here we go.' Brett pushed her chair into the lift.

Corby was lying in bed bandaged and surrounded by monitors. He was playing with a phone, but looked up in surprise when they came in. 'You going home, Mum? When can I go?'

'Oh, darling boy . . .' Leonie leaned over to kiss him, clasping his hand. 'Soon, I hope. How do you feel?'

'All right. It's so boring in here.'

'That's a pretty fancy phone,' said Brett. 'You playing games or watching something?'

Corby put the phone to one side. 'Just texting friends.'

Leonie put out her hand. 'Is that a new phone? Show me, please.' Corby hesitated then handed it to her, and Leonie glanced at Brett before studying the phone. 'Where'd you get this? It's not yours.'

Corby looked uncomfortable. 'Well, Alistair gave it to me . . .'

'He *gave* it to you? Or lent it? This is an expensive phone. You can't keep it.'

'But mine got all banged up in the crash,' Corby began, sounding upset.

Leonie handed him back the phone. 'That's very nice of Alistair, but you can't keep it. When you come home we'll get you another phone. You don't need a two-thousand-dollar phone for texting your friends.'

'Hang in there a bit longer, mate,' said Brett. 'You'll be home soon.'

Corby's eyes began to fill with tears. 'What about Disneyland, Mum . . .?'

'We'll still go, darling. Yep, definitely. We'll just delay it till we're both fit again.'

Corby looked at Brett. 'Do you think I'll still be able to play soccer and stuff . . .?'

Brett smiled reassuringly. 'Yep, definitely. You'll start physio exercises soon enough. You just have to do everything they say in here. I know you'll do your best to get fit again. The sooner you're stronger, the quicker you can go home.'

'Okay. I'll try. Can you come and see me, Mum?'

'Of course, every day, sweetheart. And I'll bring some of your mates in too.' She leaned over and kissed him, saying as evenly as she could, 'I'm so, so sorry, darling . . .'

'Wasn't your fault, Mum . . . stupid roo.'

After hugs and goodbyes Brett wheeled Leonie out of the room, and they heard the sounds of a skateboarding comp start up on Corby's phone.

'Funny thing to give a kid you've only just met,' said Brett. 'Tell me more about this Alistair.'

*

Chrissie was in her element. She pulled down her face mask, pushed her protective goggles up on her head and looked at the women around her.

'See, it's quite simple when you get the angle right, and you are breathing well and no dust is blowing in your face.' She put down the electric sander.

'It makes such a difference, I love how the old paint just blows away as coloured dust,' said one woman.

'I'm not going to repaint mine. I love the old wood. I think I'll just varnish it,' said another, running her hands over the old wooden table.

'Good idea. That looks like cedar. Apparently there was a lot growing around here in the old days. I once saw an old farm gate made from cedar,' said Chrissie.

'What a waste!'

Chrissie checked her watch. 'We'll have to call it a day, I'm afraid,' she said. 'We can do a final check of our pieces tomorrow and get down to the final coat you want.'

The five women chatted as they packed up, each looking pleased with the work they'd done on stripping the pieces of furniture they'd brought along to refresh under Chrissie's guidance in the newly created Women's Shed.

Penny bustled over. 'Here, let me help you put away all that stuff.'

'Pen, don't worry, that's my job,' said Chrissie. 'It was so good of you to arrange the use of this place. I've really loved it.'

'Well, it was just sitting here empty most of the time,'

she said. 'You know, you're not the only one getting something out of this. Look how enthusiastic everyone was. You're a natural communicator.'

'Oh, I don't know about that,' Chrissie said, flushing with self-consciousness, but she felt rather pleased at the compliment.

'Are you kidding? This has been so great!' Penny waved towards the other women, who were still chatting happily and exclaiming in wonder over what they had achieved, and Chrissie grinned.

However, her high spirits faded when she walked into the apartment and saw Troy standing at the living room windows, his baseball cap backwards on his head, a beer bottle in his hand. She could tell by his stance and his demeanour the minute he turned around and glared at her that he was in a bad mood.

'Where the hell have you been?' he demanded.

'I told you I'd be at the Women's Shed this afternoon.' She walked into the kitchen, her back to him, trying to sound calm.

'And just where are our fucking kids while you're out doing this stupid shit? It's unnecessary and a complete waste of your time. Women's bloody sheds – there's no such stupid thing.'

'There is now.' Chrissie opened a cupboard and took out a coffee mug. 'And the children are doing after-school activities till 4 pm, fully supervised.'

'Don't be a smart-arse with me!' He flung the beer bottle, which smashed against the cupboard, splintering glass across the floor.

Chrissie jumped. 'What is the matter with you?' she shouted, starting to shake.

Troy glared at her. 'The matter with *me*? Look at you!

Do you think you can just do whatever you want? Just because we have money now –'

'It's my money,' whispered Chrissie, unable to stop the tears that leaked from her eyes and ran down her cheeks.

Troy's face turned purple and he leaped at her and grabbed her hair, the broken glass crunching under his shoes.

'Look at me. Whaddya mean, *your* money?' He slapped her face.

'I'm sorry, Troy . . .' Chrissie tried to pull away from him, her hand on her stinging cheek, but Troy grabbed her by the shoulder, pulling at her blouse until they were only inches apart.

'What's yours is mine. Don't you forget it. Now go and get the kids – I don't want them messing around doing God knows what. You can clean this up when you get back, and then you can try to cook something edible. And no more fucking Women's Shed. What a joke.' Pushing her roughly away, he went to the fridge and grabbed another beer as Chrissie fumbled for her handbag and fled to the front door, inching it silently shut behind her.

She leaned against it, tears spilling down her cheeks, before fishing for a tissue to wipe her face. Then she headed towards the lifts, putting on her sunglasses to hide her reddened eyes.

*

Within two weeks of becoming the owner of Totoka Island, Sarita had mobilised a small team who were enthusiastically clearing, building, installing water tanks, a generator, solar panels and a satellite dish. The half-finished main house was being transformed into an airy, if somewhat basic, pavilion. Sarita's design was for two wings on either side of the open-plan area which would be private bedroom and living areas, one facing the peak and lush forest, the other facing the sea.

Varo walked around the skeletal framework with Sarita. He had slipped easily into his newly expanded role of caretaker/site foreman/security person.

'This is some record for work here in Fiji,' he said with a smile.

'Yes, I'm pleased with how it's going,' Sarita replied. 'But I must get back to Australia to see my husband and check on things there. I need you to keep these workers on track while I'm away. The architect will come over, too, to see how things are going. The gardens and entertainment area will be next. Outdoor cooking and eating, a pool.'

'But you have the ocean,' said Varo.

'It's tidal. We'd like a pool close to the house,' said Sarita enthusiastically. 'The lagoon is too far away.'

'Lot of work,' said Varo. 'How often are you going to come here?'

Sarita shrugged. 'Not sure yet.' She hadn't told him that her husband didn't fully support this plan yet, or that her sons didn't know about it at all. 'I want my husband to see what we've done in such a short time.'

Varo nodded. 'So, you will come back before storm time?'

Sarita looked at him. 'How bad and how long is storm time?'

The big man shrugged. 'Who knows now? Everything is upside down with climate change.' Seeing Sarita's concerned expression he added, 'Don't worry, boss, these workers will make everything strong.'

Sarita glanced out at the tropical palms and thick remnant jungle. 'No short cuts, okay?'

He nodded. 'No worries. I'll make sure everyone does a good job.' Varo held up a thumb and grinned.

At sundown, Sarita walked to the beach and watched two of the workers take their launch back to the main island where they had families. They'd return at first light next morning. The three other workers were bunking down in a temporary shelter attached to Varo's place on the other side of the island.

It was the time of day she loved the most, when the sun set over the endless sea and the universe seemed to hold its breath just before the night closed in, the evening breeze rustling the palm fronds as the sea lapped gently at the shore.

She missed Ray and the boys, and despite the progress on the build and the exquisite setting, she had begun to feel strung-out and anxious. Maybe she was just tired. These were long, steamy days, the only respite from the heat being when she jumped into the sea at regular intervals. Every now and then she wondered if she was doing the right thing here, but she always quickly pushed the thought aside. She was too far in now, so the only way was forward. The family would all love the island paradise when it was done, she reminded herself.

How her life had changed. It was still hard to believe what had happened to her and her three friends. Winning a fortune was a complete turnaround in her life. She still found it hard to believe she was doing all this, and felt so happy and fulfilled.

*

Maddie sat facing the solicitor behind the desk, her parents on either side of her, the paperwork completed in front of them.

'Well, the only thing left to say is that a farm and an apartment on the Gold Coast is a pretty big outlay, Madison.' He paused as Maddie looked back steadily at him while her mother looked out the window and her father looked down at his clasped hands. The solicitor continued, 'Therefore I would suggest you speak with your financial advisor about investing what remains of your estate until sometime in the future.'

Maddie nodded. 'I will. Thank you.'

Silently they filed out of the office.

When Maddie reached her car, she looked at her parents.

'Well, it's done. I hope you'll both be happy now.'

'It's not like we're getting divorced,' said her mother, trying to sound light-hearted. 'We just want . . . different things now.'

'I know,' said Maddie tiredly. 'You two work it out. I have other things to do. I'll see you both later.'

'Is she moving out?' Maddie heard her dad ask her mother.

'She'll have to. We only rent in Fig Tree River, remember, and the owners are selling up. We have no choice but to move out. Maddie will be fine. I'll talk to you later.'

Maddie sat in her car, gripping the wheel as she saw her parents walk away in different directions. A tear ran down her cheek. This felt worse than a divorce.

She needed to talk to someone about how she was feeling. She picked up her phone and dialled Charlie, but there was no answer.

She wiped her face and scrolled through her phone, then hit another button.

Fleur's smiling face came into view on her phone.

'Maddie, how lovely to see you, so early in the morning! How are you doing, gorgeous gal?'

'Oh, Fleur. I don't feel very gorgeous. There's been a few hassles here with my parents. It's sorted now, but I just needed to hear a friendly voice . . .' She took a shaky breath.

'Do you want to talk about it?' asked Fleur gently, looking concerned.

'Not really. Well, some other time. When I see you, perhaps . . .?'

'What! You're coming over! Oh Maddie, that's wonderful. Smart move. How soon can you be here?'

'As soon as I get a passport. Then I can travel.'

'Well then, get here as quick as you can. I know you said you don't want to audition for the show, but bring your music.'

'You mean my compositions? No one will be interested in those.'

'Someone might, so bring them on paper, okay?'

'Why? I have them all in my head.'

'I thought you'd been learning notation? I can't send your head to people.'

Maddie was a bit unnerved. 'Send them to people? Are you sure?'

'Of course. This is exactly what you should be doing. In fact, it's perfect timing. Go and book the flight then text or call me with the details. You can stay here with me for as long as you want. I'm so thrilled you're coming!'

'Me too!' Maddie laughed, suddenly feeling excited.

*

Other than her parents, Maddie decided not to tell anyone her plans until everything was in place.

First she rang her mother, who said, 'Well, I guess travelling is no surprise. You had to move out and move on anyway. Has Dad started to pack up his gear?'

'He's in the process. I think he's getting excited, but he's still a bit nervous about taking a farm on again.'

'He should turf out a lot of his old stuff and buy some decent clothes.'

'Why, Mum? He'll be living on a farm, so he's going to need his old work clothes. He does love it. He went over and fixed the tractor the other day. And gosh, he loves the dogs that are there.'

'Dogs are too noisy. When he comes up here he'll need new clothes. Can't hang out with me looking like a hayseed! But Julie and I will take him shopping.'

'Good luck with getting him into Hawaiian shirts or whatever, Mum!' Maddie laughed.

'Yeah. Well, we'll do our best.'

'Mum, you know Dad isn't the type to hang out at cafés and the bowling club or wherever it is you go. I hope you'll also come down and see him at the farm. Help him get settled.'

'He said he didn't need me to help him. But Julie and I will certainly visit.'

'Okay. Well, I just want you both to be happy.'

'You get on with your life, Mads. Don't you worry about us. You know, this might turn out to be a good thing for Dad and me. We might have something to talk about when we see each other now. But you keep in touch and call us, okay?'

'Of course.' Maddie felt a rush of relief, as if she'd been holding her breath. She hadn't heard her mother sound so bright in ages. Maybe the new direction her parents were taking wouldn't be so bad after all. For the first time, she felt lucky and relieved that the windfall of money had made all this change possible. On her financial advisor's advice, she had also stashed away the nest egg that was left and arranged a modest payment to herself each month. It meant that even though she was nervous about leaving Fig Tree River and what might lie ahead, she was excited too.

*

Harry was working by the front verandah when Brett pulled up in the driveway and parked. They helped Leonie to get from the car into the house.

'Oh, it's so good to be home,' she sighed as she sank into a chair.

'How's the lad?' asked Harry.

'They say he'll be okay,' she replied, relief clear in her tone.

'Can I make you a coffee? Tea?' asked Brett.

'No thanks, I'm fine. How're things going here, Harry?' she asked.

'No problems. Haven't seen anyone around lately – maybe that dam idea has gone on the backburner,' said Harry.

'Why don't I check on that for you,' said Brett. 'In fact, I'd like to take a hike around the creek and up the hill. Get the lie of the land before I call in the experts to do an environmental assessment.'

'Of course. Harry, can you show Brett around?' said Leonie.

'Sure, want to go now?' said Harry.

As Harry and Brett pulled on their hats and were about to head outside, there were footsteps on the verandah and a call through the front door.

'Leonie, are you home at last?'

'In here, Alistair,' she called.

A smiling Alistair came through the door carrying a huge bouquet of flowers.

'Welcome home!'

'Oh, my goodness. These are beautiful. Thanks, Alistair. I just arrived, actually. This is my good friend, Brett. His sister and brother-in-law live in Fig Tree River. And Harry, my right-hand man and dear friend.'

'Ah, yes, we spoke on the phone, Harry. Great to meet you, Brett,' Alistair said as the men shook hands.

'Can I make you a coffee?' said Brett.

'I'm fine, thanks. I had a milkshake with Corby earlier. I'll put these in water, shall I? Point me to the vases,' said Alistair.

'Alistair, that reminds me, you shouldn't have given Corby that flash phone,' began Leonie.

He held up his hand. 'I know, I know, it's a lot. I just felt bad that his was smashed up in the accident. And don't worry, he can't access porn or gambling sites or anything, I locked all those. You have access to his phone at all times to see what he's watching and when he gets out of hospital you can track his location.'

'I'm impressed,' said Brett, smiling. Then he said his goodbyes before he went out to join Harry who was waiting for him on the verandah.

'Do you have kids, Alistair?' Leonie asked.

'No,' he said softly. 'My wife died before we could have children.'

'Oh, I'm sorry, that's so sad,' exclaimed Leonie.

'Thank you. Well, I'll put these flowers in water then come back.'

Leonie sighed deeply. She was happy to be home but

terribly upset that she still didn't know when Corby would be out of hospital and mobile again.

She smiled when Alistair came in carrying the vase of flowers. 'Thank you very much. You know, while I was in hospital I had a lot of time to think, and I was imagining how lovely it'd be if a balcony bar could be added upstairs at the Playhouse, overlooking the river. It could double as a small function room. All in keeping with heritage values, of course.'

'You're a big ideas person,' said Alistair. 'But taking on the Playhouse Theatre is a pretty ambitious plan. It's a lot of money, so you need to know it will be a smart business proposition.'

'Sometimes people do things for sentimental and altruistic reasons,' said Leonie.

'But that's not always smart business practice,' said Alistair.

'I guess so.' Feeling rather cooped up, Leonie pushed herself to her feet, leaning on her stick, and headed towards the kitchen.

'Hey, be careful. Are you ready for this?'

Leonie's walking stick caught on the edge of the rug, and as she stumbled, Alistair leaped forward.

'Got you!' He caught and held her as she steadied herself. For a moment, as he clasped his arms around her, Leonie felt his strong body, the drift of aftershave and his warm breath on her neck. She felt an impulse to lean into him and stay there in the protective strength of his arms.

'Oh, how clumsy of me.' She straightened up.

'Better pull up some of the rugs and mats till you're steady and have tossed the stick, eh?'

'Good idea. I'll ask Harry and our young worker, Stevie, if they can do that for me.'

'You sure you're going to be okay on your own?' he asked, looking concerned.

'I'm not alone. Stevie and Harry are a minute or two away. And I have my phone in my pocket. I'll be fine. Thanks so much for all your help, Alistair. And I must fix you up for Corby's phone –' began Leonie, but Alistair brushed the suggestion aside.

'Keeps him occupied. But he did ask for some books to read. I can go to the library tomorrow and take them to him when I see him next.'

'That's too much trouble –' began Leonie as Alistair again waved a hand.

'It's okay, really. I have time tomorrow.'

'Isn't all this out of your way?' asked Leonie. 'I'm very grateful but I don't want to put you out . . .'

'I'm staying with an old mate nearby and helping fix up some issues for him. That's what I was going to tell you when I couldn't get hold of you the day of the accident. So I'll be around for a few days, maybe a week. It's no trouble.'

'Well, thank you,' said Leonie.

'I'll check in with you again soon. Take care, Lee.'

*

Sarita found the port very busy and crowded after the isolation and peace of her island.

She'd allowed herself two days to adjust, shop, maybe go to a beauty salon and have her hair and nails done. She realised she must look like a wild woman after doing little more than bathing and swimming and using her sunblock the past few weeks. She had worn a hat woven from palm fronds that Varo had made her.

First thing the next morning, she set out from her small harbour hotel and spent two hours in a nearby beauty shop before buying herself a sundress and sandals from a local store.

Feeling like a new woman, she went to find the little café where she had arranged to meet Stuart and fill him in on her progress on the island.

As Sarita walked she passed a jewellery store where a young woman was staring at the display in the window. Sarita wondered idly if she should buy some gifts, but it was the beautiful shells used as props that caught her eye.

The woman at the window turned and saw Sarita, then gasped.

'Cousin Sarita! It's me, Dobra!'

'Oh my gosh, how lovely to see you. What a surprise,' said Sarita to her second cousin.

'You came back so soon! Why haven't you visited us? Nani would love to see you!'

Sarita felt embarrassed that she hadn't contacted the Chands, but quickly said, 'I've been on an island for several weeks, actually. I've only just returned. What are you doing here?'

'I'm here on business for my brother. And while I'm here I thought I'd buy a gift for Purnima's birthday.' She nodded at the jewellery store. 'So, have you been chilling out at a resort?'

Sarita shook her head. 'No. I've been on a privately owned island that's being restored.'

'Which island is that?' asked Dobra.

'Oh just a small, quiet place, Totoka.'

'Oh really? Is it open again? Who're the new owners, I wonder?'

'Well, me, actually. I bought it,' blurted Sarita.

The young woman clapped her hands. 'How fabulous. But where is your family and your nice husband?'

'At home in Australia. I'm doing this myself. With a lot of help, of course. It's a surprise for them . . . although Ray knows, naturally.'

'Why did you not ask us for help? We could have advised you about who to contact to hire workers, those sorts of things.'

'Oh, I didn't want to bother you. I found a great guy who hires the right people,' said Sarita. 'I'll invite you all over when I'm finished.'

'That would be wonderful. Would you come and help me choose a gift for Purnima?'

Sarita felt she couldn't refuse, but after a while she found herself enjoying her cousin's company. They laughed a lot and admired the jewellery before selecting an engraved gold bangle.

'When are you leaving?' asked Dobra. 'Would you like to have lunch with me?'

'Oh, I'm sorry, I can't! I have to meet my island contractor before he leaves. How about this evening?'

'I have to fly to Suva this afternoon as there's a cyclone forecast. Please catch up with us if you have time, before you go home to Australia.'

'A cyclone!' Sarita looked alarmed.

'Oh, don't worry too much, it could be anywhere in the area and change direction. Besides, the hotels here are cyclone safe.'

'Okay, if you say so.' Sarita smiled nervously.

They exchanged a hug and Sarita was warmed to know she really did have family in the islands now.

*

'Hi there. Been out for your morning run?' teased Alistair when Leonie answered her phone.

'Not quite, but I'm doing really well. Surprised the physio a few days ago. I've got a sort of mini-gym set up for Corby and me, now that he's home, and we're going great guns. How're you, Alistair?'

'Going well too. I have some news for you.'

'About the Playhouse?'

'Yes. It looks like I can get it heritage listed. Need to look at a few details more closely, which won't affect what you might want to do. But the hint of "heritage listed" can mean a headache to a lot of developers and builders.'

'Those with no imagination, or who don't follow guidelines and suggestions to have the new complement the old?' suggested Leonie.

'Yes, as well as those who don't want any extra costs or frills,' he chuckled.

'Great. Well done.' Leonie smiled.

'Might be a bit of an invoice attached, if that's okay? I've had to get a few second opinions on how best to tackle the building issues,' said Alistair. 'I'll come by with some paperwork in a few days. You up for going out to lunch or dinner?'

'Love to,' said Leonie. 'I'm going a bit stir-crazy inside, what with not being able to drive yet.'

'Then it's a date,' said Alistair warmly.

Is it? wondered Leonie. Then thought, *Why not?*

*

'Hi Stuart, what's happening?' asked Sarita cheerfully when they met at the café by the marina that had become their informal office.

For once, Stuart was not quite his nonchalant, relaxed self. 'I'm a bit concerned about this cyclone they're predicting.'

'Oh yes, I was told about it, but it didn't sound like something to worry about.'

'Well, the meteorological service has put out a warning and the forecast is not looking good. Your island could be right in the cyclone's path. Hard to say whether it'll stay category two or three – but neither will be very safe. Wouldn't be many places for anyone to shelter, and the satellite communication could go down.'

'But Varo is there at the moment, and he has his young daughter, Jinti, with him,' said Sarita with a worried frown.

'He didn't leave with you?'

'No. He stayed to supervise the work, and when we spoke on the phone yesterday he said his daughter was going over that afternoon. I think it's the school holidays. Do I need to get them off? I wonder if his phone is still working. What can I do?' Sarita felt a bit helpless.

Stuart shrugged. 'It might not happen. Luck of the draw with cyclones round the islands here – some get hit, some don't.'

'Well, I can't just do nothing,' exclaimed Sarita. She pulled out her phone and tried ringing the number of Varo's satellite phone, but she got an immediate automated message saying there was no signal. She tried again, with the same result. She thought hard for a minute and then asked Stuart, 'Can we hire someone to go and get them?'

Stuart stared at Sarita's concerned face. 'If, and just if, someone was stupid enough to try and get them off with a cyclone predicted, they'd charge a bloody fortune!'

'Which I'd pay,' said Sarita evenly.

Stuart's eyes narrowed and he looked at her. 'How much?'

'Depends whether they rescue them,' said Sarita.

Stuart glanced at his watch, counting to himself, then said brusquely, 'We have four hours. There and back before the cyclone hits.'

'We?'

He raised his eyebrows as he stood up. 'Let's go down to my boat and work out what we need.'

They raced along the marina and Stuart jumped on board a compact launch with *You Bewdy* written along the side, reaching out his hand to help Sarita as she climbed on.

'Your boat is called *You Bewdy*?' she laughed, and for a moment she felt less anxious.

Stuart quickly but methodically began pulling out gear and untying canvas covers. 'Okay,' he said. 'I have a big tarp. Water. First aid. Radio backup. Flares. Extra lifebelts. Spotlights, torches. For starters.'

'Food?'

'It's not a picnic, but yes, I have enough.' He glanced at Sarita. 'You're not wearing sensible clothes but I think there's a bag of things in the galley cupboard you can change into if necessary. I have a lifeboat and life jackets. I'll need you to manage the radio while we can still get reception.' He stopped and looked at her again. 'You sure you're up for this?'

Sarita nodded. 'Yes, I'll have to be, they're my responsibility.'

They headed from the lee of the island into the white-capped ocean. The sun was out and the breeze refreshing as the bow dipped between waves.

Stuart grinned and raised his arms from the wheel for a moment. 'Totoka, here we come!'

Maybe it will be fine, thought Sarita. As she looked

ahead, she found it hard to imagine anything sinister was heading their way.

Stuart had notified the harbour authority they were going to Totoka and there'd been some exchange between them that she hadn't heard clearly. She glanced down again at her phone, on which she'd continued to try to reach Varo. Nothing.

Stuart stuck his head out of the cockpit. He didn't look quite as cheerful as he had before.

'We'd better make this rescue fast. I'll moor and I'll have to stay with the boat when we get there. Where do you reckon they'll be?'

'With the phone down, they won't have any clue what's heading their way,' said Sarita worriedly. 'I'll go to the main building first. Hopefully they're camped there and not over at the lagoon side in Varo's tent.'

'Yeah. Right.' Stuart nodded. 'Has he got a boat there, for fishing maybe?'

'Yes. Just a little tinnie. I doubt he'd take that far from the island,' said Sarita, but it was another thing to worry about.

Stuart didn't answer, but pushed the throttle a little more and the boat surged forward, throwing Sarita off balance.

'Sorry! We've got to give it all she's got.'

Sarita nodded as she steadied herself.

The trip seemed to take forever as *You Bewdy* cleaved through the water. Sarita looked anxiously at the clouds banking up in the distance, and she could feel the wind becoming much stronger. Then, when Stuart gave her a wave and pointed, Sarita was flooded with relief to see the thin black line of the island silhouetted against the horizon.

When they came close, Stuart held the boat steady and Sarita jumped into the waist-deep water and waded ashore in the casual clothes and sneakers she'd found in the galley. She held on tightly to the police whistle Stuart had given her.

'Remember, three long whistles if you need help, and I'll find you. Or three short whistles, which means you've got 'em and are coming back to the boat,' Stuart called to her.

Sarita ran, oblivious to the undergrowth thrashing against her, praying that Varo and Jinti were at the main building even though it was unfinished.

Panting, she slowed when she saw the outline of the gracious structure blending so well into its surroundings, and stressed though she was, a feeling of pride and pleasure rushed through her.

'Varo . . . are you there?' she shouted. 'Hello, anyone here . . .?' Her voice rang out in the serene setting.

She listened for a moment but heard only silence. Sarita had started down the path that led across the island to Varo's camp when she heard a voice.

'Sarita! We're here,' shouted Varo, hurrying towards her and holding the hand of a small girl. *This must be Jinti*, Sarita thought, and her heart went out to the child, who looked about five years old and was clutching a toy tightly.

Flooded with relief, Sarita ran to them. 'Oh, thank goodness. You have to leave, there's a cyclone coming. Stuart is at the beach to collect us.'

'I know, storm coming. We were hunkering down as best we could. You came back for us . . .' He was visibly moved. He picked up Jinti and they began jogging the way Sarita had come.

'You knew? You have reception?' gasped Sarita as they ran.

'No. The birds, great flocks heading the wrong way. I figured something was going on.'

'They say it could be bad,' said Sarita.

Varo nodded and Jinti clung to him. As they set off, Sarita blew the whistle in three short bursts. Finally they reached the beach, waded out to the boat and scrambled aboard.

Although there was still sunshine and blue sky, the wind had picked up and the waves seemed to surge from a great depth rather than roiling over the surface. Stuart frowned as he studied the screens in the wheelhouse.

'Barometer is dropping,' he said. He moved to one side. 'Here, take the wheel while I check the weather forecast. Keep going in that direction.' He pointed at the compass.

Sarita took the helm, seeing little to guide her in any direction but keeping her eye on the compass. Struggling to keep her balance, she shifted into the seat at the wheel. She glanced back at Varo, who was cuddling Jinti. He gave her a smile and a nod.

Stuart was bent over his laptop, and after a few moments he straightened.

'What've you found?' The wind whipped her words from the little cockpit.

He didn't answer but turned the screen around, which showed her the classic swirling circle of clouds.

'Cyclone,' he said.

'How far away is it?' she asked.

Varo lifted an arm and pointed. 'Look . . .'

There was a long band of dark clouds tinged with a greenish glow against the horizon.

'Is it coming this way? How long do we have?' asked Sarita nervously.

'Hard to say.' Stuart reached under a bench and began pulling out life jackets. 'Take this, Varo. I have a kid's one in here somewhere . . .'

Sarita closed the clasp on her orange life jacket. 'Is there somewhere closer we could get to? How much further to the main island?'

'Nothing closer, we'll have to run for it. It'll miss us, collect us or catch us in its tail. Varo, take your daughter into the cabin below. You too, Sarita.'

'You sure I can't do anything for you?' asked Sarita.

Stuart gave a bit of a smile. 'Have a few words to whatever deity you think might help.'

Below deck, Jinti looked terrified. Sarita opened a drawer and found some cards and a small jigsaw puzzle. She tipped the pieces onto the table.

The three of them pored over the puzzle until suddenly the boat lurched to one side and the pieces slid away. Jinti cried out in alarm.

Stuart shouted from the cockpit. 'Sea is getting up.'

They sat in silence, Varo holding Jinti tightly, her face pressed into his chest.

Sarita closed her eyes, thinking of Ray, their children, their new home, all the plans they were making. What was she doing here?

Sarita could hear Varo murmuring to Jinti. The boat, full throttle, was making hard headway. As she sat, eyes closed, the effort and stress of the day caught up with her, and time seemed to escape, stop, drift away.

She opened her eyes. Varo gave her a gentle, relieved smile.

'Hey there. Had a nice nap?' yelled Stuart. 'We're

nearly back! The edge of the cyclone will hit the town, but most places are cyclone-safe here. We'll be okay.'

'Stuart, I don't know how I can ever repay you,' began Sarita.

'Oh, I think we can find a way,' he replied with a grin.

13

THE AIRPORT WAS CROWDED. Maddie was nervous, but having spent the last couple of weeks in a whirlwind of preparation for her trip, she was excited now too. She hadn't even owned a suitcase before, let alone the sorts of clothes she'd felt she would need in New York, so she'd made several trips to the nearest big shopping centre. The café staff and her old schoolfriends had given her a send-off a few days previously, and she'd spent time helping her father move to the farm and settle in. She'd also visited Leonie to check how she was going and to thank her again for asking her to be part of the show, which had set all this in motion. Freddy and Roger had driven her to the airport and farewelled her effusively. After checking in and going through Departures, she called her mother. The one person she hadn't spoken to was Charlie.

Maddie lost track of time as the hours passed in the plane, but watched out the window open-mouthed as they descended to land and New York City spread out below her like a scene from a movie. She couldn't quite believe any of it. She was still unprepared for the sudden shock of finding herself in the midst of the bustling JFK Airport, and went through Customs in a daze. It was the busiest place she'd ever been to.

The immigration officer handed Maddie back her passport. 'Welcome to the United States, Miss.'

Maddie smiled. 'Thank you.'

Suddenly she felt ready for anything the world might throw at her.

*

Sarita was enjoying every minute of the *lovo*, as Varo told her this feast was called. The heat radiated from the pit in the ground where a suckling pig had been cooking for several hours.

Spread on large palm leaves on the mat in front of them was a feast of taro and cassava, raw fish marinated in coconut milk, lime and chilli, as well as fresh local prawns and crab surrounded by myriad small side dishes.

But it was the warm and friendly family and friends gathered at Varo's home, Jinti's small hand in hers – the child had taken a shine to Sarita – and the singing and laughing that made Sarita wish that Ray was there to share it.

The close call with the cyclone had rattled everyone, though. Beneath the happy façade, Sarita heard concerned conversations between the islanders about their fears for their future as tourism was being threatened by increasing cyclones caused by climate change.

'It's the kids. What's little Jinti going to face when she's all grown up?' said Varo. 'Climate change is already wrecking these islands; some are already going under with the sea level rising. In the last few years we've had more cyclones and mixed-up weather than we ever used to have.' He shook his head sadly.

Sarita listened as the men and women talked local politics. Then she glanced at Stuart, who was happy with a beer in his hand and talking and laughing with a couple of young women.

A short time later he tapped Sarita on the shoulder.

'You ready to zip over to Totoka and check things out?'

'Now?!'

'Of course not! At a sensible time tomorrow morning,' he said.

'Yes. That'll be great,' said Sarita.

'It's not going to be pretty, I'd say.'

Sarita sighed. 'Let's wait and see. I'll meet you at *You Bewdy* around 10 am.'

*

Stuart looked a little seedy as they set out the following morning.

The ocean seemed friendlier than it had when they'd gone to rescue Varo and Jinti. But as they neared Totoka, Sarita saw that the sea looked slightly cloudy and there was debris floating on the surface.

She had a bad feeling. At the height of the cyclone on the night they'd returned to the main island, the howling wind had worried her even in the safety of her hotel room.

Several boats had smashed against the pier, and one had broken its moorings. She'd seen a lot of tree branches and palm fronds scattered around outside the next morning, and the town had looked like the aftermath of a riot or a reckless party: messy but fortunately not deadly. But Totoka had been in the path of the cyclone proper.

Stuart cut the engine back and peered ahead for any large debris in the water.

The first thing Sarita noticed when the island came into view was that there were no palm trees silhouetted against the sky. Stuart was silent as they drew closer.

As they rounded the point to moor in the lee of the rocks, she gasped.

'Shit,' said Stuart.

He cut the motor and they glided to the shore. Sarita couldn't believe the mess facing them. The beach was littered with debris from the forest. Trees had been ripped out of the ground, which was covered with shredded leaves, branches, coconuts and palm fronds. The magical forest walk looked like a herd of monsters had chewed and slashed a path wide enough for an army to follow.

Sarita said what they were both thinking. 'What's the building going to be like . . .'

*

It had been flattened. If monsters had chewed through the rainforest, then one of them had squashed the beautiful home-to-be flat with a giant foot as it stomped across the island, as if it were inconsequential leaf litter in its path.

Sarita stopped, her hand to her mouth, tears springing to her eyes.

'Bloody hell,' Stuart muttered beside her. He put his arm over her shoulders. 'I'm really sorry, Sarita.'

She couldn't speak. Slowly she walked forward, hoping it would all vanish and her dream building would materialise.

'It's not just this place . . . it's the whole island!' Sarita managed to say. It was utterly devastating.

'Yeah, the place is totally wrecked,' said Stuart bluntly. 'What're you going to do now?'

Sarita was just trying to absorb the enormity of what was in front of her. Making a decision was far from her mind.

'I don't know, Stuart. I just don't know.'

*

Chrissie ushered Thomas and Mia in front of her as she opened the apartment door.

They dropped their schoolbags and raced into the kitchen.

'Can we go to the park?'

'I guess so. Go and get changed and we'll have an afternoon snack first.'

They were heading back out when Troy's voice suddenly bellowed from behind them, making Chrissie jump.

'Where do you think you're going?'

Chrissie jerked around. 'Oh, I didn't know you were here. I'm just taking the kids to the park to work off some energy. We won't be long.'

'Why do you have to go out all the time? What do you do? Why can't they play in their rooms?' he snapped.

'They like to meet with their friends,' said Chrissie. 'It's not as much fun to have their friends over here. There's no backyard.'

'Well, what about you?' he said. 'You like to meet friends too?' he said accusingly.

'You don't have to use that tone of voice,' she answered as calmly as she could.

'Don't tell me how to talk! Kids, go to your rooms.'

'Why? But Dad, we want to play –'

'Mind what I say,' he yelled. 'Get to your rooms because I said so!'

The children scurried away.

'Troy,' began Chrissie, 'that's not fair. They've been cooped up at school for hours.'

'Why're you so keen to get out? Who're you meeting?'

'Troy, don't be ridiculous.' Chrissie turned away in exasperation. But he was behind her in an instant, slamming his hand down on her shoulder.

'Don't you turn your back on me!' he yelled, spinning her around to face him.

'Troy, for God's sake, stop it. Just stop it!' she shouted.

'Don't you dare yell at me. Just because you got lucky with a fluky win, you think you can be the boss around here, do whatever you like.' He gave a nasty smile. 'Don't get too big for your boots, babe.'

'Don't you threaten me,' said Chrissie, but she had started to tremble.

Troy leaned close and hissed, 'I don't have to threaten. I take action when I don't like what's going on.'

'What's that mean?' said Chrissie.

'Think back to your last stupid thing at the Playhouse, eh? A little accident and all your work gets burned up.' He smirked at her.

Chrissie stared at him. He kept smiling.

In a whisper, Chrissie said slowly, 'You...you started that fire and burned my sets down for *Percy and Ella*. You tried to stop me going there.'

'Never met any Percy or Ella.' Troy shrugged. 'But don't you think you can hang out with a couple of fellas without me noticing,' he added.

'Who do you mean? I was *working* with them,' burst out Chrissie. 'There were just a couple of guys helping with the play.'

'So you'd rather be with them than at home with me and your kids – *where you belong*?!' he yelled.

Chrissie stared at him then spun on her heel. 'That's crazy, Troy –'

Troy grabbed her by the hair and yanked her to him, wrenching her around to glare into her face. 'Don't... you...muck...around with *me*, bitch!'

He shoved her away and Chrissie stumbled then ran from the room.

Troy slammed his office door shut as Chrissie fell on her bed sobbing. For a moment she considered locking the door, but she figured Troy would just kick it in if he wanted to. He hadn't lost his temper this badly since he'd smashed his beer bottle and slapped her some weeks before. She didn't want to upset him any more.

She buried her face in the pillow as she heard him bellow to the children to do their homework.

*

Leonie stood in the front yard surrounded by three men and two women, all dressed in what looked like hiking gear. Boxes of equipment were being unloaded from two trucks. Another woman with a clipboard was supervising the group as Leonie listened.

Alistair drove up to the house and got out of his car, and Leonie walked over to him.

'Hi, what's going on here?' he asked.

'Good to see you, Alistair,' she said, smiling. 'It's the team doing the environmental study around the dam area. We're pretty sure there's endangered and protected flora and fauna there, but it has to be documented. I know there's platypus in the creek crossing for a start, and koalas.'

'Why are there so many of them, and all that equipment?' Alistair sounded surprised.

'To do it properly we need various specialists, each with their own field of expertise,' said Leonie. 'They've got night and day cameras, several drones and sample takers. We've got the A-team here,' she smiled.

'Impressive,' said Alistair.

'It needs to be comprehensive,' said Leonie firmly. 'I want this environmental study done well and ASAP. If I have to pay more to get it done quickly, then I'll do it.'

Eyebrows raised, Alistair glanced back at the group.

'Come in and I'll make us a pot of tea. They don't need my help,' she said.

They went into the kitchen and Leonie put on the kettle as Alistair sat down at the long table.

'I have good news for you,' he said.

'Do tell?'

'The Playhouse. I had a specialist heritage classifier come and look at it.'

'Oh, yes? And? Any problems?'

'Not for you! You want the Riverside Playhouse to stay as it is. The building inspection I arranged was very positive.'

Leonie passed him a mug of tea and put slices of banana bread out on a plate.

'So, by getting it heritage listed now, officially, it means heritage values can't be erased – it can't be torn down or visibly changed. Which makes it less attractive to a developer because it can't be pulled down in the future,' said Alistair. 'I've had a very thorough report done. At a cost, of course, but I think it's worthwhile.'

Leonie sat down opposite him. 'Of course. I'll make sure you aren't out of pocket, Alistair. I'm just so grateful you've been able to get it done so quickly.'

'Helps when you know the right people,' he said. 'So, where to from here? Once the theatre is secure and you're the boss, that is?' he asked.

'Another show, of course!' Leonie laughed.

'You're taking on a fulltime job there, Leonie. What about time for yourself? Are you going to have some fun? Travel? How long since you've taken a proper holiday?'

'I was taking Corby to Disneyland, but we had to postpone it,' she replied.

Alistair reached across the table and took her hand. 'No . . . I meant a different kind of holiday – you know, sunset cocktails, interesting sights and new places, delicious meals and someone to share it all with . . .'

'Oh.' Leonie felt slightly flustered. 'Well, that does sound nice, and yes, one day I'd love it, but I don't think I'm up to travelling at the moment.'

'What about starting small, with me? Why don't I take you and Corby away for a few days? There's a long weekend coming up, and I have a holiday house we could use. Just as friends, eh?'

'And perhaps invite a friend for Corby?' Leonie smiled.

'Sure, if that's what you'd like. Seriously, no pressure. You and the boys can have a bedroom each, it's at Swift Beach, two hours from here. I'm a reasonable cook, although we could eat out. There are some great restaurants down there.'

'Oh, I've heard of it. Never been there, though,' said Leonie. 'It would be nice, but I don't want to put you to any trouble . . .'

'None at all, just a thought.' He paused. 'Why don't you ask Corby?'

'Don't tempt me,' Leonie laughed. 'Let me think about it.'

*

It was a very cute cottage with lawns that ran down to the beach. Lounges and a small table in the back garden were set under shady trees looking out over the ocean. The house was level, no steps or stairs, which suited Leonie and the boys. There was a small pool that Leonie preferred to the ocean, but she loved walking along the beach at sunset with Alistair as the boys tried their luck fishing, and Corby was thrilled when he caught a decent bream.

'Two more and we have dinner,' called Alistair.

'This is so good for us,' said Leonie. 'Corby is having such fun, and I haven't felt this relaxed since I don't know when. Thank you.'

'We could do it more often – if you'd like,' said Alistair. 'I have a friend who has a house down in the snowfields, too. We often trade places for holidays. Has Corby tried skiing? Have you?'

'Good heavens no! And I'm not about to start. We have enough broken bones already. But thanks for the offer.'

'Just ask if you ever want to,' he said with a smile.

When they returned home to Fig Tree River, Alistair kissed Leonie on the cheek and shook Corby's hand.

'I've loved spending time with you both. Maybe we can do it again, eh?'

As they watched Alistair drive away, Harry stepped onto the verandah. He was holding his old hat. Leonie looked at him and smiled. The hat off meant a conversation, usually brief, but always serious.

'How was your holiday?' asked Harry.

'Really excellent!' enthused Corby. 'I caught fish for dinner and the beach was so cool. We ate in really nice restaurants, too.'

'Better than fishing and rafting down at the creek?' asked Harry dryly.

Corby caught the tone in the older man's voice. 'Well, not really. Just different.' He quickly excused himself and hurried inside.

Harry raised his eyebrows. 'Not my business . . . but what's going on?'

'What do you mean?' But seeing his expression, Leonie continued, 'Harry, there is no need to worry. There is nothing "going on". Alistair is a friend and he's helping me with the Playhouse, that's all.'

'Why?'

'Why not? He's an architect and protecting old buildings is his area of expertise.'

'But what's in it for him?' said Harry bluntly.

'Harry! I know what I'm doing. I can't do everything myself. Give me some credit.' Leonie changed the subject. 'Any problems while I was away?'

'Nope. That environmental mob know what they're doing, that's for sure. So do Stevie and I.'

'Excellent. Thanks for keeping an eye on it all. I'll see you later, I have some calls to make.'

Harry watched Leonie march indoors, then slowly jammed his hat back on his head.

*

'But Mum, where are we going?' Thomas's small legs buckled slightly as he dragged his backpack to the car.

'Just on a little holiday,' said Chrissie as she helped Mia into the back seat.

'I want to go to the park like you said,' whined the little girl.

'It's night-time, stupid,' said Thomas. 'Where's Dad?'

'Out with his mates. Now buckle your seatbelts.'

The two children were sound asleep when Chrissie pulled into the Airbnb house she'd booked in the small country town. The home was on a large block in a quiet backstreet, safe and suburban.

They grumbled and fell into their beds, too tired to ask questions, but comforted that they were sharing a large room.

'I'm right next door. I'll leave my door open,' said Chrissie as she tucked them in.

She sat on her bed and turned on her phone. There were five missed calls from Troy. She turned the phone off again and slid between the sheets, shivering; not from their smooth coolness but knowing Troy must have read her note and was trying to find her.

*

The children were exploring the house when Chrissie woke up, and as the memories of what she'd done the previous night rushed back to her, she felt more tired than when she'd fallen into bed.

She made a cup of tea from the basic supplies in the kitchen, handed the children a glass of milk and said, 'Get dressed, we're going out for breakfast.'

'Hooray, can we go to a chicken place?' Thomas asked.

'For breakfast?! I have no idea what's around here. Let's go and explore, hey?'

They sat down at a table inside the fast food restaurant, where a parade of coffee drinkers queued.

'Is this the holiday, Mummy?' Mia asked.

'Not yet, sweetie. Well, it's the start of it, I guess.'

'Where are we going?' asked Thomas.

'Oh, you'll see. First I have a bit of work to do. I have to see some people about things,' she said vaguely.

'I want to go home,' sighed Mia.

'Yeah, can we go back to Fig Tree River?' said Thomas. 'But after my soccer game at school.'

'Let's take a little trip before we decide, eh?' Chrissie smiled, trying to sound steady and strong.

After breakfast they piled back in the car and she glanced at her phone. No more calls or messages. Somehow that felt more ominous than yesterday's missed calls. She drove back to the house, noticing that there were more people about, heading off to work, no doubt. It was just after 8 am.

Chrissie unlocked the door, letting the children run in ahead of her and wondering what she should do and who she should call after her spur-of-the-moment decision to leave. It was terrifying, but deep down she knew it had been coming, possibly for years.

Walking through to the kitchen, she heard the

front door slam behind her, and then Mia called out in surprise.

'Hello, Daddy!'

Chrissie froze, then turned slowly to see Troy, holding Mia in his arms, as he walked into the kitchen with a nasty smile on his face.

'Surprise, Mummy. Thought you'd take my children for a little holiday, did you?' He put Mia down and Chrissie shrank back against the island.

'They're my children too, Troy,' she said in a quivering voice. 'How did you find us?'

Troy spun around to look at the staring children. 'Get out of here. Go to your rooms, or that big backyard you've been missing so much,' he snapped.

The children ran.

Troy suddenly moved so fast, Chrissie's head snapped back as he grabbed her shirt and shoved his face close to hers.

'You don't just piss off, you stupid bitch,' he snarled. 'Get back to the apartment right now, and don't try and call anyone. I know where you are, and what you do, every minute of the day and night – and don't you forget it! You try this again and you'll never see those kids again, ever. YOU HEAR ME!' he shouted, and shook her hard before pushing her away.

Chrissie dropped her face into her hands, sobbing.

'You will not see those kids. *Do you hear me?*' he repeated.

Chrissie stared at him. 'Troy – you can't do that,' she stammered.

'Bullshit! Don't think your money will make any difference. What's yours is mine, remember, and what's *mine* is mine! They're my children and that money is mine too.' He turned and headed from the room, saying over his shoulder, 'I'll see you back at our apartment tonight. You'll cook us a nice family dinner, and we'll have no more of this crap. Right? *Right?*' he repeated.

Chrissie nodded defeatedly. 'Yes, yes, Troy.'

The door slammed as he left.

Chrissie stood with her face in her hands as the two children crept into the room and went to her. Thomas quietly took her hand while Mia held her around the hips.

'It's okay kids, it's okay,' she whispered.

They said nothing but watched as Chrissie wiped her face and put the kettle on.

Her phone rang. She stared at the screen and saw it was Penny, who was no doubt wondering why she wasn't at the Women's Shed.

'Hi,' said Chrissie in a dull voice.

'Good morning, I'm at the shed, where are you?' Penny waited a moment, and when Chrissie didn't respond, she said, 'Chrissie? Are you all right?'

'No,' Chrissie gulped.

'Where are you?'

'Ah, a couple of hundred k's north . . . I rented an Airbnb.'

'What for? What's going on?' said Penny quietly.

Chrissie spoke to the children, 'Put the TV on in the living room, I won't be long.' Walking into her bedroom, she slowly stammered out a brief summary of what had happened after Troy had threatened her the previous afternoon. 'I left a note saying I needed some space and would call him, but he found me somehow and followed me here. And the things he said to me just now . . . I'm scared, Penny. And the kids saw it all. I can't bear that they've been exposed to this. How'd he know where I was?' she exclaimed.

Penny let out an angry breath. 'It's your phone! He can track you. Do the kids have phones? It's probably the same for them. Listen, Chrissie, I haven't known you very long, but I could tell there was something going on. And what you told me just now – it sounds to me like he is both physically violent and trying to control you. Is that right? So give me the bottom line. Is he worth going back to, starting over? Can it be sorted, do you guys need counselling – or is this something you need to get away from?'

'It's been happening for years!' Chrissie burst out in a choked voice. 'I wanted to get help for us but he wouldn't go to counselling or see anyone. I stopped asking ages ago because it only made him angry. He says there's nothing wrong with *him*, it's all me. The thing is, lately it's been getting worse.'

'Have you ever walked out before? With the kids?'

'No.'

'Why not?' she asked gently.

'I don't know . . .' said Chrissie brokenly. 'I mean, I knew he would just drag me back. Anyway, he's always sorry when he does something like this, gives me flowers and says he'll never do it again.'

'But he doesn't mean it! Look what he's just done!'

The two women were silent then Penny said, 'Here's what we do; believe me, I've been through something similar. There are organisations and groups for domestic violence victims . . . you need to face it, that's what you are, Chrissie. Now, I'll make some phone calls. You'll need a lawyer. Do you have a solicitor?'

'Oh my God, I can't do this, Troy will go bananas –'

'Chrissie, listen to me. He's mad already, right? But

you can't go back there if you and the kids might be in danger. I'll get the name and number of a refuge who can help you and the kids. Now, tell me where you are exactly.'

'Penny, I don't want to go to a refuge! I can afford a nice apartment or a hotel –' started Chrissie.

'No,' said Penny firmly. 'You need protection, advice, help. Support for the kids. Do you want me to meet you? Or will you be okay?'

'No, no,' said Chrissie miserably. 'Just tell me where to go. I feel so . . . useless.'

'Listen to me. This is not your fault. Don't speak to him or have any contact. And no more believing any bullshit he says, "I love you and the kids . . . I just lost my temper, I'm sorry . . . I didn't mean it . . ." You've heard it all before, right?'

Chrissie was nodding, then quietly said, 'Yes.'

'This is your chance, Chrissie. Is he still around the place, do you think?'

'I don't think so. He knows I'll drive back.'

'Good. Because you're not going to. Turn off your phone and buy a new one. Then text me the new number. Do you have enough money? Get as much cash out of your account as you can – go into a bank, don't use an ATM. Make an appointment with your solicitor, and tell them it's urgent. Don't contact anyone else yet, family or friends, in case Troy tries to get at you through them. Call me when you've done that and I'll give you the address of the refuge. He won't be expecting you till this evening, and he won't be able to track you if your phone is off.'

Chrissie was numb and silent.

'Chrissie, please listen to me. This is your chance. If you don't make a move now, then it might be too late.

Seriously. I know someone else who went through this . . . well, she died. He killed her. The "nicest couple", everyone thought. You're miserable. The kids aren't happy, I can tell. This is a chance for you and them to start over. You'll have support – you don't have to do this on your own.'

Chrissie took a ragged breath. 'I hear what you're saying, Penny, and I appreciate it, I really do, but Troy will go ballistic, he'll kill me if I –' Chrissie broke off, realising what she'd said.

'Yes. He well might,' said Penny steadily. 'Think of the kids. You can't stay.'

Tears rolled down Chrissie's face as it occurred to her that she could afford to go anywhere in the world. That was more than many women had. And, when she thought of her children, she knew she had no other choice.

'I'll turn off my phone and get the kids ready to go. Thank you, Penny,' she said, trying to sound strong and firm. 'When I buy a new mobile, I'll call you.'

'I'm here for you, Chrissie, okay? Remember that.'

Chrissie turned her phone off and took out the SIM card to be extra careful, but she felt as if she was going through the motions without feeling anything. The fear and shock had numbed her.

Shaking herself, she called to the children to pack their bags. Then she went into the bedroom to pack her own things.

'Why're we leaving, Mum? I thought this was a holiday?' grumbled Thomas. 'We haven't done anything fun yet. Are we going home?' he added cautiously.

'Not yet, my darling. Just a few stops to make on the way. Now, let's check that you've packed all your stuff, then we'll put the bags into the car.'

In town, Chrissie found a bank, where she withdrew

two thousand dollars, and a phone shop where she bought a new mobile.

'Right, here you go.' The young woman gave Chrissie her phone after setting it up for her. 'Will that be all?'

'Yes, thank you.' Chrissie handed over her credit card.

'Sorry, it's not working,' said the sales assistant.

After several fruitless attempts, Chrissie knew what Troy had done. She paid for the phone in cash.

'C'mon, kids.' Chrissie walked from the store and threw her old phone in a rubbish bin on the footpath. Luckily the kids didn't have phones yet, although she wondered about their iPads and made sure they were turned off and packed away in her own bag. 'Let's hit the road. We'll stop for a hamburger somewhere, okay?'

Chrissie's head was spinning, and the fear she seemed to have felt for years was ever-present. But she was also furious, and somewhere deep down a small spark burned.

*

Maddie shivered, her breath steaming in the icy night air.

'Bit of climate shock,' laughed Fleur.

'It's so cold it almost hurts to breathe,' said Maddie. 'But it's wonderful. I can't believe I'm here!'

Fleur linked her arm in Maddie's as they walked down the street from her apartment block to a local bar and restaurant.

'Is Julian here yet?' asked Maddie.

'He arrives in a few days. It took a while for him to renew his passport. He'll be staying with a composer friend.'

'Oh, yes, you mentioned that,' said Maddie. 'So tell me, just what is going on with the show? What are you planning?'

'Let's wait till we're out of the cold and sitting down with a nice glass of something.'

'It's so . . . buzzy here,' said Maddie, looking around. 'I feel like I'm in a movie.'

'New York will do that to you,' said Fleur with a smile. 'There it is, Sardi's. The food is okay, sometimes unpredictable, but we're going for the old-time atmosphere.'

'Now I really do feel like I'm an extra in a film,' whispered Maddie, walking into the glamourous restaurant with its booths and signed photos on the walls.

'How about we have a classic cocktail? I'll have a Manhattan; what about you, Maddie, or shall we look at the drinks menu? It's pretty amazing.'

'I'll have a Cosmopolitan,' said Maddie firmly, adding with a grin, 'I'm a big fan of the re-runs of *Sex and the City*!'

They sat down, ordered, and when the drinks arrived, they clinked the elegant cocktail glasses.

'Welcome to New York, Madison. It's like nowhere else you've ever been.'

'That's for sure! Especially as I haven't travelled at all!' Maddie took a sip and glanced around. 'Weren't you bored in Fig Tree River, coming from this fabulous city?'

'Luckiest place I ever fell into,' said Fleur. 'I never thought that's where I'd find my Percy and Ella, but life is full of the unexpected.'

'Now tell me, what's happening with the show?' asked Maddie. 'Are you really going to do it here? On Broadway itself?'

Fleur put down her glass. 'Well, I certainly hope so. There's lots of interest, but it's a matter of finding an angel or two, and I'm very close to securing them.'

As Maddie cocked her head in confusion, Fleur added,

'Backers. To invest money to get us up and running, until the box office receipts kick in.'

Maddie stared at her. 'But how far along are the preparations? Have you done any auditions yet?'

'We've started. It's okay, Maddie. I'm not asking you to hit the boards on Broadway – I know you aren't here for that – although you'd be fantastic.'

Maddie shook her head. 'Performing was fun in Fig Tree River, but it isn't what I really love about my music. It's the creating I like, finding the right tune, the right lyrics, to say what I want to say. And I just don't think I'll ever get over the awful nerves that go with having to perform in front of an audience. I see how confident Julian is, and I'm just not like that. I'm a composer, not a performer.'

'Many performers have had to deal with stage fright. It's not as uncommon as you'd think,' Fleur said. 'But I do understand, Maddie. Anyway, I'm confident it won't be long till the backing is in place and I have the money to start really working on this production.'

'You're creative as well as a businesswoman. You manage to fit so much into your life, Fleur.'

'You have choices in life, or circumstances dictate how things might evolve,' said Fleur quietly. 'I was not meant to be a mother or wife, as things turned out. I knew I had a musical talent – a gift – as you do, Maddie. So I chose to pursue that. I am also fortunate that I have always been secure financially, thanks to my clever parents.' She paused, adding, 'My father and mother were both smart businesspeople, and I learned a lot from them, which has come in handy.'

Maddie looked down and sipped her Cosmo, which she was enjoying, as Fleur went on, 'Charlie's video got my foot in the door here.'

'Really? That short film he did of us on stage?' said Maddie, feeling a twinge of emotion at the mention of his name.

'It wasn't so short. In the end I had him film a lot of extra background material, including the Grainger Museum in Melbourne,' Fleur added. 'It came together well and sparked quite a bit of interest when I pitched the show.'

'Wow,' said Maddie. 'And what about Ella, have you auditioned anyone for that part yet?'

'I've narrowed it down to two women. They'd both kill to do it. Especially with Julian, after they saw the video.'

Maddie laughed. 'So they haven't met him? He's such a character. Enchanting, charming, annoying and very full of himself. Although I'm not sure if he's as confident as he seems. Hard to pin down, really.'

'I think of him as being like quicksilver – mercurial, self-centred, quick tempered, runs a bit hot and cold.'

'That's a good description,' said Maddie.

'Let's order our food. You should sleep well tonight and get over your jet lag, then we'll get into all things showbizzy after that.'

'I know I keep saying this, but I can't believe I'm here.' Maddie beamed.

*

Maddie had no idea what time it was when she woke from a deep sleep. She was nestled in the cocoon of a feather doona and had slept like a log. She eased herself out of bed and opened the curtains.

It was like looking at a black-and-white photo. Tall grey skyscrapers, a wide boulevard all dusted in white, seen through misty rain – or was it snow?

She went into her ensuite to wash her face, and wondered if Fleur was awake. The bathroom was chilly and Maddie looked for a robe behind the door. To her surprise, hanging beside a fresh fluffy towel was a mink coat. Maddie carefully reached out and stroked the layers of fur. It was incredibly soft. She couldn't resist slipping it on over her nightgown.

She hesitated, but smelling coffee, she walked into the kitchen.

Fleur was smartly dressed, pouring coffee into two mugs. When she turned and saw Maddie, she clapped her hands and laughed.

'You look fabulous – even if politically incorrect – in that coat. Good morning, you slept well by the looks of it.'

'Am I allowed to wear this coat as a bathrobe?'

'If you like. I'm not cruising around outside in it,' smiled Fleur, sipping her coffee. 'It belonged to my mother, so I couldn't part with it.'

'That coffee smells good. What time is it?' Maddie yawned.

'Lunchtime! I'm dashing out to a meeting but I'll be back about 3 pm and then we can go out. I've left food in the refrigerator, so help yourself to anything you find. Just make yourself at home. Have a slow day; it's a bit frosty outside. I have several coats in the hall closet if you want to go for a walk. Have you got boots with you?'

'Ah, no. Just good sneakers.'

'Not so good for the slippery snowy sidewalks. We'll buy some boots when we go out. Okay?' Fleur put down her coffee mug and picked up her bag. 'The doorman will let you in and here's the key and the code for this door if you want to brave a slippery walk around the block.'

'I'll think about it, thanks,' said Maddie with a smile.

'There's Bloomingdale's a block or so along.' As Maddie looked puzzled, Fleur clarified, 'A pretty decent department store. Do you have a credit card you can use? I'm happy to treat you to snow-safe boots, but you'll have to wait till I come back.'

'I'll be fine. Thank you so much, Fleur. I think I'm in a bit of a daze.'

'Have your coffee, that will wake you up,' said Fleur with a smile. She picked up a camel coat and pulled a knitted cream beret on her head, gave Maddie a wave and headed down the hall radiating energy and purpose.

Maddie heard the front door click and lock.

She wrapped her arms around the mink coat. *Fig Tree River, eat your heart out*, she thought.

*

'Hello, is that you, Dobra? It's me, Sarita,' said Sarita. She was standing out on the balcony of her hotel room, phone in hand.

'Well, hello again. Are you still here? That cyclone messed up a lot of flights.'

'Yes. The cyclone delayed me. I'm in Nadi and I'd love to see you, or could I talk to your father?' asked Sarita.

'Of course you can, would you like to come over? Or shall I send the driver?'

'It's fine, I'll catch a taxi. Are you at your father's place?'

'Not at the moment, but I can meet you there in an hour. I'll call Dad now and let him know you're coming.'

'Okay, thanks very much. You sure I won't be disturbing either of you?'

'Not at all. We'd all love to see you.'

Sarita changed clothes, smoothed her hair and dropped her phone in her handbag.

As soon as the taxi pulled up under the portico of the Chand home, Dobra came down the steps to greet her with a hug. 'Come up, Mum and Dad are waiting for you.'

In the entrance hall, Sarita's cousin Aishik came towards her, arms outstretched in welcome. 'What a lovely surprise. I hope everything's all right. Dobra said you sounded concerned.' He looked at his daughter and smiled. 'We'll have tea together and you can tell us what you have been doing since we last saw you.'

Settled with tea served by the maid, Sarita was telling Dobra and her parents about the island she'd bought and the work she was doing there when Aishik cut in.

'Where is Ray? I do hope he's all right.'

'Oh yes. He's at home, back in Australia. I have been staying on Totoka overseeing the renovations.' She gave a quick smile.

'I hope you weren't there during the cyclone,' said Indira.

'No, but my caretaker Varo was on the island, with his young daughter. There was nowhere for them to shelter, but thankfully we evacuated them – my contractor Stuart and I – just before the cyclone hit the island. Unfortunately, it left the place devastated.'

'What do you mean by "devastated"?' said Dobra. 'The cyclone wasn't that bad here.'

Sarita brushed a hand across her eyes. 'It was terrible. The island is virtually shredded. Here . . .' She took out her phone, scrolled to the photos of the ruined beach, and handed it to Aishik, who frowned and passed it to his wife. As Indira gasped, Dobra jumped up and peered over her shoulder.

'You got away just in time, by the looks of it. A brave and kind gesture on your part to help your employee, my dear,' said Aishik. 'Surely you didn't have to go over there to rescue these people yourself?'

'I felt responsible. And Jinti, the little girl, is barely five. They are good people. In fact, they had a *lovo* for me, as a gesture of thanks, I think.'

'Of course, they would feel very grateful. Thank goodness you and the others were safe,' said Indira.

'Sarita, my dear, what had you built? What was destroyed?' asked Aishik.

Sarita showed them the images of the near-completed residence, the traditional bure for the caretaker, and the photo of the drawings of how the finished buildings and gardens would look. Then she scrolled down to the photos of everything destroyed.

The three passed the phone around in silence, until a noise behind them made them look up.

'What are you all looking at? My dear! Sarita!' exclaimed Purnima, leaning on her stick and holding out a hand in greeting as she entered the room. Sarita jumped up and went to her, gently embracing her aunt and leading her to a chair.

'Nani, Sarita was building a wonderful home on Totoka Island and the cyclone has smashed everything,' said Dobra.

'Oh, that's shocking news. I hope no one was hurt,' the old woman exclaimed. 'Do you need our help to rebuild?' she asked bluntly.

The group exchanged small smiles.

'Always one step ahead of us,' said Aishik. 'So how can we help, Sarita?'

'Oh, no! That's not why I came here. But I am grateful

you allowed me to tell you all about it. I think I'm still in shock, really.'

'That's what family is for, my dear,' said Purnima.

'Have you made any plans? What does Ray think?' asked Indira.

Sarita looked down. 'Actually, I haven't told him yet. Just that the cyclone delayed my flight home. I'm still mulling over what I should do next.'

'Dobra, pour her another cup of tea,' said Indira, seeing Sarita's cup empty.

'Were you insured?' asked Aishik.

Sarita shook her head. 'No. Buying it was rather an impetuous idea. I'd insured the workers for their protection in case anyone was hurt on the site, but I hadn't got around to insuring the island for weather damage and that sort of thing.'

Aishik frowned. 'I would have thought your contractor would have mentioned it?'

'It was not his responsibility. I should have done it,' said Sarita quickly. 'But I was rather swept away with the romance of it all. It was to be a surprise for my family.'

'Undoubtedly it will be,' said Aishik.

'Darling, what do you suggest Sarita should do now?' Indira asked her husband.

'Whatever she wishes. If you want to rebuild, we're here to help,' Aishik said.

Sarita sat forward. 'I'm not sure. It is such a beautiful place, and while I was staying there, I was starting to observe all the wildlife and the unusual plants. One day we watched a turtle come ashore and start to lay her eggs. It was on the lagoon side, and I wondered why she came so high up the beach. I do hope they survived.'

'I suspect the animals are smarter than us,' said Dobra.

'You may be right,' said Aishik gently. 'Sarita, I can see that you want to protect your little piece of paradise, and I understand that.'

Sarita nodded, suddenly choked with emotion.

'Have you booked your flight home?' Indira asked.

'Yes. Tomorrow afternoon.'

'Then stay here until then,' she said. 'You and Dobra can go to your hotel to collect your things. Then you can relax and have dinner with us all – your family. Our driver will take you to the airport.' Indira reached over and took Sarita's hand.

'Splendid. It's all arranged,' said Aishik.

Sarita looked around at the smiling faces of her family.

'All right, yes. I suppose it is. Thank you.'

*

Maddie was surrounded by shoeboxes. She leaned back, lifting her legs to admire the knee-high boots on her feet. The leather was soft, but treated with a wax to keep them waterproof, she was assured by the attentive saleswoman.

'How much did you say these are?' Maddie asked.

As the woman told her the price, Maddie winced. Then she smiled and turned to the sales assistant. 'I'll take them.'

14

Leonie was curled on her side. When she opened her eyes, it was to see the clear blue of the sky through the slight flutter of the curtain. It was going to be a beautiful day.

She yawned, then, fully awake, she remembered the night before, and momentarily froze – then relaxed. She took a deep breath.

Gently Alistair drew himself closer to her naked back, an arm reaching over her shoulder to cup her breast.

He kissed the nape of her neck. 'Sleep well?' he whispered.

'Eventually,' said Leonie.

He gave a soft chuckle. 'That was quite a marathon.' He hugged her, murmuring, 'My darling Lee, that was wonderful . . . it's been so long. I'm so glad I found you.'

Leonie rolled over and reached out to touch his cheek. 'Yes . . . me too.'

Sex had been far from her mind for so long. She'd missed Tony in so many ways, and she realised she'd forgotten how sex felt. Now, her body tingled.

Alistair continued to nuzzle her throat, then her shoulder. She could feel him becoming aroused again, so she rolled onto her back.

'Alistair . . . you're incorrigible. Let's get up. I'm ready for a new day!' She didn't add that she didn't want Corby and his mates suddenly coming in from their Friday night sleepover and finding her swanning around in a nightie or, worse, in bed with Alistair.

She jumped up and went into the bathroom to shower.

'I'll put the coffee on,' called Alistair.

Leonie preferred a pot of tea first thing in the morning but as she came into the kitchen the smell of coffee and toast was enticing.

'Look at you! No make-up, wet hair, jeans and a T-shirt. You look fifteen years old!' he exclaimed.

'Sorry. I just threw myself together. Corby and the boys could be heading over here any time.'

He handed her a mug of coffee and kissed her cheek, murmuring, 'I wish I had known you when you were fifteen.'

'Alistair – that sounds all wrong!' said Leonie.

'Apologies! I didn't mean it like that, just that it would have been so good if we'd met then, been teen sweethearts and married in our twenties . . .'

'We'd be divorced by now,' said Leonie lightly, but the comment made her feel very uncomfortable. Tony was the love of her life, and she didn't want anything to encroach on her memories of her life with him, even if Alistair hadn't meant it badly.

He looked contrite as he put a plate of toast in front of her. 'What would you like to do today?'

'Actually, I promised Corby and a mate of his I'd take them out to The Scrub,' she said.

'I've heard of The Scrub. It sounds beautiful.'

'Yes, it's a very pretty place, a nature conservation area. The boys are doing a school project on it. Corby's friend is doing photography and Corby is doing some sort of nature survey. I was so glad to see them show an interest in something other than sport and the PCYC. Mind you, they didn't have much choice since it's for school! You're welcome to join us.'

Alistair made a noncommittal sound, but after they'd eaten and he'd showered, he came back into the kitchen dressed, his car keys in his hand.

'If I can't talk you into lunch or dinner, I'll head off. I have an appointment on Monday. Might have some more news for you after that.'

'Thank you, Alistair. Things do seem to be progressing quickly now. I so appreciate your help with all my plans.'

'Any time.' They kissed gently and Leonie saw him to the door and waved as he drove away.

Leonie glanced over at the garden. Harry was working around the hayshed and looked up and nodded to her. Leonie smiled. He never missed a trick.

*

Maddie loved New York and when Fleur took her to Veselka, her favourite restaurant in Brooklyn, she loved that, too.

Two days later Maddie stared at her wardrobe, wondering what to wear to the new production of *The Book of Mormon* they were seeing that night. Fleur told her she could wear whatever she wanted – 'jeans or a ballgown'. Maddie settled on a mid calf-length dress and a long cashmere shawl she'd bought as she loved its soft warmth.

'You look stunning,' said Fleur. 'You're lashing out a bit here, aren't you? I can take you to some great discount places where you can buy good labels very inexpensively if you'd like.'

'Oh, I love bargains! That sounds great. When you have time, of course,' said Maddie.

Fleur smiled. 'New York is costly, until you know where to go. We're dining at a darling French restaurant in an old brownstone building near Broadway before the show. My treat. I always feel like I'm in Paris when I go there,' she said.

Once they were settled at their table, Fleur and Maddie browsed through the classic French dishes on the menu.

'New York is fun,' said Maddie. 'I think I could live here, but what would I do?'

'Same as you did at home, if you want.' Fleur laughed.

'I guess that's true.'

'Or you can fly to LA and hook up with some people I know. They'll introduce you to the right musos and recording people. You need to lay down some of your songs.'

'Make a recording? I don't know about that!' Maddie laughed nervously.

'I'm not joking. But all in good time. Enjoy my town for a bit,' said Fleur.

Maddie shrugged. 'Maybe. It's a weird feeling not being on a schedule.'

'Enjoy it while you can, sweetie.'

'*Et voilà! Bonsoir, mesdames . . .*' called a familiar voice, and Maddie nearly dropped the menu as she looked up to see Julian prancing over – that was the only word to describe it.

Maddie didn't know whether to be stunned, amused or delighted, although she was all three. Seeing Julian waltzing towards them was one shock, his outfit was quite another.

He wore knickerbocker pants and a matching fringed jacket in maroon, sage and royal blue velvety fabric, trimmed in gold over a white flouncy shirt, as well as a floppy bowtie and long socks and soft shoes.

'Julian! Wow, what a surprise,' said Maddie as he leaned over to hug her.

Fleur laughed and held up her hands in mock dismay.

'Is that your costume for the show that you're wearing?'

'You said there was no dress code here.' He did a small pirouette and sat down, looking very pleased with himself. 'Don't you just adore New York!'

'You didn't have to come in costume,' Fleur chuckled. 'But you look great. Percy would be proud. It's exactly like some of the clothes he made for himself.'

'Is that a Percy Grainger outfit?' said Maddie. 'You said he was eccentric but, well, wow. Only you, Julian, could get away with that.'

'We're trying out Percy's wardrobe. It's not all eccentric,' said Fleur.

A waiter managed to keep a straight face as he asked Julian what he wanted to drink and took down his order.

'I can't wait to see *The Book of Mormon* tonight. I missed it when it came to Sydney,' said Julian.

'So are you excited?' asked Maddie. 'I am.'

'About what in particular?' Julian grinned as he picked up a menu.

Maddie pretended to bop him on the head with her menu. 'Everything!'

'Well, it has been full-on, what with the filming and racing around pretending to be Percy.'

'Filming? What are you talking about?' started Maddie, when there was a tap on her shoulder. She turned around to find Charlie smiling at her.

For a moment she froze, and dozens of images, memories and feelings rushed through her. 'What?! This is too much!' She jumped up and hugged Charlie, then sat back down, shaking her head. 'Is that it now?' she asked Fleur. 'I can't take any more, I'm on shock and excitement overload.'

'Wait till you see the show,' said Julian, adding mischievously, '*Our* show, not the show tonight.'

'In your dreams, Julian,' said Charlie, sitting down with them. 'I can't wait to see *The Book of Mormon* again.'

'Let's order, I'm famished,' interjected Fleur.

Through the meal, they laughed and chatted as they all caught up, but Julian did most of the talking. When he and Fleur launched into a conversation about a scene in the show, Maddie turned to Charlie.

'How long have you been here?'

'In New York? Not long. I've just been having meetings with Fleur and the rest of the crew. She took me to White Plains – it's maybe forty-five minutes from here. It felt weird, being in Percy and Ella's home with so much of their memorabilia.'

'You're filming something? A documentary?' asked Maddie.

Hearing this, Fleur broke away from her conversation with Julian and smiled. 'We plan to use Charlie's film to hook the major investors for a full-scale production.'

'I thought you had angels in the wings?' said Maddie.

'I have the initial backing for a very limited season, but I think it can be much bigger than that,' said Fleur. 'I need megabucks to mount a full-scale Broadway musical. And I'm not near my target yet. The money people want me to step up to their estimate. Don't worry, kids, I'll find a way.'

'Everyone has so many plans,' said Maddie, somewhat ruefully.

'Plans, shmans,' said Julian cheerfully. 'C'mon, Fleur, where are all the rich Noo Yoikers? Maybe Percy could play for their private parties and raise a bundle!'

'You? In those clothes?' said Charlie, frowning. 'I wouldn't pay!'

'Many would!' said Julian loftily.

'Percy was a serious musician, not a clown!' retorted Charlie.

Maddie and Fleur exchanged a quick look. Charlie and Julian were still glaring at one another.

*

Sarita leaned her head on Ray's shoulder as they stared out at their garden view. He tightened his arm around her waist.

'I missed you.'

'Me too. I felt I was in another world. Well, I was, I suppose.' Sarita paused. 'Till the cyclone. Totoka was such a paradise. To see it all trashed was heartbreaking.'

'You shouldn't have gone back after the storm. Why didn't you just get Stuart to check on it?' asked Ray.

'I had to see it for myself. Even photos don't do it justice. There's a massive mess.'

'You didn't really have to stay there for so long, though, did you?' he asked gently, turning to look at her.

She nodded firmly. 'Yes. I did. I don't know why – I just felt I had to do it. I know you wouldn't enjoy being on my island as much as I did.'

Ray was moved at her pained expression. 'The cyclone was a terrible thing.'

'I'm glad no one was hurt. It was awful to see all that beauty and hard work wrecked.'

They were silent for a moment, then Ray said, 'I was worried about you the whole time.'

She reached up and kissed him, then sat down by the window. 'I can tell you one thing – I wasn't bored working on the island. I lost track of time. And I worked hard. I often wished I had Chrissie with me, because I wasn't crash-hot with a hammer and nails! Sewing is such a one-person project; this was so different. I liked working with the guys, though. Varo was a terrific foreman. I cleared and dragged and hammered where told. It was so rewarding to see it all take shape. I did a lot of explaining, too,' she added proudly. 'Until I had the drawings and plans they had no idea of the scale and style of what I was doing.'

'Well, from your photos it would have been an amazing building,' said Ray, sitting down opposite her.

'Yep.'

'So what now?' asked Ray.

Sarita didn't answer for a moment.

'Well, we won't be spending Christmas with the family on Totoka. Nor any time,' she said slowly.

Ray blinked. 'So you're selling it?'

Sarita shook her head. 'Nope.'

'What do you mean?'

'I just don't like the idea of jetskis, fishing boats, scuba-divers, bars and bistros, all the kinds of things that come with tourism.'

'Hmmm. And what were the boys and I, or whoever else might have visited, supposed to do when staying at Chez Sarita, Totoka?' asked Ray.

Sarita looked at him and smiled ruefully. 'Well, some people might get bored after a couple of days, I suppose, but if you're into snorkelling, fishing, diving, you won't be bored. I'm more a book-under-a-palm-tree person.'

'I don't understand. So now you'll just walk away from this... project?' Ray paused, debating whether to ask just how many millions she'd lost – or was abandoning. 'Really? Are you going to turn your back on a place that captivated you, that you seemed to love?'

'It's not easy to walk away, Ray. It's such a special place that just swept me up.' Sarita lowered her head. 'I feel so guilty. It was such an indulgent waste of money. I'm sorry. I never imagined it'd be so easy to spend money! I just don't want it to be for nothing.'

Sarita couldn't speak for a moment. Ray wasn't sure what to say. He reached over and took her hand.

'I'll make it up to you all in some way, I promise,' said Sarita.

'Sarita, darling, there's still more money left than we ever dreamed of having. It's what we do with it now that matters,' he added gently. 'I've been thinking, too.'

Sarita looked at him as he went on. 'We should, *must*, tell our boys about it. It's only right and fair –'

He held up his hand as Sarita went to speak. 'Please hear me out. We need to sit down with the boys and discuss it sensibly. We now have the means to give them a huge educational advantage. There are all manner of universities, different courses and internships, especially overseas, which they can take advantage of. It's an opportunity we could never have given them before, even if we'd gone into debt to do it.'

Sarita nodded slowly. 'Was it wrong to pay for them to go away camping, surfing and doing what they wanted all these months?'

'Of course not, darling! It's been a welcome break, which is exactly what gap years should be. Maybe a bit of an indulgence, but now the hard work starts – which, to me, sounds pretty exciting. Think back, what would you have done if your parents had suddenly said, "Now you've got high school behind you, where in the world would you like to study and what would you like to study?"'

Sarita looked at him, her eyes now shining. 'Oh my God! Where to start! Design, couture, maybe architecture . . . Oh, the dreams I had. Who knows where I'd be.' She jumped up and hugged Ray, and sat on his lap. 'You're right. Our boys have the opportunity to shape their lives now, rather than when we leave this earth!'

'It's going to be a long and interesting conversation,' Ray smiled. 'Now, back to business . . . Freddy and Roger are dying to catch up, and Leonie is anxious to see you, too. She had a prang with her car – hit a roo – and she and Corby were in hospital for a bit. They're fine. Back home. She seems very busy.'

'Oh, how terrible! They're okay?' asked Sarita. 'I'll look forward to seeing everyone.'

'Leonie is apparently saving the world, according to Brett.' Ray laughed. 'Well, her bit of it.'

'I know the feeling,' said Sarita. 'The whole planet needs saving.'

Ray kissed her. 'Actually, I've booked a new restaurant for dinner. Go to a beauty shop and treat yourself. Buy a new outfit,' he suggested.

'Do I look that much of a mess?' said Sarita in alarm.

'Of course not! You look exactly like a woman who has been slashing undergrowth, building a big bure, bossing the blokes, catching her dinner, and, well, I can't imagine what else . . .' he chuckled.

'There were some very magic moments when I wished you were there,' sighed Sarita.

Ray reached across and traced her face with his hand. 'I'm just glad you're home.'

*

'I'm sick of being in the car,' said Thomas.

'I want to go home,' said Mia in a tired voice.

'Which home?' said Thomas.

Chrissie glanced in the rear-view mirror and saw her daughter's pale, sad face.

'Our real home,' said Mia.

'I'll tell you where we're going. We're going on an adventure,' said Chrissie, trying to sound cheerful.

'Why're we leaving that place, Mum?' asked Thomas.

'There are some very important things I need to do, honey. But don't worry, I plan for us to have lots of fun very soon,' said Chrissie resolutely.

They stopped for a quick lunch and Chrissie carefully counted out the cash to pay for it.

It was hard to keep her head from spinning, but she knew she had to stay strong now.

Two hours later she found the Airbnb she'd booked online with her new phone and Penny's credit card. It was at the edge of a town where there was a bank, a fast food outlet, a pub and a supermarket.

'Is this the holiday?' asked Mia dubiously.

The house was very basic. 'There's a small pool out the back,' said Chrissie, trying to sound enthusiastic.

'What're we going to do here?' asked Thomas.

'Right now, rest up. I'm tired. We'll explore tomorrow.'

She turned the TV on, found a cartoon for the children to watch and took her new phone into the main bedroom. Closing the door behind her, Chrissie rang the number of the refuge Penny had sent her. Penny had made an appointment for Chrissie to talk to the facilitator. When her call was answered, she asked for Jennifer.

A warm and friendly voice came on the line. 'Penny said you'd be calling and I'm so glad you have, Christina. Now, where are you at the moment? Can you talk?'

Briefly Chrissie told Jennifer the situation she was in. 'After the last time, I just . . . left. I hadn't planned it out at all. And since he found me and I didn't go home like he asked – well, he's cut off my access to my credit card. We're in an Airbnb that Penny kindly put on her credit card – I'll have to pay her back.'

'We can get that sorted. Have you got any documents with you? You don't have to stay here at the refuge, but we can give you help with a caseworker to support you through all the paperwork, seeing as you're not going back to him.' When Chrissie didn't answer, Jennifer asked, 'You're not thinking of going back to him . . . are you?'

'No,' said Chrissie with an anxious sigh. 'But I didn't plan this, so I just didn't think things through. What should I do? How do I get my belongings, and what paperwork will I need?'

'I'll give you a list – passports, birth certificates,

bank and insurance details if possible, school reports and medical records, that sort of thing. As I mentioned, we'll assign you a caseworker who'll help you with everything. She'll go with you to the police to take out an AVO against him. Then you get a Recovery Order, and she will accompany you to court if needed, and also go with you to your home to get your things. Once you have an AVO against him, he can't do anything. You'll need your personal things, though, especially your documents.'

Chrissie felt her head spinning. 'This is all so much. I don't have a passport.'

'Have you got a new SIM card in your phone? We'll arrange to have your car checked, as well as any other devices, in case your husband has put a tracker or tracking app in them. The perpetrators can do that remotely – it's called TFA – Technology Facilitated Abuse.'

'Really? Penny thought he must be able to track my phone, but how would I know if he has a tracker on anything else?' exclaimed Chrissie.

'You won't,' said Jennifer crisply. 'Take as much cash out of the bank as you can. And make an appointment with your solicitor.'

Jennifer spoke in a calm and friendly voice and Chrissie began to feel somewhat stronger, if still overwhelmed at the wheels she'd set in motion.

'Are you sure he won't find me again? How long is all this going to take?' asked Chrissie.

'I'll give you the phone number and name of your caseworker at the refuge closest to you. While you don't have to, I think it would be good for you to go there and feel safe in order to get things sorted. We can have a counsellor speak with the children, if you'd like. They could stay there while you run around with the caseworker.

They're all lovely, caring women. You won't be alone through all this, Chrissie. Deep breaths. You're doing the right thing. For you and your children.'

Jennifer sounded so reassuring, Chrissie did feel calmer. But as she put down her phone, the enormity of it all hit her. She took a slow, deep breath. Yes. She could do this. It was time. The right time to start over. She felt so grateful for the support of women like Penny, Jennifer and the refuge. She decided to call Penny and thank her. Chrissie drew another deep breath. She was ready for whatever came next.

*

'Sounds like you had quite an adventure over there, all up,' Brett said, as he walked with Sarita along the riverbank heading into town for a coffee.

'Sort of, I guess. The island really got to me, though.' She paused. 'Made me wonder about my mother.'

'That's not surprising, when you think about it. And I think it's great that you've connected with her family now,' said Brett.

'Yes. They're very decent people. It's just made me want to – I don't know, have some link there, as you say.'

'With your island? I thought you'd given that idea away,' said Brett.

'As a family resort, yes. But it's such a special place, it's like a beautiful beacon out there – a microcosm of what could be if we look after our environment.'

'But what are you going to do with it, then? You can't just leave it to do its own thing,' said Brett.

'Really? Can't I? Not many people would bother going there if there wasn't anything on the island, and it's not an easy beach to get onto,' said Sarita.

'Hmm. Abandonment often leads to unwanted invasion by people who could harm the wildlife, set fire to the undergrowth, that sort of thing. Also, it could be hard to move them off the island if that happens, so some form of security is essential.'

'You're right. I hadn't thought about that,' said Sarita. 'I think I just need some time to work out what to do with it now.'

'Well, you could join the exclusive club of "island collectors". There's one guy who has bought an island off each continent. He installs a keeper on each one and visits his islands every year or so,' commented Brett.

'Gosh, that's interesting, but not for me!' said Sarita. 'Now that I've bought Totoka, I am responsible for it.'

Brett thought for a few moments. 'What about handing the island over to local people as an environmental commons? They can watch over it, use it for study and local customs, that sort of thing. Or it could be designated a national park, with conditions. Establish a small perpetual trust to finance any ongoing basic costs. Perhaps you could involve your friend Varo.'

Sarita squeezed his arm. 'Now I like that idea! I'll talk to Ray, and then approach Aishik and Indira and ask if they'd like to be involved. The island could be a living museum and observed and documented for decades to come, good or bad. You are clever, Brett!'

Brett smiled at Sarita's infectious enthusiasm. 'Good on you, Sarita. As an environmentalist, I have to say I like the idea too,' he grinned.

They walked a little further and as the town came into view Brett asked, 'So what's happening with Chrissie? How's she liking her new place?'

'I'm not sure,' said Sarita slowly. 'I'll ask Leonie.

I've been out of touch. Maybe it's time for a get-together, although I hear Maddie has gone to New York. She's staying with Fleur.'

'That would be exciting for her. Fleur is incredibly generous,' Brett said.

'She is, and perhaps she enjoys the company too. Let's drive over to Leonie's later, if you have time. I'm sure she won't mind us dropping in.'

*

As Brett and Sarita drove up the driveway, they saw Leonie sitting on the verandah with a man beside her. Leonie waved as they got out of the car.

'Hey! What a nice surprise! Welcome home, Sarita!' she called.

'Who's this?' asked Alistair as he rose to greet them.

'Well, you've met Brett, and this is his sister Sarita. She's been away for weeks. Sarita, this is my friend Alistair.'

With a nod to Alistair, Sarita rushed up onto the verandah and hugged her friend. 'It's so good to see you, Leonie. I heard about the crash! I'm so relieved you're all right. How's your leg?'

Brett reached out and took Alistair's hand. 'Hello again, Alistair.' He gave a slight smile.

'I'm glad you dropped by,' said Leonie, beaming. 'Pull up some chairs. I'm much better now, Sarita, thanks.'

'She's doing very well,' Alistair broke in. 'She went on a little hike and overdid it a bit yesterday, didn't you, Lee?' he tutted. 'Can I get either of you a coffee or a cold drink?'

Brett and Sarita exchanged a glance as they sat down.

'I'd love a coffee, please. White, no sugar,' said Sarita quickly.

Brett opened his mouth to remind her she'd just had a coffee in town, but then thought better of it. He looked at Alistair. 'Just a glass of cold water, thanks. Want a hand?'

'No, no. I'll be right back.' Alistair squeezed Leonie's shoulder. 'You want another one?'

She shook her head. In silence the three of them watched Alistair disappear.

Sarita turned to Leonie. 'Okay. Who's he?'

'Oh, just a friend. He's been helping me get the Playhouse heritage listed, and then I'm going to buy it, believe it or not! Let the developers try to get hold of it then.'

'So where does Alistair think you're getting the money from to buy it?' whispered Sarita. 'Have you told him about your win?'

'No! I told him I had a small legacy and was selling some cattle and land. Though frankly, that wouldn't nearly cover it all,' said Leonie. 'Stop panicking, though, Sarita. He's a good guy.'

'How'd you meet him?'

Before Leonie could answer, Alistair returned, putting a tray on the small table and sitting back down.

'Leonie says you're helping her with the Playhouse. How's that all going?' said Sarita brightly.

'Great. I had a breakthrough and found enough features to get it heritage listed. It's still a long process till it's finally signed off and the listing is official, though.'

'Sounds complicated,' said Sarita, 'and expensive too, I guess.'

'The experts we need know how to charge like wounded bulls,' said Alistair ruefully. 'Of course, I waived my fee. It's such a pleasure to help Lee, and that Playhouse is certainly worth listing.' He turned to Brett. 'What's happening with Leonie's dam, Brett?' he asked.

'My, you're across everything,' said Sarita mildly.

'I told Alistair all about the dam and how it could affect not just us but the entire Fig Tree River system,' said Leonie.

Brett clapped Alistair on the arm. 'You have a solution to that one too?' he asked, a touch snidely.

'Not my area of expertise,' said Alistair lightly. 'I saw the team of researchers and their equipment who turned up here for days to do the scientific studies, so I figured they would give Leonie more than enough ammunition.'

Sarita noticed that her friend seemed quieter than usual and was about to ask her about the environmental assessment when they all noticed Harry's ute speeding towards them, P-plates crookedly attached and Stevie at the wheel. Stevie got out in a rush and started shouting, 'Harry's had an accident! He's down at the creek.'

Brett sprinted down the verandah steps. 'Stay there, Leonie, I'll go. What's happened?' he asked Stevie.

'Take the first-aid kit,' called Leonie in a distressed voice. 'Ring me if I can help.'

As Alistair rose and moved towards the steps, Brett waved him back. 'I'll call you if I need anything.' He clambered into the passenger seat of the ute, slamming the door, and Stevie sped away.

Leonie was on her feet. 'Oh no, I hope Harry is okay. I couldn't bear it if something happened to him.' She started shaking.

Alistair put his arms around her.

Sarita looked at Leonie's stricken face. 'Don't worry, he's a tough old bugger.'

Leonie pulled her phone from her pocket and stared at it. 'Brett won't be able to call me from the creek. There's no reception there.'

'Brett will send Stevie back if he needs to, it'll be all right,' Sarita reassured her.

It seemed an age before they heard the rumble of the ute returning. Leonie stepped forward as Stevie came to a halt.

There was a general sense of relief as they saw Harry propped up in the front seat looking sorry for himself.

Brett got out and slowly opened Harry's door. With Sarita beside him they eased Harry onto a chair on the lawn as Stevie jumped from the back of the ute.

'It was a snake, he said. He leapt away from it at the last moment, and fell and rolled down the slope,' said Stevie.

'Did it bite you, Harry?' asked Leonie anxiously.

'No, I didn't let the bugger near me. Stop bloody fussing,' Harry grumbled as Leonie and Brett examined him. 'It just came out of nowhere. Didn't see it till it was almost too late.'

Stevie leaned down towards Leonie.

'I reckon he's got a bit of a problem with his eyesight,' he said quietly. 'That's why he didn't see the snake. I've been telling him to go and get glasses.'

'Nothing wrong with my eyes,' said Harry. 'And my hearing's good too, young fella!'

Stevie and Leonie exchanged a look.

'Okay, mate. Let's get you inside where I can keep an eye on you,' said Leonie, patting Harry's shoulder.

'Should we take you to the hospital?' asked Sarita.

'No, no, I'll be all right . . .' Harry struggled to get up. 'Bit battered and bruised but nothing broken.'

Between them, Stevie and Brett helped Harry onto the verandah.

'Come into the guest bedroom. You need to lie down there, Harry,' Leonie said firmly as she hurried inside.

Sarita looked at Alistair. 'Looks like Leonie's going to be tied up a bit.'

'Harry doesn't strike me as the type who likes to be mollycoddled,' said Alistair. 'He's worked here a long time, I gather.'

'You bet. He was here when Leonie came as a bride and he worked for Tony's father before that. He's like family. There's nothing he wouldn't do for Leonie and Corby,' said Sarita pointedly.

'How nice,' said Alistair flatly. As Brett and Stevie returned from settling Harry, Alistair added, 'I'll go see if I can do anything for Lee.' He headed inside.

'I'll be around if I'm needed,' said Stevie as he went back to the old ute.

'You did well, mate,' said Brett. 'I'd hate to think what would have happened if you weren't there to help him.'

'No worries. See you.'

Brett sat down and looked at his sister. 'What do you make of that Alistair?' he asked in a low voice.

'Not for me to say, of course, but I'll say it to you – he's not my type, that's for sure. Too smooth.'

'He seems keen, though. Bit over-the-top keen.'

'Hmm. You're right. He is very keen,' she said thoughtfully.

'Do you think he knows about her money?' said Brett, even more quietly.

Sarita frowned. 'Leonie says she hasn't told him. But he's probably seen this place and what she's spending and thinks she might have some inheritance, or something. He could have put two and two together.'

Brett shrugged. 'Harry's accident could actually be fortuitous for Leonie. Alistair will want to keep up appearances and move out. I doubt Corby knows what's going on.'

'She's entitled to a life, Brett. I just wish it was with someone else.'

'Mmm, I think I agree,' Brett said. 'Anyway, let's go and say goodbye. See if Leonie or Harry need anything. Maybe you can just tell her to be alert?'

'I can't do that when I've got nothing to base our worries on,' exclaimed Sarita. 'She won't care what I say, anyway. She could tell me to piss off, that it's none of my business, and she'd be right.'

Brett nodded. 'Yeah, I understand.'

They poked their heads around the door of the guest room where Harry was lying on the bed. Leonie was handing him a glass of water.

'Glad you're okay then, Harry,' said Brett.

'Right as rain. I don't want to be any bother,' said Harry.

'Sleep it off. Here, I have some sleeping pills,' said Alistair.

'Don't take pills,' muttered Harry.

'Just have a bit of a nap, Harry. I'll check on you later,' said Leonie gently.

Alistair headed for the front door. 'I'm going into town, Leonie wants a few things.' He looked around. 'Bye all. See you in a bit, Lee.'

They farewelled Alistair and all moved back out onto the verandah as he drove away. Sarita turned to Leonie. 'Is there anything we can do for you?'

'No. But this has given me a bit of a shock. Don't you worry – Alistair will help me look after Harry.'

'He's staying with you?' said Sarita delicately. 'You two haven't known each other for long, have you? You jumped in the deep end pretty quickly.'

Leonie shrugged. 'Sort of. He's only here when Corby is staying with a mate. He's been very helpful,' she added, with a look at Sarita that said 'don't go there'.

'So, are you okay with what he's done for you at the Playhouse?' asked Brett.

'Well, it's costing me a bundle, but if the building is given a heritage listing, it will be safe in perpetuity,' said Leonie. 'I couldn't have done that without Alistair.'

'Do you have any documentation about it? I'd be interested to see it,' said Brett. 'I could give it a once-over for you, from a legal perspective.'

'It's all in a folder on my desk in Tony's old study. It's clearly labelled – help yourself.'

As Brett walked away, Leonie looked at Sarita. 'You don't approve?'

'Leonie, it's not my business. I'm happy if you're happy,' said Sarita. 'But I guess, if you want my two cents' worth, I'd say Alistair doesn't seem your type. He's so different from Tony.'

'I'll never find another Tony,' sighed Leonie. 'Alistair's very attentive and generous. He dotes on Corby. He never had children.'

Sarita just nodded. 'Okay, let's sit down while I wait for Brett. It's been an eventful day. That Stevie is a good kid.'

'He's matured a lot since he's been here,' said Leonie. 'Harry has really taken him under his wing. But I think Stevie's right – I'll ask Harry if he'll agree to go to the optometrist.'

Brett strolled out to join them, holding a folder of papers. 'There's a lot of work in here.'

'Alistair seemed very thorough,' said Leonie. 'I left it to him. All the processes involved are a nightmare, by the sounds of it.'

'And expensive. And, I hate to say it, Leonie, but most of this looks unnecessary,' said Brett. 'I'll have to have a closer look to be sure, but I think he's figured out you must have enough money to waste on all this.'

'What do you mean, Brett?' asked Leonie in surprise.

'I know it's not my field, but I can see there's a mass of stuff in here that you simply didn't need to do and is super costly. Do you know the solicitor he's got handling this?' asked Brett.

'No. Alistair said it's a friend of his. He has a lot of good contacts.'

'That's not good,' said Sarita. 'Jobs for the boys?'

Leonie shrugged. 'I have no idea what he's done. Take it away if you want, Brett, Alistair has copies. I just want to make sure the sale goes through on a heritage building with no fuss and no fanfare.'

'And I won't sleep easy unless I am sure you're not being ripped off,' said Brett.

'Okay, fine. Thank you. I will appreciate your legal opinion and I'm sure Alistair will be grateful if you do find any discrepancies,' said Leonie crisply.

Brett didn't look convinced. 'I'll bring this back in a day or so, okay?' he said.

Leonie looked at the brother and sister, so different in looks, both so united in her best interests. Her shoulders slumped a little.

'Thank you, truly. I'm just feeling a bit overwhelmed at the moment. Now, I think I should check on Harry.' She stood and went inside.

*

Maddie sat quietly in the background during the audition for the singer to play Ella's role in the new production of *Percy and Ella*. While there had been some changes and a lot more orchestration, the songs she'd sung in the original production at the Playhouse felt like they were etched into her soul.

Both performers had beautiful voices and the right look for the part. Maddie could tell one was extremely nervous but she thought she had the sweeter voice.

Later, alone with Fleur, she mentioned the woman she thought the better of the two.

'But I suppose you chose the confident singer?' Maddie asked.

'No. Actually, I chose the nervous one, Sophia. By the time she's been through weeks of rehearsal, she'll have lost her nerves,' Fleur smiled.

'Hard for the other singer who didn't get the role,' said Maddie.

'That's showbiz. She's got talent, she'll make it,' said Fleur.

Maddie shook her head. 'I'd be devastated. I'm not cut out for constantly putting yourself out there for rejection.' Before she could say anything more, Charlie joined them, setting down his camera.

'Hard choice, Fleur.'

'That's my job, Charlie. Did you get enough footage?'

'Plenty. Those two were great. What's next?'

'I have a meeting with a money man. You can't film that.'

'Why not? He might be too embarrassed to knock you back on camera,' Charlie laughed.

'Wishful thinking, Charlie, but no, I'd rather you didn't film it. I'll see you both later. Dinner?' asked Fleur.

'Sorry, Fleur, I'm editing,' said Charlie. As Fleur nodded and walked away, he turned to Maddie.

'What're you up to now?'

'Spoiled for choice here,' she grinned. 'New York's every bit as amazing as I imagined.'

'I haven't had time to discover much. Why don't you take me somewhere you like?'

'I thought you said you were editing your film?' said Maddie.

'I changed my mind.' He suddenly looked serious. 'I'd like to catch up with you, Maddie.'

Maddie was torn. She did want to spend time with him, but she was finding it difficult to just socialise as friends, knowing he had moved on.

'Ah, I guess so. Do you want to ask anyone else to come along too?'

'You mean Julian? Who else do you know here? I don't know anyone but the guy I'm staying with, and he's in rehearsals all the time. Don't worry about it. I just thought –' He leaned down and picked up his camera.

Seeing him cradling the bulky camera brought back memories of the times they'd shared together when she'd accompanied him on filming jobs. How she'd joked that his camera was like a kid or a dog – never out of his sight.

'No, wait. I mean, yes. I'd love to. I've found some little places here that do great food. Not too expensive,' she added.

Charlie looked at her solemnly. 'You sure? Okay. Let's go.'

'Great,' said Maddie, smiling, suddenly feeling that special warmth she always had with Charlie. But it was tinged with faint regret that there was still a barrier between them. She didn't want to be 'just good friends', but she didn't want to lose his friendship altogether, either. The day he brought a girlfriend along to meet her would be the day they'd part ways for good, she thought. But for now, here they were, on the other side of the world, swept up in the excitement of a new city, a new career, perhaps, and the privilege of seeing a magical world of new opportunities, of dreams and possibilities, open before them.

*

It was early afternoon when Chrissie drove into Fig Tree River after having met Jennifer at the solicitor's office.

School wasn't finished for the day, and the early evening rush, little as it was, had yet to start. As she'd hoped, it was a languid afternoon with few people around.

'Can we see our old friends when school is finished?' asked Thomas excitedly.

Chrissie had no intention of them seeing anyone, and, hopefully, none of her friends would spot her. She drove around into the backyard of her mother's house and hurried the children inside.

'Well, it's about time!' exclaimed her mother as she hugged the children. 'I haven't seen you for weeks and weeks.' She kissed Chrissie on the cheek, saying, 'Is everything okay? You look very strained.'

'Just tired, Mum. Long drive.'

'C'mon, let's have some afternoon tea. I've been so looking forward to seeing you. Such short notice, though, Chrissie. I haven't even had a chance to tell Dad yet. How long are you staying?'

'It's just a quick visit, Mum. I can't stay this time. I just wanted to catch up, and pick up some things I left here. But a cup of tea would be lovely.'

'Is my bike still here?' asked Thomas.

'Yes, there's a lot of your things in Poppy's garage,' said their grandmother, smiling. 'Is that what you came for?' she asked Chrissie as the two children ran off.

'They have fancy new ones Troy bought them but it's such a pain taking the bikes up and down in the lift,' said Chrissie tightly.

'Have you come for your tools? They're still in boxes in the garage. Oh, and there's all that paperwork you left in the drawer in the bedroom.'

'That's all I want,' said Chrissie, her voice suddenly shaking.

Her mother sat down opposite her and reached out, touching her hand. 'What's going on? Is everything all right?'

Chrissie looked at her mother's concerned and caring face. She shook her head. 'No.'

'It's Troy?'

Chrissie nodded, then managed to say, 'I've left him. The kids don't know . . . I'm in the middle of it all. Jennifer from a women's refuge is helping me.'

'A women's refuge? Oh, Chrissie. Good grief, you don't need that, just come back home, here,' exclaimed her mother.

She stood up and made a pot of tea, then brought it over with a tin of homemade biscuits.

'This must be hard for you. But . . . I can't say that I'm surprised, and I'm sure your father will feel the same. Dad has been very cranky at the way Troy's been spending your money. Can't you lock it up in the bank or something?'

'Mum, that's not the problem. Yes, he's spending the money – I couldn't stop him – but he's being . . . well, aggressive. Controlling. And I'm scared for me and the kids,' she added quickly.

Her mother looked horrified. 'Well, that's it then. You can't go back to him. Just walk away, you can afford your own place,' she said firmly. 'Even if you couldn't, there would always be room for you and the kids here.'

'Thanks, Mum, but it's not that simple. Troy gave me business papers to sign. It was easier to do that than argue. I don't know what they were, really. I don't care, I just want to leave with the children and start over somewhere new.'

'We'll help you in any way we can, sweetie,' said her mother gently. 'Troy has such an ego. He'll want to make you the bad guy.'

'Yes, I know. Jennifer helped me take out a restraining order against him and it comes with all kinds of restrictions. He can't come near me or the kids without permission.'

'I don't think he'll take any notice of that. He has always thought he can do whatever he wants. And he does,' said her mother briskly.

'That's exactly what's happened, Mum. He's shut down my bank account, and he was tracking everywhere I went on my phone.'

'I hope he hasn't followed you here,' exclaimed her mother.

'No, they've stopped it now. The refuge arranged it. But I have to get back there. I just need to get these papers. Thanks for everything, Mum.' Chrissie was on the verge of tears.

'You know,' said her mother gently, 'I rather hoped this day would come. You haven't been yourself for such a long time. Don't worry, darling. We're here for you and the kids.'

'Thanks, Mum.'

When she'd finished her tea, Chrissie sat on her parents' bed and thumbed through the envelope of her papers.

Suddenly her mother burst into the room. 'Chrissie . . . I can't find the children!'

'What do you mean? Maybe they've gone down the road to Thomas's mate's house? I told them not to leave the backyard, but he was so keen to see his friends . . .'

Forty-five minutes later they had exhausted all the places the children could be.

'Okay, I'm calling the police,' said Chrissie's mother.

'No, I will.' But as Chrissie picked up her mobile, her parents' landline rang. She snatched it up. 'Hello? Oh my God – it's Thomas,' she told her mother. 'Thomas? *Where are you?*' she shrieked. 'Thomas, oh my God . . .' She listened for a moment, then said to her mother, 'Troy has them . . . WHERE ARE YOU?' Chrissie screamed into the phone. 'DON'T HANG UP!'

'What's he saying?' asked her mother, ashen-faced.

Chrissie looked down at the silent receiver. 'Thomas says they're on the highway and Daddy is taking them for a holiday. Then the phone went dead.'

Chrissie stared at her mother. Then burst into sobbing tears.

15

MADDIE STOOD STILL, HANDS thrust in her pockets, staring up at the elegant skyscraper towering above her. The wind whipped her hair, and, as she lifted a hand to push the strands away from her face, a familiar voice spoke behind her.

'See why it's named after the keeper of the winds?'

Maddie turned and smiled at Charlie. 'So you've even researched this Aeolian Building? Why are we meeting here?' she asked.

'It's a sad but significant symbol in Percy Grainger's life. His mother Rose jumped from the eighteenth floor in 1922. Percy never really recovered.'

Maddie looked up at the now modernised building. 'She must have been terribly unhappy,' she said. 'Fleur told me that Mrs Grainger was ill for a long time. She was devoted to Percy, as he was to her.'

Charlie nodded in agreement.

'I've also been researching Grainger and his music,' said Maddie enthusiastically. 'I admire his passion as a pianist and composer. He collected and recorded folk music in obscure places that would have been lost otherwise.'

Charlie and Maddie walked over to the entrance to the building, to read the plaque on the wall.

'Are you including this in your film?' asked Maddie. 'Working on it must have been so interesting,' she added, wishing she could have been involved too.

'Yep. My trip here to make a film was Fleur's idea. It's basically all shot and I'm just editing the last of it before shooting the opening night of the show. I'll fill you in over lunch if you can put up with me for that long.'

He took her hand and they started walking.

Maddie stopped and pulled her hand free. Taking a deep breath she said, 'Why are you doing this, Charlie? I've really loved spending time with you, but I feel like you're giving me mixed messages here and . . . it's painful. I don't know what to think.'

Charlie gave a quick smile. Then stopped, his face serious. 'I'm really sorry, Mads. Not seeing you, not being with you, talking stuff over with you . . . I've been an idiot. These last few months I've been so lonely, and so jealous. I realised . . . *I love you*! I don't want to lose you. Especially to that goofball.'

'Who, Julian?! Don't be stupid!' Maddie wanted to laugh but was too stunned at this sudden turnaround. 'I was never interested in him. He's not my type at all. Plus, at the end of the day, Julian is only interested in Julian!'

'Well, that's true.' Charlie chuckled quietly and took

her hand in his again. More seriously he added, 'I backed off when you said you'd won that money. That was your key to the door, to freedom, Mads. I didn't want to hold you back or influence you in any way.'

Maddie took a moment to think, then said softly, 'You've said that before, but you've never given me the chance to say what I think, what I want.'

Charlie was about to reply but Maddie put up her hand. 'Please let me say what I need to. I feel that I'm at some sort of crossroads. The money is nice, of course, but it's not the most important thing in my life.' There was a catch in her voice.

Charlie turned her around to face him.

'So? What *is* the most important thing in your life now, Mads? Your career? You have the opportunity of a lifetime with Fleur's help. And now, with your money, you can travel, do great things! Start a business, whatever you want. So? What's most important to you?'

They stood facing each other in the middle of the pavement, people passing on either side of them, time seemingly suspended.

'You,' said Maddie.

Charlie let out his breath, suddenly aware he'd been holding it. He reached for Maddie and hugged her to him, bending his face to hers.

Then both of them were oblivious to passers-by, who continued to stream past them, some directing a smile at the two entwined figures as they kissed.

*

Maddie chose an Italian pizzeria that Fleur had taken her to, and they settled in a quiet corner.

'Tell me more, Charlie,' said Maddie after they ordered

a pizza to share. 'About the film you're doing with Fleur, I mean. What comes first, the musical, the movie or the TV series . . .?' she grinned.

'The musical, of course.' He leaned forward. 'But all jokes aside, I *am* thinking of helping Fleur adapt the script for a film. Would you write a song for it?'

Maddie flung up her hands. 'Whoa! That would be cool! Let me think about that. The show we did in Fig Tree River stands up really well.' She looked thoughtful. 'But I love the idea of taking it to the next step on screen . . .'

'I know just the cinematographer I'd use too,' said Charlie.

'And Sarita could do the costumes! Did you ever see those sketches she did for Fleur, just in case? I thought they were completely over-the-top but now that we've seen Julian in that crazy copy of what Grainger apparently wore, I'm not so sure!'

They both laughed, then Charlie said, 'Seriously, though, first up let's help Fleur get this show on the road.'

Their pizza arrived and Maddie reached for a slice, then paused and looked at Charlie.

'I know what I'm going to do.'

Charlie stared at her, waiting.

'Fleur is struggling to get the finance for the show. So I'm going to be one of her "angels".' She paused.

Charlie smiled. 'You'll need a name for your production company.'

'What did Percy call his music machine invention again?' she asked.

Charlie applauded. 'He called it the Free Music Machine.'

'Then that's it.' Maddie reached her hand out across the table. 'Free Music Productions it is. Okay, partner?'

Charlie had his mouth full of pizza, but he nodded enthusiastically, giving her a thumbs-up, before swallowing and shaking her hand across the table. 'Sounds good to me.'

*

Leonie heard her name called and walked out to the verandah to see Brett and Harry standing by the steps.

'Hi, Brett. You're back up again? You seem to be spending more time here than in your office in Sydney,' she said. 'I hope you didn't have to come back up because of me.'

'Nope. I'm doing some things for my sister and Ray. But I had to come by, so I was just yarning to Harry about the dam at the back.'

'Is there any update on things?' asked Leonie.

'You bet,' said Brett.

'Okay, come on in.'

Brett clapped Harry on the shoulder. 'Good to see you getting about. Those new glasses suit you.'

'Nothing wrong with me,' said Harry staunchly as he turned away, trying to hide the stiffness that lingered in his gait.

Brett followed Leonie into the study.

'Ah, you've tidied things up,' said Brett.

'Yes – Alistair wanted a space to work and I was using the kitchen table.'

Brett paused. 'Leonie, could I pry and ask if Alistair is moving in with you?'

Leonie looked at Brett. 'I could say that's none of your business,' she said firmly.

'And I could say I don't think it's a wise move,' said Brett calmly, adding, 'And it's not just me.'

Leonie turned away. 'Oh for God's sake, tell people to butt out of my life.'

'Leonie, I'm worried, and with good reason.'

'Like what?'

'I've been through those documents of Alistair's more thoroughly now. I hate to say it, but most of it is waffle and extraneous padding which adds up to unnecessary but horrendously expensive invoices. He's spending your money like there's no tomorrow. *Please* tell me you haven't told him about winning the lottery.'

'No. But once again, I could say it's no one's business but mine,' said Leonie stiffly.

Brett sighed. 'Leonie, Sarita and I are very worried that Alistair suspects you have money and is taking advantage of you because of it. Maybe he thinks it's a family inheritance – I don't know – but, well, you're vulnerable. How many years ago did Tony die? You're lonely and a sitting duck for a schmoozer like him. I know you don't want to hear this, but as your friend, it would not be right if I didn't try to warn you, even at the risk of facing your anger about it.'

Leonie was stony-faced. 'Explain the invoices and documents to me.'

'Certainly. Let's sit down.'

Twenty minutes later, Leonie leaned back in her chair as Brett shuffled the papers back into the folder.

'There's probably fifty grand worth of charges here that are totally unnecessary,' said Brett. 'And the sale of the Playhouse has not yet been formalised.'

Leonie shook her head, looking dazed. 'Alistair said he'd handle it all.'

Brett bit his tongue, holding back the 'yeah, I bet he did' that sprang to mind.

'Look, Brett, it doesn't matter. I can afford to pay this –'

'Leonie, that's not the point. Alistair is ripping you off.'

'Have you and Sarita and Ray been getting together to discuss him?' Leonie sounded hurt.

'We only have your best interests at heart,' said Brett gently. 'You four winners have had a life-changing experience. There's good and bad aspects to that. Ray is deeply concerned about the effect the whole island deal has had on my sister. Maddie is terribly upset at her parents essentially splitting up. Chrissie sounds miserable living in Port Haven, and we're all worried you're being seduced by a con man! There, I've said it.'

'And on the bright side . . .?' Leonie gave him a quizzical look. 'Brett, I appreciate what you are all thinking, but you're wrong. Alistair is considerate and attentive to me and Corby.'

'But Harry is the one Corby goes to first if he needs to talk, I reckon,' said Brett.

Leonie's mouth tightened and Brett knew he was right.

'Leonie, just think for a minute. Has Alistair suggested taking an overseas holiday together, or going on a trip when Corby is at camp or at a sleepover, or perhaps that you could go into business together? Has he ever suggested that the farm is too much work, or perhaps that he has always wanted to do some philanthropic works that, by the way, need investors?'

'Stop it!' shouted Leonie. 'What you're saying is ridiculous.'

Brett reached out to her touch her arm, realising he'd hit a nerve. 'What do you know about his background, his family, his work, his late wife's details?'

'I don't need to know any of that,' muttered Leonie. 'I see how Alistair treats us, and he's thoughtful and caring.'

'Fine. Ask him to pay for something.'

Brett stopped speaking. Leonie was silent, staring at him.

'I don't need to do that. I trust him.'

Brett closed his eyes and took a breath. 'Okay, then, please just get advice before you do anything. We just want you to be happy, but safe.'

'I am happy, Brett. Thank you and Sarita and Ray for worrying about me, but I'm a grown woman and I can look after myself and my son,' Leonie said evenly. 'And as a matter of fact, Alistair *has* mentioned us all taking a trip . . . maybe to Europe.' She paused and gave Brett a straight look. 'And yes, I will be paying. First class, all the way. But it's something I want to do, too.'

She turned away and firmly changed the subject.

'So what's happening about the dam?'

Brett drew a breath. 'Well, there's news there. It's great news, actually. The outcome of that environmental and scientific survey was massive. The report is long and very detailed – I know it must have cost a fortune, but my God! What they found! Your Tony was certainly on the right track. You can't imagine the wildlife that's up there. Anyone wanting to put in a dam there is going to face enormous obstacles.'

Leonie gave a sigh, realising how worried she'd been. 'Oh, thank God. I'm so glad to hear it.'

'Yep, nature rules! The habitat is crammed with living things from snakes to rare frogs, to birdlife you can't believe, wallabies and roos, platypus, insects and bandicoots, rare bush orchids, native grasses, koalas, of course . . . and there's more.' Brett stood up. 'Is Stevie around?' he asked.

'Yes. Why?' Leonie looked confused.

'He and Harry have some news for you, too.'

Leonie gave him a look but got up and went to the back door, where she clanged a loud bell.

'They'll think it's smoko or that I'm in trouble,' said Leonie.

'Good system,' said Brett with a grin.

Stevie and Harry appeared quickly, as if they'd been waiting for the call, both looking cheerful.

Leonie glanced at Brett.

'What's going on?'

'Do you want to tell her, Stevie?' said Brett.

Leonie glanced at Harry. 'Why do you look like the cat that got the cream?' she said.

Harry nudged Stevie.

The young man ran his fingers through his thick dark curls and stood a little straighter.

'Well, Mrs Foster, there won't be any dam,' he announced.

'Really? How can you be sure?' asked Leonie, turning back to Harry, who broke out in a great big smile.

Harry nodded at Stevie who went on, 'When I was looking around up there, I was having a real careful check for anything unusual or important. And . . . I found these stones. In a circle, old fella stones, Uncle Clarrie said . . .'

'It's a Bora ring,' interjected Harry, unable to hold back the news. 'Sacred site. Really old one. The Elders are thrilled to find it. We didn't want to tell you till it was all confirmed.'

'You're kidding me! How wonderful,' exclaimed Leonie.

'That means it can't be touched,' said Brett. 'It's a men's ceremonial initiation place.'

'The team who did the survey for you are asking the Elders to check it out,' added Stevie. 'Document it because it's old and nobody knew about it.'

'It'll be off limits for sure, I reckon,' said Harry.

Brett clapped his hands together. 'Right. Well, any other problems, give us a call, since we're on a roll,' he said with a grin.

Leonie felt better than she had in ages. 'How about a celebratory pot of tea,' she said.

*

Despite the good news about the dam, Leonie had a restless night. She got up and tiptoed down to Corby's room to quietly check he was all right, something she hadn't done in a long time, then lay in bed in the dark, unable to go back to sleep. She couldn't understand the sudden and overwhelming rush of loneliness that overtook her. Her life was busy, yes, and she'd had her fair share of ups and downs, but it was blessed in so many ways. And now, thanks to Brett – even though she still had mixed feelings about what he'd said – the purchase of the Playhouse didn't seem quite so complicated, either. Why, then, was she feeling so down? Eventually, as dawn broke, she pushed these thoughts to one side and got up to face her day's work.

At lunchtime she was walking towards the kitchen when she heard the back screen door slam.

'Hidey-ho!' called Alistair. 'Ah, there you are. Surprise – not! I thought we could head out to dinner tonight? Try someplace new. What do you feel like?' He drew her into his arms. 'Apart from me, of course,' he murmured.

Leonie gently wiggled from his arms. She would prefer to go out with Alistair, she thought, than have dinner with him at home. Times alone with him when Corby was staying over at his friends' places had become a little predictable. The glass of wine on the verandah, the arms around her waist from behind as she cooked and he nuzzled her neck. They ate, cleared the dishes and then went to bed and made love. Sleep. Sometimes he left before Leonie awoke, leaving an ardent note behind explaining some early-morning appointment. She'd kept her rule that he only stayed over when Corby was away.

Alistair pulled a bottle of champagne from his shoulder bag.

'Just off the ice at the shop! Let's celebrate.'

'Oh, what are we celebrating?' said Leonie, and suddenly found herself wondering if he'd put it on her account at the shop as usual, then chided herself for being petty.

'Us? Whatever you'd like. Do we need a special occasion?' He poured the champagne into two flutes and handed her one.

'Of course not.' Leonie turned away, but Alistair caught her other hand.

'My beautiful Lee . . . I've been thinking, and I think it's time. I have a great idea, a plan, for us both.'

'What sort of plan?' asked Leonie cautiously.

'There's so much more we could do together.' As Leonie went to speak, he put a finger to her lips. 'Hear me out. It's time you stopped letting this place drag you down. I see how exhausting it is for you. You could begin a new life, travel, start up an exciting new business –'

'Alistair!' Leonie looked alarmed.

'Listen, listen, I'm not finished,' he smiled. 'Sell this

place, and let's invest in a new company – together! There are so many exciting projects we could be doing. After the success we've had with the Playhouse, we could restore heritage buildings in all the small towns around here, imagine it! With my expertise and your sensible charm,' he enthused, ignoring Leonie's stunned expression, 'we'd make a great team!'

Leonie was utterly shocked. She took a moment to gather her thoughts. 'Alistair, how could you suggest this? Sell this place? This land? This is Corby's inheritance! I'm helping carry out Tony's dream. I could *never* sell this place. Do you know what you're asking?'

'But Lee, what's the point of this place, really? Nothing happens here. A few cattle and old horses – worth peanuts! It's not being used to its full commercial potential.'

She knew he was deliberately downplaying the value of her property. 'Well, to you, maybe. But this land – the soil – is the most valuable thing on this property. We work with nature to ensure that it remains good land, with clean water, biodiversity and protected wildlife! How can you have missed the importance of that to me, when you've spent all this time here, with us?'

Alistair gave a harsh laugh. 'C'mon, Lee – don't go all hippy-dippy greenie on me. Land means bucks: for buildings, developments, big crops. But it's too much hard work. Don't you want to be in a business that brings in the dollars but means we can live a freer life, with the world at our feet, not out here in the middle of nowhere? We can have so much fun together, you and me – travel, live the good life.' He held open his arms, but Leonie took a step backwards.

'This *is* the good life,' she said slowly. 'It's what Tony and I wanted, dreamed of, worked for. And I don't hear much room in your plans for Corby. He comes first for me, and this place is his, too.'

Alistair broke in, 'We'll create a far bigger inheritance for Corby, together! There's better ways to do things now. I have lots of ideas –'

'Stop! Alistair, no! Listen to me.' Leonie fumbled for words, trying to work out how to make him see how badly he'd misread the situation, and how ridiculous his suggestions seemed to her. He didn't understand her at all. Brett's words suddenly came back to her like sharp arrows. Was Alistair really after her money? An easy life for himself? He clearly had no idea what this land, this place, meant to her. She suddenly understood how deeply different they were. How could she not have seen it before?

Oblivious to her stunned reaction, Alistair put down his champagne flute and went down on one knee, fumbling in his pocket. 'Lee, darling . . . there's something I want to –'

'Oh . . . oh,' Leonie gabbled.

'Anyone home?' Harry called from the verandah, the screen door banging behind him.

'Bloody hell.' Alistair scrambled to his feet.

'Mail's here,' called Harry.

'Thanks, I'll get it in a minute,' called Leonie faintly, and turned back to Alistair.

'Alistair, look –'

'Lee . . .' Alistair frowned. 'I want you to marry me. I have such plans for us; it could be so wonderful. Sell this place and we'll see the world, start our own future, together.'

Leonie took a deep breath. 'I'm sorry, Alistair, but the answer is no. I can't and won't leave, let alone sell this place,' she said steadily. 'I intend to keep on doing what

I do. Here. For Corby. For Tony, for myself!' She paused, seeing his shocked and angry face. 'Maybe I'll pass on dinner tonight.'

Alistair downed the last of his champagne and put his glass on the table, saying, 'You are making a terrible mistake, Lee. I can offer you so much – we could really be a team.'

'I don't think so, I'm sorry,' she said again, more firmly this time.

'How can you say that, Lee? You will have such regrets.'

'Then I'll have to live with them. And actually, I prefer to be called Leonie.'

Alistair frowned, his face blank, his eyes cold. 'I won't call you again.'

'Goodbye, Alistair.'

He strode from the room, and she heard his feet stomp down the front steps and his car roar away.

*

A short time later, Harry walked into the kitchen.

Leonie turned as he dropped a pile of just-picked beans on the table.

He looked at her. 'You all right?'

'Never better,' said Leonie, and realised she meant it. She felt lighter, clearer. 'Alistair just left. For good.'

'Right-oh.' Harry walked back outside.

Leonie stared at the older man's back. She knew damn well he had a big grin on his face.

*

Later, as Leonie drained her glass of Alistair's champagne, her phone rang.

'Hi Sarita,' she began, but before she could break her news about Alistair, Sarita gasped, 'Chrissie just rang me in a panic. She's at her parents' place in town. Troy has stolen her kids!'

'What do you mean, stolen?' asked Leonie in alarm.

In a rushed breath Sarita explained what had happened.

'My God. We knew something was up, but I had no idea... Did she call the police?' asked Leonie. 'What's happening?'

'I'm not sure. I'm heading over to her mum's place now to see what I can do.'

'I know where Chrissie's parents live, I'll meet you there,' started Leonie, then stopped. 'Wait – why don't we call Wade Franks at the police station? That might be quicker.'

'Good idea. Maybe he's already on the case, but he can fill us in,' said Sarita. 'I'll call him now – see you soon.'

Leonie raced outside. She quickly arranged with Harry to pick Corby up from school for her, then jumped in her car.

*

A police car was outside Chrissie's parents' house. Her father was standing at the front door.

'Thank you for coming,' he said to Leonie as Sarita pulled up behind in her car. 'This is all so dreadful.'

The group in the living room was sombre. Chrissie's mother was talking quietly with Wade, and Sarita went to join them. Leonie sat down beside Chrissie and took her hand as the young mother spoke tearfully.

'I thought I had everything covered – I did what Jennifer at the refuge said. How could he just be hanging around here at the very moment I come here with the kids? I haven't been in Fig Tree River for ages.'

'Don't beat yourself up. We'll get them back safely; he's trying it on. He's probably mad you got the better of him, stood up to him,' said Leonie. 'But he'd never harm the kids.'

'He hit me,' said Chrissie grimly. 'The kids saw it. They'll be terrified.'

'Oh my God! That's horrible! Has he done it before?' gasped Leonie.

Chrissie hesitated then said, 'Yes.'

'Why didn't you tell us? Report him? How long has this been happening?' asked Leonie.

'It's been going on for ages, but it was getting worse. He used to always be so sorry afterwards, and would try to make up for it. Not so much lately. And anyway I felt it was my fault . . .'

'Chrissie! No way! You can't blame yourself for this.'

Leonie paused as Sarita and Wade walked over to them.

'He won't get far, Chrissie, as you have an AVO out on him, which he is now breaching,' said Wade. 'We have cars looking for him and an all-points bulletin out for all the vehicles registered in his name. Your husband must have a new phone number as we can't track the number you gave us. Do the kids have phones?'

'No. They're a bit young so we hadn't got them phones yet. They have iPads, but I kept them turned off just in case.'

Leonie shook her head. 'I can't believe this technological tracking stuff.'

'There's a lot to keep up with,' said Wade. 'How do you think we find people in the middle of nowhere? Infrared imaging tracks heat sources. And police can use

GPS boundaries to know when there's a phone conversation happening in a specific area. Plus, you would be amazed at the spyware for sale on the open market. Oh, the stories I could tell.'

Wade lowered his voice, turned away and said to Sarita, 'The hard part will be getting the kids away from Troy when we find the car.'

Then he cleared his throat and turned back to Chrissie. 'Do you know if Troy owns a gun?'

Chrissie's eyes widened. 'No . . . not that I know of, anyway,' she said shakily.

As Leonie reached out to pat Chrissie's shoulder, Wade and Sarita quietly stepped away.

'I didn't want to alarm Chrissie, but I had to ask,' said Wade.

'I understand. Come to think of it, she was always anxious not to upset Troy,' said Sarita sadly.

'I did wonder why Troy never turned up at the theatre, and why she never spoke about him,' said Wade. 'Not an uncommon scenario, unfortunately.'

They walked back to Chrissie. 'We should have realised what was going on, when it was so difficult for you to meet up with us and when you said you couldn't do the show. I guess Troy was making it hard for you? I'm sorry, Chrissie,' Sarita said.

Chrissie shook her head. 'You weren't to know, Sarita.'

'Yes,' Wade agreed. 'You even worked at home to make those –' He suddenly stopped. 'Those sets you made, that caught fire. I bet only your things were damaged, not Troy's.' Wade looked at Chrissie. 'Did Troy have anything to do with –'

Chrissie nodded, her eyes filling with tears again.

'Sit tight, Chrissie,' said Wade grimly. 'We are throwing everything at this. You'll be the first to know when there are developments.'

*

Roger and Freddy came over as soon as they heard the news and were soon making tea and coffee for the group gathered in the living room.

Wade kept glancing at his phone.

Chrissie looked at her watch. 'It's been two hours,' she murmured.

Sarita nodded. 'Want a cup of tea?'

Chrissie shook her head. Then the landline rang again and she jumped. 'Thomas rang me on Mum and Dad's phone before,' she said.

'Answer it,' Wade said gently.

Shaking, Chrissie managed a hesitant, 'Hello . . .?' Then she gasped. 'Mia! Where are you, darling? What's happening?' She tried to keep her voice as calm as possible, then listened and nodded. 'Is Thomas all right? Yes, we're coming, darling, it'll be ok–' She listened a moment then stopped and looked at the phone. 'She's hung up.'

The room was silent, everyone frozen in place. Then Chrissie burst out, 'They're in some town, Mia didn't know the name. She says Thomas got the phone away from their father. She's hiding in the toilet at a café across from the Wanderlust Motel – where or what is that?'

Wade was immediately on his phone repeating this news as he strode towards the door. 'I'm on my way,' he said as he hung up.

Chrissie jumped up and rushed across the room. 'I'm coming with you.'

'No, Chrissie – it could be dangerous. Please wait here, a liaison officer will stay here with you.' Wade shook his head and hurried outside.

'They're my kids, I should be there!' sobbed Chrissie.

He stopped and turned back. 'All right, but you can't come with me. Get one of the others to drive you and do exactly what the other officers and I tell you. Do anything else and it could harm the kids,' Wade said quickly, then raced down to the waiting police car.

Sarita was scrolling through her phone. 'Got it – it's the only place with a name like that within two hours of here. Let's go.'

As the three women ran from the room, Chrissie's mother called, 'Take care and call us!'

'Be careful,' shouted her father.

*

Leonie drove in silence, Sarita plugging the address into the car's navigation system and watching the speed limit, and Chrissie hunched in the back, arms tightly folded, hugging herself and biting her lip.

'What kind of car does Troy have?' asked Sarita.

'Which one? He has several now,' said Chrissie tightly.

'I see. Spending your money, eh?'

'Our money, unfortunately. He's entitled to half – or so he keeps reminding me,' said Chrissie.

'Right. I see. I can understand what's been going on, Chrissie,' said Sarita.

'I don't think so.' For a moment Chrissie felt she was going to crumble apart. 'This has been going on a long time. The money has only made it worse. The woman from the refuge told me Troy's behaviour is classic and predictable coercive control. I always thought it was me . . .' Her voice trembled. 'I just want my kids to be safe.'

'Of course you do. I'm calling Ray,' said Sarita.

She quickly filled her husband in, listened for a moment then, after hanging up, said, 'Ray and Brett are on their way as well.'

Leonie nodded and glanced at the car's navigator, which indicated they were getting close to the small township. As they approached, she pulled over. 'I'll call Wade, see what's happening.'

'Shouldn't we just keep going?' fretted Chrissie.

'Let me call first,' said Leonie. 'I don't want to arrive if the police don't want us there yet.' She dialled, then sat listening and nodding. 'Okay. Yep, got it.'

Chrissie looked anxious.

Leonie hung up and turned to Chrissie. 'Mia is still locked in the toilet in the café across the road from the Wanderlust Motel, and Thomas has locked himself in his father's car in the motel car park, but they are both safe. Wade says Troy is being interviewed by two policemen,' Leonie explained as clearly as she could. 'There's a roadblock either side of town, but they'll let us through. Sounds like the kids are refusing to come out until you're there.'

She started the car again as Chrissie slumped with relief and gave a tearful smile. Then Chrissie said darkly, 'He'll never forgive me for this. He'll try something again, I know it.'

'I believe that's the pattern. You just need the right protections and procedures in place,' said Leonie.

'Everything just seems so hard,' said Chrissie. 'He made everything my fault – always told me I'm useless and hopeless. In his eyes the only thing I've ever done right is win that money. I don't think he'll ever leave me alone.'

'Listen, Chrissie,' said Leonie as she drove, 'you're absolutely doing the right thing. You've made the move to get out of there, you've got your kids away from that terrible situation. It might not be easy, but you'll be able to move forward and put him out of your life now.'

'How? They're his kids too . . . he'll always be part of our lives. There's no escape,' she said bitterly.

Just then they arrived at the motel, and the women saw the police cars and a small group of people standing around.

'Oh my God . . .' cried Chrissie.

'I'm going to go and tell the coppers who you are. So just hang on. It's going to be fine,' said Leonie steadily.

Chrissie watched for a moment as Leonie went over to the nearest officers, then she stepped out of the car.

'Chrissie, wait here. Let's find out what the cops have told Leonie,' Sarita cried out, but Chrissie had already hurried away.

Troy's car was in the parking lot with a police officer watching over Thomas, who was bravely sitting inside it.

Suddenly Troy emerged from the café across the road from the motel, walking between two police officers. They moved to one side and stood in a small group in intense conversation.

Then, as if a starter's whistle had blown, there was an explosion of energy and confusion.

Chrissie started running as fast as she could towards Troy's car.

Thomas, seeing his mother, unlocked and opened the door and ran towards her, calling out, 'Mum, Mum!'

The police all turned to see Chrissie screaming, 'Thomas!' as she ran. Troy suddenly pushed past the policeman he was speaking to and broke away. As the second officer chased after him, Troy reached his car, swinging an elbow and knocking the policewoman who'd been watching over Thomas to the ground.

Thomas reached his mother just as another officer ran towards Troy's car, which was now reversing at speed. Troy spun the wheel, then accelerated forward across a garden bed and rocketed out onto the main road.

Two police officers ran to their vehicle and set off in pursuit, siren blaring.

Chrissie hugged Thomas to her. 'Oh, my darling. Are you okay? Let's get your sister.' They both hurried towards the café.

Inside, Chrissie knocked on the toilet door. 'Mia, it's Mum, sweetheart. It's okay now, you can come out, I'm here.' Slowly, the door opened, and a terrified face looked up at Chrissie.

Speechless with relief, Chrissie pulled her children into a tight hug and thought she'd never let them go. Finally Thomas wriggled free and looked up at her.

'That was so bad, Mum. Dad scared me. I got his phone when he wasn't looking and I gave it to Mia when he couldn't see, then she started crying, saying she wanted to go to the toilet, and Dad stopped here so she could go.'

'But I was just pretending,' said Mia proudly. 'Daddy had Nana and Poppy's number in his phone, so I rang it.'

The policewoman who'd been looking after Thomas in the locked car came running in.

'How are you all? Are the kids okay?' she asked Chrissie, who could only nod and wipe away her tears. When she looked up again, she saw Brett standing in front of her, smiling but looking anxious.

'Oh Brett, thank you for coming. It's so nice to see a friendly face. You've all been so good to me. What's going to happen now?' Chrissie asked him as they all made their way towards the door.

'You keep going forward, I'd say, Chrissie. No going back now,' said Brett gently. 'Sarita filled us in. I'm so sorry this has happened to you, but the main thing is that it's over.' As they walked, Mia looked up at him and slid her little hand into his.

When they got outside, Sarita, Leonie and Ray hurried over to them.

Leonie looked down at the young girl, who still appeared very shaken. 'That was very clever of you to call your mum,' said Leonie.

'Thomas and me thought of it together,' Mia explained. 'But I couldn't talk any more when someone came into the toilet. Where's Dad?'

'He's left here, sweetie,' said Chrissie quickly.

'I didn't want to go with him!' said Mia. 'He was being really mean.'

Thomas leaned against Chrissie. 'We're staying with you, Mum,' he said firmly.

Brett was staring at the police who were talking together in the car park. One of them was speaking intently into a radio. He turned back to the group, saying, 'How about you all sit down and order something to eat and drink. I'll just be a minute.' He threaded his way between several tables of curious onlookers over to the officers.

'Are you a friend of the family?' one of them asked.

'Ah, yes, I am. What's happening?' Brett could hear sirens again.

'There's been an accident. Yet to be confirmed, but it seems the father just ran off the road into a tree.'

Epilogue

NEW YORK CITY, SIX MONTHS LATER

Maddie was watching the morning breakfast show on TV as she ate her toast and Vegemite.

'Why are you watching that?' asked Charlie, towelling his hair dry from the shower.

'Come and see. Julian is being interviewed – and he's wearing a Percy outfit.'

'Only Julian could look so at ease in striped knickerbockers. Is he on because of his Obie Award?'

'Yes. And he's just mentioned that a film is in the works. That's us!'

'Well, that might be a bit premature, but it looks more promising every day, thanks to you,' said Charlie, giving her a kiss. 'You're so clever *and* talented.' His kiss lingered. 'Umm, want to go back to bed?'

'Don't tempt me,' laughed Maddie. 'I have a big day today, or have you forgotten?'

'No way.' He grinned at her. He was still in awe of how her organisational abilities, her charm and confidence at scoring meetings with the heads of studios, distributors and bankers had developed.

'And soon I'll be tackling the movie capital, too – I have appointments set up in LA with a lot of heavyweights who are genuinely interested. None of these Hollywood lunches I've heard about, I'm meeting them in their offices, all strictly business. Of course, it's much easier to get in the door now that *Percy and Ella* is such a hit. Fleur says it's going to run for the rest of the year at least. But the best meeting of all is going to be our Riverside Players reunion in LA.'

'Why not wait till the girls get here to New York to see the show? That's going to be a helluva night, and you could have the reunion then?' said Charlie.

'Business,' said Maddie. 'Fleur is in Germany and Amsterdam too, as both places are interested in having the show there. They might invest in the film, too. So she will meet us back here with the others, who will all be seeing the show for the first time.' Maddie paused, then said, 'I know they'll love it.'

Charlie grinned at her. 'I love seeing you come out of your shell, Mads. It was always there, this confident version of you – you just had to trust in it, let it out.'

Maddie smiled back at him. 'It's hard to imagine now. What if I'd never taken that chance, hadn't been brave enough to take the part of Ella? What if I hadn't come to New York?' She looked thoughtful. 'Fleur has been such a mentor to me. I'm so grateful to her.'

Charlie glanced at Maddie as she turned back to the TV screen to watch Julian. For someone who'd hardly ever been out of her small country town, she'd made New York her backyard in no time, and now they were together renting a Manhattan apartment on the twenty-fifth floor. Yet there were times when she was still simply Maddie, the shy and sweet young woman he'd fallen in love with the moment he saw her.

Charlie knew he'd follow Maddie to the ends of the earth.

*

'Ray, why not come with me? We can travel around America together,' said Sarita.

'Nope. This is a girl thing with your mates. I don't want to be the only bloke tagging along. I'll hold the fort here. Wade and some other fellows and I are going to go to Sydney for the weekend to watch the footy final.'

'Oh, nice, you'll enjoy that,' said Sarita, who had no interest in football at all. 'Before we head to New York I'm planning to go to the Academy Museum in LA – they've got thousands of costumes from movies on display.'

'You will love that,' he smiled. 'Give you plenty of inspiration for the costumes for Maddie and Charlie's movie! But I've been thinking, after that we should go back to Fiji and catch up with your family. Aishik rang me a few days ago and asked me to look over the financials for their philanthropic foundation for the island. I told him I'm sure you'd want to be there for the public announcement of the plans.'

Sarita nodded. 'Definitely. We should go when the boys have a break so they can come with us. I know they're loving uni and have grand schemes for the future, but Fiji is part of their heritage too, so I'd like them to know it.'

Ray gave her a hug. 'Sounds like a plan. But first, you go and enjoy your time with your friends.'

*

'Are you excited?' Brett asked Chrissie. 'About New York and LA?'

She nodded slowly. 'I feel like this time away will reset my clock. Or my life! I've never travelled overseas. And Thomas and Mia are besides themselves about going to Disneyland.'

'And what about your plans, Chrissie?' He paused. 'You have surprised everyone – I mean, with what you're doing for Troy. It must be hard on you.'

'Depends how you look at things, Brett,' she said. 'You and Wade were wonderful in helping me retrieve my money from Troy, even with those papers he made me sign. That money has given me the means to be magnanimous, as some say, but I don't see it that way. Troy's life as he knew it is over. He's in a very nice nursing home, with top-class care, though he's still not really aware of where he is, which I suppose is a blessing. He's confined to a wheelchair but the staff take him out on trips. There's no way of knowing if he'll regain any more of his cognitive abilities. He seems happy and placid. The children visit him and tell him what they've been up to and he just smiles and nods.'

Brett found it hard to imagine Troy as placid. 'You're a beautiful woman, Chrissie. Inside and out. I admire you,' he said softly.

'Thanks. I know many people are wondering why I bother doing all this,' she sighed.

'And why do you?' asked Brett.

Chrissie gave him a straight look. 'He's the father of my children, Brett. I don't want my kids to ever say I neglected their father or was unkind to him. He wasn't the best husband. Not at all. But there was some good in our marriage – and that's Thomas and Mia. I'd never turn my back on their dad.'

Brett pushed aside the thought that some women would have walked away, or just handed over the money for Troy's care and moved on. He was tempted to ask her if she would be so generous if Troy was still the old Troy, but he bit his tongue. Fate had decided otherwise.

'Well, you still have a life to live,' said Brett gently. 'What are you going to do with yourself?'

Chrissie gave a broad smile. 'Oh, I have it figured out. My friend Penny and I are going to establish a local Women's Shed in Fig Tree River, where women can learn skills as a recreational hobby, or a job training opportunity, all for free. But my big plan is to set up and fund a good women's refuge, like the one Jennifer works for. One that puts women and kids first, and helps them get on their feet again.' She smiled. 'I might start a chain of them around the state, because sadly they're desperately needed,' she added. 'And I plan to do some fun things just for me!'

Brett smiled at her. 'Wow . . . they're big plans.'

'So what are you doing with *yourself*?' asked Chrissie suddenly.

Brett shrugged. 'Ah, well, I'm hanging out with Harry and Stevie at Leonie's place while she's overseas with you all. I love it around here, so I'm kind of thinking I might base myself up here, as I can work from anywhere, and through helping Leonie with the dam issue, I've made some good contacts here.'

Chrissie grinned. 'Be nice to have you in the area, Brett.'

Brett nodded, and they smiled at each other.

*

The recording studio was cluttered with gear, instruments, a piano, drum kit, chairs. Outside the soundproof windows the LA traffic snaked along the freeway. Behind the adjoining soundproof control room, a cluster of people watched Maddie through the glass. Two sat at a large desk adjusting dials, sliding knobs, watching screens.

In the studio, Maddie bent over her guitar, her eyes closed.

In her mind she was walking beside the Fig Tree River, holding Charlie's hand as sunset turned the world around them gold.

'Ready when you are, Maddie.'

She adjusted her headphones, not looking at the control room as she began to gently strum her guitar.

> *I thought I was just little old me*
> *that I'd live out my days on this river*
> *that my songs would be heard*
> *by the water birds*
> *and the shadows on my bedroom walls . . .*

The group listened in silence, and a young woman wiped away a tear. 'Oh my God . . . it's beautiful,' she whispered.

The musical director shook his head. 'She's a natural. Stunning. God, where the hell has she been? Wait till we get the backing track on this. Number one material.'

The final notes of Maddie's voice and guitar drifted to silence.

In the control room all was quiet as they stared at her, mesmerised.

The producer at the control panel gently pressed the intercom.

'Just beautiful, Maddie. What's it called?'

Maddie smiled shyly. '"River Song",' she answered. 'It's about my home.'

*

The gardens were manicured, movie-set perfect, and white umbrellas bloomed on green lawns by an azure pool. No doubt famous people were sipping from crystal glasses behind tinted windows.

The four women sat at their table by a palm tree so real it looked plastic, as Sarita described it. Older palms screened the garden oasis in the heart of Beverly Hills.

'Can you believe this place?' said Chrissie. 'Totally OTT, yet I feel soooo at home!'

'I could just spend the whole week right here,' said Leonie. 'So could Corby. He loved Disneyland.'

'I'm really charged up after seeing those film costumes,' said Sarita enthusiastically. 'I have so many ideas now, I don't know where to start – especially for Ella's dresses.'

There was much to laugh and comment on, food to order, jokes and tales to tell.

Their waiter arrived with champagne and filled their glasses. 'I hope you have something to celebrate, ladies.'

As he walked away, the table was silent as each paused, then lifted their glass.

'Well, what will we toast?' said Leonie. 'I know it's through sheer luck that we're here – and it hasn't all been smooth sailing.'

'God, when I think of the disaster on the island. I lost so much money, but it's going to be fine, now, I think,' said Sarita.

'I just cringe at how stupid I was about Alistair. What an idiot I was not to see through him!' said Leonie.

'You were lonely; you didn't want to see,' said Sarita.

'And I nearly didn't go to the lunch when we bought that ticket! God, to think I was scrabbling around in Troy's damn car looking for coins . . .' Chrissie smiled.

Maddie stared at her. 'Wait, Chrissie – that was Troy's car? Fleur and I thought it was yours . . .' She paused, wondering whether to continue.

'My little car was in for a service. Troy wouldn't drive me to the lunch so I took his work car. It was the one and only time I think I ever drove it. Why?' Chrissie looked at Maddie's shocked face.

'Ah . . . well, Fleur was sure that was the vehicle that tried to run me off the road on my bike. Fleur was behind me and stopped. It's how we became friends, I guess . . .' Maddie paused. 'She recognised it when you were looking for the money to buy the ticket, so we thought it was yours.'

The table was silent as they all looked at Chrissie, who shrugged. 'It must have been Troy, to be honest. He had a temper. Didn't like cyclists getting in the way. But I'm glad you were okay, Mads. I guess if I hadn't taken the truck, I wouldn't be here today.'

'Did anyone ever tell Fleur that we won?' asked Leonie.

Maddie raised her hand. 'Um, I did. But only a little while ago, when I offered to back her show,' she admitted shyly. 'It looks like I'll get my money back and then some.'

'Well. I'll drink to that,' said Sarita, raising her glass. 'So, here's to . . .?'

'How about: to luck, love, friendship, mistakes and moving on. And helping each other!' said Chrissie.

They clinked glasses, smiling and laughing, and drank.

'I think we've managed our great luck better than

many winners do,' added Sarita. 'We've made mistakes, but we kind of know where to go now.'

Maddie nodded. 'I'm starting my real life in ways I could never have imagined. The money makes it easier, of course, but I would never have been brave enough to do any of the things I'm tackling and trying without you guys,' she said.

'It rather makes us family,' said Leonie. 'No matter where we all end up.'

'And Fleur's the fairy godmother,' added Maddie. 'Best bucks we ever spent, buying that ticket!'

'Here's to us!'

They toasted again and sipped the excellent sparkling wine from the Santa Maria Valley. But each was thinking of the gift out of the blue that had changed their lives – a simple lucky spin of the wheel of fortune.

Or was it?

It was what they did from here that really mattered.

Author's Note

Ella Strom and Percy Grainger on their wedding day

AUSTRALIA'S PERCY GRAINGER (1882–1961) defies even the wildest of imaginings.

As a child, Grainger showed prodigious talent as a pianist and later became, for some time, world famous as a composer, concert pianist, music arranger, collector and preserver of folk music (using an Edison Bell cylinder phonograph), and musical inventor (of the Free Music Machine). He also composed and created pianola rolls, and was a conductor and lecturer.

Perhaps it is because Grainger's genius was so diverse that he did not achieve iconic lasting fame in any one area.

Percy Grainger became his own extraordinary biographer, historian, visual artist and archivist. He documented his passions, frustrations and innermost feelings, as well as his ideas, opinions, and controversial views on race, religion, love and sex (including his predilection for masochism), through his immense collection of writings and correspondence with friends, associates, and especially between himself and his mother, Rose.

Percy was the only child of Rose and John Grainger (an engineer who designed the Albert Bridge in Adelaide), who, when he gave his wife a son, also passed on syphilis. Rose left her husband to his philandering and devoted her life to her child.

There has been much speculation about whether Percy's relationship with his mother was incestuous, although the consensus seems to be that Rose Grainger simply took her adoration for her golden-haired, talented son to an obsessive level – which potentially did Grainger no favours at times. Rose's death in 1922 from suicide (thought to be partly as a result of the very painful symptoms of her disease) affected Grainger deeply.

Percy had several love affairs, but his romance with beautiful Scandinavian poet and architect Ella Strom, long after his mother had died, led to a devoted and lasting marriage. They married in 1928 on the stage of the Hollywood Music Bowl after a packed concert by Percy. Their home in White Plains, New York, where they lived for decades after World War I, is heritage listed as a national monument to Grainger and his music.

*

Grainger's colourful personality (including designing some of his own clothes) and sheer creativity in so many areas has perhaps overshadowed his multitudinous musical talents. He found the immense popularity of the ditty 'Country Gardens' – a mere bagatelle to him, and sometimes the only credit recognition of his name – very frustrating.

Grainger challenges us to reflect not only on the inner life of the artist, expressed so often in flamboyant, idiosyncratic forms, but also on the wider role of the artist in society. His desire was to influence, educate and mould public taste to create an appreciation of the history of music, music-making in its universal and cross-cultural dimensions, and to unflinchingly expose his personal aesthetic.

Percy's sheer volume of work, comprising compositions, performances, musical arrangements and experiments, and preservation of folk music – let alone his ruminations in letters and diaries, his souvenirs, clothes, musical instruments, obsessive collections, including personal belongings of his mother – are preserved in the Grainger Museum, which Percy and Ella established in the grounds of The University of Melbourne. This immense collection, from the minutiae to the madcap, the personal to the private (for example, his whips and sadomasochistic paraphernalia), as well as his prolific correspondence, illustrates his genius.

*

I think it was Melbourne filmmaker Paul Cox who first mentioned Percy to me.

I then met British film director Ken Russell again in Melbourne in 1983 (I'd previously interviewed him as a young reporter for London's *Daily Mail*) when he came out to direct his (typically) flamboyant and controversial version of the opera *Madam Butterfly*, and asked him if he would make a film based on Percy Grainger.

It was a no-brainer, we thought, so we embarked on

a decades-long journey to bring Percy, Rose and Ella to the big screen.

Ken and Percy were a match made in heaven – or hell, depending on one's viewpoint. Ken and I never gave up hope, and came so close so many times.

Sadly, we never got Ken's script to the screen, although I treasure the remarkable friendship we shared through decades of our lives. I promised Ken I'd never give up, so it occurred to me that perhaps Percy could become a musical production? Therefore, instead I gave the idea to Fleur, Leonie, Maddie, Sarita and Chrissie in my novel *River Song*.

There will only ever be one Percy Grainger.

Di Morrissey, 2024

On the River

Lyrics by Hester Fraser

I thought I was just little old me
that I'd live out my days on this river
that my songs would be heard
by the water birds
and the shadows on my bedroom walls
but this voice that started as a whisper
is now calling to the moon and stars
and I could wander the banks
of this river I love
but I don't think it would be enough
anymore . . .

so I'll pack up my things and go
but don't you worry, I'll be back
this story must be told
and it won't wait
something inside of me
is demanding to be free
but my heart will always live
on the river

I used to stand at the edge of the water
look straight across to the other side
watch the fish jumping high
and the gulls in the sky
peaceful in this beautiful place
but now I wriggle my toes in the water
my imagination starts to dream
and far distant shore
holds no interest anymore
now I wonder where the river goes . . .

so I'll pack up my things and go
but don't you worry, I'll be back
this story must be told
and it won't wait
something inside of me
is demanding to be free
but my heart will always live
on the river
but my heart will always live
on the river
on the river
on the river
on the river

Scan the QR code below to hear 'On the River'